WICKEDLY
POWERFUL

DEBORAH BLAKE

BERKLEY SENSATION, NEW YORK

**BERKLEY
SENSATION**

**An imprint of Penguin Random House LLC
375 Hudson Street, New York, New York 10014**

WICKEDLY POWERFUL

A Berkley Sensation Book / published by arrangement with the author

ISBN: 978-1-101-98744-5

PUBLISHING HISTORY
Berkley Sensation mass-market edition / February 2016

PRINTED IN THE UNITED STATES OF AMERICA

10 9 8 7 6 5 4 3 2 1

Cover art by Tony Mauro.
Cover design by Sarah Oberrender.
Interior text design by Kelly Lipovich.

Penguin
Random
House

To Kathy, whose years of service in a real-life fire tower inspired this story and whose strength and love inspire me. Thanks for all the help with the book, and for being my friend. BMC misses you. And not just because of all the great baking. This one's for you, babe.

To Caere, whose entire town mourned the loss of the nineteen Prescott Granite Mountain Hotshots crew members who lost their lives fighting the Yarnell Hill fire in 2013. Your personal grief made it all more real for me, and I remember thinking then, "What on earth is it like to be the one man who survived?" That thought stuck in my head and became a part of this book. Thank you for that, and for all the other things you have given me over the years. I wouldn't be here and writing if it weren't for you.

And for all those who fight fires, in any capacity, everywhere. Thank you.

ACKNOWLEDGMENTS

As always, this book only came to be with a lot of help from a lot of people. In particular, my friend Kathy Fraser, who has spent many a summer high up in a fire tower in Wyoming and who kindly let me pick her brain, and then even more kindly read the entire book as I was writing it and gently told me when I was getting things egregiously wrong. Any remaining mistakes are my own. People often say, "Without you, this book wouldn't exist." In this case, that is nothing short of the truth.

I am fortunate enough to have a fabulous agent who not only takes care of the business aspects of my writing, but also reads my work before I inflict it upon my lovely editor, Leis, and tells me when I'm getting things egregiously wrong (you are starting to see a pattern here, I suspect). In the case of this particular book, I could tell about halfway through the first draft that Something Was Very Wrong, but I couldn't tell what or how to fix it. Elaine gave me terrific editing notes that pinpointed the problems, and then my heroic writing partner Lisa DiDio brainstormed with me until we figured out how to fix it. Then Leis made it even better, as all good editors do. If you like this book, it is probably because of them.

Thanks also to my first readers, who did a stalwart job of giving me feedback and catching mistakes. Thanks especially to Karen Buys, who provided a second pair of eyes for proofreading at a time when I was so burned out I didn't trust my own.

And really huge appreciation to all the folks who read and/or bought the first two books in the series and said, "We want more!" Here you go!

ONE

THE EARLY MORNING fog blanketed the area surrounding the fire tower, stippling the windows with condensation and cloaking the ground below in mystery. Even the twittering of the birds was muffled, as if the world itself had fallen away behind the mist.

To Sam Corbett, perched on a stool in the tower with his coffee mug gripped between tense fingers, the fog looked like smoke and brought back nightmares.

Eventually, he set down the cooling coffee and turned his back to the windows, doing push-ups and crunches and working with the free weights until he had an excuse for the sweat on his brow and the tremors in his hands, and the sun had burned away the fog and welcomed in a bright new day.

The radio crackled around the time he was going into service, and Tiny's voice from down below gave him a heads-up to expect a scout troop within the hour. Sam scowled, feeling the scar tissue pulling at the skin on the left side of his face. He hated having people invade the tower; it was *his* space, *his* sanctuary. But of course, it wasn't, not really. It was a job. And visitors were part of the job. Few of them stayed long anyway, after they'd met him.

At about nine thirty, Sam heard the clatter of feet outside, along with the usual preadolescent griping about the absurd number of stairs that had to be climbed to reach the top of the tower. He grabbed his Yankees cap, a souvenir of a long-ago trip to the Big Apple—a place far, far away from these woods around the Black Mountain in Wyoming, both geographically and spiritually—and tugged it down low over his forehead. The shadow it cast didn't so much hide as soften the effect of his disfigurement. For Sam, this fire tower was as close as he could get to hiding, and as evidenced by the gangly figures currently wandering around the catwalk outside, it wasn't close enough.

Sam went out the door and greeted Dennis, the scout leader, and the two women with him, probably mothers to one or another of the shouting, laughing boys they were attempting to herd. He had met Dennis before, but the moms were new, and didn't do a very good job of covering up their shock at the sight of his face.

"Hey, Sam," Dennis said cheerfully. The scoutmaster was a thin, energetic man who ran the general store in the nearest town. He happily made up boxes of groceries and necessities for Sam and had them delivered to the tower so Sam didn't have to come into town as often; the two men got along well. "This is Claire and Felicia. They're helping me out today. Ladies, this is Sam Corbett. He's manning the fire tower this season; it's his second year here, so he's practically an old pro."

"Hello," Sam said. He didn't say much these days, not liking the permanent rasp of his voice, damaged by the smoke he'd inhaled at the same time his face had been burned. He'd give the boys the tour, but Dennis would do most of the talking. The gregarious store owner didn't mind, and it made things easier for everyone.

"Hi," Felicia said, looking at the view instead of at him. She was a little plump, and still trying to catch her breath from the climb. "Thanks for having the boys here. I can't believe anyone lives up in this tower for four months. Don't you get lonely? I'd never be able to stand it."

Sam shrugged. "I get more visitors than you'd think," he said. There was no point in adding that he preferred the solitude; loneliness was a constant companion, no matter where he lived. "And someone needs to watch for fires. I'm happy to do it."

Claire, the other mother, had been studying him unobtrusively, eyes hidden behind big designer sunglasses. She was blond and pretty, and stood a little too close for comfort. Sam had met her type before, and he had a bad feeling about what was coming.

Sure enough, she pulled off the glasses and stared at him more openly. "Sam Corbett. Weren't you one of the Hotshots crew they called in a few years ago to deal with that terrible forest fire up on the ridge? I remember reading about what happened."

He kept his expression neutral through long practice. "Yes, I was, ma'am. Shall we gather up the boys now?"

Felicia clapped her hands to her mouth. "Oh. Oh, that explains the . . . I mean, oh dear, I'm sorry. For, you know, the fire and everything." Tears sprang into her eyes, and Sam's stomach knotted. He didn't know which reaction he hated worse—the voracious interest or the pity.

"Hazards of the job," he said, as he always did. "I got off easier than some."

Dennis rescued him, blowing a whistle to bring the scouts over for their informative tour of the tower.

"Boys," the scoutmaster said, "this is Mr. Corbett. He's going to tell you all about his job as a fire spotter, and show you how he watches out for fires so he can keep the forest— and us—safe."

"Do you have to run down all those stairs to put out the fires?" one skinny boy asked with a hint of awe. He was staying well back from the railing, unlike some of the others. Not everyone liked the heights up there, but they'd never bothered Sam. Heights didn't scare him. Nothing scared him anymore. He'd already been through the worst and survived. More or less.

"He doesn't put the fires out himself, stupid," one of the other boys said with a sneer. "Real firemen do that. He just sits up here with a pair of binoculars and watches."

"Now, Tommy," Dennis said, with the air of someone who has repeated himself so often, the response was automatic. "We don't call anyone stupid, do we? And Mr. Corbett's job is just as important as that of the people who actually put out the fires. In a way, he is a firefighter too."

Sam tried not to grimace, hearing the echo of his own voice inside his head. That was the same thing he told himself every day. That the job he was doing was vital to the effort; that he was still doing his part, in the only way he now could. It was the one thing that kept him going.

The problem was, he didn't really believe it, any more than that young scout did.

SAM SHOWED THE boys around the inside of the tower, and let them each take a turn looking out through the big binoculars in different directions. Most took their turns eagerly, almost hoping to be the one to spot a fire. He told himself not to be angry with the youngsters; to them, the prospect of seeing actual flames was an abstract idea, an adventure, not a grim reality. But he could still feel his teeth clench and his shoulders tighten.

Peter, the smallest of the scouts, squinted seriously as he looked through the lens, then pointed out into the forest with one slightly grubby finger. "Mr. Corbett? Who lives down there in that little house?"

Dennis and Sam exchanged glances. There weren't any residences in that quadrant, and the ranger station was too far away to be seen from the tower.

Sam held out his hand for the glasses. "Let me take a look so I can see what you're talking about," he said, expecting something like a large, vaguely house-shaped boulder. Instead, once he'd adjusted the binoculars, he spotted the structure Peter was referring to—except that it wasn't a house, exactly, more like a modern gypsy caravan on wheels, parked in a clearing in the forest.

"Huh," he said. "Just somebody camping, I guess." *Or someone who had wandered into the woods and gotten lost. That happened occasionally too.* Out of habit, he swung the glasses around to check out the surrounding area, and felt his hands grow clammy at the sight of a column of gray and white smoke, shooting up less than a mile from where the caravan stood.

Dragging a harsh breath in through scarred lungs, he turned to Dennis and said quietly, "You need to take the boys down now. Right now."

Dennis's eyes widened, but he didn't ask any questions, just called the scouts and the two moms together, had them say a quick thank-you to Sam, and hustled them out the door and down the stairs. As soon as the last pair of sneakers was on the top step, Sam ran over to the two-way radio.

"Dispatch, come in," he said. "It's Sam. I've got a smoke." He quickly relayed the coordinates, as well as the information that there might be a civilian in harm's way.

The dispatcher called it in, sending the first response team on their way, then switched back to Sam and asked a few more questions about what he'd seen.

"So, this caravan you spotted," the dispatcher said. "Did you see anyone near it?"

"Nope," Sam said. "Whoever it was could have been inside, or out hiking." *Or just maybe, setting a fire.*

They'd had too many fires already this season . . . some caused by a series of fluke lightning storms, but there had been a couple that no one had been able to explain. No sign of campers being careless with their campfires, or any indication that some moron with a cigarette had decided to go for a walk in the woods. Just fires, when there shouldn't have been any. They'd been lucky so far and Sam had spotted them all while they were still easily controlled. But sooner or later, they were going to run out of luck.

In Sam's experience, you always did.

TWO

BELLA YOUNG SAT on the flip-down steps of her traveling caravan and stretched her long legs out in front of her as she looked at the surrounding forest with satisfaction. After being stuck in the dry mountains of Montana battling wildfires for weeks, mingling with local firefighters, she was happy to be back among the peaceful environment of the trees, listening to squirrels and blue jays squabble instead of people.

It wasn't that Bella didn't like people, exactly. She just liked trees and animals and mountains better.

In a way, that made her the most traditional of the three Baba Yagas who watched over the United States. After all, the original Baba Yagas, powerful witches tasked with guarding the doorways to the Otherworld, keeping the balance of nature, and occasionally—if absolutely forced into it—helping out some worthy seeker, had lived in the deep, dark forests of Russia and its Slavic neighbors.

These days, Bella's sister Babas Barbara and Beka mostly handled the eastern and western sides of the country, leaving Bella happily stuck in the less-populated middle. That was just fine, since she and people, well . . . Let's just say there were issues. Big, big issues.

The Black Mountain forests, on the other hand, suited her to a T. She hoped that whatever urge had brought her here was due more to wanderlust and less to some mysterious magical crisis. She was due for some rest and relaxation. Or at the very least, fewer things blowing up.

She took a deep breath, reveling in the sharp, resinous tang of pine needles and the deep, musty aroma of decaying leaves. Compared to the auto fumes of the city, they smelled better to her than the most expensive perfume.

"Isn't that the best smell in the world, Koshka?" she said to her companion, who currently bore the guise of a gigantic Norwegian Forest cat (since it was difficult to either fit or hide a large brown and gray dragon in a small caravan).

All Baba Yagas traveled with their own Chudo-Yudo, although each dragon chose a different form. And pretty much anything else they wanted. Even the powerful High Queen of the Otherworld rarely argued with a dragon.

Bella called hers Koshka, which was Russian for a female cat. It was something of an inside joke, since he was neither female nor a cat . . . nor Russian, if you came right down to it. Bella's mentor Baba, who had found her as a child and trained her for the job, might have been from the mother country, but dragons came straight from the Otherworld.

"It's not bad," Koshka replied, showing off an impressive set of incisors in a wide yawn. "I prefer the aroma of tuna, myself." He looked back through the open door toward the compact kitchen space inside, in case Bella had somehow missed his point.

Bella rolled her eyes. "Seriously. Smell that; it's practically ambrosia."

Koshka dutifully lifted his dark pink nose into the air, the wide ruff around his neck and tufts of fur in his ears making him look a bit like his wilder cousin, the lynx. "Huh," he said.

"What? You don't like pine all of a sudden?" Bella shoved herself up off the steps so she could go open a can of tuna.

"No, I don't like the odor of smoke in the middle of a

forest," he said. "Can't you smell it?" He pointed his entire massive forty-pound body toward the west. "I don't know why they bother to put those puny noses in the middle of Human faces. They're not good for anything."

Bella lifted her head and sniffed deeply, but still couldn't detect anything out of the ordinary. But she didn't doubt Koshka for a minute. "Let's go check it out," she said, and they set off at a fast lope through the trees.

LESS THAN A mile from her caravan, they came upon the source of the smoke; she clearly would have scented it soon enough, even with her *puny* Human nose, since there was a bonfire the size of a Buick burning away merrily amid a pile of leaves and downed tree limbs. Bella looked around for any signs of whoever started it, but the area was empty except for her and her faithful dragon-cat.

"*Shit*. Fire again," she said with feeling. Bella had a love/hate relationship with fire. It was the element she was strongest in, just as Barbara was most attuned with earth and Beka with water. But in her experience, that made for as many problems as it did solutions. Still, there was clearly no one around to wrestle with this particular fire but her, so there was no point in wasting time.

"Want some help?" Koshka asked. As a dragon, he wasn't even mildly intimidated by fire. If he was in his natural form, he probably could have just sat on it. As a dragon, he was bigger than a Buick too. Much bigger. But it wasn't a good idea for him to change where anyone could possibly see him, and it was broad daylight in a public forest.

Bella gritted her teeth. "I've got it," she said. After all, if there was one thing she had experience with, it was putting out fires. Unfortunately, she was also usually the one who started them, but it made for good practice for situations like this.

She held her hands up to the sky, gathering her power until it made her fingertips tingle and her long, curly red hair crackle like the flames it resembled. Then she lowered her hands until they were aimed at the fire, making a circling motion. The energy flowed smoothly out to surround the burning tinder, encompassing it in a bubble of magic. Then she snapped her fingers, and all the oxygen within that bubble disappeared. A few minutes later, the fire had died down to a few barely smoldering embers, and she snapped her fingers again to return the air to normal.

"I love that trick," Koshka said, walking over to sniff at the edges of the burned area. "Pah!" He yanked his nose away in a hurry, stalking off with his tail held high. "That stinks."

Bella glanced back over her shoulder as she followed him, moving faster as she heard the sound of incoming men and machinery. Someone must have spotted the smoke from the fire and reported it. Which was good, but she didn't want to be seen lurking around the area of a suspicious fire. Her cover as a traveling artist was solid, but there was no sense in subjecting it to unnecessary scrutiny if she didn't have to.

"What stinks?" she asked, moving faster. "The fire?"

"No," the dragon said. "Whatever was used to start it."

"Oh," Bella said. She'd been hoping it was just a fluke of nature. There hadn't been a storm for days, but sometimes a lightning strike could smolder for a while before bursting into flame. "That's bad news."

"It gets worse," he said, growling under his breath as he waited for her to catch up to his bounding pace. "Whatever it was, it had the faint scent of magic on it."

"SHIT," Bella said.

"With a side of crap," Koshka agreed. "Now, what about that tuna?"

⚱HREE

THE FIRE WAS too far away for Sam to see any details of what was happening on the ground, but he could tell when the smoke disappeared, and breathed a sigh of relief, letting go of a weight he hadn't been aware of carrying. He'd continued checking the surrounding area, but it appeared that this was an isolated incident.

The radio crackled and the dispatcher said his name.

"Corbett here," he answered. "Looks like your guys got the fire out. Nice job."

"Huh," the dispatcher said. Sam had never met Willy, the person on the other end of the radio, but he knew the sound of the man's voice better than he knew his own, especially these days. That was Willy's "I'm not happy" grunt. His "everything is great" grunt sounded completely different.

"Something go wrong down there?" Sam asked, his heart suddenly hammering in his chest. "Someone get hurt?"

"What? Oh no, nothing like that." Willy's tone went apologetic. "Sorry, Sam, didn't mean to alarm you. No, everything was fine. In fact, the fire was out when we got there. It had clearly been going pretty well for a bit; the lower branches of a few nearby trees showed some signs of char. But there was nothing left except warm ashes by the time we showed up. Kinda weird, really."

"Weird how?" Sam asked. "Some camper let his campfire get out of control, then poured water on it. It happens. We should just be glad whoever did it didn't panic and run away instead."

"That's just it," Willy said. "No water. In fact, no sign of whatever put the fire out at all. Just a nice round circle of ash, like somebody upended a bowl over it."

"Huh," Sam said in unconscious echo. "That *is* kind of weird. Still, the fire's out, and that's what really matters."

"I suppose so."

"Did you check on that caravan I told you about?" Sam asked the dispatcher. "Maybe whoever owns it knows something about our mystery."

Willy laughed. "I doubt it. The guys went and knocked on the door; said the thing was really cool, like some kind of gypsy wagon, only with a truck to pull it instead of horses. I've heard they have modern versions of those caravans, Vardos, they're called, but I've never seen one." He sighed. "Maybe I'll get one when I retire, and wander around the country in it."

Sam smothered a rare smile. Willy was chatty, and despite the fact that they'd never met, Sam knew enough about the other man to fill a book—including the fact that he'd never been more than fifty miles away from the place he'd been born, and had no real desire to be anywhere else.

"So what made them so sure the owner didn't have anything to do with the fire?" Sam asked.

Willy guffawed. "They said that they knocked for a while, and finally a little old lady answered the door. They said she didn't exactly look like the type to go wandering through the forest setting fires; said she had a cat that was almost as big as she was, so she must have been tiny. Apparently she asked them in for tea and served it to them on real china. Man, I wish I'd been there."

Sam was mostly glad he hadn't been. Still, a little old lady sounded like a pretty unlikely suspect for a firebug. If they even had one, and the fire hadn't somehow started accidentally.

"Did they ask her if she'd seen anyone else around?"

"Yup. Said she told them that if she wanted to be surrounded by people, she would have stayed in the city. Then glared at them until they all put their cups down and left." More laughter hiccuped across the airwaves.

"Good enough," Sam said. But it wasn't, really. He went out of service at 1900, and at seven o'clock in July there was still plenty of light left. As soon as he was off duty, Sam was going to go have a look at the remains of the fire himself.

BELLA WAITED UNTIL the sun was almost ready to go down before she returned to the scene of the fire. She'd wanted to go back and see if she could sense the magic Koshka mentioned. But she needed to be sure the firefighters were gone before she banished her old lady disguise. The guise of an old woman, like the traditional Baba Yaga, was easy to put on. Besides, it often helped that Humans tended to believe that an old crone was of no account. In truth, the hardest part was not laughing while attempting to stay in character.

But now the forest was empty again, except for the creatures who belonged there, so Bella and Koshka padded silently back down the animal trail that had led them to the other clearing, hoping to discover something useful. Or, in Bella's case, hoping to discover that there was nothing to discover.

Unfortunately, a crew full of firefighters wearing heavy boots and pulling along well-used pieces of equipment had left the place stinking of Humans and their tools and not much else.

"I swear the scent was here," Koshka said, swinging his large head to and fro, and making the local birds scatter for safer environs.

"I'm not doubting you, Koshka," Bella said, poking at the ashes with a pointy stick. "But I don't know what you expect me to do about it now. Maybe it was here. Maybe it wasn't. Even your fabulous nose can't be right all the time. If we decide to stick around, we'll just have to keep our eyes open."

Koshka made the little coughing noise that passed as a laugh when you were a dragon-cat, and Bella gave him a sharp look. "What?"

He sat back on his rump with a thud. "You do realize we're not alone, right?"

What? So much for keeping her eyes open. Bella turned around and spotted a shadowy figure at the edge of the clearing, barely visible in the oncoming dusk.

"Hello?" she called, and it took a few steps forward, materializing into a tall Human man wearing worn jeans and a slightly rumpled light blue denim shirt. He kept his face turned partially away from her, looking at the sizable burn mark on the forest floor, but what she could see was attractive enough to make her heart skip a beat—like a Greek god with a straight nose, a strong chin, and longish blond hair that brushed his collar. Her mentor Baba had sworn she'd met Thor once, and this man looked much as Bella had imagined the thunder god might. Broad shoulders, muscular arms, and all.

Certainly his expression was thunderous enough, the half that she could see of it, although he seemed to make an effort to smooth it out when she greeted him.

"I'm sorry," he said, his voice sounding a bit rough, as though he had a cold. "I hope I didn't frighten you."

Allergies, maybe, she thought. Not something the Babas had to worry about, thankfully, since drinking the enchanted Water of Life and Death not only made their magic stronger, but also gave them increased health and longer lives than most Humans.

"Not at all," she responded. "Very little frightens me."

The corner of his mouth edged up slightly. "Not even bears? I could have been a bear, you know."

Bella snorted. "Actually, I rather like bears. They're normally quite agreeable, unlike many people."

"Know a lot of bears, do you?" the man asked, sounding amused.

"Only a few," Bella answered quite truthfully. "I'm a lot more familiar with dragons."

A rusty laugh escaped well-shaped lips, as though the man was out of practice with the act. "I've met some unusual folks in these woods, but never anyone who claimed to know dragons."

He looked at the burned spot again, and his smile slid away into the shadows. "Unfortunately, I doubt a dragon did this." He was silent for a moment. "So, have you been in the woods all day, or are you lost?"

"I'm not lost," Bella said, skipping over the other part of the question. "I'm traveling through the area doing some painting. I've got a caravan parked about a mile from here." She nodded her head back in the direction of her home. "I'm Bella, by the way. Bella Young."

"Sam Corbett. I'm the fire spotter in the local tower. I saw the smoke from the fire earlier and called it in." He didn't offer his hand, or move any closer, but she thought she detected a suspicious glint in the eye turned toward her. "The guys said they met an old woman at that caravan. Nobody said anything about a gorgeous redhead, and that doesn't seem like something they'd forget to mention."

Bella blushed, grateful for the gathering gloom. *The Greek god thought she was gorgeous? How about that.* "I must have missed them. That was my Baba; she was visiting me for the day, but she's gone now. It's just me and Koshka here."

Sam looked around the clearing. "I thought I heard you talking to someone. Who is this Koshka person, and where is he?"

Koshka rose out of the shadows at her feet, where his brown and gray fur and absolute stillness had rendered him practically invisible in the dusky evening light. Once he stood up, though, he was pretty hard to miss.

"Holy crap!" Sam said, taking a step forward as if unable to believe his eyes. "Is that a *cat*? That thing must weigh thirty pounds."

"Closer to forty," Bella said cheerfully. "And that thing,

as you call him, is my companion Koshka. He's a Norwegian Forest cat. They get quite large."

"I'll say." Sam's gravelly voice was a mix of awe and admiration. "He's really impressive. Such beautiful markings; I've never seen anything like him."

Koshka preened, a deep purr rumbling up out of his furry chest. "Tell him I think he's pretty too." Of course, to the Human, it would just sound like meowing, unless the dragon-cat decided otherwise.

Bella rolled her eyes. "He says thanks, and right back atcha." There was no way she was going to call this hunk of a guy "pretty."

"Uh-huh." Sam appeared to be considering the dubious nature of her sanity. She wasn't offended; she did the same, from time to time.

"So, you and your large friend there have been wandering through the woods? I don't suppose you've seen anyone else in your travels?"

The unspoken "or set the forest on fire yourself" hung in the air between them like an arrow paused midflight. She ignored it.

"I'm afraid not," Bella said. "Well, it was nice meeting you, but I should probably get back to the caravan before it gets any darker. Wouldn't want to be eaten by bears now, would I?"

"That would be bad," Sam said seriously. "Probably give the bear terrible indigestion."

It would if one tried to eat Koshka and suddenly found a huge dragon inside its stomach.

"I definitely wouldn't like to be responsible for that," Bella said with a smile. "Maybe I'll see you around some-time."

"Maybe. Were you planning on staying in the area?"

"I haven't decided yet. You know artists," she said. "We just go where the muse sends us." She gave him a cheerful wave good-bye and set out along the trail back in the direction she'd come from.

Upon reaching the caravan, they were greeted by the welcoming glow of a lantern over the door. Magic, of course, although it looked like a regular lantern to anyone who didn't know better. In its former life, the now-updated gypsy wagon had been a traditional Baba Yaga's wooden hut on chicken legs, moving through the forest from place to place, and only found when its owner so desired or fate willed it to be so. Its appearance might have changed, but the enchantments that were at its core were much the same as they'd been for a thousand years.

Woman and cat paused in the doorway, purposely not looking back into the woods.

"You realize he followed you back here," Koshka said.

"I know," Bella said in a low voice.

"Maybe he wanted to make sure you got back safely," the dragon-cat suggested. "Or he followed you because he thinks you're cute."

"Sure," Bella said, a little wistfully. She'd been alone for a long time, and now that her sister Babas had both found love with wonderful men who somehow managed to deal with the fact that Barbara and Beka were powerful witches straight out of fairy tales, she'd found herself dreaming that such a miracle could happen to her too.

But somehow, she didn't think that the handsome prince she'd met in the forest had fallen deeply, madly in love with her at first sight. More like deeply in suspicion, if anything.

"Or, he could have followed you because he thinks you're a crazy, fire-setting menace," Koshka added, a hint of laughter in his voice.

"In that case, he'd be right," Bella said, and went inside to pour herself a hefty glass of wine.

A SHARP TAPPING noise woke her sometime around two a.m., pulling her out of a dream about a semi-naked muscular blond god.

"You might want to get that," Koshka said with a yawn from where he was sleeping at the foot of the bed. It was a small bed, and he took up most of it, leaving one of Bella's legs dangling half on and half off the platform that stretched across the back of the caravan.

Bella rubbed her eyes, peering around, and the tapping noise repeated itself, coming from the small round porthole window over the bed. *Huh.* Bella snapped her fingers, lighting the candle on the wall sconce, and cranked the window open a couple of inches.

Brisk, pine-scented nighttime air came flowing in, along with a tiny winged being about the size of Bella's palm. Most of the paranormal creatures that used to live on this side of the doorway had left years ago, summoned back to the Otherworld when the Queen and King decided that it was too dangerous to continue to coexist with Humans. But some, like the tree sprite whose gossamer wings hummed in front of Bella's face, couldn't leave their homes. Those that hadn't died out altogether remained, hiding and lurking in the places that Humans were less likely to go. Bella had met the occasional sprite in her travels, since she tended to spend most of her time in the forests where they lived, but they were solitary creatures, and rarely made themselves known.

Having one of them rap on her window in the middle of the night was definitely a first.

"Are you the Baba Yaga?" the small being asked, in a voice almost too high-pitched to hear.

"I am one of the Babas, yes," Bella said. "Are you in need of assistance?"

"Not me, Baba," said the sprite. It looked like a miniature, somewhat androgynous Human, if Humans were three inches tall with diaphanous wings like a dragonfly, and a long tongue that could unroll itself to catch insects or sip sap from a tree. "I carry a message for another. 'Give to Baba Yaga,' he says." It looked curiously around the caravan. "Told me to look for a big, shiny silver can."

Bella choked back a laugh. That was one way to describe Barbara's Airstream trailer, she supposed. "That home belongs to another Baba Yaga. Did this person want you to look for her in particular?"

The sprite shook its head, shaggy bark brown hair slipping down over its wide-set eyes. "No. Just said, 'Find a Baba' and told me about that one's hut. You are a Baba. You will do." It held up one little hand. "Wait." It flew back out the window, moving so quickly that Bella could hardly see it, even knowing it was there.

"What do you suppose that was all about?" Bella asked as Koshka padded up to join her at the head of the bed.

"Sounds like you might be here on a Baba mission after all. I told you that nagging feeling you had was probably a summons." He licked one massive paw, not terribly interested.

Bella sighed. Sometimes a Baba was *Called* to deal with a problem, usually by someone who was familiar with the old tales and knew that such a thing was possible. A summons could be as obvious as a written invitation, or as subtle as a sudden yearning to drive in a completely different direction from the one where you'd been heading. A Baba didn't always know she'd been Called until she got to where she was going.

Bella had already begun to suspect that her presence here had something to do with the mysterious fire she'd found. But what that had to do with a tree sprite bearing a message from someone looking for a Baba Yaga was anyone's guess.

She sat up on her knees as the sprite flew back in through the open window, carrying something almost as big as it was, its wings laboring as it struggled under its unlikely load. Bella's respect for the little creature rose a couple of notches; how far had it carried this unwieldy package, looking for the right person to give it to?

The sprite dropped its burden gratefully into Bella's outstretched hand, and she took a closer look at what it had brought her. At first glance, she thought it was a small scroll, tied with a black string. But on closer examination, the paper appeared to be made out of thin, once-white leather, and the thong was a tight braid crafted out of straight black hair. A sinking feeling started in her stomach and made its way up to her heart.

"Where did you get this?" she whispered. "Who gave it to you?"

The little being gave an approximation of a shrug, wings fluttering a little slower. "Two days' travel, maybe three?" Sprites didn't have much sense of time or distance, so that didn't really help her. "From the place of the rising sun," it added.

It had come from the east, then. That at least gave her a direction. It wasn't much, but it was something. Assuming the sprite hadn't been distracted along its journey.

"Did you see the man who gave you this? Did he have long black hair in a tail, and a dangling mustache?" The tie binding the message looked as though it could have come from Gregori Sun, her favorite of the three Riders who had always assisted the Baba Yagas—Sun, Mikhail Day, and Alexei Knight.

No one, not even the Babas, really knew much about the Riders; just that they were powerful, immortal, and always there when a Baba needed them. Until recently, when Day had disappeared after helping Barbara with a problem out on the East Coast. Sun and Knight had vanished a little later while out looking for him.

Still, no one had been terribly worried. After all, the Riders (who rode black, red, and white enchanted steeds that manifested these days as a black Harley, a red Ducati, and a gleaming white Yamaha) were nigh on invincible. Even the haughty rulers of the Otherworld treated them more like favorite cousins than like subjects to be ordered about.

But Bella was worried now. The message the sprite had brought her could only have come from the Riders, or at least two of them, if the white leather and black hair were anything to go by. And she couldn't imagine a situation that would cause the men to send a tiny sprite for help, but she could see the evidence of desperation in the palm of her hand. The hair that held the tiny scroll rolled tight still had a few roots at the ends, as if it had been pulled out by force rather than neatly cut, although the braiding itself was arranged and precise, much like Gregori himself. The scrap of dingy leather must

have been torn from Mikhail's white leather pants, but Bella
had never seen the Rider anything but immaculate. The other
two always teased that he could roll around in the mud and
still come up sparkling.

"Who gave you this?" she asked again. "Was he slim and
dark? Huge and hairy like a bear? Tall and blond and handsome?"

The sprite shook its head. "I saw him not, Baba," it said.
"I flew far from home in search of mushrooms, and followed
a singing ribbon of magic to a tiny hole in some rocks. Faint
it was, the call, and stopped as soon as I arrived. When I
answered, this was pushed out through the crack, and a voice
whispered to take it to the Baba Yaga. It said something about
the shiny silver can, then said, 'please, please, please.' Then
there was nothing more."

Bella pulled off the dark tie and unrolled the piece of leather with shaking fingers. The writing on it was faint and
brownish red; it looked as though it had been drawn on pains-
takingly with the tip of a fingernail, rather than spilling neatly
from a pen. She had to brighten the light inside the caravan
to make it out at all.

"Is that . . ."

Koshka leaned his large head in close and touched the
pink tip of his tongue delicately to the surface of the message.
"Blood. Yes. With a hint of magic in it." If a cat could look
worried, Koshka did.

"What does it say, Baba?" the sprite asked curiously.

There were only three words, each written in straggling
capital letters. The message said:

CAVE
HELP
BRENNA

That was all. But it was enough.

OUR

BELLA YAWNED OVER her cup of tea, feeling the effects of her interrupted sleep and the hours that followed spent questioning the sprite for any details the small creature could remember and then mulling over the contents of the note and what it could mean. The pungent steam of the peppermint leaves in her cup did its best to prop open her drooping lids as she eyed the tiny parcel on the table before her.

"What do you think, Koshka?" she asked her irritatingly alert companion. Dragons could go weeks without sleep if they felt like it. Unlike the mostly Human Babas. "Should I contact Barbara and Beka and tell them about this?"

Koshka reached out one claw and delicately touched the scrap of leather, then sniffed at the claw before retracting it. "What good would that do? They're both busy with other things. They wouldn't be able to do anything but worry, and you're doing enough of that for all three of you."

Bella bit her lip but didn't bother to deny it. How could she *not* worry, with the Riders missing and this disturbing evidence that they were in some kind of trouble? She couldn't even imagine what kind of mess the powerful immortals could get into that they couldn't get themselves out of—or, for that matter, what on earth she could do about it if they were dealing with something too big even for their combined skills to triumph over.

"Maybe I should bring it before the Queen," she said dubiously. Her mentor Baba had always taught her that it was better to keep off the Queen's sometime chancy radar whenever possible. But this was an emergency, wasn't it? Or, at least, an alarm bell that could possibly mean an emergency. Oh yeah, the Queen would love that.

Koshka dropped his head down onto his paws, stretching out to take up most of the limited space on the drop-down table and causing Bella's teacup to wobble precariously. She grabbed at it, watching the leaves slosh around in the bottom of the cup and wishing that she could read the answers she needed in their ragged patterns. Sadly, she wasn't that kind of witch.

"I'd leave the Queen out of it for now," Koshka said. "No point in riling her up if you don't have to."

Bella opened her mouth to argue, but was distracted by the sound of knocking coming from the front of the caravan. But not from the door.

"You had to mention her name, didn't you?" Koshka muttered as he jumped off the table.

It did seem rather as if just thinking about her had summoned the monarch, Bella thought. Or at least, the monarch's representative, since the Queen would never deign to rap on anyone's door, and only someone from the Otherworld would be knocking on the inside of the cupboard that also doubled as the hidden entrance to that magical world. Although occasionally the Babas would travel that way as a shortcut to see one another, which gave Bella a moment's hope.

Until she twisted the knob twice to the right and once to the left, and opened the door to see a four-foot-tall orange salamander dressed in a top hat and tails. Definitely *not* a Baba Yaga.

"Good day, Baba," the salamander said, bowing politely. "I bring greetings from my mistress, Her Most Royal Majesty

Queen Morena Aine Titania Argante Rhiannon. She bids me to convey her desire that you attend Her in Her gardens, as promptly as possible." He bowed again, almost dislodging his tall hat.

"And by promptly, you mean . . . ?"

"Now, if not sooner," the messenger confirmed. He bowed once more, this time in Koshka's direction. "Chudo-Yudo, sir. A good day to you too." And then he turned and disappeared back into the swirling mist that was all that could be seen of the Otherworld from this close to the other side, the tip of his orange tail disappearing last like the Cheshire Cat's smile.

"Well, crap," Bella said, closing the cupboard door behind him and banging her head against it gently a couple of times. "What do you suppose that was about? She called us all to a meeting not too long ago and then canceled it. Now she's summoned me again. Do you think she somehow knows about the message from the Riders already?"

Koshka shrugged with the confidence of one who knew he had to stay behind and guard the caravan and therefore didn't have to go and face the Queen, a woman known for both her exquisite beauty and her occasional cataclysmic fits of pique. "I don't see how she could have, but maybe you'd better take it with you to show her just in case."

He looked her up and down. "And if I were you, I'd get changed first. Somehow I don't think that the Queen would be amused by bunny slippers and a tee shirt that says, 'Have fun storming the castle.'"

FRONDS OF LEMON yellow willow branches swished slowly back and forth along the sides of the path, despite a notable absence of wind. Translucent dragonflies with outsized iridescent wings darted through the leaves, their high-pitched choral song echoing up into the boundless sky. Bella smiled at a small gnome woman who was sweeping the steps of her hut, its roof not much higher than Bella's waist. The little woman waved before she went back inside; everyone in the Otherworld knew the Baba Yagas.

Bella loved the Otherworld, although she wouldn't have wanted to live there. It was a little too unpredictable for her tastes, as was its Queen. But Bella found the multihued forests charming and the varied flora and fauna (and people) fascinating. If she hadn't been on her way to court, she would have taken more time to wander the endless trails and enjoy the way the land shifted and changed with every step. As it was, though, she walked as fast as she could without breaking into an undignified trot, and got to the royal gardens only slightly out of breath.

With one last tug at her scarlet tunic and one last check to make sure her black silk pants were neatly tucked into her boots and her rebellious hair was still clinging precariously to its jeweled pins, she took a deep breath and walked down the crushed crystal pathway that led through a carved ebony gate.

Once inside, she made her way toward where the Queen and King sat amidst a crowd of elegant beautiful courtiers, all dressed in vibrant silks, satins, and velvets in as many colors as the flowers that surrounded them. The scents of gardenias and roses filled the air, and birdlike creatures swooped and dived among the abundant growth. There was no true sun in the Otherworld, but in the virtual daytime the light was bright and clear and the air was almost effervescent in its purity.

The last few nobles in her way took notice of her presence and shifted gracefully to allow her passage with the haughty manner of people who had intended to move anyway, their helpfulness only the most minor of coincidences. Bella didn't take it personally. Anyone who had lived for thousands of years tended to develop a bit of an attitude, in her experience.

Her eyes widened when she spotted both Barbara and Beka, also decked out in their formal going-to-court, don't-want-my-head-chopped-off best, but as protocol demanded, she ignored them until she'd paid homage to the royal couple.

The Queen and her consort were a study in contrasts,

although both of them were gloriously regal and inhumanly attractive. The Queen glittered from her silvery-white hair, arranged in complicated braids looped around the top of her head and topped with a crown of diamonds and amethysts the color of her icy purple eyes, to the tips of her silver shoes. Her gown was a froth of frosted blue lace, sprinkled with aquamarines, sapphires, and chalcedony that made it look as though she had captured a piece of the sky and wrapped it around her slim, straight-backed form. The King wore more muted tones of topaz and amber silk, and his dark hair and neatly pointed beard gave him an air of self-contained dignity, although his emerald-colored eyes, a shade brighter than Bella's own, held a hint of humor and affection as he greeted her.

"Ah, and here is Our final Baba Yaga," he said, his voice as melodious as the birdsong in the air around them. "Thank you for coming on such short notice."

As if she'd had any choice. The King and Queen ruled the Otherworld and all the paranormal creatures on either side of the doorways. The Babas weren't under their control, strictly speaking, but they did report to the Queen and depended on her to provide the Water of Life and Death that boosted their powers and prolonged their lives. Besides, Bella wasn't sure if anyone had ever told the Queen "no" and lived to tell the tale. She certainly wasn't going to find out what happened if you tried it.

Of course, she wasn't foolish enough to say any of that out loud, instead bowing deep first to the Queen and then to the King. "I am at your service as always, Your Majesties," she said.

The Queen waved one graceful hand, at once an acknowledgment of Bella's words and a motion for her to move back a few steps to stand with her sister Babas.

"What's going on?" she whispered to Barbara, who looked tough and striking in her usual head-to-toe black leather, her cloud of dark hair restrained in a jeweled net, and a sharp silver sword hanging from an ornate belt. Standing on Barbara's other side, Beka's shimmering green and blue skirt and top looked even more vivid than usual, her long, straight blond hair tied back with a matching ribbon.

Barbara gave a minute shrug and whispered back, "No idea," and gave Bella a brief squeeze, which was the equivalent of most other people's full body hug.

The Queen leaned forward on her seat, which appeared to have formed itself from a small, sturdy tree that grew directly from the ground underneath her, no doubt at her command. Decorative vines twined around the arms and back, turning from shades of blue to yellow as they flowed from her chair onto the King's.

"My dear Baba Yagas," she said. "We are concerned."

"Oh *hell*," muttered Barbara, then endeavored to look innocent when the Queen raised an elegant eyebrow in her direction. It wasn't a look she carried off well, but luckily the Queen chose to ignore the interruption.

"As I am sure you are all aware, Our friends the Riders have been out of contact for an unusual amount of time. They have not been seen either in your world or in the Otherworld."

Of course, she didn't use that exact word, but rather a musical ancient phrase that Bella's mentor had told her translated to something roughly along the lines of "the one true place." To Bella's ears, it sounded like chiming bells, slightly off tune for Human ears.

"Have any of you by chance heard from them since We last spoke to you?"

Beka bit her lip and Barbara looked worried. All three of them shook their heads. "No, Your Majesty," they chorused.

Bella couldn't decide whether to mention the note or not. Did it count as hearing from the Riders if she couldn't be sure it came from them? Her "no" wavered in uncertainly after the other two.

The Queen tapped an ornamental fan on the arm of her throne, once, twice, three times, as if coming to a decision.

"Very well," she said. "Enough waiting. It is not like the Riders to disappear with no word to Us or any of the Baba

Yagas. We are out of patience. It is time for them to return home."

"Your Majesty," Barbara said, "I bow to your great wisdom in this matter, of course, but how are we supposed to get them to return home if we don't know where they are or why they haven't been in touch?"

"Simple," the Queen said, seemingly mollified by Barbara's court manners. "Bella will find them for Us."

FIVE

BELLA SWALLOWED HARD. "I beg your pardon?" She added a belated half bow. "Your Majesty, why me?"

The Queen leaned forward, the faceted gems of her crown glinting in the faux sunlight. "We heard from your sister Beka that you'd seen some sign of the Riders on your travels. Is this true?"

"Well, I did think I spotted Sun's and Knight's motorcycles when I was in Montana a few weeks ago, battling some wildfires. But there were a lot of firefighters called in from outside the area, and I only saw them for a minute; I really couldn't be sure. I told Beka I thought someone who looked like Alexei Knight waved at me from a rapidly moving black Harley, but it could have been just a really huge Human."

The Queen gave the smallest of frowns. "How unfortunate. We were hoping for something more certain."

Bella sucked her breath, praying that the Queen wasn't in one of her more volatile moods. She wasn't sure how her next piece of information would be received.

"Actually, Your Majesties, I was planning to come see you today anyway," she said. Nobles who had begun drifting away subtly wafted back; it could be boring, being immortal, and anything that broke the patterns of the lengthy days was worth paying attention to. Either that, or they were hoping to see the Queen turn Bella into something amusing, like a statue. Or a swan. Or a statue of a swan.

"How intriguing," the King said, as his lady settled back into her seat with a rustling of silks and the tiniest of sighs. "Pray tell Us why, Baba Yaga."

"I believe I may have received a message from the Riders, although I can't be certain it came from them, or that it was directed toward me," Bella said. Next to her, Barbara let out a gasp and Beka said, "What? When?"

The Queen sat up even straighter. "At last. They have returned, then, Our three horsemen? We are pleased to hear it."

Bella shook her head. "I'm afraid not, Your Majesty. In fact, if the message I got was truly sent by them, then I think they might be in some kind of trouble."

The Queen's tinkling laughter soared up over blossoming elderberry bushes and twining lavender and violet roses. "The Riders? In trouble? My dear girl, the Riders eat trouble for breakfast and then twice for lunch. Whatever are you talking about? True, We are somewhat concerned about their overlong absence, but that is hardly the same thing as believing that they have met with some circumstance they could not handle. It is much more likely that they have simply gotten distracted by women or fighting. Or fighting women, one supposes." Courtiers tittered behind peacock feather fans.

But Bella stood her ground. "Normally, I would agree, Your Majesty, but a sprite brought me this note late last night, and I think it came from them." She pulled the tiny scroll out of the embroidered leather pouch that hung around her waist, and held it out so that the royal couple could see it.

The King frowned, his eyes darkening from emerald to malachite. "What *is* that thing you are holding? It does not look much like a message to me. In fact, it looks more like rubbish."

"I think it is a tiny scrap of leather off of Mikhail Day's trousers, Your Highness, tied with a few strands of Gregori Sun's hair." She took a couple of steps closer so that the Queen and King could see more clearly, although faerie eyes were so much better than Human ones, it was probably unnecessary.

The Queen sniffed. "Mikhail would never allow his garments to become so soiled," she said. "Clearly someone is having a joke at your expense. This sprite you speak of, perhaps."

Bella shook her head, and repeated the story the little winged creature had told her. "What reason would she have for making up such a tale, Your Majesty?"

"Perhaps the message came from someone else, then?" the King suggested. "The Riders are age-old, well experienced, and immortal. What could cause them to be in such dire straits that they would need to use their own clothing and hair, and the services of a passing sprite?" He shook his head. "No, I cannot believe this missive came from them, Baba Yaga. Perhaps their unaccustomed absence preys on your mind, and so you mistake this scrap of leather for something of theirs. Quite understandable."

Barbara, always the most assertive of the three Babas, stepped forward and said, "Perhaps we should ask her what the message says."

The Queen's brows rose, but she gestured with one white hand to indicate her willingness to listen.

Bella unrolled the tiny scroll with trembling fingers, although she'd already memorized the brief message. "There are only three words, Your Majesties, and my Chudo-Yudo confirms that they are written in blood that carries the scent of magic within it."

The garden grew so silent, even the grass temporarily stopped growing.

"Well?" the Queen said. "And what are those words?"

"The note says: Cave, Help, Brenna."

At the mention of Brenna's name, a ripple spread outward from the center of the circle surrounding the royals, as whispering voices repeated the message to those standing behind them who had been too far away to hear Bella's quiet voice.

Barbara's hand went involuntarily to the hilt of her sword, and Beka's normally cheerful face turned ashen. Brenna had been Beka's mentor, had raised her and trained her, but reluctant to give up the power of a Baba Yaga, had also purposely undermined her confidence in her magical abilities to the point where Beka had almost walked away from the role she was meant to play. When that course failed, Brenna had colluded with a handsome Selkie prince and, eventually, tried more than once to kill her.

In the end, Beka had triumphed, but Bella was sure the betrayal still stung. To put it mildly.

It certainly bothered the Queen, who had declared Brenna a traitor to the court, her life forfeit if any found her, and forbid the utterance of her name anywhere in the Otherworld.

Oops.

The King held out a calming hand as his consort started to rise. Beneath the Queen's feet, colorful piles of artistically coiled vines drew back from her anger, as if justifiably fearful of being singed.

"We did ask her to tell Us the words of the message," he pointed out. "It is hardly her fault that one of those words is anathema to Us."

White lines pinched the Queen's nose as her face tightened with barely restrained wrath. "Surely not even Brenna would dare to imperil the lives of the Riders," she said with a hiss.

"I don't believe we can dismiss any possibility when it comes to that woman," Barbara said. Her tone was calm and even, but Bella could see her hands clenched in fists at her sides. "She tried to kill a Baba Yaga. The woman"—Barbara carefully avoided uttering the forbidden name—"is completely, totally, nut-cracking insane."

Another wave of muttering went through the assembled nobles at Barbara's bluntness, but no one disagreed. It was a well-known fact, although little discussed in polite circles, that in rare instances, too-long use of the potent Water of Life and Death brought on a kind of madness called Water Sickness. This was one of the reasons why Baba Yagas eventually stopped drinking it and retired to a quiet life in some luxurious corner of the Otherworld, leaving their newly trained replacements to take their places. Only Brenna hadn't wanted to give up the power of being a Baba Yaga, and had stalled too long. Eventually, the Queen had forced her to retire and give up her position to Beka, but by then, the damage was done.

Of course, Barbara's theory was that she'd been unbalanced all along, but no one mentioned that either. The only thing scarier than an out-of-control Baba Yaga was one who was both out of control and, as Barbara had put it, "completely, totally, nut-cracking insane."

The Queen looked from the note to Bella, and tapped her chin thoughtfully. She and the King exchanged glances, communicating in the silent fashion of longtime couples.

"Very well, Bella," she said, finally. "You have piqued Our interest. We believe this matter to be of some concern, although it is to be sincerely hoped that your suppositions about the origins of this mysterious message will be proven incorrect. You have Our permission, nay, Our command, to investigate and report back to Us."

Barbara and Beka both stepped forward in unison, although it was Beka who spoke, unusually firmly. "We'd like to help, Your Majesties."

The Queen dismissed the offer with a wave of her diamond- and ruby-encrusted scepter. "Brenna is old and no longer has access to the Water of Life and Death, and Bella is still young and at the height of her power. Bella should have no problems handling her, *if* she is behind this, which We doubt. You both have your own duties to attend to, and more than enough to do as it is. Bella knows where to find you if she needs your assistance. We had already intended to task her with this mission. Her news merely gives Us one more reason to do so." Her tone made it very clear that Bella had better *not* need assistance, if she knew what was good for her.

"Well, this was certainly interesting," the Queen said, rising gracefully and taking her consort's arm as he rose along with her. "But I do believe it is time for tea."

Swell, Bella thought. *So all I have to do is solve the mystery of where the Riders have vanished to, based on the tiniest of clues, and how, if at all, a deranged former Baba Yaga is involved. Piece of cake.* Suddenly she wished that tea was a nice, strong martini.

MIKHAIL DAY LIFTED his head a scant millimeter off the rough, uneven floor and then dropped it down again, exhausted by just that small effort. The scent of damp rock and musty air and rusting iron surrounded him, making him long for clean summer breezes.

He thought wistfully about some of the ocean shores he'd visited in his long life, with their crashing waves and swirling sand, bright blue skies and joyfully soaring sea birds. But that distraction only worked for a moment, and then the craggy cave walls crouching like motionless prehistoric beasts curved in around him again, making his chest tighten with newfound claustrophobia.

He was starting to think that he would never see the ocean again. Or feel the wind on his face. They were going to die in this dark pit in the marrow of the world, and it was all his fault.

"You okay, Mik?" Alexei's deep voice sounded hoarse as it echoed off the rock around them.

The three Riders were all encased within the same cave, but it was just large enough that none of them could touch any of the others, no matter how hard they strained to reach out with torn, bloodied fingertips. Spell-armored cages chained them in their separate spots, such that they were unable to move other than to sit up or lie down. Not that it mattered anymore; none of them was strong enough to break loose, even if the bars had been made of tin. Although Alexei had nearly ripped his arms out of their sockets trying, in the beginning.

"I'm fine," Mikhail whispered. But of course it wasn't true. None of them were fine, least of all him.

The witch had captured him first. He'd been so cocky, so proud—he'd never seen it coming. In all their thousands of years of existence, nothing and no one had ever truly threatened the Riders, although plenty had tried. So when he'd stopped on his way out to aid Beka on the West Coast, he'd assumed he would stride in as he always did, rescue the damsel in distress, and leave her sighing pleasantly over his handsomeness and gallantry as he rode away on his enchanted white Yamaha. He'd always had a weakness for a good damsel in distress.

Alas, this time the damsel was anything but good. Evil, in fact, one might be tempted to say. Especially if one ended up chained to a cold, uncomfortable cave floor, being tortured over and over again and drained of one's lifeblood and magical energy. And to make things even worse, to have been used as bait to lure in the two other men who were both companions in battle and friends of the soul, and be forced to watch them endure the same agonizing treatment.

Yes, he thought, *evil* was not too strong a word for her. He hated Brenna with every wounded fiber of his being, and if wishes made things true, she would be the one writhing in pain, her own essence trickling away into the gray dirt.

Alas, for the moment, that fervent wish might as well have been the breeze on some distant beach, for all his chances of attaining it. Their cages seemed unescapable, and none of their gifts—not Alexei's strength, nor Gregori's wisdom, nor his own charm—could get them out. They could only hold on as each of them was bled again and again, and pray that one of the Baba Yagas had received Gregori's message and was able to figure out its obscure clues in time.

Sadly, time seemed to be something they were running out of fast.

$\mathcal{S}$IX

SAM PACED THE small space; thirteen steps in one direction, then turn and thirteen steps back again. From force of habit, he maneuvered around the small rickety table, the neatly made single bed, and the miniature kitchen with its once-white propane stove and dorm-sized refrigerator. Every time he swung back toward the south he could see the smoke, its gray-black plume rising up above the tall ponderosas in the distance.

Part of him ached to be down there, attacking the fire with chain saw and polaski and sheer teeth-clenching grit, struggling through the smoke and the exhaustion and the blisters until the job was done. He could almost feel his heart beating in time with those who were, his mouth dry and his muscles tense in sympathy. They'd been battling this one for two days; two long days during which Sam watched and waited and battled with his wish to be in the midst of the fire, his relief that he wasn't, and the guilt that came with both.

Finally, just before dark, he could see the smoke dwindle, mixing with the early evening clouds until it disappeared into the gloom. The two-way radio for the county zone officer clicked and buzzed at him, bringing the news that the fire was under control and all those fighting it were safely back at base. A few had been selected to stay overnight, keeping an eye out for flare-ups, but the crisis was over.

"Any hint of what started it?" Sam asked, feeling the tightness in his neck starting to ease.

Click. "Nope. Just like the last couple. No lightning that anyone saw, no sign of a campfire or careless smoking, although this one was burning pretty hot by the time we managed to hike in to the site, so no way to tell for sure. We lost some old growth trees and about ten acres, but kept it from taking one of those new cabins, so we're calling it a win." *Click.*

Sam rubbed the back of his hand over gritty eyes. "Good to hear," he said. "Your guys did a great job. Too bad about the trees, but at least you saved the rest of the area."

Click. "Speaking of which, I'm sending a little present your way." *Click.*

"What?" Sam thought he heard a chuckle in the other man's voice, but it was hard to make out through the crackling static of the radios. "What are you talking about?"

"You'll see." The other man signed off, leaving Sam slightly puzzled, but mostly just grateful that they'd made it through another fire without anyone getting hurt.

He'd reheated some stale coffee from the morning and was halfheartedly sipping at it while trying to read when he heard footsteps on the stairs. It was pretty unusual to have visitors at this time of the day; the tower was sixty-nine feet up, with seventy-five stairs to climb. Intimidating enough in the daytime, even more so in the waning light of the slowly setting summer sun. In fact, there was only one person who occasionally showed up this late, his closest "neighbor," Tiny, who lived with his wife in a cabin not far from the tower.

Tiny was, in fact, about six foot six, which must have made it interesting for him in the days when he had worked the job Sam had now. The ceiling of the tower wasn't much higher than Tiny was. At somewhere past seventy, Tiny was still active and fit, and he occasionally subbed for Sam on the rare occasions Sam needed to make an unavoidable run into town.

"Hey, Sam!" Tiny said, knocking perfunctorily and ducking his head as he came inside. His gray hair was pulled back into a short ponytail, and he wore a denim shirt, blue jeans, and a well-worn pair of hiking boots. A knapsack slung over one shoulder was emitting much better aromas than anything Sam ever cooked, and there was a small cardboard box tucked under his other arm.

"Evening, Tiny," Sam said, getting to his feet. "Do I smell Mrs. Tiny's three-alarm chili?" He actually didn't mind having the older man around. Unlike most people, Tiny didn't care about Sam's history or his scars and didn't seem at all self-conscious around the former Hotshot. He was blunt and straightforward, and sometimes in his company Sam would actually forget for ten or fifteen minutes that he wasn't the man he used to be. Tiny had lost part of three fingers to a chain saw before Sam had met him; maybe this made him more accustomed to disfigurement than most. Or maybe it was just his easygoing nature.

"Yep, that it is," Tiny said, placing the bag carefully on the table. "I was coming up here anyway, so she insisted I bring you up a couple of meals' worth. She thinks you don't eat enough. Silly woman would feed the entire world if they'd sit still long enough for her to do it." The words might have sounded critical, but Sam could hear the pride and affection in Tiny's voice.

"Well, you tell her I said thank you. You know I love her chili. But to what do I owe the honor?"

Tiny snorted. "What, you thought we wouldn't notice all that wood you cut and stacked for us a couple of days ago? Or maybe we'd think it was done by elves?"

Sam shrugged, looking away. He liked helping the older couple, who were both kind and didn't seem to mind acting as a buffer between him and the rest of the world. He just didn't like being thanked.

"No big deal. I was out taking my walk before I went in service and saw the logs sitting there. Figured I could use the extra workout. I'm going to get fat sitting around up here in the tower all season if I'm not careful. Especially if your wife keeps sending up her fabulous cooking."

He didn't mention that having her husband use the ax made Mrs. Tiny nervous. (Her real name was Lisa, but nobody called her that.) Left to himself, Tiny would have chopped the entire stack anyway, and probably done just fine, but it hadn't taken Sam long to do it. Anyway, the physical labor helped him sleep, a little.

"You said you were coming up here anyway? What for? I thought you said you weren't going to play chess with me after that last time."

Tiny snorted. "I swear you cheated. Checkmate in six moves. That was just plain rude. But no, I came by to bring you something. One of the guys who worked on the fire dropped it by, said the county warden told him that you had a soft spot for critters."

He put the cardboard box down next to the chili and opened the top. Two huge yellow eyes blinked up at Sam, set in a round ball of fuzz with a gray beak in the middle.

A smile tugged at the scar tissue around the left side of his mouth. "That's a baby great horned owl, isn't it?" Sam asked softly, not wanting to spook the small bird. "It's awfully young to be on its own. Where's its mama?"

"Lost in the fire, they think," Tiny said. "Leastwise they found this little guy on the ground under a tree, spotted some charred remnants of a nest, but not much else. Paul said you nursed a baby squirrel they found last season, thought you might want to try your hand at this one."

"I don't mind trying," Sam said. And it was true. It gave him something to do with his downtime, and even if it was kind of silly, saving that squirrel had made him feel like he'd actually won a tiny battle with the fire. "But he belongs with a certified wildlife rehabilitator."

Tiny rolled his eyes. "'Course he does. But our local rehabilitator is in the hospital for the next few months. Some kind of car accident, I think. So you might as well try your hand at keeping him alive, if you feel like taking him on. It's either that or he can go back into the woods."

Sam reached out one cautious finger and ran it over the soft feathers on the top of its head. "You know they eat things like mice, right? Did you bring some with you along with Mrs. Tiny's chili?"

"Ha!" Tiny had a laugh like a tuba. "Are you kidding? We spend all our time trying to keep the mice out. I start fetching them in, my wife will kill me. You're on your own there, fella. But I'm sure you'll think of something." He clouted Sam affectionately on the back and clomped his way back toward the door.

Sam looked down at his new companion. "I don't suppose you are willing to try some of Mrs. Tiny's chili instead, pal?"

The bird bobbed its head up and down, *eep*ing repeatedly as if having a one-sided conversation only it could understand. Sam glanced out the window at the encroaching dusk. If he could jury-rig a couple of traps quickly enough, he could still get them set out before full dark. In the morning, maybe he could call Dennis on the cell phone and see if he could dig up something helpful in his storeroom and bring it with him on his next trip to the tower. Or maybe a pet store in town carried mice for people who had snakes. In the meanwhile, Sam would just have to see what he could come up with.

"You may have to settle for raw chicken," he told the owl. "But I'll do the best I can."

SAM HAD A flashlight tucked into his back pocket, but it was still just light enough to see without it. He'd ridden the four-wheeler down to the main trail, but from there he hiked the rest of the way. Sam loved the forest at dusk when the nocturnal animals started to make their rounds and all of the people were gone, except a camper or two.

And one wandering painter, apparently.

He saw Bella before she saw him, and took a moment to

soak in the glorious sight. Her red hair was carelessly pulled back into a ponytail, a few errant waves escaping to curl around her heart-shaped face. She wore what looked like a man's blue work shirt with the sleeves rolled up and a pair of worn jeans. Sam had never seen anything more beautiful in his life. There was just something about the woman, a kind of a glow he couldn't explain. Not that he was interested, of course. Just . . . intrigued.

Tugging the brim of his cap as far down as it would go, Sam cleared his throat. "Evening," he said. He hoped he didn't startle her too badly.

Bella turned around with a bright smile, not seeming at all alarmed by his presence. "Hi, there. Sam, isn't it? We've got to stop meeting like this."

He ducked his head, turning a little to hide the damaged side of his face. His slightly too-long hair swung forward, as it was supposed to, covering a little bit more. "I don't know," he said. "It could be worse. At least you're not a bear."

"Maybe I'm a bear in disguise," she said lightly. "You never know in the forest. Appearances can be deceiving."

Sam chuckled. "You sound like my grandmother. She used to read me fairy tales when I was a kid. She especially liked the ones with witches in them; even predicted I'd meet one someday."

"Really? Your grandmother predicted you'd meet a witch?" Bella raised an eyebrow. "And did she think that was going to be a good thing or a bad thing?"

"You know, she never said. But since most of the stories she told me involved witches that ate small children or turned people into things, probably not so good." He thought about it for a minute. "Although I'd still kind of like to find out for myself."

Bella made a small choking noise. He thought she was probably trying not to laugh at him. He didn't blame her. She must think he was an idiot. Talking to women these days made him uncomfortable, and he tended to babble.

"So, you believe in witches?" she asked. Her green eyes gleamed at him in the soft evening light.

He shrugged. "In the forest, almost anything seems possible. At least to me."

"Oh, to me too," Bella agreed. "Forests are definitely magical places."

Sam took a few steps closer. He could tell when she saw the scars, because her eyes widened briefly. But she didn't seem all that shocked and didn't ask him about them, which he appreciated. For a moment, it was almost as though they were two normal people, chatting amidst the trees. He knew it was an illusion, but it was one he treasured just the same.

"It's a little late to be wandering around," he said. "There really are bears in the woods, and someone saw some mountain lion tracks the other day. You should probably be heading back to your camper."

"It's a caravan, actually. Kind of like a hut with legs, only the legs are wheels," she said. "And I was more or less wandering in that direction. I was out sketching and kind of lost track of time. Artists, you know."

Sketching? Sam hadn't noticed a sketchbook, but now she pulled one out from behind her back, so he must not have been looking very carefully. Probably too distracted by the rest of her, which he definitely found pretty damned distracting.

"Can I see?" he asked.

"Oh. Ah . . ." She hesitated. He thought maybe she was shy about showing her work, especially to some random guy she kept bumping into in the middle of the woods. But finally she shrugged and handed it over.

He had to tip it sideways to catch the fading light, but then he was genuinely impressed by what he saw. There were charcoal, ink, and pencil sketches of all sorts of wildlife; a chipmunk standing on its hind legs holding a nut, a marmot on the ridge, even a deer with two fawns who looked like they were posing. Page after page of chickadees, nuthatches, flickers, and bluebirds. There were also pictures of interesting trees covered with moss or mushrooms.

These were the same things that fascinated him, the textures and shapes and life of the woods all caught on paper.

Then he turned a page and saw why she'd hesitated. He saw himself, that first time they'd met. An idealized version, since Sam knew he'd never looked that good, even before things went to hell, but recognizably him. It gave him a funny feeling in the pit of his stomach, looking at the sketch she'd done based on his right side, which was all he'd let her see, and he shut the notebook and handed it back to her.

"Nice," he said, not meeting her eyes. "I like the one of the deer."

"That was a lovely morning, meeting up with Mona and her girls," Bella said. Her hand brushed his as she took the notebook, and a tingle ran up his arm.

"You call the doe Mona?" Sam said, startled out of his self-consciousness for a moment.

"Well sure," Bella said. "What else would I call her? That's her name."

Sure it was. And no doubt the deer had told her so. All their conversations seemed a little odd, and Sam was pretty sure she was having a laugh at his expense. He almost didn't care.

BELLA COULD HAVE kicked herself. Twice. First she'd forgotten to bring the sketchbook with her while she went out searching for any trace of the Riders, and she'd had to conjure it magically out of the caravan and hope that Sam didn't realize she hadn't had it all along. And then she made that stupid comment about the doe's name. She clearly spent way too much time hanging out with a dragon-cat and not enough with regular people. She was out of the habit of normal conversation. The poor guy was going to think she was a nutball. Which was too bad, because she still thought he was the best-looking man she'd ever met. And he seemed funny and nice too. A triple threat to a woman who was interested. Which she wasn't, alas.

The scars had startled her for a moment, since she hadn't noticed them the first time they'd met. Then she'd realized that he purposely kept his head turned slightly to the left most of the time, probably so they wouldn't be so obvious. She recognized them as burn scars—she'd know better than most what those looked like—but it seemed rude to ask. Besides, to her mind they didn't make him any less handsome. Just more interesting.

She'd never understood Humans' obsession with perfection and normality. Of course, she'd spent a lot of her formative years wandering around the Otherworld with her mentor Baba, where normal came in more shades and sizes than most Humans could imagine, so she supposed her view was a little different than most.

"So, you know why I'm in the forest at this hour. What's your excuse?" she asked. "I mean, other than hunting for witches." She snickered, thinking how amazed he'd be—or maybe appalled—to discover he was standing and talking to one right now.

He held up what looked like a pile of twigs tied together with twine. "Believe it or not, I'm trying to set traps to catch mice."

Bella blinked. In her experience, most people didn't go looking for mice on purpose, although the ones she'd met had always seemed quite pleasant. "Is this some kind of strange Wyoming hobby I haven't heard about, or are you just getting lonely up in that fire tower?"

A tiny smile hovered at the corner of his mouth. "Neither. I'm trying to take care of a little owlet some of the firefighters found today. His nest burned, along with his mama, and the local wildlife rehabilitator is out of commission. So I'm filling in until they can find someone with more experience. The mice are for his supper, if I can catch any."

"Ah," she said. *Damn. Good-looking, funny, and really nice. It figured. Too bad he was Human. Off-limits. Not for all Baba Yagas, necessarily, but definitely for her. Especially since it seemed like she was going to run into him every time she went out searching for the Riders. She couldn't afford to let some guy distract her, no matter how appealing he was.*

"Owls go through a lot of mice in a day," she said. "Even

small owls. You're going to have a hard time catching enough, even with that, um, interesting contraption."

"Hey!" Sam said with mock indignation. "I worked for at least fifteen minutes on these things, and I've got them scattered within a mile's radius of the tower. I even used my best stinky cheese to bait them."

Bella bit her lip. Did he even have any idea of how adorable he was? She was willing to bet he didn't. Of course, she could magically lure some mice into his cages, but she didn't think she needed to. Not when she had the ultimate secret weapon.

"I've got something even better than stinky cheese," she said. "Come on back to the caravan with me and I'll show you."

"Okay," Sam said. "But only so I can protect you from bears, not because I don't have faith in my ingenious traps."

"Fair enough," Bella said, hooking her arm through his. "Protect away. I'm feeling safer already."

SEVEN

THEY WALKED A ways in companionable silence, and then Bella said, "So, you said there was another fire? I didn't see any smoke."

Sam's mouth turned down, and he pulled his arm away from hers, although she didn't think he did it consciously. "It was off to the south. About thirty miles away. You might have caught a whiff or two, but otherwise it was far enough away not to affect this area. Took them two days, but they got it under control this afternoon. Nobody got hurt."

There seemed to be a special emphasis on that last statement. She wondered if it had anything to do with his burns, but decided not to ask. She got the feeling that any mention of fire made him defensive, which she thought was kind of strange for a guy who lived in a fire tower, but what the hell did she know about Human norms?

"That's good," she said. "So did you spot it from the tower?"

He nodded.

"That's cool. It must be a great job, staying up in that fire tower for months at a time, helping to keep the area safe."

Sam gave her a funny look. "Most people's first response is to ask if it gets lonely."

Bella laughed. "I know what you mean. People say the same thing about me traveling around in the caravan. They obviously don't realize how restful it is to be away from people." She waved an arm around to indicate the trees around them. "Besides, you get to protect all this. That's fabulous."

"It is," he said. "But it's not like being on the ground fighting fires."

Bella suppressed a sigh. As far as she was concerned, there was nothing romantic about fighting fire. It wasn't her friend, but it wasn't her enemy either. At least not most of the time.

"I suppose not," she said. "Well, here we are." The lights of the caravan were warm and welcoming in the encroaching darkness. A shadow detached itself from the bulk of the caravan and materialized into a ridiculously large feline with a long ruff around his neck.

"You remember Koshka, right?" she said, leaning down to pat her companion on his wide head.

"Who could forget such a magnificent cat?" Sam asked, causing Koshka to purr and wrap himself around Sam's ankles.

Bella rolled her eyes. "Yes, he is magnificent, isn't he?" More so in dragon form, but the less said about that the better. "He's also the solution to your mouse problem."

Sam looked confused. "What do you mean? I admit, cats are great at catching mice, but it isn't as though you can ask him to go fetch you one and he'll do it."

She smirked. "Want to bet?" Humans. It was almost too easy. "How about you cook me dinner if you lose?"

"Sure," Sam said, probably thinking she was kidding. "But I warn you, my cooking is elemental at best."

"No problem," Bella said. "I'm all about the elements." She turned to Koshka and said, "Okay, stop sucking up to our guest. Yes, you're gorgeous and we all know it. Can you make yourself useful and go catch me a few mice?"

"*Mice?*" Koshka huffed indignantly. "I'm a damned dragon! I don't fetch mice." Of course, to Sam it would just sound like a peeved meow.

Bella bit back a giggle as she bent down to whisper in one tufted ear. "I know. I know. But Sam is taking care of a baby owl and he needs mice to feed it. He put together a pathetic attempt at a trap, but he's never going to be able to catch nearly enough to feed a youngster that way. I thought maybe you'd be willing to help out."

"It would be a lot easier if I just ate the owlet," Koshka suggested. But after a glance at the bundle of twigs in Sam's hand, he shook his head from side to side and slunk off into the woods.

Bella turned to Sam, who was looking a bit bemused. "Would you like a beer or a cup of tea while we wait?"

"Uh, sure," he said. "A beer would be great. And I love the way it seems like you and the cat are actually having a conversation, but you don't really expect him to come back with a mouse, do you?"

She fetched a couple of beers, and they sat down together on the steps of the caravan. "I guess we'll have to see, won't we? But just for the record, I like my meat rare and my potatoes crispy."

The two of them sat side by side, chatting about Sam's days in the fire tower and Bella's travels (albeit with some of the good bits left out). She had a moment to wonder at how comfortable it all seemed before a gray-brown form misted out of the forest and deposited a pile of mice at their feet. Four, she thought, or maybe five. It would at least keep the little owlet alive until Koshka could find more. Sam's eyes were so big, she thought they might fall out of his face.

"What the hell?"

"You needed mice. You've got mice. And also, you owe me dinner." She went inside and got a small basket to put the mice in, and Koshka very neatly picked each one up and deposited it inside. Bella handed Sam the basket with a grin. "Ta-da!"

Sam looked from her to Koshka and back again, then

down at the basket. "That is either the best-trained cat on the planet, or the guys are playing a *really* complicated practical joke on me."

Or I just sent my dragon into the woods to fetch rodents for you because I'm the wicked witch your grandmother warned you about.

Bella just smiled. "Like you said, in the forest anything seems possible. Maybe he ran away from the circus when he was young."

Sam shook his head. "Uh-huh. Well, thank you, Koshka. I appreciate it."

Koshka licked one paw, looking as smug as a dragon could while still in cat form.

Bella and Koshka watched Sam walk away, Bella feeling strangely wistful in a way she couldn't explain.

"Thanks, Koshka," she said. "I owe you."

"Damn straight. Do you have any idea how terrible mice taste?"

"Not from personal experience, no," she said. "I don't suppose a can of tuna would help take away the taste?"

"We can only try," said the dragon-cat in a martyred tone, and he stalked up the stairs into the caravan with his bushy tail held high.

SAM STOOD FOR a few minutes at the entrance to the clearing where Bella's caravan was parked. He was hidden behind a thick stand of bushes, but he wasn't spying, he told himself; just watching to see if she did anything suspicious. The resinous fronds tickled his nose, and a bead of sweat ran down the back of his shirt. He should give this up, climb on his four-wheeler, and go back to the fire tower.

Yet for some reason, his legs didn't move and his eyes stayed focused on the woman as she sat by a small fire pit, roasting a marshmallow and talking nonsense to her gigantic cat. Not exactly criminal behavior, although she'd somehow gotten the little bonfire started amazingly quickly, between the time he'd walked away and when he'd stopped and turned around to watch her. She must have had it primed and ready to go. It looked safe enough, anyway, the pit deep and surrounded by rocks, with no wind to blow an errant spark outside the depths of the hole.

Her red hair was muted in the glow of the fire and the one dim light that hung above the caravan door, but it still brought back memories. Good ones, mostly, although these days good memories brought as much pain as bad ones. But he didn't think his fascination with Bella had anything to do with her hair, despite the fact that his lost love had also been a redhead.

They were nothing alike, outside of their shared hair color. Heather had been stocky and strong, her round face and sturdy arms covered with the freckles he'd loved to tease her about, pretending they were a road map that could lead to his heart. As placid as an Irish lake in the sunlight, Heather had been calm and straightforward whether fighting fire or making love.

This Bella, on the other hand, was mysterious and exotic—the only thing straightforward about her was her steady green gaze. Taller and more willowy than Heather, her face was a creamy white touched with peach on her high cheekbones, and her hair was longer, curly and wild as it tumbled down her back. If she had any freckles, they were in places he couldn't see. No, the two women couldn't have been more different.

And yet there was something about her that tugged at him, like a compass pointing north. He didn't understand it and he didn't like it. So it was easier to call it suspicion, if that would allow him to stand there for a few more minutes, listening to the sound of her tenor voice echo through the clearing like birdsong on the first warm day of spring.

DUSKY WATER RIPPLED then stilled, until the scrying bowl was as dark and silent as the grave. Brenna bent over the water and peered into the surface as an image slowly appeared. These days, she tried not to use such magics; they were tricky to hold and drained what power she had left all too quickly. But she needed to see the man from the fire tower, and it was hard to watch him any other way.

She'd figured out days ago that since her plan required the forest to burn, the fire watcher—Sam, his name was— would have to go. And the sooner the better.

It was tempting to just kill him. Unlike this new, soft, younger generation of Baba Yagas, Brenna had no qualms about an occasional death here or there. After all, they were supposed to be keeping the balance of nature; she supposed the planet would be grateful to have a few less Humans running about making a mess of things. But his death or disappearance would attract attention, and that was the one thing she was trying to avoid at all costs.

So she'd done a little research instead; put on her harmless elderly hippie guise and wandered about town asking seemingly aimless questions of the locals, puttering around in a rusty brown truck she'd liberated from behind a nearby barn.

Brenna missed her old hut, transformed many years ago into a brightly painted school bus, and the mortar and pestle that had become a little blue Karmann Ghia. But they were long gone, passed on to her replacement, along with her Chudo-Yudo and her share of the Water of Life and Death. For now. Until she got them back, and more with them.

Small towns were all the same in her experience; lots of people who knew way too much about everything that went on, all too eager to share what they knew with anyone who asked. She'd gathered all sorts of information that way, in the diner and the grocery store, at the one gas station and the tiny post office. Then she'd taken what she'd learned and gone to the library (open three days a week from nine until noon, for a wonder) and used the Internet to fill in the blanks. Brenna wasn't fond of the modern world, for the most part, but even she had to admit that computers could be quite handy at times.

A curious man, this fire watcher; dedicated to his job, from what people said, but oh, such a tragic past. Brenna laughed quietly to herself, careful not to let her breath stir the water. It didn't seem as though it would take much effort to make him leave. He was barely holding on as it was, from the sound of it. Post-traumatic something or other. The name didn't matter to her, as long as it got her what she wanted.

The picture in the scrying bowl was clear, albeit miniature, as though seen from far away. Brenna watched as the man walked down the many steps of the tower and mounted his mechanical steed. Four-wheelers. Another Human abomination. Loud and disruptive in the otherwise peaceful forest. Still, she supposed he had to get around somehow, and at least it made him easy to track.

He stopped periodically, laying down odd contraptions whose purpose she couldn't discern. Eventually she parked the machine and walked off the path until he came across a woman.

Brenna gripped the edges of the silver bowl so hard they cut into her hands, but she managed to keep the gasp from slipping past her lips. What was *she* doing here?

Gah. That was all Brenna needed, a Baba Yaga running around, getting in her way. Still, at least it wasn't Barbara. That one was a terror. But the redhead, Bella, well, she could be handled. Or avoided, even better. But handled if necessary.

Was her presence here a coincidence, or had she been *Called* to deal with the fires? Either one was a possibility. One was more of a problem than the other, but nothing Brenna couldn't deal with.

Brenna looked on as the fire watcher and the Baba Yaga talked, deep in the forest. *Redhead. Redhead. Why did that remind her of something she'd seen or heard about recently?*

Brenna scowled fretfully at the dim reflection of her own wrinkled face, overlaid on the images in the bowl. She could feel her true age creeping up on her now that she no longer had the Water of Life and Death to stave it off. The whitening of her hair was annoying, the aches in her bones even more so. But worst of all was this fog in her mind.

Sometimes it seemed as though her thoughts were

squirrels, dashing here and there, chasing shadows, flitting from place to place. It took more and more effort to focus, but focus she must if her plan was to succeed and the power that was rightfully hers was to be returned, along with her youth.

Nothing would stop her. Certainly not some damaged former firefighter and a Baba Yaga who spent most of her adult life hiding from Humans and her own lack of control. Brenna chuckled to herself. At least she didn't need to worry about them teaming up to work against her; neither one would spend any more time in the company of others than could be helped.

Ah yes! A redhead! Brenna laughed out loud as she remembered where she'd come across another whose hair was as bright as Bella's long locks, and a brilliant idea popped into her head. The movement jarred the bowl, causing the water to slosh and the images to disappear. But no matter. She had what she needed anyway. The poor fire watcher was as good as gone already. As for Bella, well, hopefully she was just passing through. If not, Brenna thought, chuckling again, there was always that temper. Worse came to worst, she could probably get Bella to burn the forest down for her.

IGHT

THE FLAMES ROARED like wild beasts as they surrounded the fire shelter, creating violent winds that tugged and pulled at the fragile layers of aluminum, silica, and fiberglass. Inside the shelter, Sam hugged the ground, breathing through the bandana he'd pulled up over his face right before deploying the "shake and bake" in a last-ditch effort to survive a raging forest fire that had suddenly changed direction and surrounded him and his Hotshots team.

He knew that his friends were all huddled beneath their own shelters, facedown, feet pointed toward the oncoming flames. Some of the team were within touching distance, but inside the belly of the inferno, all he could hear was the sound of his own rough, labored breathing and the pounding of his heart.

But in the dream, he could hear them screaming as they died.

Wake up! Wake up! Like all the times before, Sam knew he was dreaming, knew the worst had already happened, that there was nothing he could do, nothing he could have done. Still his heart raced and sweat poured down his body, just as it had on that terrible day. The memory of heat seared the inside of his nostrils and dried his mouth, and still the dream unwound like a horror movie with no plot other than death and destruction. And fire. Always the fire.

Sam could feel the ravenous flames as they passed directly over him, clawing and prying at the shelter, looking for any opening to slide through and steal his precious remaining oxygen. Could sense when the beast finally moved off, seeking trees to devour and brush to feed its insatiable hunger. Listened frantically for any signs of life outside of his own tiny bubble of safety. Heard nothing but his own ragged breathing, echoing in his ears.

"Ryan!" he called to his best friend. "You okay out there?" No answer.

"Heather! Heather! You okay?" His fiancée, so proud to be one of the few female Hotshots in the country—the last time he'd seen her she'd been deploying her own shelter, no more than two feet away, grinning that maniac grin as she waved to him one last time.

In the dream, there was screaming. Sobbing. Cries for help. In real life, there had been only silence. Even the wind had vanished.

Sam reached a hand up to touch the side of the shelter. Too hot. The rule was to wait until it cooled. And he tried. Tried to wait until he was sure it was safe. But he knew they were out there. His friends. His lover. Nineteen other wilderness firefighters who'd fought side by side with him. And in the end, he'd gotten out too soon.

Air that was still superheated had seared his lungs. He'd tripped and fallen on his way to Heather's shake and bake, barely noticing the agonizing pain on the left side of his face where it hit the smoldering ground. Frantically, he'd called her name, all their names. But he was the only one left. All the others had died, curled up in their shelters, victims of a fire that burned like a demon on a piece of land too slanted and tangled to protect them.

And in a fluke of unreasonable luck, the main force of the fire had veered around his shelter, leaving him alive.

Alive, alone, and filled with grief that burned hotter than any fire.

Gasping for oxygen, Sam shot upright in his narrow bed, sheets tangled around his legs, torso dripping with sweat as if he'd truly been back in the shelter. Muscles cramped and burned. The scar tissue on his face itched as if freshly healed. But nothing about Sam was truly healed. The nightmares proved that, forcing him to relive the worst day of his life, over and over again.

Sam swung his legs over the side of the bed and staggered over to the sink to get a glass of water. He drank it down fast and cold, wishing it were whiskey. But he'd tried that route the first few months after he left the hospital, and it didn't help. The oblivion was only temporary, and his fireman's soul was too used to needing to be ready to jump up at any moment, prepared to do battle with the fire. So he stayed sober. And suffered through every minute of every day.

All Sam had ever wanted to be was a firefighter. As a boy, he'd been obsessed with the wailing red trucks, the helmeted men and their gear. As he got older, he was drawn to the wilderness with its majestic beauty and fragile ecosystem. Joining the Hotshots felt like a natural progression of that dream. Being part of an elite team of firefighters, even when it meant spending days facing unimaginable danger, coming home covered with minor burns, exhausted and filthy, was all he could have asked for. When Heather joined the team and they fell in love, life was perfect.

Until the fire turned his life into an unbearable tumult of never-ending pain and guilt. The shrink they'd made him see—after—had talked to him about survivor's guilt. How hard it was to be the one who lived. But the man had no idea. No idea what it was like to go on without his friends, without the woman whose laughter used to rise up like sparks from a bonfire into the night. No idea what it was like to ache to fight fires, but be unable to do the one thing that had given his life purpose.

Sam had tried, once, to join another team. He'd broken down on the first day and had to admit to himself that he'd never be able to face the flames again. In the end, he'd retreated to the fire tower. It was at once a place for him to hide and the best compromise he could find; a way to fight the fires without having to be near them. It didn't feel like enough, but it was the best he could do.

Most days, it was *almost* an acceptable existence. Nights like this, it felt like the third circle of hell. The only thing that kept him going was the knowledge that it would shame the memory of his lost comrades if he threw away the life he'd somehow been gifted with when all those who mattered to him had lost theirs.

A faint glow from behind him made him turn around. The glass slid unnoticed out of his grasp and hit the floor, bounced on the braided blue rag rug in front of the sink, and rolled under the table.

She stood in the middle of the room—Heather, looking much as she had the last time he'd seen her alive, her fire gear draped over one shoulder, helmet tucked under the other arm.

Sam reached out one hand, and then pulled it back, clenched into a fist. It wasn't her. He knew that. It wasn't as though he didn't believe in ghosts; of course he did, with the grandmother he'd had and all of her tales. In fact, he'd waited after the disaster, waited night after night for Heather's ghost to appear. First in the hospital, then, figuring its antiseptic stink and hissing machines had kept her away, back at home. Waited, but she never came.

So why would Heather be here now? She wouldn't, would she?

"Sam," she whispered, her voice almost as rough as his, almost too low to hear. The sound was as unfamiliar as her face was dear. But maybe that was how the dead sounded. How would he know?

"Sam," she said again. "I saw you with her. In the woods. With that woman. Have you forgotten me so soon, my love?"

He took an involuntary step backward, his bare skin shocked by the chill metal of the sink. "What?" he asked. "What woman? Forgotten you? No, never." Part of his brain thought, *Crazy man, talking to an empty room*, and the other part just thought, *Heather*, and drowned in rippling waves of pain and sorrow.

"The woman in the forest. Red hair, like mine. Not me. Not for you. Stay away."

The figure seemed as solid as the chair, the floor, the lump in his throat. She looked just like Heather. But why would Heather care if he talked to a passing stranger? She'd never been the jealous type, in life. Of course, who knew what the dead felt?

"I could never forget you," he said again. "I think of you every day." A single hot tear ran down over scarred tissue and was ignored. "Are you really here?"

"Leave the woman alone. Leave this place. You do not belong here. You should not be here. Leave. Leave. Leave." The eerie whisper rose to a strangled shriek that made the hair stand up on the back of Sam's neck.

Out of nowhere there came a crashing clap of thunder, and Sam spun around to see a jagged bolt of lightning split the sky. When he turned back, there was nothing there. No one there. Just the screen door of the tower swinging open and then closed in a sudden gust of wind.

Sam staggered over to latch it shut on numb feet, flicking on the small light by his desk. Nothing. No one. Just an empty room with an unmade bed and a splash of water on the floor where his glass had landed. Unbroken, thankfully, unlike his heart. And maybe his mind.

Had she really been there? Had Heather's ghost finally come to see him, only to tell him to give up the fire tower that was his last refuge? Or was it just his own guilt, caused by his momentary attraction to a woman other than the one he'd lost? Because he'd seen a woman with red hair like hers?

Or maybe it was the option he dreaded most, that the PTSD was getting worse, and this was either hallucinations or his subconscious warning him that he wasn't competent to do the job others depended on him to do. Or both. His shaking hands made that as likely an answer as any, although maybe it was normal for anyone to tremble after being visited by the dead. He'd been so far from normal for so long, he couldn't even hazard a guess.

Sam knew from experience that he'd never get back to sleep, so instead he grabbed some of the mice that had appeared on his doorstep right before he'd gone to bed. His doorstep that was sixty-nine feet and seventy-five stairs above the ground. Which either meant that Bella had climbed all that way to drop off food for the owl and not even knocked on the door to say hi, or her huge cat had somehow known to leave the mice at his door. Sam wasn't sure which idea he found more disconcerting.

He settled himself and the owlet in front of the south-facing window, his attention half on the feeding and half on the bright stars of the cool night sky. Once he'd thought heaven was up there somewhere. Now it was just a cold and empty void, much like his soul.

A nip from the owlet's tiny beak forced his attention away from the stars. For such a tiny ball of fluff, it seemed very determined to live. Maybe a little of that would rub off on him. He could only hope.

BELLA STOOD UNDER the fire tower in the moonlight, watching Sam feed the tiny owl. Even from a distance, his tenderness toward the bird was obvious. As was his suffering. She didn't really understand what had pulled her here in the first place, but she could practically feel his grief and pain sliding down from the tower like a shadow.

"There are reasons you don't get close to Humans," she reminded herself, not worried about anyone else overhearing her scold herself out loud. At this time of night, there was no one else around. Just her and a tormented man feeding a tiny owl.

But despite the reminder, she couldn't stop herself from sending out a sliver of magical energy, letting it float up on a wisp of fog. A few minutes later, she could see Sam leave the window, and a few minutes after that, the lone dim light went out as he settled back into bed.

Bella stood guard under the tower for another hour, as still as a statue. But if anyone had asked her, she couldn't have told them why.

THE NEXT DAY, Bella pulled out all the stops. Magically speaking, that is. She gathered together the basics—candles, incense, herbs, and crystals—and placed them in careful order on top of her portable altar. Then she added three small additional items, all gifts given to her by the Riders over the years. A dainty green and white porcelain teacup Gregori gave her to celebrate the day her mentor retired and the caravan became officially Bella's. A golden necklace that Day bestowed upon her for some birthday or another. And a polished piece of red agate that Alexei picked up somewhere on his travels and gave her because he said it reminded him of her hair.

Now she would use the agate, and everything else, to find her lost friends.

Of course, she had tried magic initially and it hadn't worked. But that had been a simple finding spell. This was something that went a step further, reaching deep inside to find the ties that bound them all together with love and shared experiences. It was a little risky, because it tapped into the core of her own essence, but desperate times called for desperate measures, right?

As the first rays of dawn slid through the open window, Bella cast her circle, lit the candles and the incense, and said the spell that would send a tiny sliver of her soul out searching to find Day, Sun, and Knight, wherever they were.

Except that it didn't work. Yes, her consciousness rose from her body and followed the light up into the sky. It meandered here and there, giving her a bird's-eye view of nesting birds, a small herd of deer drowsily cropping grass in a small meadow, and even a mountain lion slinking along a shadowy path. But every time she tried to redirect her energy to find one of the Riders, she ended up circling aimlessly, following her own depressing thoughts as they spiraled ever inward.

In the end, she had to admit defeat. She didn't think the Riders were dead; she wouldn't let herself think that. But wherever they were, it wasn't accessible through this kind of spell. She didn't know if they were blocking their connection to her for some reason, or if something or someone else was. All she knew was she wasn't going to find them this way. The sputtering candles, drowning in pools of melting wax, pretty much epitomized the way she felt.

BELLA SAT ON the steps of the caravan, sipping a cup of strong tea (Russian Caravan, delicious for both its taste and the irony of its name) and trying not to panic. The strong morning light streaked the clearing, making the surrounding trees seem even taller and darker and casting interesting shadows. None of which contained the answers to her problems, alas.

A sudden stinging sensation jolted her out of her reverie, and she glared at Koshka until he removed his sharp claw from her thigh.

"What the hell was that for?" she demanded to know.

The dragon-cat plopped down on the step next to her, causing what felt like a small earthquake.

"I asked you a question three times and you didn't answer," he said. "So I figured I'd get your attention another way. We don't have time for your brooding."

"I'm not brooding. I'm thinking deep thoughts."

"Right," he said. "Deep thoughts that are depressing and worrying you. They have a word for that, you know. I think it's, um, let's see . . . brooding." He lifted one hind leg and licked it thoroughly, the feline equivalent of a frustrated eye roll.

"I'm just a little concerned, that's all," Bella said. "The Queen of the Otherworld gave me an assignment: find out where that message came from and if it has anything to do with the Riders. So far, I haven't made any progress, and in case you haven't noticed, the Queen does not react well to people failing to do what she asks of them."

Koshka dropped his leg back down with a thump and

head-butted Bella gently. She almost fell off the stairs, but appreciated the supportive gesture anyway.

"You've only been on the job for a few days," he said reasonably. "And you've been out looking during all the daylight hours there are."

"Yes, but I haven't found anything. No clues as to the origin of the message. No sign that the Riders were ever in this area. Nothing." She sighed. "If I don't come up with something soon, the only thing I'll be looking for is a new career."

Koshka smirked at her. "Yes, but you found an attractive Human in a tower. That's very appropriate in a fairy-tale kind of way."

Bella flushed. "Oh shut up. There's no fairy tale here. I just keep running into him in the forest."

"Uh-huh. And now he has to make you dinner sometime."

"I was kidding about the dinner. But it makes sense to keep in touch with him," Bella said, not sure if she was justifying it to Koshka or to herself. "He sees all kinds of things from the top of that tower and talks to the locals more than we do. Maybe he'll come across something that can help us."

"Hmph," the cat said. "Nice rationalizing. But I'm not sure you need him to talk to the locals for you. Something tells me you're going to get the chance to do that for yourself sooner than you think."

For a moment, Bella couldn't figure out what the heck he was talking about, but then she heard what his large, tufted ears had picked up on already—the rumbling sound of multiple vehicles making their slow progress down the bumpy access road that led to various camping spots throughout the national park they were in. The vehicles could be on their way to someplace past where she was parked, of course, but she didn't believe in coincidences.

It looked like they were about to have company.

A MOTLEY COLLECTION of cars and trucks came to a stop about six yards from the caravan, and an equally motley assortment of people piled out of them. Bella counted a dozen in all, mostly middle-aged or older, although there was one young man who looked to be about nineteen who lent a supportive arm to a tiny elderly woman with wispy white hair and gnarled limbs. Eight men and four women, all wearing well-worn practical clothes and the distinctive air of people who worked hard for a living. The old woman wore black from head to toe, with the exception of a colorful embroidered shawl she had tied around her shoulders despite the warmth of the summer day.

Bella flashed for a moment on the story Barbara had told her of her latest adventures and the angry mob of locals who had come to drive her out of town. But these people seemed more wary than irate, and as far as Bella knew, she hadn't done anything to attract attention, either good or bad. So it was with more curiosity than concern that she stood up and walked down the steps of the caravan to greet her visitors, Koshka trailing along behind her as unobtrusively as was possible for a dragon disguised as a gigantic cat.

"Good morning," she said. "Can I help you folks?"

One man stepped forward, clearly nominated to be the spokesman for the group. He was strongly built, with graying brown hair and a neatly trimmed beard, and despite his plain jeans and scuffed work boots, he had an air of quiet authority about him.

He took off his baseball cap and held it politely in his hands before saying, "My name is Bob Winterholler. My brother-in-law was one of the firefighters who was here earlier this week. He told me he met an old lady at this caravan, and I was wondering if it would be possible to speak to her."

"That's interesting," Bella muttered under her breath.

"Told you so," Koshka said in a smug tone. "Didn't I tell you you'd probably been *Called* here?"

Bella scowled at him. After all, there could be a perfectly reasonable explanation for why this group of people had come seeking some old lady they'd never met. Maybe they were selling Girl Scout Cookies. Or passing out religious pamphlets.

"Shut up," she said.

"Excuse me?" Bob looked taken aback.

"Oh, sorry, not you. So, um, was there some particular reason you wanted to talk to her?" *Let it be pamphlets, let it be pamphlets.*

The elderly woman hobbled to the front of the group; the youth with her, a grandson or even great-grandson maybe, seemed to be supporting most of her weight, but she still stood up as straight as her bent back would let her.

"We believe that she may be the one that we seek," the old woman said. "The one called Baba Yaga."

Dammit. Why couldn't it have been pamphlets? Bella felt the mantle of her office settle over her with the weight of history and eons of belief, as the air in the clearing grew thick with magical potential.

"And why do you seek the Baba Yaga?" she asked. From here on in, there was a proper ritual to things. It was tradition, and tradition was the rule.

A slight widening of the creases around the old woman's eyes said she recognized this.

"There are always fires in this area, and sometimes they are bad," she said in a thin, strong voice, a little querulous with age. "But this year there is a wrongness about them. Some are normal, but others seem to start out of nothing. They threaten the trees and the land, and all those who must fight them, many of whom are family to one or another of us."

"We had a fire a month ago that charred damn near half my ranchland," one man said. "I lost over a hundred head of cattle, and the firefighters barely stopped it from taking my house."

"What does this have to do with the Baba Yaga?" Bella asked.

Bob indicated the entire group and the old woman in particular with a wave of his hand. "We're all local, descended from Russian-German families. Most of us grew up hearing stories about Baba Yaga, although I have to admit that until recently, that's all we thought they were. But when the fires started, Mrs. Kneis told us that she could sense something unnatural in them. It's a gift she has, you see, and we all respect it, and her. So when she told us we should call the Baba Yaga to help us, well, we did."

A few of the others looked slightly embarrassed, as though realizing how silly it sounded when spoken out loud, but Bob didn't seem at all fazed, and cast an affectionate look toward the woman he called Mrs. Kneis.

"When Mike, my brother-in-law, told me he met a little old lady in the woods in a strange traveling house, we all thought that maybe it was her—Baba Yaga—come to answer our prayers."

Bella sighed. "Baba Yaga isn't someone you pray to, you know. She's not a goddess." *Maybe once, way back in the history of the world. But not now, and not for a long time. Now she was mostly just one of a few overworked magical women who would really rather not grant boons to worthy seekers if it was at all avoidable.*

"We do not seek a goddess," Mrs. Kneis said, taking another unsteady step forward. "We seek the Baba Yaga and ask for her aid. Is she here?" She stared defiantly into Bella's green eyes with her own watery pale blue ones, as if daring Bella to deny it.

She needn't have worried. She'd used the right words in the right way, and Bella had her role to play. The ground shivered slightly, and a faint mist surrounded the clearing as destiny settled over them all.

"I am she whom you seek," Bella said. "I am the Baba Yaga."

INE

THERE WAS A buzzing hum as the group discussed this among themselves, clearly not buying it.

Bob cleared his throat. "Uh, not to be rude, miss, but we're looking for the Baba Yaga. The old woman the guys met the other day, not her assistant or kin, or whatever you are."

Koshka smothered a chuckle, which ended up sounding a little bit like he was about to cough up a hair ball (not that dragons did such a thing, no matter what form they happened to be wearing). "I love this bit," he said.

Bella didn't. She longed for the good old days when if you said you were the Baba Yaga, everyone took your word for it, by golly. Not that she'd been around then, but still, it must have been nice.

She turned to Mrs. Kneis, certain that if anyone in this crowd knew how things *really* worked, it was her. "Grandmother," she said, using the term as a polite title, as people did in the old country. "Perhaps you would like to explain it to them?"

The old woman smiled, her wrinkles falling in on

themselves like old linen sheets piled on a bed. "Baba Yaga doesn't have to look like a crone, although she often takes that form since everyone knows that us old ladies are full of wisdom." She turned her head to look at Bob. "You think all lumberjacks have to be big and burly, just because you are?"

"But the woman my brother-in-law met was old. He said so," Bob insisted. "This can't be her."

Bella thought it was probably lucky he was dealing with her, and not Barbara, who tended to be a bit on the cranky side and not very patient with Humans. Or anyone else, for that matter, although these days she made an exception for her new husband, Liam, and their adopted daughter, Babs. Still, they'd wasted enough time. She looked down at Koshka and winked.

"Oh my," she said loudly. "How very rude of me, keeping such an esteemed elder standing in the hot summer sun." Bella looked at Mrs. Kneis with a smile. "Can I get you a chair?"

The old lady nodded gratefully. "That would be much appreciated. I'm afraid my legs aren't what they used to be, and my poor great-grandson must be getting tired of holding me up." The youngster protested, and she patted his arm.

Bella's smile widened as she snapped her fingers and transported a small green and pink tufted chair from inside the caravan to a spot about a foot to the left of Mrs. Kneis. Bella was a little afraid she'd give the poor woman a heart attack, but Mrs. Kneis just sank onto the seat gratefully. Big Bob, however, gave out a satisfying high-pitched shriek, and a few of the others gasped audibly.

"Now that we've established my credentials," Bella said briskly, "we should probably get on to the bargaining part of the program. That's when you tell me what you want me to do for you, and what you're willing to give me in exchange for my help."

"You're not going to ask for one of our firstborn children, are you?" one woman asked in a trembling voice.

"Not usually," Bella admitted. "Unless you happen to have one that likes to clean and doesn't eat much."

They all looked at one another and shook their heads.

Bella sighed. "Fine. Then no, no children. The traditional choices are accomplishing three impossible tasks, or a year or two of servitude, or giving me your most precious treasures— you know, things like that."

"Oh right," Bob said. "Mrs. Kneis told us about that. We put together as much um, treasure, as we could." He went back to his truck and pulled out a small wooden chest that looked like it had been in someone's family since before they emigrated to America, then came back to stand in front of Bella.

She opened the lid and looked inside at the assorted accumulations of a number of lifetimes. There was a roll of paper money, which probably represented every spare penny they could put together between them. She ignored that, reaching her hand inside to finger a gold watch, a necklace decorated with a pretty amethyst pendant, what looked like a genuine Fabergé egg that someone *really* should get authenticated, and some other interesting odds and ends.

Finally, she pulled out one object, a simple wooden comb, meticulously hand-carved with figures of tiny rabbits and birds and decorated with a few small seed pearls and shiny crystal beads. Its monetary value was probably less than anything else in the box, but Bella had a feeling that to its owner, it was priceless.

She smiled down at Mrs. Kneis, sitting in Bella's battered pink and green antique chair as if it were a throne, and leaned over a little to bring them closer to the same level.

"This is lovely. Is it yours?" Bella asked.

"It is," the old woman answered, reaching out the tip of one gnarled finger to touch it gently. "My husband made it for me when we were courting, back in the days when people did such things. He didn't have much money, so it's not really valuable. Not like some of those things in the chest there. But it was the first thing I ever owned that wasn't a hand-me-down from one of my sisters or just something practical for everyday use. And he put so much love into it; I figured maybe it would be worth something.

"My Henry's long gone now"—she patted her sparse white bun held up with simple black bobby pins— "along with most of my hair, I'm afraid. Better to add the comb to the treasure chest, I thought, although most here figured it wasn't worth the bother."

"Well, they'd be wrong," Bella said softly. "A Baba Yaga knows true treasure when she sees it." Then more loudly, so the others could hear, "I will take this in payment."

She handed the chest back to an openmouthed Bob and said, "What is it you wish from me in return for your treasure, so freely given?"

"Uh, we want you to stop the fires. Or leastwise, find out what or who is causing them, and put an end to it if that's possible," Bob said.

"Keep our people and our homes safe," Mrs. Kneis added. "And save the forests, as much as you are able."

"So be it," Bella said, feeling the promise vibrating through her bones and down into the ground beneath her feet. "I will do what I can." Koshka growled low under his breath, seconding her vow.

For a moment there was silence, and then the gathered crowd seemed to realize that they'd accomplished what they'd come for, as odd as it seemed, and began to retreat to the vehicles they'd arrived in. Some of them nodded to Bella before they left; one or two even assayed a clumsy bow. In the end, only the old woman and her great-grandson were left.

"Go wait by the car, Jeffery," Mrs. Kneis said, sounding slightly out of breath. "I want to ask the Baba Yaga something."

"But—" The young man looked torn between wanting to protect his great-grandmother and the habit of doing what she said without question.

"I'll be fine," she said firmly. "Go on now. I'll wave for you when we're done."

Jeffery walked away reluctantly, glancing back over his shoulder as if to make sure the wind didn't blow her away.

"Koshka," Bella said in a quiet voice. Nothing more, but

for once he didn't argue and went to sit on the steps of the caravan. Not far enough to keep him from hearing, of course, but at least it gave the old woman the illusion of privacy.

"You wished to speak to me, grandmother?" Bella knelt on one knee in the dirt, lessening the distance between them.

"I am old, Baba Yaga," Mrs. Kneis said. "And I am nearing the end of my days. I've no regrets about that; it has been a long life and a good one. I bore five children, and four of them lived. Twelve grandchildren and more great-grandchildren than I can count. Did my best for my family and my community. I figure that bringing you here is my last act of any note, and that is good enough for me. Not many can say they met a Baba Yaga, now, can they?" She gave a light laugh that conjured an echo of the sweet young girl she'd once been.

"That is true enough," Bella said. "But not what you wanted to talk to me about. You told your great-grandson you had a question for me? I will answer it, if I am able to."

They sat in silence for the space of a few heartbeats, the old woman and the younger. Bella was content to wait; magic always was, even if those who wielded it could sometimes be impatient.

"I miss him," Mrs. Kneis said, almost too quietly for Bella to hear. "My Henry. We loved each other from the hour we met, and I miss him every day. But I've never been sure, you know, even though I've gone to church my whole life. What comes after. And I wondered if you could tell me, Baba Yaga, since you are said to wander far. Do you know what lies beyond? Will I see my Henry again?"

Later Bella thought she might cry for this woman, but for now, she wore the mantle of the Baba Yaga, and so she was calm when she spoke. The magic came at her call, giving her a vision so clear it might have been drawn by an artist in vivid pastels.

"Your Henry, he was tall and blond, and when he smiled, there was a crooked tooth at the front?" Bella could see him, standing behind his wife, one hand resting gently on her shoulder.

"Yes," Mrs. Kneis said in a wondering voice. "That's my husband. He used to try and hide that tooth behind his fingers, but I loved his crooked smile. You can see him?"

"I can," Bella said. "He is waiting for you. And when your time comes, he will walk at your side again, into whatever waits. I promise it will be wonderful. On this, you have my word."

Bella stood up, staggering a little under the weight of knowledge, which could be a heavy burden at times. Not so much, on this occasion. She could see the old woman's great-grandson crossing the clearing toward them, no doubt tired of waiting, and bent down to whisper in her ear.

"Not long now," she said. "You will see your Henry soon."

The elderly lady gave her a brilliant smile, her eyes filled with happy tears. "I thank you, Baba Yaga. It has been a great pleasure to meet you."

"The pleasure has been all mine, grandmother," Bella said with all sincerity. "I hope we will see each other again." They both knew they would not.

After Jeffery's dented Toyota drove away, Bella and Koshka sat on the steps for a while, watching the dust settle.

"Nice old lady," Koshka said finally. "What do you think? Two days?"

"Maybe three," Bella answered. She was glad to have met Mrs. Kneis; glad enough that she almost forgave the woman for sending the rest of them to ask her for help.

"She's lucky," Bella said after another minute.

"Because she's dying?"

"Because she is going to be with the love of her life. I envy her that."

"You could still find one, you know," Koshka said, blowing a few smoke rings through his nose now that there was no one around to see. "Your sister Babas did."

"Yeah, well, they didn't have the unfortunate habit of setting the people they liked on fire," Bella said with a sigh. "Somehow I think that would take all the shiny off a relationship."

"Hmph," Koshka said, settling down with a thump and putting his large head across her knees. They'd had this discussion enough for him to realize he wasn't going to change her mind. "Well, I guess you're officially on the job now."

Bella held up three fingers and waved them through the air. "Jobs," she said morosely. "I have to solve the problem of the fires for the locals, find the origin of the mysterious message the sprite brought, and *somehow* figure out where the Riders have gone and bring them back to the Queen. How the hell am I supposed to accomplish all that, Koshka?"

The dragon-cat pondered her question thoughtfully for a second. "I think we need . . . snacks."

Bella rose to her feet, dislodging the feline with a grunt. "I think we need a damned miracle. But I guess snacks are as good a place to start as any."

BRENNA POKED THROUGH the magical tools on the make-shift worktable she'd set up in one corner of the cave, looking for an empty vial among the cluttered piles of books and herbs and bubbling pots. The wooden table looked like a cross between a witch's altar and a mad scientist's laboratory. Fitting, really, since she was a bit of both these days. Alchemy—an uncertain endeavor under the best of circumstances, and a dusty old cavern in the middle of nowhere certainly wasn't that. Still, needs must.

"Aha!" she said, turning to display the glass container to her captive audience. "Here we go. Now whose turn is it?" She pulled a dull pencil from her untidy bun and sharpened the end with her teeth. She'd twisted her frizzy gray hair up to get it out of her way. It was never a good idea to have stray ingredients falling into one's potions. Then she picked up the notebook she was using to track her work, meticulous in that, if not in her general neatness.

"Ah, Day, my darling boy, it looks like you're up again." She tapped the pencil against her teeth fretfully. "A pity. You're not looking all that well."

Of course, none of the Riders looked *well*, exactly. How could they, since she only fed them enough to sustain them, and bled them repeatedly under varying and unpleasant circumstances? She'd carefully set up her magical restraints so that none of them could hurt her; it just wouldn't do to have them interfere with her work. She didn't much care if she hurt them. In theory, the Riders could live forever, and they were damned tough—they could take whatever punishment she dealt out in the name of progress. Probably. If not, too bad.

"Use me," Alexei said, his voice low in a growling plea. "I am stronger. My blood will be better. Let him rest for a day or two before you bleed him again, and use me instead."

Tap, tap, tap. The pencil knocked against her teeth as she pondered. Perhaps the bearded giant had a point. After all, the whole purpose of the potion she was creating was to make her stronger, both physically and magically. Perhaps it wasn't good to let the source of the main components become *too* weak. So hard to say what would make a difference and what wouldn't when one was dealing with an obscure ancient manuscript written in faded scrawling calligraphy by a discredited wizard. Tut.

"What do you think, Mikhail?" she asked the man once considered the handsomest of the Riders. With his pristine white clothes covered with dirt and blood and his long blond hair hanging in matted hanks, she doubted the women would be so impressed with him now. "Shall I let your friend take your turn, or do you want to be the one to contribute to science today?"

"You can hardly call what you are doing science," Gregori Sun said from his patch of rocky floor. Even battered and filthy, he kept his usual calm, even tone. "It's barbaric and a waste of time. Not to mention our blood. I still do not understand what you hope to achieve with this nonsense—besides eventually having the Queen feed your heart, eyeballs, and liver to her pet falcons. Not necessarily in that order."

"Bah. Don't talk to me about the Queen." Brenna spat on the floor. "It is her fault that you're here. I wouldn't have to go to these lengths if she hadn't forced me to retire from my job as a Baba Yaga. And given away my share of the Water of Life and Death."

"All Babas have to retire eventually," Gregori said. "Most are grateful to finally be able to rest and enjoy their lives."

"What's left of them, you mean. Who would be happy to grow old and die, watching her power slowly ebb away along with her vitality?" Brenna shook her head at his foolishness. "Not I. But the Queen insisted, so I must find my own way. If that means creating a potion using your blood, then so be it. I have nothing against you three; you were always helpful. It's nothing personal."

"Then let us go," Alexei suggested.

"Oh, I can't do that," Brenna said in a reasonable voice. "This ancient tome I found hints at the potential to create a potion that will replace the Queen's enchanted Water, but it requires the lifeblood of immortals, and let's face it, there aren't all that many of you around. I'm banished from the Otherworld for trying to kill that silly Beka, so it isn't as though I can stroll in and snatch one of the Queen's courtiers. And you were willing to come to me, which made things so much easier."

Mikhail rolled over and stared at her balefully, well aware that it had been his weakness for damsels in distress that had gotten them all into this in the first place. He licked cracked lips, trying to work up enough moisture to speak.

"You're mad," he said. "The Water Sickness is upon you."

"Pfft." Brenna stirred a large cauldron with a wooden spoon. "There's no such thing as Water Sickness. No one goes crazy from drinking the Water of Life and Death for too long. That's just a myth the Queen tells so that none of us Babas will hold on to our power long enough to threaten her." She cackled, enjoying the way the sound bounced off the cave walls. "Well, I have a surprise for her. Once I've completed my lovely potion, that is."

Gregori lifted himself up onto one elbow. "I fail to see how the blood of immortals will give you the power you seek. It simply is not possible."

Brenna waved her wooden spoon through the air, spattering

droplets that hissed and burned when they hit the dirt. A little more cautiously, she placed it into a silver bowl next to the cauldron.

"Foolish man. You know nothing. You may be the brains of the Riders and have lived for thousands of years, but I have discovered secrets even you have never seen." She patted the large leather-bound book that had pride of place in the middle of her worktable. "Inside this manuscript are the writings of a man far wiser than you. I have based my potion on his work."

"Who is this man?" Gregori asked.

She ignored him, raising one increasingly gnarled finger into the air to make sure he was paying attention. "But his theories were flawed; they did not go far enough, which is why he never succeeded in his task, and why I will."

Brenna smiled down at the cauldron, currently bubbling softly and emitting a scent both noxious and strangely inviting. Its color was the green of new moss, tinged with a hint of gray the exact color of a dead man's skin. It was her creation, her masterpiece, and it would make her great again. Just as soon as she perfected it.

"What do you mean, he did not go far enough?" Gregori asked, sounding incredulous. "How could anyone go further than this barbarity?"

She sighed at the limitations of small minds. No wonder no one else had ever come up with the solution.

"The wizard postulated that the blood of immortals, taken unwillingly and with great pain, would lend everlasting potency to this brew. I believe the formula never worked because it was missing an additional component. After all, the power of the Baba Yagas comes from nature, from the elements themselves. But to create this potion, those powers must be twisted, perverted in ways that the gods never intended. Fire, that's what he needed."

"Fire?" Gregori looked baffled, poor dear. She tried one last time to explain.

"The agony of the dying trees, plants, animals, and birds as they succumb to the fury of the flames will feed my magical abilities. I capture it with sigils and enchantments and channel it into the cauldron to mix with your blood and all the other ingredients I have gathered. Together, they will create a potion that will give me back my power and enable me to live forever. And that, my darling Gregori, is worth any price."

"You are insane," Gregori said. "Are you truly indifferent to the cost to the natural world and Human lives?"

Brenna shrugged. "They are of no consequence to me. And I may be insane, but at least I'm not the one trapped in a magical cage, helpless and hopeless, am I?" She smiled at him cheerfully as she held out the glass vial. "So lovely of you to volunteer, darling Sun. Hold out your arm now. Time to begin again."

ᛏEN

A TREE BRANCH swung back as Bella worked her way through the forest, smacking her in the face like the tail of a too-large and overly exuberant dog. Pine pitch stuck to her hands as she pushed it out of the way.

"Cut that out," she muttered. "You're not helping."

Of course, this wasn't the Otherworld, so the tree hadn't done it on purpose. But after a morning spent trying to follow the sprite's not very helpful directions had gotten her nothing other than hot, sweaty, and annoyed, she wasn't really in the mood to fight with Mother Nature.

She'd started out the easy way, of course, trying to track the Riders by magical means. But something seemed to be blocking her, and so she'd finally ended up searching the old-fashioned way by looking under every rock and tree for some hint of the Riders' passage or the sprite's wandering journey. Unfortunately, there were a lot of rocks and trees.

It would have been helpful if Koshka could have come out with her, but it was his job to guard the Water of Life and Death hidden within the caravan, and that meant that at least one of them had to be close enough to sense an intruder at all times. He would go out searching on his own later, since the dark didn't slow him down at all. Meanwhile, she was ready to call it a day and head back to a warm shower and a cool beer.

Another branch slapped her in the rear, and as Bella swiveled around to glare at it she caught a glimpse of someone slipping off into the forest behind her. It wasn't the first time she'd sensed another person in the vicinity, but whoever it was clearly didn't want to be seen and didn't seem to mean her any harm. Some hiker accidentally crisscrossing her path, maybe, or a homeless vet who'd taken to the woods rather than deal with the vagaries of an indifferent system. She didn't care who it was, as long as he or she didn't get in the way of that cold beer. But goddess help anyone who did.

INSTEAD OF HEADING back to the caravan like any sane witch would, Bella walked up the stairs to the fire tower. All the stairs. She was in pretty good shape, but damn, that was a lot of stairs. *Sam must have thighs like iron*, she thought, and then tripped on the next step, nearly dropping the bag of dead mice she was carrying. She would have loved explaining that to Koshka, who had brought them back for her after his early morning run. "Sorry, but I dropped them when I was thinking about Sam's thighs. Could you please get me some more?" The dragon-cat wouldn't have stopped laughing for a week.

Koshka had already left some mice off late last night, but baby owls needed to eat a lot, and besides, it gave her a good excuse to get a view of what lay off to the east from a different perspective. She was hoping she'd be able to pick out some of the landmarks the sprite had mentioned if she was looking from the air instead of the ground. The fact that she got to spend more time with Sam was just a bonus, no big deal.

At the top of the tower there was a small, square cabin, with windows on all four sides that started about midway up the wooden walls. It was surrounded by a deck with a waist-high metal railing. Modern, functional, and slightly shabby around the edges, it wasn't much to look at. There was no privacy it all, since the glass went all the way around. But the view was spectacular. For a moment she just stood there, lost in appreciation of the beauty spread out beneath her, forests and mountains as far as the eye could see.

"Impressive, isn't it?" Sam's raspy voice made her jump as he came up to stand by the rail beside her. "I didn't expect to see you today."

His tone didn't sound welcoming, and she noticed that he kept the burned side of his face turned away from her. He'd obviously thrown a shirt on when he heard her coming up the stairs, but hadn't bothered to button it. Unlike his scarred face, the rest of him seemed . . . perfect. Or at least, perfectly distracting. But their easy camaraderie of the darker hours seemed to have vanished with the light.

She dragged her mind back to why she'd come and held out the bag. "Sorry to show up unannounced. I don't mean to intrude on your work, but Koshka wanted me to bring these to you while they were still fresh. More or less."

No smile. "That's very kind of you. I found the other batch before I went to bed, but I didn't hear you climb up to drop them off or I would have come out and thanked you."

Bella eyed the coffee cup in his hands longingly, but he didn't offer her any. She was starting to get the feeling he didn't much like guests. Or maybe it was just her. "Oh, that wasn't me. Koshka brought those up himself. He can be surprisingly light on his feet for such a big cat. Maybe he picked it up from the acrobats at the circus."

Sam gave her a strange look. "Uh-huh. He seems quite . . . remarkable."

"You have no idea," Bella said, forcing down a laugh. "So do I get to meet the patient? Or would you rather not have me walking around in your space?"

Sam shrugged. "No worries. Part of the job is showing people around the fire tower. Forces me to keep the place neat, so it's not all bad." He opened the door and waved her in ahead of him.

Bella thought that *neat* was something of an understatement. Calling the interior of the tower neat was like calling Koshka large. There was a narrow single bed against one wall, its sheets and blankets tucked in military fashion. Rows of wooden cupboards ran under most of the other windows, much like in her caravan, making the most of the limited space.

There were few personal items on view, only a couple of framed pictures and a stack of books on top of one of the cupboards. The institutional green paint was peeling a little around some of the windows and the door, but everything else that was visible was almost painfully clean and tidy. The only thing out of place was a plate that held a crust of bread from a late lunch. And a wide box in the middle of the table that was letting out a pitiful *eep*ing noise.

"Oh," she said, peering inside to see two huge yellow eyes gazing back over a gaping beak that clacked open and shut as if to remind her that she'd brought his meal. "He's adorable!"

"And hungry," Sam said, tipping the sad little carcasses out onto a paper plate. "I meant to go out and check my traps this morning before I went into service, but I had a rough night and overslept. Thanks again for bringing these by." He bit his lip. "I mean, thank the cat for catching them."

"I will," Bella said. "But really, he's happy to have any chance to show off his hunting skills."

Sam held one of the mice up by its tail over the box and then hesitated. "Here, you want to have a go?"

She wasn't sure if he was trying to chase her away, but if so, it wasn't going to work. Anyone who lives with a cat learns to deal with the occasional rodent. At least these ones were dead already. Besides, life and death were part of the natural circle. Creatures had to eat to survive. It was just the way of the world. If Sam thought she was going to squeal at the sight of nature in the raw, he had a lot to learn.

Bella fed the owlet, cheering as he gulped down his food with a greedy intensity that bode well for the little guy's future recovery. And she grinned to herself when she heard

Sam mutter under his breath, "This has got to be the weirdest first date in history." It wasn't a date, of course, but he had a point.

After they were done, Sam showed her how he used a large set of binoculars to search for signs of smoke, pointing out the radios and a series of notebooks in which he kept track of any incidents. He seemed more animated when he was talking about the work, but Bella could tell the moment when he realized he was facing her, and turned away. She wished she could tell him that it didn't matter, but she knew already that he'd never believe her.

"If there's nothing else," he said gruffly, "I should probably get back to work. Conditions are dry, which means a high chance for fire."

Sam moved toward the door, his desire for her to leave not even subtle anymore, but she ignored the hint and went to stand in front of the windows that looked out over the view to the east.

"What's out in that direction?" she asked, aiming the big binoculars at hills that didn't look any different from the ones in every other direction.

"Trees, mountains, not much else," Sam said. His hand twitched as if he wanted to grab the glasses away from her, and his shoulders were so tense they caused his shirt to bunch up over the broad expanse of his muscles. "A few cabins. Most of it belongs to the national park, like the part you're camped in. Why?"

Bella pulled a picture of the Riders out of her back pocket and showed it to him. "A few friends of mine were headed in this direction to go camping, and they seem to have disappeared. I figured that since I was here anyway I'd have a look around for them." She put the binoculars down on top of a cupboard and handed him the photo. "You haven't seen them, have you?"

Sam raised an eyebrow. "Interesting bunch. Sorry, no. I'm pretty sure someone would have mentioned if they'd seen three guys on motorcycles like those. Especially if one of them was as large as the bearded giant on the Harley. But I can ask around, if you like."

He handed the picture back and moved toward the door again. This time she followed, although slowly.

"Are there any caves that you know of in the area? My friends like spelunking." Okay, Bella didn't know for sure that the Riders liked climbing around in caves, but she was guessing that in their long lives they'd probably done it plenty of times, so it wasn't exactly a lie. Besides, she couldn't come right out and ask if Sam could think of any caves that someone could use to hold three magical prisoners in. He already thought she was weird enough, what with the mouse delivery.

He shrugged. "Don't think so. There may be some though."

Bella smothered a sigh. She missed the witty, friendly Sam she'd chatted with the other night. But apparently he was an illusion, fostered by starlight and darkness.

"Okay, thanks." She put one foot outside and then turned around again. "By the way, have you seen anyone else in the woods?"

"Besides you? Mostly just the usual—a few locals, some hunters, a couple of backpackers. Why?"

"Oh, it just felt like I was being followed earlier. I thought I caught a glimpse of someone."

"You were probably imagining it," Sam said. "Lots of people get jumpy alone in the woods."

Bella rolled her eyes. Alone in the woods was the way she liked to be. And trying to have this conversation was reminding her of why. She hated being treated like some wimpy woman. It annoyed her. Which usually wasn't a good thing for the annoyer.

"I don't imagine things," she said through gritted teeth. "I'm not the imaginative type."

"You're an artist," Sam said, sounding surprised. "I thought you were all imaginative types. Either way, it was probably just an animal. Nothing to worry about."

Not for a Baba Yaga, it wasn't. "I wasn't worried," Bella

said. "Just asking. Thanks for showing me around. Sorry I bothered you." She shut the door behind her a tiny bit more forcefully than was strictly necessary, while magically erasing the tiny char marks her fingertips had left in the paint. Hopefully the walk down all those stairs would burn off the rest of her temper before she accidentally set the forest—or one particular irritating man—on fire.

SAM WATCHED HER go, feeling torn between his usual relief at having his space back to himself and regret at losing the glow Bella seemed to carry with her presence. He wanted to kick himself for acting like such a jerk.

No wonder she'd stormed out without a backward look. She'd come bearing gifts, and he'd acted as though she was carrying the plague. Hadn't even offered her a cup of coffee, although he'd clutched the one in his hands the entire time she'd been there. *Idiot.* He was so out of practice being around women, he couldn't even act like a normal human being with the only one he'd ever met who didn't seem to notice or care about his scars or his raspy voice.

Of course, maybe she was just a good actress. There was something distinctly odd about all the questions she'd been asking. He wasn't sure what she'd been after, but Sam was pretty certain she hadn't climbed all those stairs just to bring the owlet its dinner. Maybe something to do with those three guys she was asking about. They looked pretty shady. Could she be some kind of bounty hunter? She sure as hell hadn't come visiting for the pleasure of his company. Which was a good thing, since he'd defaulted to his usual tactic of being downright *un*pleasant, so she would leave as soon as possible.

So why was he so sorry that it had worked?

ELEVEN

BELLA SPENT THE rest of the afternoon searching toward the east again. She'd spotted what she thought was what the sprite had described as "the very tallest tree ever, with moss like a frog's belly in spring" from the window of the tower and forged her way resolutely in that direction. Underneath the tree, she'd thought for a moment that she sensed a shiver of power, but it vanished before she could be certain.

Maybe Sam was right and she *was* imagining things. There was a first time for everything. Like not being able to stop thinking about some guy. That, missing lunch, and the long, fruitless search made for a crabby Baba.

Back at the caravan, Koshka greeted her with an affectionate lick and the announcement that they'd had company while she was gone: someone snooping around.

"One of the townspeople?" Bella asked. "Or, uh, Sam?" Not that she cared if he decided to come around. She was still a little annoyed at him. Or at herself, for being insensitive about his obvious discomfort around others. Either way, she didn't care. Probably.

She had a sudden alarming thought. "Hey, it wasn't Brenna, was it?"

Koshka laughed, an odd coughing sound somewhere between a purr and a revving truck engine. "Not unless she is currently disguising herself as an adolescent Human, and somehow I can't see even crazy Brenna doing that."

"An adolescent? You mean a teenager?" *Why would a teen be sneaking around the caravan? Looking for something to steal, maybe?* Bella didn't have much experience with Human children. She hadn't grown up around them, what with being raised by an aged Baba Yaga in the woods. "How old was our visitor?"

Koshka lifted a hind paw and scratched idly behind one large ear. "How am I supposed to know? All Humans look more or less the same to me. Not a child. Not an adult. Female. That's the best I can do." He lowered the paw. "But I'm pretty sure she's been here before; this isn't the first time I've caught her scent around the camp. Never too close, but definitely hanging around."

"Huh. Maybe I should go see what she's up to," Bella said, cracking her knuckles together. She was still unsettled after her encounter with the prickly version of Sam, despite all her attempts to shake it off during her walk through the forest. She snapped her fingers fretfully, and sparks flew out.

"Not in the mood you're in," Koshka said. "You'd just scare her off. I'll go check her out myself." He disappeared into the woods before Bella could argue with him.

JAZZ SAT AS still as she could on the bank of the creek, watching her fishing line drift through the water as though it had nothing better to do than waft to and fro. It certainly wasn't catching a fish, the useless thing. Truth was, Jazz sucked at fishing. She could curse out the line all she wanted, but she suspected she was doing it wrong. She only caught little fish, and the last one was days ago.

She'd caught a rabbit in a snare once, something she'd read about how to do in a book. But the book didn't say anything about how the rabbit would look at you with its big brown eyes, and she'd ended up caving and letting it go.

You'd think she'd be tougher after living in the woods for all these months, surviving off of whatever she could catch or find—she'd brought a book on what you could eat in the wild; she wasn't an idiot—or steal from campers. But this week the pickings had been scarce, and she was hungry.

Jazz thought maybe she could get some food from that cool wagon-house she'd spotted, but weirdly, she could never find a door in the stupid thing although the red-haired lady living in it always seemed to be able to get in and out.

Suddenly a gigantic cat appeared next to where Jazz was sitting, startling her so much she almost fell into the water. For a minute, she thought it was some kind of wildcat, on account of it being so very, very big, but then she recognized it as the one she'd seen hanging around the wagon and let out her breath in a big huff.

"Hey, cat," she said, reaching out a hand carefully. Jazz liked cats. One of the places she'd lived had a bunch of cats. She'd liked the cats a lot better than the people who owned them. They'd been real assholes. "Whatcha doing out here?"

She could swear that the cat's answering meow sounded almost like he was saying, "I could ask you the same thing."

Jazz laughed at herself; she'd clearly been on her own in the woods too long. But she answered anyway, since there wasn't anyone around to call her a weirdo or judge her talking to animals like a crazy person.

"I'm just trying to stay out of trouble, cat," she said. "Speaking of which, aren't you going to get into trouble if you don't go back to your little traveling house?"

The cat meowed again, sounding indignant.

"Oh sure, I get it. You're a cat. No one is the boss of you."

The cat blinked big green eyes at her. Or maybe they were yellow. It was hard to tell in the muted shadows under the trees.

"Hey, you get no argument from me," Jazz said. "No one is the boss of me either. Life is way better that way, don't you think?"

"Me-ow."

Right, now the cat was arguing with her. Jazz couldn't have said why it felt like she could understand everything the animal said, but she did.

"Fine, maybe the lady you live with is nice, but not everyone is, you know." She shifted a little on the hard dirt and twitched her line the way the books all said to, so that a fish would think the worm on the end was alive. Nothing. Apparently the fish hadn't read the books.

The cat let out a big yawn, showing teeth like razors and a gullet the size of the Grand Canyon, then batted at her makeshift fishing pole, making her drop it on the ground.

"Oh nice," Jazz said. "Now my fishing technique is being dissed by a cat." She picked the pole back up and dusted it off. "I suppose you could do better?"

The cat yawned again and strolled down to stand motionless by the side of the creek for a moment. Then one huge paw flashed out almost faster than Jazz could see and came back up with a sizable trout speared on its scythe-like claws. With an attitude she would have called smug in a human, he dropped it into her lap before sauntering off in the direction of the wagon.

Jazz gazed at the retreating cat and then down at the fish still wiggling wetly on her ragged jeans. "Huh," she said. "Is it just me, or was that kind of strange?" She sighed. "Great. Now you're talking to fish too. Dude, you have got to get a grip."

"I'M PRETTY SURE she's living rough in the forest," Koshka reported to Bella. "I didn't smell any other Humans on her, and she's too skinny. I don't think she's getting enough food." He shook his massive head. "Someone needs to teach the girl how to fish. I don't think the forest is her natural environment."

"Don't look at me," Bella said. "I use magic to catch my fish. Besides, I don't have time to babysit some lost kid.

Maybe I should report her to someone. You know, call the authorities."

Koshka plopped down next to her on the steps of the caravan, making the entire traveling house rattle. "The *authorities*? Since when do Baba Yagas have anything to do with the *authorities*?" He snorted. "I mean, other than Barbara marrying one of them." They were all still trying to wrap their minds around that turn of events, since the oldest of the United States Babas was also the least likely to follow rules of any sort. Yet she'd ended up marrying a seriously law-abiding sheriff. Bizarre. And a little amusing, for those on the sidelines.

"What do you suggest? I ignore the kid and let her starve?"

"I think if she was going to starve, she probably would have done so already," Koshka said. "But you could try leaving some food out for her and see what happens."

"What happens will probably be that she tries to hit me over the head with a tree limb and then search the caravan for drugs and alcohol," Bella muttered.

Koshka rolled his eyes. They both knew he had better intuition about Humans than Bella did, but she hated to admit it. "And if she does, the hut will kick her out on her ass and I'll bite her. After which you get to say, 'I told you so.' But we both know that isn't going to happen. So how about you just be patient and do it my way, and we'll see how it all plays out. I have a good feeling about the girl."

"Pfft," Bella said, getting to her feet. "I'll think about it. In the meanwhile, I'm going to do another spell to look for the Riders, now that I have a better idea of which direction they might be in. I think if I can narrow the focus of the search spell, I might be able to break through whatever seems to be blocking it."

"Great," the dragon-cat said. "On your way to get your supplies, make me a tuna sandwich, will ya? In fact, make three. I'm feeling unusually hungry."

"You're not fooling anyone, you giant softy," Bella said. But she got the tuna out anyway.

*   *   *

AS THE AFTERNOON went on, Sam felt worse and worse about how rude he'd been to Bella. After all, it wasn't her fault that he'd seen a ghost or had a hallucination or whatever it was. Not her fault that she happened to have nearly the same shade of red hair as Heather. Or that, despite everything, he found her incredibly attractive.

Not that he had any intention of doing anything about it, unless you counted feeling guilty, but it had clearly triggered something in his subconscious. Which he'd then taken out on her. He might not be the man he'd been before the fire, but he didn't want to be *this* man either.

His mother had always said, "If you mess up, then make it right." He wasn't a kid anymore, and his parents were across the country running an RV park in Florida, but he could see his mom standing in the sunny kitchen he grew up in, arms on her ample hips and a frown on her flour-kissed face as she waited for him to act the way she'd taught him to.

Sam wasn't sure how to make things right with Bella, but he had an idea for a place to start.

He hit one of the few numbers on speed dial in his government-issued cell phone and said, "Hi, Tiny, it's Sam."

"Yo," Tiny said. "What's wrong?"

"Nothing," Sam said. "Does something have to be wrong for me to call you?"

There was a brief pause. "Well, yeah, usually," Tiny said, a hint of laughter in his voice. "You don't exactly call to chat."

Sam tried to remember the last time he'd called anyone just to chat and failed. He sighed. One issue at a time.

"Actually, I was calling to see if you could help me with something," Sam said.

"Shoot," Tiny said.

"You know that woman in the caravan who is parked off Wilson's trail?"

"The pretty redhead? The one with the gigantic cat? Sure, a couple of the guys mentioned seeing her."

Sam wasn't surprised. Tiny's family had been in the area for generations, and he knew everyone for miles. If there was news, Tiny always heard it, more often sooner than later. It didn't hurt that twice a week he delivered a batch of Mrs. Tiny's famous pies to the diner, then sat around and had coffee with all of his cronies.

"What does she have to do with this?" Tiny asked. "Is she causing some kind of trouble down there? You need me to send Lisa to go beat her up?"

"Very funny." Sam tried to visualize the plump and cheerful Mrs. Tiny beating anything other than a bowl of batter and failed miserably. "No, it's just that she was up at the tower earlier this afternoon and said something about looking for a few friends who she thought might be in the area. I figured if anyone had spotted these guys, you'd probably know about it."

"Huh," Tiny said. "Okay. Did she say what they looked like, these friends of hers? I mean, it's tourist season. We get all kinds through town this time of year."

"Oh, I think these three would have stood out," Sam said. "She showed me a picture of them. One was a good-looking, tall blond guy dressed in white leathers standing in front of some kind of white motorcycle. Another one had dark hair and kind of Asian features; that one was wearing red leather and had a bright red Ducati. You know, those racing bikes?"

"Sure, I've seen 'em," the older man said. "Look damned uncomfortable to me, riding all bent over like that. And the third one?"

"A huge bear of a guy, long brown hair, braided beard, black leather, and a big Harley," Sam said. "You can see why I'd think someone would remember them if they came through together."

"I guess so," Tiny said with a whistle. "Sounds like an interesting bunch. I guess artists hang out with all types." Sam could almost hear the shrug through the phone. "I haven't heard anything about anyone fitting that description, but like I said, it's tourist season. Might be they didn't stand out enough for anyone to mention. Tell you what; I'll make a few calls and get back to you, okay?"

"You bet," Sam said. "I appreciate it."

"No problem," Tiny said. "That's what neighbors are for. Oh, hey, how's that little owl doing? Is it still alive?"

"Yup. In fact, Bella, the woman from the caravan, her cat has been fetching mice for me to feed it. Figured I'd see if I could say thank you by finding out if her friends were here."

"A cat that fetches mice, huh?" Tiny said. "Now I've heard everything." He chuckled to himself and hung up.

AN HOUR LATER, he rang back.

"That was fast," Sam said.

"Hell, I just called Ellie at the diner," Tiny said. "I would have gotten back to you sooner but that woman could talk the ear off an elephant. Had to hear all about her bunions before I could ask if she knew anything about your lady friend's buddies."

"She's not my lady friend," Sam said, his voice sounding harsher than usual.

"Sure, of course not," Tiny said. "Didn't mean anything by it, Sam." He cleared his throat. "Anyway, at first Ellie didn't think she'd seen 'em, because the day they came into the diner, there was only two of them, she said. The big one and the skinny Asian one. Her words, not mine. You know how she is."

"Uh-huh," Sam said. "No sign of the blond guy on the white motorcycle?"

"Apparently not. And I asked her, but she can't remember when she saw them. Maybe three or four weeks ago, she said, but it could have been less, could have been more. Diner's pretty busy in the summer, and she just wasn't paying that much attention. Wouldn't have noticed them at all, probably, except she said the big one ate five burgers, three orders of curly fries, and six pieces of Mrs. Tiny's pecan pie. Now *that* stuck in her head. Said she'd never seen anyone eat so much in her life."

Sam smiled at that, having met Ellie. She lived to feed people; Bella's friend must have made her day.

"Well, thanks, Tiny," he said. "I'll pass that along the next time I see Bella."

"Bella, huh?" Tiny said. "Pretty name."

An unasked question hung in the air. Sam ignored it. The answer was no, anyway.

"I need to go check for smoke," he said instead. "I'll talk to you later."

"Uh-huh," said the voice on the other end of the phone with a chuckle, and then its owner hung up.

Sam rolled his eyes and put the phone down on the table, picking up the binoculars in its place. Maybe he'd go down and see Bella when he went out of service and tell her what he'd found out. Maybe. Maybe not.

BELLA WAS COMING down the steps of the caravan when she suddenly looked up and saw Sam. Her heart skipped a beat, and a small crimson gout of fire flared into existence, dropping from her fingertips onto the ground below.

"Shit!" Sam said, racing over and stamping it out. "How the hell did that happen? Are you okay?" His face was white as he checked to make sure the flames were out.

Shit squared. Bella couldn't believe she'd done that, lost control just because a gorgeous guy showed up. What was she, a teenager? Now the fire spotter was going to think she was some kind of pyromaniac or something. *Way to go, Bella.*

"Uh, sorry," she said. "I'm not usually that careless. I promise. I'd just lit a match to start up the barbeque and you startled me into dropping it." She crossed her fingers behind her back. She hated lying, but she couldn't come up with a better explanation without saying something like, *Sometimes I set things on fire by accident when I'm nervous or upset. That* would go over well.

Sam stared at the grill, which was a good foot and a half away from where they were standing. Bella could feel her cheeks heat, hotter than the fire she'd created.

"Can I help you with something?" she asked, trying not to sound defensive. After all, she didn't owe him any explanations; the flames were out, no harm done, and besides, a few hours ago he acted like he couldn't wait to see the back of her.

He blinked at her, his head turned slightly away as usual. She fought the impulse to grab his somewhat stubbly chin and turn it around to face her, just to prove he didn't need to hide. Somehow she didn't think it would go over well, no matter how good her intentions.

"Um, actually, I kind of came to help you," he said, surprising her.

"Really?" She raised one eyebrow. "I wasn't aware I needed help."

Sam shuffled one booted toe against the dirt, raising a small cloud of brown-gray dust that smelled of pine and summer. "I was rude before," he said, not looking at her. "When you came to the tower. I'm sorry. I didn't sleep well and I was a little short with you."

Well. Whatever she'd expected him to say, it wasn't that. "That's okay," Bella said. "You weren't all that bad."

He shrugged, but finally looked directly at her, although he backed up a few paces as soon as he realized how close they were standing. Bella tried not to take that any more personally than his attitude from earlier, although a tiny sigh escaped her lips. He would be so much more pleasant to be around if he didn't act like she had the plague or some kind of communicable disease. Of course, what she did have was worse, but he didn't know that.

"You're being kinder than I deserve," Sam said. "But I do have a little information for you about your friends."

"My—you mean Sun, Knight, and Day?" Bella could feel her jaw drop open. "You found them?"

"Are those their names?" Sam shook his head. "And, no, I'm sorry. I didn't mean to get you all excited. All I found out was that two of them were here sometime within the last month or so, maybe the last couple of weeks. I thought that might help though."

"It does," Bella said firmly. *At least she knew they'd been in the area at some point. That was more than she'd known for sure before.* "Wait, did you say two of them? Not three?"

"That's what Tiny said. He's my closest neighbor and pretty much has his finger on the pulse of whatever goes on around here," Sam said. "I asked him if he could ask around, and he found out that Ellie, the woman who owns the diner in town, remembered seeing two of your friends a while back—the big one apparently ate enough food for ten men and won a place in her heart forever."

Bella chuckled despite her concern. "That sounds like Alexei Knight, all right. I once saw him eat most of a pig roast all by himself and wash it down with an entire keg of beer. Then he complained when all there was for dessert was watermelon."

Sam gave her a look she couldn't decipher. "Sounds like quite a guy. Are you two close?"

"Oh, very," Bella said. "He practically helped raise me."

"Ah," Sam said. "I thought maybe he was your boyfriend or something."

Bella didn't know whether to laugh or be appalled. "Good gods, no. More like an eccentric uncle. All three of them, really." The budding laughter slid away on a wave of worry. "The woman at the diner was sure there were only two of them?"

"I guess," Sam said. "The big fellow and the dark-haired one. Ellie said she didn't remember seeing the blond."

The corner of Bella's mouth twitched. "She would have remembered," she said. "Women always do." She thought about it for a minute. "Actually, that kind of makes sense, now that I think about it. My sister Beka said that the last time she saw the Riders, Knight and Sun were looking for Day."

"The Riders? Is that some kind of bike club?" Sam asked. "And I didn't know you had a sister. Is she an artist too?"

Bella bit her lip. A bike club. Not unless it was the kind of club that Alexei could use to knock someone over the head in a fight. "Beka isn't exactly my sister. It's a little hard to explain. I guess you could say we're closer than family. And I suppose she's an artist; she makes jewelry to sell at craft fairs and farmer's markets and such. When she's not diving for buried treasure."

"Seriously?" Sam gave her the look he usually saved for when he thought she was telling him some tall tale to explain Koshka's unusual abilities. Of course this time she wasn't exaggerating.

"Yup. She's more at home in the water than I am on land," Bella said. "Beka does a little diving, a lot of surfing, and spends some time helping out on her husband's fishing boat. Of course, they're newlyweds, so I think she mostly does it so they can make out when the fish aren't biting. True love, you know. It's completely sickening."

"I suppose it must be," Sam said gruffly, turning his face away again. "Anyway, I just figured you'd want to know your friends were here, even if it was a while ago. I should be getting back before it gets dark." He frowned at her, brows drawing together over shadowed eyes. "Try and be more careful with matches, okay? The last thing we need is another fire."

Without another word, he turned and walked away. A minute later, she heard the muffled sound of his four-wheeler's engine. Too bad she'd been inside when he'd arrived; if she'd heard him coming, maybe she wouldn't have made such a fool of herself. Of course, that still wouldn't have stopped her from opening her big mouth.

She couldn't believe she'd made that crack about true love. She never talked to anyone other than Barbara about Beka, and all the Babas tended to tease one another. Clearly she'd offended him somehow. Bella didn't understand what it was with her and Sam; she was either completely at ease with him or falling all over herself like an idiot.

This was what came of being raised in the woods by a Russian fairy-tale witch. She could hold her own with an ogre or a tornado, but she was completely unequipped to deal with actual people. Dammit.

Oh well. At least after this he probably wouldn't want to

have anything to do with her, and that would take care of that problem. And now that she knew for sure Alexei Knight and Gregori Sun had been here at one point—and just might still be around—she was definitely going to do that spell. As soon as her heart went back to beating normally. Dammit squared.

ALEXEI WAS BROODING in his magical cage when he felt *something*. A ripple or shiver in the air. Something. He lifted his head from his knees and glanced over to where Brenna was muttering over her damned potion again, but whatever he'd sensed hadn't felt evil. The brew Brenna was stirring, on the other hand, reeked of death and despair, reminding him of a murky swamp he'd once spent three days slogging through back in Russia. Fetid air mixed with decaying frog carcasses plus rank, muddy water filled with snakes. Not his fondest memory. Although even that had been better than this damned cave.

Alexei glanced at the other two Riders to see if either of them had noticed anything odd. Mikhail was out cold, his body curled up in a fetal position on the damp ground. Alexei couldn't tell if his friend was sleeping or unconscious, but even from six feet away he could see that Mikhail's face was too pale beneath the bruises and his breathing was shallow and uneven. The blond Rider had been captured weeks before the others and therefore had suffered the worst from the malignant attentions of the crazed witch.

Alexei scraped one large hand over his matted beard, tugging on it to keep himself from cursing out loud and drawing Brenna's attention. He wasn't at all convinced that she was right about the twisted magic giving her immortality, but he was beginning to believe that theirs was being drained away. Even he, once the strongest of the strong, felt weak and shattered; the others were in still worse shape. In truth, Alexei was no longer sure that any of them would survive this experience. Perhaps he was imagining the strange sensation—wishful thinking, or maybe the start of hallucinations.

But when he looked over at Gregori, the other Rider gave him a subtle nod. Alexei's eyes widened. "Baba?" he mouthed, and Gregori twitched one shoulder in an abbreviated shrug. Clearly he didn't know.

Suddenly, Brenna stopped stirring, plopping her spoon down on the table and turning around to sniff the air. Alexei could see Gregori's lips tighten in concern. If their message *had* miraculously reached one of the Babas and she was searching for them, Brenna couldn't know. Brenna couldn't know. The words echoed through Alexei's head as if Gregori had said them out loud. After all these centuries together, it often seemed as though they no longer had to speak out loud to understand each other. They exchanged frustrated glances as Brenna spun in place, her nose practically twitching.

Alexei knew what he had to do. He might be weaker than usual, but he was still the strongest of them all. With a berserker yell, he threw himself against the bars that created an impenetrable cage around each Rider. They'd each tried testing their prisons in the beginning, so he knew exactly what came next. But there was no choice. Not if there was any possibility that the strange sensation meant even the tiniest chance of rescue.

The magic burned his fingers and palms, raced through his body so his bones felt like they were being etched by acid, his brain drowning in flames that fired the connections between neurons until all he could feel was pain. The smell of charring flesh rose from his hands, and still he clenched the bars, holding on until he blacked out and slid mercifully to the cold, hard ground.

The last thing he saw through blurring eyes was Brenna bending over him and cursing, completely distracted by his act of defiance. *Got you*, he thought. And then there was nothing.

TWELVE

BELLA WAS WOKEN out of a sound sleep by a loud thud, followed by the jarring sensation caused by an overly large cat bounding onto the bed, then onto her stomach, and then stretching his head up to the open window. She was so startled, she accidentally set the comforter on fire and had to beat it out with her hands. Luckily, she was immune to her own flames, but she was going to have to remember to renew the magical fireproofing on her belongings. As soon as she got through killing Koshka.

"What the hell has gotten into you?" she asked groggily. "And also, *oof*."

"Did you hear that?" Koshka asked, ignoring her. He didn't even wait for her to answer, which was good since she hadn't heard anything because *she was asleep*, before he bounded off the bed again and over to the front of the caravan.

"Make a door and open it, you stupid hut!" he yelled, and then ran off into the night, leaving Bella sitting there with her mouth open and a cool breeze blowing through the tee shirt she slept in.

She listened intently for a minute, but still didn't hear anything. Finally she waved her hand to shut the door, pulled the covers back over her head, and said something rude about how the only thing crazier than dragons or cats was a cat who actually was a dragon. "Probably just a really big mouse," she grumbled and fell back to sleep.

WHEN KOSHKA RETURNED at last, the sun had been up for a couple of hours, and Bella was sitting on the steps blearily drinking coffee. She put the cup down when he trotted slowly into the clearing, blinking when she took in his unusually bedraggled appearance.

"Good grief," she said. "You look like you've run for miles over rough terrain. Backward. Where the heck did you disappear to?"

The dragon-cat made a sound deep at the back of his throat and gave her a pitiful glance. Bella took the hint and snapped her fingers, producing a bowl of water from inside the caravan.

After he'd gulped down the entire thing, Koshka said, "I *did* run for miles over rough terrain. Although I'm pretty sure I was going forward most of the time. I spent hours trying to follow the echo of a memory of a sound. I heard it last night, carried on the wind." He shook his massive head. "I don't know what the sound was, but I'm telling you, Baba, there is something wrong in this forest."

"I know," Bella said, getting up to fetch him more water and an extra-large portion of tuna before sitting back down and picking up her coffee again. This time she held the warm cup more for comfort that anything else, a shiver running down her spine. "It's as though the trees are whispering unhappy secrets to one another, but I can't quite make out what they're saying. It's driving me crazy. It's like I can hear it, but I can't hear it. So you think the sound that you chased last night had something to do with whatever is going on here?"

"I'm sure the noise I heard was connected to the Riders somehow, but I couldn't tell you why." Koshka inhaled the tuna and then licked his chops, looking more like himself. "Just a gut feeling. But as you know, my gut is never wrong."

"The Riders?" Bella sat up straight, sloshing coffee over her bare foot without even noticing. "Are you sure? Where are they? Did you find them?"

Koshka rolled his eyes. "I would have started with that, if I had. So no, I didn't find them. But I'm pretty sure I can point you in the right direction; I got quite a bit farther than you did yesterday, I think."

Bella drooped. For a minute there, she'd thought she was actually going to make progress on at least *one* of her assignments. If she didn't have something good to report to the Queen soon, she was going to end up on the short list of "people most likely to be turned into something they weren't going to enjoy being." Besides, she really wanted to find the Riders.

"Great," she said. "But you have to stay here while I'm out trying to follow the trail. How am I supposed to know where you went?"

Koshka licked a paw and rubbed it over one ear. Not that he couldn't magically clean himself, but he enjoyed playing the role of a cat. He'd told Bella once that he'd spent a very long century disguised as a dog and he was never going to do it again.

"You worry too much," Koshka said to Bella. "Have a little faith. I marked the trail for you, of course."

Bella made a face. "Oh great. I'm going to have to sniff all the bushes for dragon-cat pee. I can't wait."

Koshka made a face back, wrinkling his wide nose. "Don't be ridiculous. Even I don't have that much pee in me. I put a mark on the trees as I went past. You should be able to follow it, at least as far as I got."

She patted him on the head, then scratched underneath his chin the way he liked until a tiny ribbon of smoke trickled out of his nostrils. "I'll leave in five minutes. You're the best dragon-cat ever."

"Of course I am," Koshka said. "Was there ever any doubt?"

SAM PACED BACK and forth in the fire tower, restless and twitchy without knowing why. He didn't even go into service for another hour, but he couldn't stop looking out the windows anyway. His morning run, racing the sun as it rose in the sky, should have helped, but if anything, it only made him edgier. It was as if his blood was boiling as it moved through his veins. Something was wrong. He could feel it in his bones.

It probably didn't help that his dreams had been filled with images of roaring fire and a red-haired woman with even hotter curves and lips. His binoculars swung back in the direction of the clearing where Bella's caravan sat. Not for the first time that morning. Or even the tenth. She drew him like a lodestone pulled at iron, a natural force that couldn't be explained.

Sam could see her now, sitting on the steps petting her cat. As he watched, the sun slid through the trees and hit the exact spot where she rested, making her glow like an angel. Too bad he had a feeling she was anything but. In fact, he was certain she was trouble. But even so, trouble had never come in a more beautiful package.

BELLA PICKED HER way through the woods, following the trail Koshka had left for her. True to his word, he'd put tiny claw marks on the trees he'd passed, spaced just far enough apart that she could always see the next sign as she paused to get her bearings. Unlike those of a normal cat, Koshka's claw gouges gave off a glow when she looked at them with her magical sight, although no one else would have seen them even if they'd been looking.

She'd made her way a couple of miles to the east, well past the tall tree she'd found previously, when she heard a faint cry for help. It was much too high-pitched to be one of the Riders, and she debated for a second, torn between checking it out and staying on task, when she caught a whiff of smoke, which made her break into a run. She burst out into a small, clear space and instantly saw the fire on the far side, burning in the same abnormally circular fashion as the first one she'd seen.

This one was further along, though, and had started to edge beyond its original boundaries, creeping through some underbrush and about six feet up a couple of nearby old-growth trees. Up in one of the trees, a young girl crouched in a notch still out of reach of the flames, but not for long. Bella thought she was probably about fourteen or fifteen, although it was hard to tell.

The girl had short brown hair that looked like it had been hacked off with a knife, ragged jeans, and a backpack slung over her shoulders. She was yelling for help, stopping occasionally to cough from the smoke drifting upward, and there was a hint of panic in her eyes, although Bella could tell she hadn't completely lost her head.

The girl looked relieved when she saw Bella enter the clearing. "Hey!" she called. "Can you help me? Call the fire department or something? I'm kind of in the shit here!"

"You sure are," Bella yelled back. "What did you do, start a campfire that got out of hand?" She started wildly running through options in her head, while trying to keep the girl calm.

"Are you serious?" The girl looked indignant as only a teenager can. "I was sleeping up here, and when I woke up, the fire was already burning. I'm not stupid enough to start a fire and then climb up a damned tree to get away from it!"

She held up a hank of rope that she'd obviously used to tie herself to the tree while she was sleeping, although unfortunately Bella could tell it wasn't nearly long enough to get her to the ground. And it wouldn't matter if it was, since if she went down the tree, she'd be heading straight into the flames.

The girl coughed again, and a frantic note started to creep back into her voice. "Please go for help. I'm freaking out here."

Bella was trying not to do the same, but she could already tell that there was no way there would be time to fetch help. By the time she'd returned with anyone, the fire would have overrun the rest of the tree. As it was, smoke was starting to fill the clearing and two neighboring trees were smoldering at their bases.

She only had one choice. Magic. If she used her magic, there would be no hiding it. But if she didn't, the girl was going to die.

SAM WAS ALMOST relieved when he spotted the smoke. After feeling so on edge all morning, it was good to have something to blame the anxiety on. He zoomed in on the fire, double-checking against known landmarks so he could give the dispatcher specific details. For a minute, he thought the bright red that caught his eye belonged to a bird, or maybe an isolated flare-up. Then his heart thumped, skipping a beat, as he recognized it as Bella's hair, distinctive even at that distance, even though he couldn't make out her features.

At first he thought she was alone, but when he spotted someone up in a tree, his pulse raced even faster. Grabbing up the two-way radio, he called dispatch first and then the county zone warden.

"Bill, we've got a smoke in quadrant three. I've got at least two civilians in harm's way; looks like one of them is trapped." He explained the situation, and the warden swore.

"I'll call the state helicopter, see if we can get them to fly us in. I don't know if I've got any guys close enough to get there in time, otherwise. Start calling the volunteers, will you? Shit." He clicked off without any further ado, focused on the job.

Sam made the calls, beside himself with worry. The fire was close enough to the tower for him to see what was happening, but he wasn't allowed to leave the tower to go to their aid—and even if he could, he wasn't sure he would have been able to bring himself to get that close to the flames. He watched in anguish as the growing smoke obscured his view, clutching at his radio as if it were a lifeline. Waiting for news. Waiting for someone else to run to the rescue because he couldn't.

THIRTEEN

BELLA PEERED THROUGH the growing smoke and tried to figure out how the hell she was going to save the girl. She knew she was going to have to use magic and just try to explain it away afterward somehow, but she couldn't use the spell she'd used the last time. If she pulled all the oxygen out of the air to kill off the fire, it would kill the girl too.

No choice. She was going to have to go for the less subtle and harder to cover up, and make it rain. Her sister Baba, Barbara, was better at that than Bella, but after you've spent your entire life accidentally starting fires whenever you lose your temper, you learn all the ways to put them out too.

Bella took a deep breath, choking on the smoke briefly and then pulling herself together. Magic took focus, and it was tough to do when someone was screaming, flames were crackling, and your lungs were starting to feel a little crispy around the edges. Nonetheless, she made herself narrow all her attention to the necessary swirling motions and brief incantation and then nearly cheered as the first fat drops fell out of the sky. A minute later, rain came down in a deluge, drenching her, the girl, and thankfully, the fire. Also about a mile square around the clearing, but oh well. Barbara really was better at this than she was, but at the moment, Bella didn't much care.

The rain fell for another little while, as the girl sat amazed and relieved up in the tree, waiting for the trunk to cool enough to be safe to climb down. Bella sent a sliver of healing energy up into the teen's lungs to ease her coughing, and then used some more on herself. They were both too drained to talk, for which Bella was grateful. She was just debating the merits of doing one more *tiny* bit of magic to make the tree cool off faster (since no matter how tempted she was to disappear, Bella couldn't, in all good conscience, just take off and leave the girl up there by herself) when a fire crew hauled ass into the clearing.

"Holy crap," one of the guys said when he saw Bella. "We thought we'd lost you. Thank God that rain showed up out of nowhere. We didn't even have anything predicted for today. You must be the luckiest woman on the planet." He started directing his men to check for hot spots, using a strange tool that had an ax on one side and a hoe-like thing on the other.

Bella pointed up into the tree. "I think she's the lucky one. I could have made it out, but there was no way she was going to. The fire must have been started by a lightning bolt from the same freak storm that caused the rain. Just one of those crazy things." It was a feeble story and at least a partial lie, but it was the best she could do under the circumstances.

A couple of the other firefighters climbed part of the way up and helped the teen down from her perch. She seemed astonishingly composed despite her ordeal, and ran over to Bella and gave her a big hug.

"Thanks!" the girl whispered, before turning back to face the chief. "That was the scariest thing that ever happened to me," she said, eyes open wide. "Gosh."

Gosh? Bella didn't know what the hell was going on, but she was pretty sure that she was going to need to borrow one of the firefighters' shovels to dig through whatever bullshit this girl was about to lay down.

"Can you tell me anything about how the fire started, young lady?" the chief asked. "Did you see lightning?"

"Gee, no, I'm sorry," the girl said, brushing a hank of hair out of her face with a smudged hand. "My aunt and I were hiking through the woods and we got separated. I climbed a tree to see if I could spot her." She favored him with a cheery grin. "I'm really good at climbing trees. Better than any of the boys I know. I'm not afraid of heights at all. Anyway, I guess I fell asleep up there, what with the early start and how comfortable the notch was and everything, and when I woke up, the fire was already burning and I was, like, trapped. I screamed, and then my aunt came, and then it rained and put out the fire. And then you came." She beamed at him as if he and his crew were superheroes, radiating innocence from every grimy pore.

Aunt? Bella tried not to choke, and the crew chief looked dubious—rightfully so. But he clearly couldn't come up with any explanation that fit better.

"Are you the woman from the caravan?" the chief asked Bella. She nodded.

"Sam in the fire tower mentioned you, although he didn't say anything about a niece. He's going to be real relieved to hear that you're safe. He spotted you from the tower; I think he's been going half out of his mind with worry, knowing you were down here in the midst of this. I'm going to give him a call on the radio, let him know you're both okay."

He moved off for a moment, radio crackling. Bella had just opened her mouth to say something to the girl when he came back.

"I think you took about five years off that man's life, ma'am," he said a touch grimly. "And he didn't have any to spare, by my way of thinking. Not after what he went through."

"Does this have anything to do with his scars?" Bella asked. "I kind of wondered what happened, but I didn't want to ask."

"You don't know?" The chief's bushy eyebrows rose in disbelief.

"I'm not from around here," Bella explained.

"Well, sure, but the story was in all the papers. For a while there, Sam Corbett's name was almost as well-known as Mick Jagger's."

"Who?" Bella told herself, not for the first time, that maybe she should spend more time out in the world.

The chief shook his head. "That's okay. I don't like rock music either. More of a country and western fan myself. Anyway, Sam was one of the members of a Hotshots team that got caught behind the lines when a huge forest fire doubled back on their position. They deployed their shelters just like we're trained to, but the fire was too hot. They all died. Everyone but Sam. That's where he got the burns."

"Man that sucks," the teenager said from Bella's side. Bella had almost forgotten about the girl, listening to the chief tell his story.

"It does," Bella said, suddenly glad she hadn't asked Sam about it. It didn't sound like the kind of thing that someone would want to talk about. "I'm glad he's okay."

"Oh, I'd say he's far from okay, ma'am," the fire chief said, his lips twisted. "He lost his fiancée, his best friend, and the rest of his team in that fire. And I suspect a lot more than that, although not the kind of things you could list on a piece of paper. I'm not sure how he keeps going, to tell the truth." He caught himself and scowled, probably feeling like he'd said too much to a stranger.

"Look," he said in a more distant tone, his attention already turning back to his men as they worked. "This has been a real bad year so far for these kinds of sudden flare-ups. You take my advice, you'll move on and camp somewhere else."

Bella couldn't tell if he was just being nice or if he thought that they'd somehow had something to do with the fire, but she wasn't going to stay here and argue with him.

"Thank you for your help," she said. "You and your men provide an amazing service to the rest of us. We really appreciate it." She put one arm around the girl and steered her out of the clearing and back in the direction of the caravan.

But as soon as they were out of sight of the others, the teen said, "Thanks again for saving me from the fire. Maybe I'll see you around sometime," and started to walk away into the woods.

"Not so fast, missy," Bella said, grabbing one strap of the girl's backpack. "Where do you think you're going?"

The girl tried out the wide-eyed look on her, although Bella was a lot less impressed than the crew chief had been. She didn't think innocence and this child had had much to do with each other in quite some time.

"Um, I've got to get home," the teen said. "People are going to be, like, looking for me."

"Uh-huh," Bella said. "Somehow I doubt that. Either way, I've got some questions for you first. And I'm thinking you might have a few questions for me too, about what happened back there in the clearing."

To her surprise, the girl just laughed, sounding more genuine than she had a minute before. "Why would I have questions? It's pretty obvious—you're a witch and you put out the fire by magically calling down rain. And I really appreciate it, but I have to get going now." She started edging away, only to be brought up short by Bella's grip on her backpack.

"I don't think so, *niece*. You and I are going to have a nice little talk. Besides, I have a cat that thinks you need to eat more. You'll discover that it isn't a good idea to argue with him. Or me, for that matter." She switched her grasp to the girl's thin arm instead. "I hope you like tuna. We eat a lot of damned tuna."

SAM PUT THE two-way down on the table as gently as if it were made out of glass. He felt a bit like that himself. Except that if he had been glass, maybe things would have been a little clearer.

He was relieved to hear that Bella was safe—more than relieved, downright thank-you-God-he-didn't-believe-in grateful. But there were all sorts of things about the story the crew chief told him that didn't add up. Where had the niece come from, for instance? First there had been a grandmother who was there and then not there, and now a niece that Bella had never mentioned? Not that he knew her all that well. Or at all, come to think of it.

It was also a hell of a coincidence that Bella had been at the site of two recent fires, both of which had started and been put out under mysterious circumstances. It wasn't that Sam suspected her of setting fires—at least, he hoped like hell he didn't suspect her, because he really liked her—but something was off here.

He'd been hoping to avoid seeing her again; keeping his distance was force of habit by now, and a lot more comfortable than the alternative. Especially after that comment she made about true love, not that she could have known how much that would hurt, for someone who'd had true love and lost it. But after today, he didn't think he could stay away. He was tortured by the idea that she could have burned to death while he sat in the tower doing nothing, but he wasn't sure if he was planning to check on her or check *up* on her. Maybe both. She was a confusing kind of woman.

GREGORI WAS TRYING to meditate. Not easy to do under the best of conditions. In a dank cave after being bled and tortured and starved, nearly impossible. But he knew it was the best way to keep body and spirit intact under these trying circumstances. Besides, he could tell that his unbreakable calm drove the witch crazy, and that was almost as soothing to his soul as the meditation itself.

He had finally reached the point where the smells and noises of his confinement faded away, leaving only the internal spaces of his mind, when he heard a high-pitched shriek followed by cursing in at least three different languages. *Now what?*

A wooden spoon went hurling through the air and smashed against the cave wall, and Gregori gave up with a sigh and opened his eyes.

"These instructions must be wrong!" Brenna said, clearly talking to herself rather than any of the occupants of the cave. She mostly ignored the Riders unless she wanted them for something. "I don't understand why the spell isn't working."

She rifled through the pages of the huge book she'd been using, muttering darkly. "This was the second time. The second time the energy simply cut off just as it was being channeled in from the forest's suffering. It doesn't make sense. I did everything right. Drew the runes and sigils. Set the blood circle. Triggered the magic. Lit the fire.

"But I must be doing something wrong. Impossible. Impossible. The fires should be working. Sometimes they work. Sometimes they don't. It doesn't make any sense."

"Perhaps it does not make sense because the spell itself is flawed," Gregori said, speaking as calmly and rationally as he could.

He had tried before to reach through her madness to the woman underneath. After all, they had worked together for many long years, when she was still a Baba Yaga. The Riders had helped her often, saved her skin more than once. Surely there must be some vestige of humanity left in her. Some shredded remains of sanity. If only he could persuade her to give up this unattainable dream of immortality, perhaps she would let them go and he would no longer have to watch his friends suffer.

It was worth the attempt, even if so far each time he had tried she had only become more and more convinced that he knew some secret that he did not.

"Flawed. The spell is not flawed," Brenna said. A vein throbbed in the center of her forehead like a warning light. "I have followed the directions. I've felt it working. Already I am stronger, my magic as powerful as it was when I was drinking the Water of Life and Death. It *must* be working."

"It is doing something, Brenna, but that doesn't mean it does what you think it does," Gregori said. "And each time, the effects wear off. The costs are too high and it does not last. Surely you must see by now that the potion you seek cannot be created. Not by these means. Not by *any* means.

Immortality cannot be bought with the lives of others. You are either born to it or not."

Brenna threw another spoon, then a huge chunk of black crystal veined with emeralds, and finally, a small cast-iron cauldron. The last one clanked into the wall next to Gregori's head, shattering off pieces of rock that flew like shrapnel. One shard sliced open his cheek, and blood dripped wetly down his face.

"Noooo!" Brenna screamed, picking up a double-bladed black athame and waving it through the air. She clumped over to stand in front of Gregori's cage. "You lie! You and the others, you don't deserve to live forever. You've already had so long, while I grow old without the Water that is due me for my many years of service. I will make it work. You. Will. Help. Me."

She gasped for breath between each of the last words, stabbing him through the bars with every utterance until the knife was more red than black. Only the sound of her potion bubbling over, causing the fire beneath it to hiss and sputter, finally distracted her from her ranting.

Brenna picked up the spoon she'd thrown first, brushing the dirt off on her already stained and malodorous skirt, and returned to her stirring and muttering, Gregori forgotten for now.

"My brother, you have got to stop provoking the witch," Alexei said in his deep growling whisper. "It never gets you anywhere."

"Look who is talking," Gregori said, sinking to the ground and checking his wounds; the fact that Brenna had to reach through the bars had kept the knife from going too deep. This time. "Even with several new holes in my arm and side, I look better than you do."

The huge man's hands were still burned and oozing from when he'd thrown himself on the bars of his cage to distract the witch. Still, they each did what they could. What they had to. And they hung on, hoping against hope. Because, really, what other choice was there?

Gregori seated himself gingerly back into lotus position,

and went back to meditating. All they could do now was wait, and it was as good a way to spend the time as any other.

ONCE BELLA MADE it clear that she wasn't going to take no for an answer, the girl came along without much of a fuss. Bella wasn't sure if it was the prospect of seeing Koshka again, or the mention of a tuna sandwich, but she didn't care, as long as she didn't have to argue about it.

Back at the caravan, Bella made lunch while Koshka made what passed for small talk when only one of you spoke Cat.

"Here you go," she said, putting a plate in front of the girl, along with a glass of iced tea. She did the same for herself and for Koshka, although the dragon-cat got a bowl of milk instead.

"So, do you have a name?" Bella asked her guest, watching her plow through two sandwiches in as many minutes. She put one of hers on the girl's plate without comment.

"You can call me Jazz," the girl said. "Good sandwich. Thanks. Is that dill?"

"Yes, it is," Bella said, not interested in being distracted by a discussion of ingredients. "Is Jazz your real name?"

"It is now."

O-kay. "And would you like to tell me what you're doing in the woods on your own?" Bella said. "Don't bother with that innocent look either. I'm not buying it."

Jazz sighed and put down the last uneaten corner of her third sandwich. "I suppose now you're going to threaten to call the authorities."

Koshka made his laughing noise and Bella glared at him.

"I'm not all that big on following the rules," she said. "But I am concerned that you're okay. After all, I did just save you from burning to death in a tree. That kind of makes me responsible for you."

"It so doesn't," Jazz said, sputtering with indignation. "I've been taking care of myself for a long time. I don't need you or anyone else to be responsible for me."

"Uh-huh. How old are you?"

"Eighteen."

"Try again."

"Fine. I'm sixteen." The girl crossed her arms over her narrow chest and glared, as if daring Bella to prove she was lying. Of course, Bella didn't have to prove anything; she had a secret weapon.

"Mwrow," Koshka said.

"Sorry, try again. The cat says you're not sixteen."

Jazz sighed. "Jeez. I can't believe you're taking a cat's word over mine. Okay—I'm fifteen. But I've been living in the woods since early spring and getting along just fine, so you don't need to worry about me."

"How about you let me decide that once I have all the facts," Bella countered. "You can begin with why you've been living in the woods—and don't bother trying to embroider the truth, because Koshka here is better than a lie detector."

A dramatic teenage sigh gusted in Bella's direction, but once that was out of the way, Jazz apparently reconciled herself to the inevitable.

"Look, I know that you won't believe me, but I swear, I'm way better off living on my own than I was in any of the places I've spent the last ten years," Jazz said, looking down and fiddling with a loose thread on her jeans as she talked. "My mom died when I was five, and nobody had any idea who my father was. Just a blank line on my birth certificate, I guess. Anyway, there was no one else to take me in, so I've been bouncing around from foster home to foster home ever since."

Koshka left his spot by Bella's foot and sat down by Jazz instead, laying his big, blunt head on her knee. She seemed to draw comfort from his warm presence and petted him absently while she went on. Bella made a mental note to give the dragon-cat whatever treats he wanted later.

"Not a good experience?" Bella guessed.

"Pretty sucky, actually," Jazz said in a grim tone. "The best ones were where the people just took the money from the state and mostly ignored me. The worst ones . . . Well, let's just say that this last place I got to be a combination of slave labor and punching bag. Not a great combo. When Mike, the husband, started looking at me like he wanted to add something else to that list, I took off. And I'm not going back."

The girl lifted her head to stare defiantly at Bella, but if she was expecting an argument, she was in for a surprise.

"I don't blame you," Bella said as calmly as she could. "The woman who raised me rescued me from a bad foster home too. I was a lot younger than you are, so you've probably had to deal with some crap that I missed, but my Baba decided to take me because I was being locked in a closet for weeks at a time when I was four, so I get what you're talking about."

"Jeez, that's messed up," Jazz said. "For real? You're not just saying that to get me to trust you?"

"I would never do that, Jazz," Bella said. "I may not always agree with you, but I promise I will never lie to you."

"That would be a first," the girl muttered. "But okay."

"So you ran away?"

"Yeah, back in the spring. I got as far as I could before I found this park, and I decided to stay here for a while. It was cold in the beginning, but it seemed like a safe place, before the fires started. After today, I don't know about that, but I don't have anyplace else to go, and as far as I'm concerned, even when they're on fire, the woods are safer than the outside world."

Since Bella felt more or less the same, she didn't feel like she had much of a rebuttal for that either.

"Now that we've gotten the basics out of the way, do you want to tell me why you find it so easy to believe that I'm some kind of witch who can do magic? After all, that's not the way most people would react." Bella didn't even try to deny the witch part—she was pretty sure that ship had sailed.

Jazz snorted. "I read all the fairy-tale books I could get my hands on when I was growing up—even the grimmest stories were better than real life—and I know magic when I see it. I'm not stupid, and I've been looking for it my whole life. I *knew* it had to be real. I just knew it. So when I saw you call the rain to put out the fire, I figured you must be a witch. You are, aren't you?"

Bella nodded. "I am. I'm a Baba Yaga, in fact. You might not have read any stories about the Baba Yagas, because they're from Russia and not all that well-known here in the United States. Plus, of course, they got most of it wrong, because, you know, fairy tales." She peered at the girl. "Knowing that I'm a witch doesn't freak you out?"

"Are you serious?" Jazz grinned at her, suddenly looking even younger than fifteen. "I mostly think it is way cool. I mean, if you're not planning to eat me or anything."

"Nah," Bella said. "I just had a big lunch."

The girl giggled and then pointed at Koshka. "So what's his story? Is he some kind of enchanted prince or something?"

Koshka sneered at her as only a cat can. "Don't be ridiculous. I'm something *much* better than that—I'm a dragon in disguise."

"Wow, that *is* better," Jazz said. "And how come I can understand him now when I couldn't before? It just kind of felt like I almost could, you know what I mean?"

"Koshka can make himself understood by anyone he chooses, or not," Bella said. "Looks like he chose you."

"*Cool*," the girl breathed, and she leaned over to grab the last of her sandwich.

Bella shook her head. She couldn't decide if it was good luck or bad luck that she got the one teenager in the world who still believed in magic. Nor did she have any idea what the hell she was supposed to do with her now that she had her.

AS SOON AS he went out of service, Sam was walking toward the door before he'd even made up his mind to go. He stopped, one foot in and one foot out, and asked himself what the hell he was doing. It wasn't even dark yet. It wasn't as though he had to see her face, make sure for himself that she was really okay. He was just going to ask her some pointed questions, that's all. It could wait for an hour or two.

He told himself that again while he scooped up the box with the owlet in it, figuring it would make a good excuse for a visit. And again as he walked a little too fast down the stairs and then rode the four-wheeler down the path that led to the section of forest where the caravan was parked.

Hopping off the four-wheeler, he walked almost without thinking in the direction of the clearing. Even so, he was a bit startled to find himself there when he stopped at the edge of the trees to catch his breath.

Bella looked up from a small portable barbeque grill, and her smile when she saw him made his heart skip a beat. For a moment, it seemed like the entire clearing glowed with light.

"Sam! This is a surprise," she said with what seemed like genuine enthusiasm, although he couldn't imagine why after the way he'd treated her the last couple of times they were together. "You're just in time for dinner."

"Dinner?" he repeated, feeling stupid. He hadn't expected to be invited to dinner and hadn't brought anything. Except the tiny owl, of course, which was hardly helpful.

"You haven't eaten yet, have you? It isn't anything fancy," Bella said with a laugh. "I'm not much of a cook, to be honest, but I can char meat with the best of them." She mistook his hesitation for something else and pointed at a bucket of water sitting at the ready next to the grill. "Don't worry; we're being careful with the fire."

She gestured toward a skinny, smallish teenage girl with chopped-off brown hair and a wary expression. "After today, I think we're both feeling a little paranoid about anything with flames on it."

"I don't blame you," Sam said, walking slowly into the clearing. "Are you both okay?"

"We're fine. Truly," Bella said. "So have you? Had dinner?"

"Um, no, actually," Sam said. "I usually just make a sandwich or something. I'm afraid I'm not much of a cook either."

"We have tuna," the girl piped up. "If you're, like, a vegetarian or something."

Sam didn't know what to say. On the one hand, there was a part of him that couldn't think of anything he'd like better than to stay and eat with Bella. But he didn't even know if he remembered how to have a normal conversation with regular people anymore; something that wasn't centered around fighting fires or giving tours of the tower. And his face would probably frighten the girl or make her feel sick.

He took another step forward into the light, figuring he might as well get it over with. "Um, I'm not a vegetarian," he said, fighting the temptation to pull his cap even farther down over his eyes.

"Great," Bella said. "Then you'll join us. Jazz, can you go grab another steak out of the fridge, please? And maybe a beer while you're at it?" She turned back to Sam. "Would you like a beer? I've got Blue Moon, if you like that."

"A beer would be great," Sam said hoarsely. He sat down in a third folding chair that he hadn't remembered seeing when he'd first looked into the clearing, the owlet in its box almost forgotten on his lap.

The girl she called Jazz bounded up the three steps into the caravan and bounced back down again with a platter full of meat in one hand and a beer in another. She gave the steak to Bella and then brought the beer over to hand it to Sam, peering into his face with unself-conscious interest.

"Cool scars, dude," she said. "Here you go." She turned back to Bella without missing a beat. "Can I have a beer too, *Auntie* Bella?"

"Hell no," Bella said. "And don't be rude to our guest."

Sam found, much to his surprise, that he didn't mind the girl's comment. Maybe it was because she didn't appear fazed by the scars, any more than Bella had been. Or maybe he just preferred straightforward comments to morbid fascination or cringing pity, which were the responses he usually got.

"That's okay," he said. "I mean, as long as she thinks they're cool." He felt an unaccustomed smile tugging at the corners of his mouth. It had been so long, he almost didn't recognize the sensation.

"Way cool," Jazz affirmed. "Like tattoos, only without the ink. You know, like the way some of the natives in Africa use scars to show which ethnic group they belong to or for spiritual reasons." She shrugged when Sam stared at her. "What? I read a lot, okay? I know stuff."

"Sure you do, kid," Bella muttered. "Everything but when to shut up." She turned to Sam. "Sorry again. She's not used to polite company."

"That makes two of us," Sam admitted. "It's fine. I kind of like the idea of my scars marking me as a member of some special group. Although God knows what group would have me."

Bella yelped, probably because her gigantic cat had accidentally put his claws into her leg. "Ow!" she said. "Koshka would like to make sure that I tell you that you are welcome to be a part of our little group anytime. If, of course, you want to be."

"Uh-huh," Sam said. "The cat told you that."

The feline in question opened his mouth in a wide yawn that showed lots of sharp teeth and said, "Mrrrow," in a definitive tone.

"There, see?" Bella said.

Sam looked at Jazz. "Do they always sound like they are having an actual conversation?" he asked jokingly.

"Sure," the teen said. "That's because Koshka is really a magical dragon turned into a cat."

The cat made a rude noise and meowed again.

"Oh right, sorry. A magical dragon *disguised* as a cat." Jazz grinned at him.

Clearly they were all as crazy as loons, but somehow that made him more comfortable in their company, rather than less. Which probably meant he was crazy too. No surprise there.

Bella took four steaks off the fire and put them on plates along with salad and roasted potatoes. The steaks smelled heavenly as only charred meat under an open sky could, and Sam could feel his mouth start to water. It had been so long since he'd had anything approaching an appetite, he was startled when his stomach rumbled loudly.

"You'd better give Sam his first," Bella said with a laugh, and she handed a plate and some silverware to Jazz. She then put a plate down in front of the cat, who waited politely for everyone else to be served.

"Hey!" the girl said, spotting the box on his lap when she gave him his dinner. "Is that a little owl?"

Sam put the box on the ground next to his chair so he'd have room on his lap for the plate. "Yep. I've been taking care of it for a few days since some of the firefighters rescued him in the woods. The cat has been fetching me mice to feed it. Didn't your aunt tell you about it?"

Jazz's eyes shifted off to look at something in the distance. "Um, sure. I just forgot."

Right. "Funny about that, because she forgot to mention to me that she had a niece staying with her."

"Oh, didn't I mention her?" Bella asked, not even trying to act like she wasn't bullshitting him. "I guess it just didn't come up."

Sam took a bite of his steak, savoring the rich juiciness and smoky flavor. For a couple of minutes they just enjoyed the food, the cat eating almost as neatly as the others, although without the benefit of any cutlery besides teeth and claws.

"So," Sam said finally. "How on earth did you two get caught in that fire this morning? I've spent all day trying to figure out how poor Jazz got stuck up in that tree with the flames underneath her."

Bella and Jazz exchanged looks and then recited a tale exactly like the one the fire chief had passed on to him. It didn't sound any likelier on the second rendition.

"You fell asleep in the tree waiting for your aunt to come find you?" Sam said when they were done. "And the fire didn't wake you up until it was too big to escape?"

Jazz shuddered, her fear seeming a lot more real than her story. "That fire must have come on really fast," she said. "I woke up and it was just *there*. Although I admit, I am a really heavy sleeper. One family I lived with used to roll me out of the bed to wake me up."

"Family you lived with?" Sam asked, raising one eyebrow.

"She means our relatives," Bella said. "We all visit one another a lot. You know, for the summers and such. I have sisters. Sort of sisters."

Sam sighed. These two were the worst liars he'd ever met. Hopefully that just meant that they hadn't had much practice. And not that they were both dangerous lunatics.

"Uh-huh," he said.

Jazz jumped up from her seat and gave him a wide-eyed look. "Gee," she said. "Can I look at the owl? He's so cute."

Nice subtle way to change the conversation, kid. "Sure," Sam said. "It's time for another feeding anyway." He turned to Bella. "Do you think you could get—" He blinked, realizing the cat was already gone. "Oh. Damn, that is one smart cat."

"You have no idea," Bella said dryly.

"I think we should give it a name," Jazz said, still doing her "look how innocent and adorable I am" act.

"The cat? I thought his name was Koshka," Sam said, confused.

"No, the *owl*, silly." Jazz rolled her eyes. "Jeez."

"Oh." Sam hadn't even thought about naming it. After all, it was more likely to die than not, and if it lived, it would just go back to live in the forest where it belonged. "It's not a pet, Jazz. It's a wild animal."

"Well duh," the girl said. "So are you saying wild animals aren't entitled to names too? What are you, speciest?"

"Speciest?" Bella bit her lip, clearly trying not to laugh at Sam's predicament.

"You know, like people are prejudiced against black people and they call them racist, and people who don't like old people are called ageist. Sam's clearly got something against wild species, so he's speciest." The girl crossed her arms and looked stubborn as only a teenager can.

"I am not speciest," Sam said with mock indignation.

"Which isn't a word, by the way. Heck, I'm trying to save the thing, aren't I? I don't see you getting up every few hours to feed it dead mice."

"Dead mice?" Jazz said. "Ugh. Gross."

"Aha!" Sam pointed at her. "You're miceist!"

Bella laughed, her head thrown back to expose the smooth line of her throat, and Sam suddenly lost his train of thought. While they'd been eating, the sun had set, and the sight of Bella standing in the moonlight laughing took his breath away. He didn't think he'd ever seen anything so beautiful in his life.

And that was more terrifying than any fire.

FOURTEEN

KOSHKA CAME BACK in a few minutes with an improbably large pile of tiny mouse carcasses, along with a few other small critters. Jazz made a face and volunteered to wash the dishes inside the caravan, which might have been more impressive if she had actually taken them with her as she bolted for the door.

After the little owlet was fed, Sam fought the desire to get up and run for the safety of the tower and his solitary life. His reaction to Bella both alarmed and confused him. He'd been resigned to a lifetime alone and thought himself incapable of ever feeling for another woman the way he had for Heather. He didn't understand what was happening to him, but he didn't see it ending anywhere good.

For one thing, although Bella was welcoming enough, there was no indication that she felt anything other than friendship for him. How could she, with his scars and his sputtering social skills? Besides, they'd just met—didn't even really know each other—and she was only passing through on her way to somewhere else. Plus there were the lies, of course.

And yet, the way the dim light above the caravan door lit up her face and her fiery hair made him want to stay, despite himself.

Jazz came back out after a while and sat around the small stone fire pit with them, the bucket of water on one side ("just in case") and the owlet on her lap.

"Can we call him Charming?" she asked Sam.

Sam wasn't sure how anyone could tell what kind of personality a young owl had, but he supposed it didn't matter. "I guess so," he said. "But I'm not sure the name suits him. Screechy is more like it."

"Not that kind of charming," Jazz said, rolling her eyes. "You know, like Prince Charming. Because you never know, maybe he's an enchanted prince under an evil spell."

"Life isn't a fairy tale, you know," Sam said.

"Wanna bet?" The teen smirked at him then handed back the box with the owl in it. "I'm getting eaten alive by bugs. I'm going inside. Night, Sam. Night, Auntie dearest." She blew what looked like a sarcastic kiss, if there was such a thing, in Bella's direction and headed into the caravan.

Sam stood up too, figuring that this was as good a time as any to make his escape. It had been nice to pretend to be like everyone else for a few hours, but he could feel himself turning back into a pumpkin.

"Um, I should go too. Early morning and all that. Thanks for dinner. It was great."

"You're welcome to join us again sometime," Bella said, standing up and coming over to stand next to him. "I think Koshka likes you." She rubbed the spot on her leg where the cat had punctured her earlier.

"Right. Well, I don't know." Sam looked at the ground, scuffing one boot in the dirt. "I'm usually not very good company."

"I'm hanging out with a teenager and a temperamental cat," Bella said with a small smile. "The bar is set very low around here. But it's up to you."

Sam didn't even feel like he'd been entitled to the delicious meal he'd already eaten, much less an invitation to any future dinners. "Look," he said abruptly, the words forcing themselves up and out of his throat. "I wanted to say I was sorry."

Bella blinked up at him, and he suddenly realized that she was about six inches shorter than he was. She had such a large presence, he'd never realized she was actually fairly petite.

"What? Sorry for what?" she asked.

"Not coming to your rescue earlier," Sam said, still looking at the ground, his voice even raspier than usual. "I could see you from the fire tower, and I could tell you and Jazz were in serious trouble, but all I did was talk on the radio and look out the window. I feel terrible about it."

Bella sounded baffled. "But that's your job, isn't it? You spotted us and sent help. That's what you're supposed to do. I didn't think you were even allowed to leave the tower and go fight the fire yourself; wouldn't that have been deserting your post or something?"

Sam hugged the box with the owlet close to his chest. His stomach hurt and he felt like he couldn't breathe. The steak he'd enjoyed had turned into molten lava in his gut. "Yeah. I guess. I just feel like I should have done more and I'm sorry. I should go now. Thanks again for dinner."

Ignoring the hurt and puzzled look on Bella's face, Sam turned and bolted for the four-wheeler parked on the path back to the fire tower, suddenly feeling like the forest was closing in around him. This had been a mistake. He'd thought he could pretend everything was okay, but it wasn't. He wasn't. And he never would be. Bella deserved better.

BELLA WATCHED HIM go, feeling torn and confused. On the one hand, it was a relief not to have to keep telling Sam lies he obviously didn't believe. On the other hand, the clearing somehow felt colder and emptier without him. She moved back to sit by the fire pit, snapping her fingers to make the flames grow a little higher. It was just the chilly night air, nothing more.

She rubbed one hand over her heart, not understanding

the ache she felt there. Empathy for Sam's pain, she decided. After all, they hardly knew each other. She was no Jazz, to believe in fairy tales. Witches, yes. Love at first sight and happily ever after? No. At least not for a Baba Yaga.

Poor Sam. She recognized survivor's guilt when she saw it, although that wasn't something that Baba Yagas dealt with much either. When you outlived most of the people you knew, it was too much of a luxury to indulge in. Better to avoid connections with Humans in the first place—especially if you have the unpleasant habit of setting them on fire by accident—and stick to the paranormal folks who were made of tougher stuff.

So survivor's guilt was more of an abstract concept to Bella, and in Sam's case, she really didn't understand it. He wasn't responsible for his friends' deaths. He wouldn't have been responsible if something had happened to her and Jazz today. She wished she could have found the words that would make him feel better. He'd looked so sad.

Bella sighed. She didn't understand the guilt, but she was definitely starting to identify with the feelings of inadequacy. So far she was failing miserably at both the mission she'd taken on for the locals to discover and deal with the source of the fires *and* the task the Queen had given her, finding the Riders. She didn't know how to help Sam, and she had no idea what she was supposed to do with a teenage runaway. At this rate, she was going to go down in history as the world's most useless Baba Yaga.

She put her head down on her knees, struggling to find her usual optimism. Instead, she just saw a vision of Sam's scarred face and defeated eyes. Augh.

"Um, Bella?" The door to the caravan opened, and she looked up to see Jazz standing there uncertainly, her backpack slung over one thin shoulder.

"Hey, kid," Bella said, sitting upright. "Where do you think you're going?"

Jazz looked around, clearly checking to see if Sam was still there. "I thought I'd take off, now that we don't have to play niece and aunt anymore."

Bella shook off her rare bout of melancholy; she didn't have time to be self-indulgent. There were jobs to be done and teenagers to wrangle. Tomorrow was another day.

"I'm kind of enjoying having a niece," she said more cheerfully. "I've never had one before. I'd sort of like to see what it feels like in the morning. So why don't you turn your butt back around and I'll make up the pullout bed for you. There's one built right into the wall of the caravan; it's very cool. And I'm almost completely sure that it is more comfortable than the crook of a tree."

Jazz glanced out at the trees and then back at Bella, her expression hard to read in the dim light. "Yeah?" she said.

"Yeah," Bella answered, putting out the fire with another snap of the fingers and getting up to follow her in.

The girl stared at her for a minute without speaking and then said, "Cool," and walked inside.

"It kind of is," Bella muttered.

A CRASH OF thunder jolted Sam out of a deep sleep filled with unsettling dreams; he was sitting up in his boxer shorts, legs slung over the side of the bed, before he was even aware he was awake. The chill of the floorboards radiated up through his bare feet as he ran through scenarios fraught with lightning and fires, his head half in dreamland and half aware of his surroundings.

He'd been dreaming about Bella again, some strange mix of fantasy and reality where they both ran next to giant cats in a land filled with brown and green mushrooms that towered over their heads with snapping embers of fire chasing at their heels. So for a moment he thought it was her he saw standing in the middle of the fire tower, glowing red-gold in the moonlight that came through the wide expanse of the glass walls.

A second look showed him it wasn't, and a combination of disappointment, guilt, and fear caught in his throat and made his breathing ragged and his heartbeat uneven.

The ghost stared at him across the room as if she could read his thoughts and found them wanting.

"Heather," he said. Then, "You're not real."

"Oh, Sam," Heather said sadly. "You don't love me anymore. You love her. That woman."

"What?" His head jerked up. "No, of course I don't. I will always love you, Heather. Always." Hot tears forced themselves to the edge of his eyelids, threatening to spill over. *Real men don't cry*, his father always said. He'd spent months fighting back the emotion; toughing it out in silence . . .

"You need to stay away from her," Heather said, her voice a rough echo of the thunder building outside. "Stay. Away. From. Her."

Sam took one step toward her, and the figure held up a hand as if to stop him from coming any nearer. His shoulders drooped. Maybe the ghost was right. If seeing Bella was going to keep making things worse, he should stay away. His eyes darted to the kitchen drawer where he'd shoved the pills the doctor had given him; pills he'd refused to take. Tranquilizers could make you drowsy, and a fire watcher couldn't afford to be anything less than alert at all times. Sam lived in fear of someone finding out he'd been prescribed them and thinking he was unfit for the job.

Of course, he was standing mostly naked in the cold moonlight having a conversation with a dead woman. Maybe they'd be right.

As if she'd read his thoughts again, Heather said in that strange whispery voice, "You should not be here. You should go. Go home, Sam."

He shook his head, sleep-tousled hair flopping into his eyes, remembering the too-empty rooms of his apartment, a place where he drifted, much like the ghost in front of him. At least here in the fire tower he felt alive. Tormented and losing his mind, maybe, but at least he felt *something*, unlike the numb nothing that awaited him back in the land where people expected him to act normal and be okay.

"I need this job, Heather," he said, suddenly desperate to

make her understand. The old Heather—the living Heather—would have known why he had to be here without him having to explain. That had been one of the best things about her. She embraced the battle like he did. "I need to stay and fight the fire, at least in this small way."

Outside the windows the storm growled and rattled, like some mystical creature part lion and part scorpion, its tail banging against the windows as sharp claws scrabbled across the metal roof. His exposed skin crawled with goose-flesh, although whether it was from the cool air, the storm, or the presence—or not—of the ghost of his dead fiancée, it was hard to say.

"Go home," she said again. "You should not be here. You will cause other deaths as you caused mine. Go home. Leave. Leave. Leave."

Sam staggered as if he'd been shot. He couldn't believe that Heather would say such things. But did that mean it was just his warped subconscious? Maybe he didn't want to believe that she might hold him responsible for her death. Or that she could think he was so dangerous to others he shouldn't be doing the only job left on earth that had any meaning for him.

"Heather, please," he said, taking another step closer. But the glowing figure shivered in the moonlight, a ball of incandescent swirling orange and red materializing in one translucent hand. She lobbed it in his direction, and as he ducked involuntarily, Sam thought he saw an expression of rage cross Heather's normally placid features before he raised his arms protectively over his head.

When he straightened up a moment later, the room was empty, the storm dying away. But the experience trembled through his body and rocked his spirit long after he'd walked around turning on all the lights and scanning the darkness for spots of newly born fire, accusing dead women, or anything else that didn't belong.

Sam paused for a long time, standing in front of the drawer that held his pills, fingers tight on the metal knob with its peeling white paint. In the end, he took his hand away and went to bed. But sleep eluded him as his mind spun about in fevered circles between bad options and worse: either he was being haunted by the woman he loved who seemed to be telling him to stay away from the one person whose company he enjoyed and leave the job that gave the shattered remains of his life some kind of meaning . . . or he was finally, irrevocably, losing his damned mind.

MIKHAIL DAY WATCHED through slitted eyes as Brenna made her way out of the cave, huffing as she climbed the steep incline that led to the surface through the dim slivers of the early morning sunshine. He was pretty sure she'd rolled him (and the others after him) down that incline to get them into the cavern, since he'd woken up that first day with bruises he couldn't explain. Unlike the bruises he had now, whose origins were all too clear.

"Good riddance," Alexei muttered. "Feel free to get eaten by bears while you look for your stupid poisonous berries and mushrooms, you old witch."

Gregori shook his head. "I am not so certain that would be such a good thing, much as I would enjoy the idea of that one ending up on the inside of anything's stomach. After all, if she does not return, we will all starve to death in our cages."

"A better fate than the one that lies in store for us if she does return," Mikhail said, his voice little more than a whisper. "I am very much afraid I have led us to our end."

"Fah," Alexei said, waving one huge hand through the air. "Baba Yaga will come. You will see."

"Do you really think that Barbara, Bella, or Beka got our message?" Mikhail asked, pulling himself up on one elbow. Sitting up seemed like more effort than it was worth. "Last I knew, Barbara was in New York State, Bella was in Montana, and Beka was in California. Can sprites fly that far?"

Gregori gave his typical noncommittal shrug, barely a twitch of one shoulder. "Who can say? They are Baba Yagas. They could be anywhere. And as for sprites, to be honest, I have never paid much attention to such things. But they are very small with wings of matching size. It is hard to believe that one would get very far. It seems more likely that we are on our own."

"Nonsense!" Alexei roared (albeit quietly, just in case Brenna came back unexpectedly). "You felt that tremor in the energy fields the same as I did. There's no denying it was something magical."

"Something magical, yes," Gregori said practically. "But that does not guarantee it was a Baba Yaga."

Mikhail put his head back down, although he still faced toward the others. "I certainly hope it was one of the Babas, after what Alexei did to himself to distract Brenna in case it was."

"Fah," Alexei said again. "It was nothing." His Russian accent, strongest of them all, especially when he was under stress, made it sound like, "It vas nut-tink." It made Mikhail pine for home and earlier days, when things had been simpler and the worst thing a Rider was likely to come up against was a rogue ogre or some annoying princeling trying to overthrow an area the Babas held under their protection.

Mikhail peered through the bars at his friend, whose hands were still oozing and raw. "I wouldn't call it nothing, my large brother. You can't even use your hands."

"Ha!" Alexei said, making a rude gesture to prove Mikhail wrong. "I can use them. I am just reserving my strength until I can wrap them around the witch's scrawny neck." He scowled. "I am more worried about you, Mikhail. Can you hang on until the Baba comes to get us? You have been here longer than Gregori and I, and you are not looking well."

"Nothing a good bowl of borscht couldn't fix," Mikhail said, coughing a little and holding his ribs so the others couldn't see him wince. "I am not so weak as I seem. I'm merely trying to lull Brenna into a false sense of security. Sooner or later, she will lower her guard and I will get us out of here."

He coughed again, feeling broken ends of bones rasping against one another. The pain from that was barely noticeable in the sea of agony from everything else. But worse still was the pain in his soul.

"This is all my fault. It should be me who gets us out of this situation, since I got us into it. If I hadn't allowed the witch to fool me, falling for her tricks like some young puppy still wet behind the ears, you would not have followed me here to be trapped like animals in a cage."

"Who are you calling an animal?" Alexei growled. "It is no more your fault than it is ours. After all, we fell into her trap as well."

Gregori sighed. "There is no point in wasting our energy arguing over this again. None of us expected a Baba Yaga to turn on us. It is unheard of. Just as it is unheard of for a Baba Yaga to have to come to the rescue of the Riders, instead of the other way around. The world has gone insane and no one is to blame."

Mikhail didn't agree with him, but Gregori was right about one thing: there was no point in arguing. If he could, Mikhail would sacrifice his life to buy the freedom of his friends. He only hoped he would have a chance to do so.

"Maybe a Baba is really coming," he said. "Anything is possible." But he didn't really believe it, and he didn't think the others did either.

FIFTEEN

JAZZ OPENED HER eyes, confused for a moment to be looking at a curved wooden ceiling instead of a canopy of trees.
Then she remembered the day before—the fire that nearly
claimed her life and the woman who rescued her who turned
out to be a real, honest-to-Grimm witch. She sat up carefully, removing the blanket that covered her as she looked
around the inside of the caravan.

Early morning light peeked in through partially drawn
curtains, barely illuminating the tidy cupboards and neatly
arranged furniture, most of which was tucked against the
walls when it wasn't in use. At the far end of the compact
traveling house a motionless form indicated that Bella was
still asleep.

Jazz swung her legs over the side of the bed, thinking furi-
ously. It had been nice sleeping in an actual bed, even one that
folded out from a wall. And it had been great to eat as much
as she wanted for a change. But trusting adults had never
worked out well for her, and every instinct in her body was
telling her to get out now while she still could. After all, hadn't
most of the witches in her storybooks turned out to be evil?

On the other hand, Bella *had* saved her from the fire. There was nothing evil about that, as far as Jazz could tell, although it was always possible that she'd only done it so she could use Jazz for some other, even worse purpose. She didn't have to trust Bella in order to stay, just for a few days until she'd had another couple of good meals. On the *other* other hand, there was always the possibility that Bella would turn her in to the cops or social services for "her own good." Jazz had too much experience with people making lousy decisions because they thought they knew what was best for her. It was too risky. Better to take her chances in the woods.

She slipped her feet into her sneakers and grabbed her backpack, trying to move as silently as she could. One step toward the door, then another, sliding her feet on the smooth wooden floor so they wouldn't make any noise.

Suddenly she bumped into something solid that hadn't been there a minute ago. Looking down, she saw a pair of yellow eyes gleaming up at her in the dim dawn glow.

"I wouldn't," Koshka said. "It's not safe out there."

She still couldn't get used to the fact that she could understand the talking cat. Dragon. Whatever. "Like I'm safer in here with the wicked witch," she said.

"I heard that," a sleepy voice said from the rear.

Jazz could swear she heard the cat snicker.

"I was just going to stick my head out and see what the weather was like," Jazz said, crossing her fingers behind her back. She hated lying, although she did it when she had to. Too many people had lied to her over the years. She figured this one wasn't exactly a lie—she'd check the weather, and then keep on going.

Bella yawned and sat up in bed, her curly red hair sticking up in every direction like a fiery halo. She sure didn't look evil. Although in Jazz's experience, that didn't mean much. In the last family she'd run away from, the father seemed like every kid's dream dad—until he shut the door.

"Carrying your backpack?" Bella said. "Wouldn't it be easier to just open a window and stick your head out?"

Jazz grimaced. Even half asleep, the woman was way

too observant. "Look, nothing personal. I just have trust issues, okay? I'd rather be on my own. It's easier that way."

Bella rubbed one hand across her face. "Hey, I get it. I'm a loner myself. Except for Koshka, of course."

At Jazz's feet, the dragon-cat let out a purr that sounded like an outboard engine.

"Great," Jazz said. "So I'll just be going then. Thanks for dinner and the bed and everything."

"Koshka was right when he said it isn't safe out there," Bella said, getting up and padding across the floor in bare feet. She was wearing an oversized tee shirt with a picture of Margaret Hamilton from *The Wizard of Oz*. Underneath the pointy green face was printed, YOU SAY WICKED LIKE IT'S A BAD THING.

"Uh-huh." Jazz aimed one finger at the shirt. "Or in here?"

"Oh please," Bella said. "Where's your sense of irony?" She pushed a button on the coffeemaker, and the scent of roses filled the caravan. Weird. "Look, I'm working on trying to solve the mystery of whatever is causing these fires and put a stop to it. Just stick around until I've done that, so I don't have to worry about you getting trapped in another tree. After that, if you want to leave, I won't stop you."

Jazz looked down at the cat, and Koshka shrugged, looking like an earthquake on a fur mountain. "She has her faults," he said. "But she doesn't lie."

"Oh yeah? She told the firefighters and Sam that a sudden rainstorm came up and put out the fire."

"And one did," Bella said. "I just didn't mention that I'd made the rain happen. You're the one who said the fire must have been started by lightning. And for all we know, it was."

Jazz thought back through what she could remember of their conversations. She didn't think Bella had lied to her—she'd even admitted to being a witch when Jazz said she was one.

"Fine," she said. "I'll stay for a couple of days, but you have to promise you won't call the authorities on me."

Bella laughed. "The 'authorities' I deal with aren't interested in runaway girls, I assure you. But I promise not to tell anyone you're not my niece as long as you stick close until I can figure out what to do with you."

"Huh." Jazz rolled her eyes. "I've got an idea. You want to figure out what to do with me? You could start by making me breakfast. I'm a growing girl, you know."

TINY RAPPED PERFUNCTORILY on the door to the fire tower and ducked his head as he came in, putting down a plate that smelled delectably of grease and sugar on the table where Sam sat, head slumped over a steaming cup of coffee.

"Mrs. Tiny made donuts," the tall man announced unnecessarily. "So I brought up your mail. Seemed cruel to keep all these calories to myself."

He patted his still-flat belly and put a small pile of envelopes and circulars down next to the donuts before going to help himself to a cup of coffee and sitting opposite Sam.

"Nothing personal, my friend," Tiny said, peering across the table at Sam. "But you look like five pounds of shit in a one-pound bag. Something I should know about?"

Sam took a gulp of coffee and shook his head. "I'm okay. Just having some trouble sleeping."

"I figured," Tiny said. "What with the bloodshot eyes and the fact that you're trying to inhale that coffee. Have a donut; they're good for what ails you." He shoved the plate closer to Sam. "What's the problem? The PTSD giving you nightmares? I had those for years after I got back from Nam. Nothing to be ashamed of."

Sam winced. He wasn't surprised that Tiny had guessed about the PTSD. After all, the older man knew his history and had already told Sam that he'd dealt with the issue himself years before. Still, he hated to have anyone mention it. Speaking it out loud seemed to give it more power.

He took a donut and nibbled at one powdery edge. "It's not that," he said. "I mean, yeah, I have nightmares, but I'm kind of used to them. That's not what's keeping me awake nights." He glanced over one shoulder as if the ghost might appear, even though it was almost seven in the morning on a crystalline clear day.

Tiny leaned back in his chair, a trace of tannish brown cinnamon sugar decorating his denim shirt. "Well, what is it then? Worried about the fires? We all are, but you can't spot 'em if you can't keep your eyes open, now can you?"

"It's not that either," Sam said, putting the donut back down. He wasn't going to say it. No way. "Don't worry about it, Tiny. I'm fine."

"Son, if you were any farther from fine you'd be in Nebraska," Tiny said with a chuckle. He had an entire assortment of slightly askew sayings; Sam had never been sure if they were local colloquialisms or if the older man just made them up on the spot. "Come on, you know you can tell me anything. After all, I told you all about me and Mrs. Tiny and the picnic table."

Sam shuddered. "I know. And I wish you hadn't. I've never been able to look at that poor, innocent hunk of wood the same way since." He sighed. "Okay, I'll tell you. But I warn you, you're going to think I'm crazy." *And maybe I am.*

"I'm pretty sure you're the sanest man I know," Tiny said. "'Course, considering the company I keep, that might not be saying much. So, what's going on?"

Sam took a deep breath. "I think I might have a ghost." He waited for the laughter.

The older man just looked thoughtful. "Here at the fire tower? We never had one before, leastwise not one that I ever heard of. Not in the years I was working here, anyway, before I married Lisa."

Most people assumed that Tiny and his wife were an old married couple, but in fact they'd been high school sweethearts who'd lost touch and hadn't reconnected until after Lisa's first husband had died suddenly and she'd come back to the area to heal about five years ago. She and Tiny reconnected, fell right back into love, and got married about a year later. That was when he'd given up working the fire tower in the summer, not wanting to miss one more minute with the woman he'd never stopped waiting for.

"You believe in ghosts?" Sam said, a little taken aback by the other man's casual acceptance of his announcement.

Tiny rolled his eyes. "'Course I do," he said. "My granny sat in her rocking chair most nights after she died, just rocking back and forth even when there was no wind. We tried to get rid of the damned thing once; my mother said it gave her the willies. But as soon as we took it out to the shed, things started moving around the house. Vases would fall over, little stuff like keys would disappear, and my dad's favorite coffee mug somehow ended up upside down in the cat's litter box. That was the last straw. They brought granny's rocking chair back inside and put it right back in the corner of the living room." He chuckled. "You bet I believe in ghosts. Besides—"

"Besides?" Sam asked.

"Well, you've got to understand the people around here," Tiny said. "There's a large group of Russian-Germans; folks whose families were Germans who first relocated to the Volga region of Russia under Catherine the Great and then emigrated here when things went to hell later on. They tend to be a close-knit community, and even all these years later, many of them believe in the things their ancestors believed in back in the Old World. That includes a lot of stuff most other people would consider fairy tales or superstition, including ghosts."

"Huh." Sam drank some more coffee. "I had no idea. Your family is part of this community?"

"You bet," Tiny said. "My ancestors helped settle this area. Believe it or not, I'm considered a highly respected man around these parts." He chuckled again, but then the grin on his face morphed into something more serious. "In fact, I might know of someone who can help you, if you really are being haunted."

Sam was torn between hope and alarm. "Really? You mean some kind of exorcist or something? I don't think I'm up to dealing with incense and chanting in Latin."

"Not an exorcist," Tiny said. "A witch."

$\mathcal{S}$IXTEEN

"A WITCH," SAM said. "You want me to go see a witch about my ghost problem. I'm beginning to get what you mean about me being the saner one here."

"What, you don't believe in witches?" Tiny asked.

Sam shrugged. "Theoretically, sure I do. But I've never actually met one."

Tiny laughed. "Yes, you have."

Sam was beginning to wish he could hook his coffee up to an intravenous line; maybe this conversation would make more sense. "You're not trying to tell me Mrs. Tiny dances naked under a full moon, are you? Because somehow she doesn't seem like the type."

"Lisa does plenty of dancing, but none of it naked, more's the pity," Tiny said with a twinkle in his eye. "No, the witch I'm talking about isn't anyone local. You see, there's some hereabouts, in that same community I was talking about, that think there's something that doesn't feel right about the fires this year. You can't tell me you haven't felt it too. Fires popping up in places they shouldn't, burning in ways that don't seem natural."

"I figured that was just me being twitchy," Sam admitted. "Or not knowing the patterns of the way things burn around here well enough."

"Well, maybe we're all being twitchy," Tiny said. "But when the elders start saying something is really, really off, most of us pay attention. So they called in what you might say is specialized help, using the old ways."

"Specialized help is a witch?" As a Hotshot, Sam was used to being considered specialized, but this was a little outside of his usual definition of the word.

"Not just any witch," Tiny said. "If there is such a thing as 'just any witch.' We only know about the one type: Baba Yaga. So that's who we called. And we must have done it right, because she came."

Sam scratched his chin, feeling the rasp of stubble under his fingernails. If he was going to shave before he went into service, he was going to have to do it soon. But he was having a hard time tearing himself away from this bizarre but fascinating conversation.

"I think I remember hearing stories about her when I was a kid," he said. "Wasn't she an ugly crone who lived in an enchanted hut and flew through the sky in a cauldron, or something?"

"Mortar and pestle, actually," Tiny said, as if they were talking about models of cars and not magical modes of transportation. "Although these days, the Baba Yagas have updated some, so they blend in better with the modern era. Or so I'm told. It's more of a job title than one particular person. And I don't know about the others, but the one we've got is anything but ugly." He chuckled again.

Sam got the distinct feeling he was missing something.

"So has this witch found anything, um, abnormal about the fires?"

Tiny lifted one shoulder. "No idea. I'd guess not, since no one has said anything to me and the fires are still going on. Maybe there's nothing to find after all. But she's powerful and magic, so I'm guessing that if anyone can help you with your ghost problem, it's her."

Sam gazed down into the depths of his mug. "I'm not absolutely sure it *is* a ghost, Tiny. It might just be all in my head." He didn't dare look up for fear of seeing pity in the other man's eyes.

"If it is, it is," Tiny said calmly. "But it wouldn't hurt to talk to the Baba Yaga about it, seeing as you already know her."

"I do?" Sam sat up straight in amazement. "I don't think so. I'm pretty sure I'd remember meeting a wicked witch in the woods."

"Oh, I think she's only a little wicked," Tiny said, grin widening. "And since she's disguised as a wandering artist living in a caravan, I don't expect it is all that obvious. On purpose, no doubt."

Sam could feel his mouth drop open. *Bella?* That wasn't possible, was it? Or was it? "Huh," he said. "I suppose that would explain a few things." *Like improbably large cats who fetched mice.* "But I'm not sure I'm buying it. You're not pulling my leg, are you? I mean, Bella, a fairy-tale witch? It seems kind of far-fetched."

"Right," Tiny said. "Says the man who can't sleep because he's being haunted."

"Oh. When you put it like that, maybe I should consider going to talk to her about it."

"What could it hurt?" Tiny asked, grabbing one last donut and stuffing it in his mouth as he stood up.

That was the question, wasn't it? If seeing a red-haired woman had started this all off in the first place, would going to see her again make it better . . . or worse?

THE FOREST STAYED calm for a couple of days, for which Sam was grateful. He dealt with a chatty family visiting from Japan who had never seen such tall trees before, another troop of Boy Scouts, and one very lost hiker. But no smokes and no fires.

Every morning, Sam decided to stay in the fire tower come evening, and every night he ended up eating dinner at the caravan anyway. It was as if his feet took him there of their own volition. But he didn't mind, not really. He found Jazz amusing, Koshka both intimidating and adorable in his own odd way, and Bella . . . Sam didn't know what he thought about Bella. But somehow watching her in the dimming summer sunlight made him feel better than he had in a long time. Besides, Jazz and Koshka were helping him with the owlet, which was growing stronger with every passing day, and he didn't have to cook. Win-win.

Every evening he resolved to talk to Bella about the ghost, whose intermittent appearances were growing more and more unpleasant. Or ask her if she was really a witch. And every night he chickened out. Maybe he just didn't want to hear the answer.

So for the most part, he tried not to notice that this was more time than he'd spent with other people in years. As long as he didn't pay attention to what was happening, he didn't have to decide whether it was okay or not. But the nightmarish visitations were beginning to fray his nerves and make him wonder if the answer was "not."

JAZZ WOKE UP every morning sure that this would be the day she'd be on her way, and yet every night she went to sleep in the caravan anyway. Bella wasn't like any other adult she'd ever met, which Bella said was because she'd been raised in the woods by a witch out of Russian fairy tales, but Jazz thought was most likely just because of Bella being Bella.

Bella was funny and kind, even though she made Jazz do her share of the chores around the caravan, and Jazz knew somehow that Koshka would never let anything bad happen to her. Jazz even liked it when Sam came and hung around in the evening, although she didn't like most men as a rule.

She didn't get that creepy vibe off of him, and besides, it was clear—to her, at least—that he had a serious thing for Bella, although he hardly even looked at the red-haired woman. Instead he told bad jokes and played rummy with Jazz. She had already won almost twenty bucks off him, and he didn't even sulk about it, which made her like him more. At first his scars were kind of shocking, but after a while she didn't even notice them anymore. He was just Sam.

Jazz had even convinced Bella to teach her a few basic bits of magic, like lighting a candle without a match and making a glass globe glow. Bella told her she had a natural talent, which made her feel like glowing herself. Nobody had ever said she had a talent for anything, much less something as way cool as magic. She thought she might stick around, for another day or two, just to check it out. But something, some itch at the back of her head honed by years living on a knife's edge, told her that nothing this good could last. Something bad was coming and coming soon.

BELLA SPENT THE next couple of days searching the woods for any sign of the Riders or anything else out of the ordinary. She hadn't smelled so much as a whiff of smoke or the tiniest scent of magic. It was a big forest, and she was only one woman. She was feeling both frustrated and nervous—not just because she would have to report back to the Queen soon empty-handed, but because she had a bad feeling that something was about to break. The moon would be full in another day, and besides, it was *too* quiet.

Bella felt guilty about how much she was enjoying her evenings with Sam and Jazz when she wasn't accomplishing any of the things she was supposed to be doing. She had always thought of herself as the consummate loner, needing only her faithful dragon-cat for company. She knew these pleasant nights were just a temporary aberration and kept reminding herself not to get used to it.

She really should be spending her time doing something more useful. If only she could figure out what that might be. And she'd better come up with some answers fast. The Queen wasn't going to be satisfied with, *No, I haven't found any signs of the Riders, but I'm getting much better at gin rummy. And I think I might be falling for a completely inappropriate guy.* People had been turned into swans for far less. Something bad was coming; she could feel it in her bones. If she didn't find any sign of the Riders soon, she vowed to tear the forest apart with her bare hands.

BRENNA WAS FRUSTRATED and annoyed; rarely a good thing for anyone around her. She was never the most patient witch even at the height of her power and influence, as that idiot child Beka would attest. She'd spent days going over and over the ancient book of instructions (if you could call anything so vague by that name) for creating the immortality potion and doing small experiments to try and figure out where she'd gone wrong.

She had no more answers than when she started, and it was beginning to piss her off. To make things worse, she was almost certain that Bella was doing something to put a stop to what magic she did manage to create, and that stubborn fire watcher *still* hadn't gone away, despite her best efforts to drive him out.

It was time to do something big. The moon was going to be full that night. Time to go all out. Perhaps the smaller fires she'd set simply didn't cause enough anguish to the forest. Today she would bring on the mother of all magical storms and see how it liked that.

Stupid trees and bushes. Stupid wild animals. Stupid young Baba Yagas. She was tired of being thwarted. She could feel her strength and power waning without the boost she used to get from the Water of Life and Death. Every day of her two hundred eighty-nine years of life weighed her down like ice on a glacier. The potion's limited effects were only temporary and wore off faster every time she used it.

To muster the magic required for this kind of storm, even with all her skill and experience, she would drain all three Riders at once, a task she approached with the first hint of joy she'd felt in days. Brenna found the fear in their eyes to be almost addictive, their screams of pain a balm to her troubled soul. Well, she probably didn't have a soul, but still, the screaming made her feel better.

She ran from cage to cage, as gleeful as a child let out of school early, stabbing and kicking and tormenting them as she pulled the blood from their wounds with a combination of magic and twisted science. None of them had the strength to resist, nor dared to do so for fear of what she might do to the others. The first time Alexei had tried to fight back despite his enchanted chains, she'd nearly sawn Mikhail's arm off with her athame. He had healed that time—it was earlier then, before their powers to heal themselves had waned, but none of them had ever tried anything like that again.

As she poured more and more of their blood into the cauldron, even with the muted effects of their strength, it started to make a difference. Brenna could feel her vitality returning as she breathed in the magic, the energy running into her extremities like the pins and needles of returning circulation. It burned like acid, like the sun, like lava from a volcano of never-ending life.

"This," Brenna whispered to the gods. "This is mine. I swear to you, I will never give in to weakness and age. No matter how many trees have to burn. No matter who has to bleed. This is mine. Mine. Mine. Mine." Her laughter leapt to the roof of the cave and swirled down around her like ashes.

$\mathscr{S}$EVENTEEN

THE STORM STARTED normally enough, with light rain and some intermittent rumbles of thunder. But as the day went on, it grew wilder and wilder until the entire fire tower shook with the force of the winds and the constant lightning. Sam could feel the panic building inside, making his stomach muscles quiver and his hands clench.

He tried to focus on doing his job, but the visibility was so bad, he wasn't sure he could see a smoke if there was one. And there was almost certain to be one with all this lightning. There was rain, but not enough to put out a truly fierce fire. There was one coming—he could feel it in his bones—and he was helpless to do anything about it. All he could do was to wait and watch, and hope he caught it early.

Part of Sam wanted to run down to the caravan and warn Bella to be careful. Wanted to keep her safe against the possibility of harm, even though he knew she was smart and alert and didn't need him for that. Of course, he couldn't leave the tower anyway, even if there were some point to it. So he just watched and waited for the worst to happen, getting tenser and more tightly wound by the hour.

* * *

THE RAIN STARTED as a drizzle and kept getting worse, the intermittent thunder and wild winds making it impossible to go outside and search. Instead, Bella set Jazz to working on another magical task—this time moving a shiny copper penny from one side of the dining table to the other. It seemed simple, but in truth it was nearly impossible unless you had the knack for it.

Bella leaned back in a chair across from her and sketched the girl as she sat staring at the coin. It was as good an excuse as any to watch her closely, since the exercise was less about keeping Jazz entertained on a rainy day and more a matter of testing the scope of her natural ability. Not that Bella was going to tell her that.

There were always human beings with some talent for magic, little gifts that eased their lives or changed their luck, or more often than not, got them deeper into trouble. But very few had the aptitude that was required to become a Baba Yaga. Even with the boost in power that came from drinking the Water of Life and Death plus years of training from her mentor Baba, a girl had to be born with a certain potential and into the right (or wrong) set of circumstances.

For the first hour, Bella watched in silence, with only the scratching of her colored pens on paper and the sound of the storm outside as music to draw by. She waited for Jazz to get bored, to get frustrated, to bounce around in her usual fashion and give up. Instead, on Bella's pad a picture grew of a teenage girl sitting in front of a table, her face set and determined, her posture straight but relaxed. The ragged hair and holey jeans seemed a strange contrast to the intensity in the girl's eyes.

As the storm grew louder, Bella found it harder and harder to concentrate. At around noon, she said quietly, "Do you want to take a break for lunch?"

Jazz just replied, "Nope," without taking her eyes off the penny.

At one, Bella asked, "Do you remember the three basics of magical work?"

"Focus, intent, and belief," Jazz said, still not looking up. "Got it."

At two o'clock, Bella said, "If you're tired, you don't have to keep going."

"I'm fine," Jazz said. "Stop bothering me."

"Okay." Bella and Koshka exchanged glances, and Bella pointed at the cupboard where the tuna was. The dragon-cat just shook his shaggy head. Bella went back to sketching, the *skritch, skritch, skritch* of her pencils loud against the quiet of the room.

At around a quarter after three, a particularly violent clap of thunder made them all jump, rattling even the caravan with its magical protections, although Bella probably could have driven it across the floor of the ocean if she was insane enough to want to. Bella was about to say something to Koshka when she heard a whoop from across the table.

"I did it! Come look!" Jazz said, jumping up and down in her seat. "Look, I moved it!"

Bella thought maybe Jazz had simply jarred the table when the thunder had startled her, but when she checked, the girl was still sitting a couple of inches away, and the penny was smack dab in the middle of the circle Bella had drawn in chalk on the woven tablecloth.

"Impressive," Bella said, raising an eyebrow. "Good job."

Jazz grinned from ear to ear and held one hand up in the air. "High five!"

Bella just looked at her. "What?"

The teen snorted. "Man, you really were raised in the woods, weren't you?" She stood up from the table and stretched muscles stiff from hours of sitting in the same position. "Holy crap, I've had to pee for, like, forever. I'll be right back." She headed off toward the tiny bathroom tucked into the back corner by the bed.

Koshka raised himself up on his hind legs and peered at the coin. "I can't believe she did it. It took you two years to master that one."

"Hey," Bella protested. "I was only six."

"True," Koshka said in a thoughtful tone. "It's too bad you didn't find Jazz when she was four or five."

Bella grunted in agreement. It was common practice to start training a new Baba when the girl was very young. It was thought that the mind and spirit were more flexible at an early age, better able to adapt to the concept of magic. Not that Jazz seemed to be having any problems with that.

"Are you going to say anything to her?" Koshka asked.

Bella sighed. "No. There's no point in getting her hopes up. The Queen would never agree to let me train someone as old as Jazz. It's too bad."

The bathroom door slammed and Jazz said, "What's bad?"

Koshka and Bella exchanged looks. "The storm is getting really bad," Bella said. And that wasn't a lie either. She looked in the direction of the fire tower. "I hope Sam's okay."

"I'm sure he'll be down for dinner later," Jazz said.

BUT SEVEN THIRTY rolled around and he didn't come. By eight there was still no sign of him. The rain drummed on the roof of the caravan, and Bella's skin crawled. Cabin fever, probably. She was used to being stuck in the converted hut with Koshka, but having another person there, even one undersized fifteen-year-old, made it seem unbearably small. Or maybe she was just fretting about Sam.

"It's no wonder he didn't come out in this rain," she said, talking to herself out loud. "He's probably still watching for lightning strikes, even though it is getting dark. He told me that lightning starts most of the fires in this part of the country."

"Sam probably hates lightning storms," Jazz said. "I wouldn't blame him."

Bella picked her head up in surprise. "What do you mean?"

"I looked up his name on the Internet," Jazz explained. "The article I found said that they thought the fire that killed the Hotshots crew Sam was on was probably caused by lightning. I wonder if he has a tough time on nights like this, like, thinking about it and everything."

How could he not? Bella thought. "How did you get on the Internet?" she asked.

Jazz stared at her. "I just used my tablet." She pointed at her backpack. "I charged it and hooked up to your Wi-Fi."

Bella blinked. "My caravan has Wi-Fi?" It never had before. Usually if she wanted to check something online, she went in to the nearest town.

"Well, duh," Jazz said, and Koshka gave a snort that was more dragon than cat, causing a faint ribbon of smoke to eddy in the air above his head.

"I think the caravan likes her," he said to Bella meaningfully.

"Apparently it does," Bella agreed, absently rubbing her arms. "Does it seem cold in here to anyone else?" It shouldn't. The caravan had its own magic—and often its own mind—and was always just the right temperature.

Jazz nodded, looking worried. "Can I tell you something and not have you think I'm crazy?"

Bella shrugged. "You're asking the witch with the talking dragon-cat; what do you think?"

"Good point," the girl said. "It's just, well, when I was concentrating on moving the penny, I thought I heard the storm talking."

She paused, obviously waiting for Bella to laugh at her. But Bella didn't feel the least bit inclined to do so. If anything, Jazz had just confirmed something Bella had been feeling for the last couple of hours. So she merely asked, "What was it saying?"

Jazz bit her lip. "Nothing specific, really. I don't know how to explain it, exactly. It was like cursing."

"Cursing?" Bella raised both eyebrows this time. "What do you mean?"

"You know, a bunch of bad words. The kind that someone will threaten to wash your mouth out with soap if you say them? That kind of cursing," Jazz said, the "duh" unsaid this time. "Only it wasn't like I was actually hearing the words themselves, just a kind of feeling."

"Dammit," Bella said. "I was afraid of that." She ran over and shoved open a window, purposely making a hole in the protections that kept the storm away from the inside of the caravan. "Do you smell anything odd, Koshka?"

The dragon-cat bounded up onto the counter underneath the window and stuck his large nose out through the open space. "Pah!" he spat. "Magic. There's magic in the wind. I knew the hair was standing up on the back of my neck for a reason."

"Who could make a storm this strong with magic?" Jazz asked, only the slightest quaver in her voice betraying her fear. "Could you?"

"I could," Bella said. "But not easily. My sister Baba, Barbara, could do it, or Beka, I suppose. In fact, the only ones I can think of who could create this kind of unnatural natural phenomenon are Baba Yagas." She and Koshka looked out the window and then at each other.

"*Brenna*," they said together. "It has to be Brenna."

JAZZ WATCHED WITH a mixture of fascination and trepidation as Bella laid out a few basic magical tools: an athame, a chalice, a rough celestite crystal, and a candle the exact color blue of a cloudless sky.

"What are you going to do?" Jazz asked. "Can I watch, or will I be in the way?"

"You can watch if you like," Bella said. "But there won't be much to see. Sort of like when you moved the penny earlier; most magic happens inside the person doing it. I'm just using a couple of simple items to magnify my focus while I try to stop the storm."

"With magic, you mean?"

Bella nodded. If it was started with magic, in theory it could be stopped with magic. Of course, in theory Brenna shouldn't have had enough power left to cause more than a sprinkle, so there were a lot of things that didn't add up here.

Including the answer to the question of why on earth Brenna would *want* to create a storm of this magnitude. But that was something to deal with later. For right now, Bella just wanted to make it stop before lightning set the entire forest ablaze.

She lifted the chalice, filled with **mead** crafted from the purest spring water, and saluted the **goddess** who watched over witches. Then she dipped the tip of the athame into the mead and sketched a circle onto the table in front of her with the wine. Once that was done, she placed the crystal and the candle into the middle of the circle and easily lit the wick on the candle with a thought and a snap of her fingers.

Closing her eyes, she called on the powers of nature that all Baba Yagas were connected to and commanded them to banish the wind, rain, and lightning.

It didn't work.

Again and again, she threw her energy into the storm, but it just bounced right off. The storm was too powerful. Or the one who sent it was.

"Dammit," Bella said, finally admitting defeat. "I'm not getting anywhere. I need to focus my magic more tightly, aim it right at the source of the storm. But for that I need to know where the storm is coming from, and I can't tell that from here."

"Does that mean you're giving up?" Jazz asked, sounding like a kid who had just seen Superman without his cape.

"Not at all," Bella said. "One of the first things you learn about doing magic is that you have to be flexible. If you try something and it doesn't work, you may need to change your approach, that's all." She tapped her fingers on the table, then snapped them to extinguish the candle. "I need to look at the storm from a different vantage point. Maybe if I can get to higher ground, I'll be able to tell where it is being generated. I'm going to the fire tower."

"Are you sure that's a good idea?" Koshka asked.

"Not at all," Bella said. "Do you have a better one?"

The dragon-cat sighed. "Sadly, no. Go on, then. I'll watch over things here."

Bella gathered a few supplies together and pulled a reasonably waterproof hooded cloak out of the closet (which was, for the moment, miraculously actually a closet). Slinging it over her clothes, she tucked her supplies into the pockets sewn inside and turned to give a quick hug to Jazz. It was a mark of how freaked-out the girl was that she actually tolerated the hug without making a snarky remark.

"You'll be safe here with Koshka," Bella told the girl. "And the caravan won't let anything happen to you either."

"But what about you?" Jazz asked. "You're going out into that storm. What if a lightning bolt hits you?"

"I'm a Baba Yaga," Bella said with a smile. "It wouldn't dare."

BELLA PULLED HER transportation out of its special storage compartment underneath the caravan and hoped that what she'd told Jazz what true. It probably wasn't the smartest thing in the world to be riding her little red Enduro dirt bike into a raging storm, even if it was powered by magic instead of gasoline. But it would take too long to hike to the fire tower on foot, and she needed to save her energy for another try at calming the weather.

Traditionally, Baba Yagas had traveled through the forests of Russia and the surrounding lands in large enchanted mortars that were steered with huge pestles, but these days such a thing would stand out a bit too much. So each of the Babas inherited an updated version from her mentor and persuaded it to transform into a vehicle that suited her own particular needs and tastes. Barbara, for instance, rode around on a glossy royal blue BMW classic motorcycle, while California surfer-girl Beka drove an improbably well-preserved Karmann Ghia with a tie-down for her surfboard.

Bella's choice might have been a little less flashy, but it was much more practical for the forests and badlands in which she tended to spend most of her time. She had a truck (which was essentially a magical extension of the main hut) for pulling the caravan, but for short trips, the zippy little dirt bike couldn't be beat.

Of course, riding it in the rain through intermittent lightning bolts wasn't going to be much fun, but at least it would handle the muddy trails better than virtually anything else, and hopefully its magic would help Bella to stay upright and relatively safe on her trip.

She pulled her cloak around herself as tightly as she could, tucking the ends under the opposite thighs to hold them in place, pulled on her helmet (she was a Baba Yaga, not Superwoman), and started off into the dark and stormy night.

IT TOOK NEARLY twice as long to get to the fire tower as it had the last time she'd gone; the wind and the rain fought her the entire way, the bike swaying and slipping on what had been easy paths. The darkness didn't help either. The full moon was hidden behind sullen clouds, and the dirt bike's headlight barely made a dent in the gloom.

When Bella finally reached the base of the tower and started climbing the stairs, she could have sworn there were suddenly a lot more than the original seventy-five—not that seventy-five hadn't been more than enough to begin with. It felt as though the wind was trying to blow her off on purpose, whipping her cloak around her like the wings of a demented bat and tangling her long hair into knots. The thunder rattled the steps beneath her feet, and she clung to the railing as if it were a lifeline.

Once at the top, she paused for a moment to catch her breath and then banged on the door. She could see Sam inside, sitting at the small kitchen table, his shoulders hunched and his head in his hand. He clearly didn't hear her knocking over the sound of the storm, so finally she simply opened the door and went in, her hand slipping for a moment on the wet metal knob.

"Sam?" she said softly, not wanting to alarm him.

He jolted upright, eyes wide. "Bella! You startled me.

What the hell are you doing out in this? Are you crazy? How did you get here?"

Nice to see you too, she thought. And, *Probably, but that's not the point.*

"Sorry," she said, dripping on his floor. "I did knock. And I have a dirt bike."

Sam shook his head like a man rousing himself from a nightmare and got up from the table to grab a towel. "No, I'm sorry," he said. "I'm not great with thunderstorms, and this one is a doozy."

"You have no idea," she said under her breath, taking the towel gratefully and rubbing it across her hair. He looked like a man who was barely holding himself together, his hands trembling the slightest bit when she handed him back the towel. "Are you okay?"

He shrugged, shoulders tight. "Sure. You want to tell me what the hell you're doing coming out in this mess? Not that I'm not glad to see you." He looked anything but—like a man who was feeling wretched and was uncomfortable being seen with his defenses down. She didn't blame him, and normally she wouldn't intrude, but it couldn't be helped.

Bella tried to think of a good way to tell him that she needed to get a better look at the storm from this vantage point without using the words *witch* or *magic* and failed miserably.

She opened and closed her mouth a couple of times and finally said, "I'll explain later, but you have to believe me when I say it is important. Can you just trust me for now?"

Sam stared at her without speaking, studying her face. Something he saw there must have convinced him. "Okay. What do you need? Can I help?"

She almost sagged with relief. Or maybe that was the weight of the urgency riding on her shoulders. "Did you happen to see where the storm started? The specific area or at least the general direction?"

He pointed out the window. "Toward the east. It came in from there, where you can see the two mountainous areas meet in a kind of notch. But they hadn't predicted bad weather for today, and there was nothing on the radar. Until, suddenly, there was."

The east. It figured. Bella thought that might be a narrow enough area to focus on, especially with the distinctive feature Sam had indicated. Of course now she was going to have to work major magic without it looking like, well, major magic. Although the poor guy looked so wretched, she thought she could probably have ridden a unicycle while singing "The Star-Spangled Banner" and he might not have noticed.

"Do you want me to make you a cup of tea?" she asked. "You look like you could use one."

Sam winced. "That obvious, huh? Sorry. I should have offered you some, since you're the one who just came in from the storm. How about I make the tea and you do whatever it is you need to do." He was clearly curious, but at least she had managed to distract him for the moment, as he moved off to heat up the kettle and pull out a couple of mugs from a cupboard.

While he did that, Bella moved to the window facing east. She pulled her cloak with its magical tools tucked into the pockets close around her, ignoring the drip, drip, drip of water sliding off of it onto the floor. Breathing deeply and evenly, she put both hands against the window, directing her energy through the glass and out into the storm.

Closing her eyes, she visualized an army pushing back the rain, the wind, the lightning; her magical warriors fighting back against those of the witch who sent the storm. Again and again she shoved her will against the might of the tempest. And again and again she failed.

"Dammit!" she said, then jumped when a hand appeared with a steaming cup of tea.

"It's not going well, I take it?" Sam's raspy voice said, bringing her back to reality with a thud. "Whatever *it* is."

Bella wrapped her hands around the mug, grateful for its warmth. The more she fought the storm, the colder and more drained she got. It was as though the elements were absorbing everything she threw at them, using them to feed the storm instead of stop it.

"Crap!" she said. "I'm an idiot!"

Sam blinked at her, diverted for a moment from his own misery. "I doubt it," he said.

"No, really, I am." Bella took a cautious sip from the cup and put it down with a thunk. "I've been trying to use force against a wild animal when what I really need to do is soothe its soul. I can't believe I didn't remember one of the most basic lessons my mentor taught me: in the face of an unbeatable foe, it is better to sneak in under its defenses than to face it head-on. I've been going about this all wrong."

"You know you're not making any sense at all, right?" Sam peered into her eyes as if trying to discern the depths of her madness.

"Not at all unusual," Bella said with a tight laugh. "You'll get used to it." She gave him a quick hug, more for her own benefit than his, and said, "Thank you for the tea. I have to go outside now. Don't worry; I'll be fine."

"Don't worry?" Sam roared. "There are gale-force winds out there and the platform is sixty-nine feet off the ground. You're out of your mind." He reached out a hand to stop her, but she had already stepped out the door and onto the platform outside.

EIGHTEEN

THE WIND WAS even worse on the platform surrounding the tower cabin than it was on the ground below, and the rain misted her vision and made the surface slick underneath her feet. But it didn't matter; she could feel the rightness of her new approach bubbling in her veins like wine.

Fighting the storm had just fueled its fury; it had been born out of hate and anger, and couldn't be combated with the same things that had created it. So instead, Bella started to sing. She sang an old Russian lullaby, one that her own Baba Yaga had sung to her when she was a small child. Its melody was soft and haunting, the words gentle and soothing.

"Baby, baby, rock-a-bye, in our little corner is a green garden with a scarlet flower," she sang, the Russian words translating themselves into English automatically in her head. "The flower is under the sun and little Ilusha is asleep. Please, my children, don't make noise and wake Ilusha up. He is sleeping in the cradle, he's not crying nor is he screaming. He sleeps tight all night long. Please, my children, go and bring us that little flower. That scarlet flower for little Ilusha."

She lowered her voice, singing even more quietly, as the wind began to drop and the lightning stopped flashing. "And when the sun comes up, he will sing and dance, and we will take him into the garden, my little Ilusha." She hummed a bit more, but the lullaby had done its work. The rain grew heavier, hopefully soaking any fires that might have been started by the lightning, but the storm itself had been lulled to sleep. Bella wished that her old mentor could have been there to see it.

Of course, someone else had been, and now there would be no escaping the need to explain.

SAM STOOD BY the door when she went back inside, his eyes wide and a strange expression on his face that she couldn't quite decipher. He took her dripping cloak and hung it on a hook, then handed her a towel and a steaming mug of tea. They both sat down at his small kitchen table. All the while she waited for him to ask her about what she'd done. But when the question finally came, it wasn't the one she'd expected.

"You really are a witch, aren't you?" he said, sounding more impressed than intimidated.

It looked as though she was going to have less explaining to do than she'd thought. Which was good, considering how exhausted she was.

"How did you know?" she asked Sam, breathing in the warm steam gratefully as she held the mug between chilled fingers. She'd dried her hair as well as she could with the towel and patted mostly futilely at her clothing, but she was still soaking wet and chilled to the bone.

Normally she'd just snap her fingers and magic herself dry, but she'd used up too much energy fighting the storm to indulge in such a trick, even if she felt comfortable doing it in front of Sam. "And how long have you known?"

"My neighbor Tiny told me a few days ago," Sam said, eyes on the floor. "I was having an . . . unusual issue . . . and he told me that he was part of the community that called you in to deal with the fires."

"An unusual issue?"

"Is it true?" Sam asked. "Do you really think there is something supernatural behind these fires?" She noticed he'd neatly sidestepped her question.

Bella shrugged, causing a cascade of droplets to hit the floor underneath her. She scrubbed at her hair again, feeling it curling into unruly ringlets because of the moisture. Bah.

"There was certainly something magical behind this storm," she admitted reluctantly. Baba Yagas didn't usually share information with normal Humans. But it had worked for her sister Babas, Barbara and Beka, and besides, Sam was right in the middle of this mess; protocol be damned, as far as she was concerned, he deserved to know. "Does that mean there is something supernatural involved in the fires themselves? Honestly, I don't know yet."

"But you did come here to look into the fires," Sam said. "Just like Tiny said."

"I was *Called* to do that by the locals, yes," Bella said. "Although I didn't know that when I first got here. You don't, always. I'm also looking for my friends the Riders." She sighed, trying not to shiver as the cold and damp worked their way into her marrow. "To be honest, I'm beginning to think that the two problems might be related. Not in a good way."

"You don't think they're setting the fires, do you?" Sam started to rise from his chair.

"No, no. Absolutely not." Bella scowled and gestured at him to sit back down. *As if the Riders would ever do such a thing.* "My concern is that the same person is behind both the fires and the Riders' disappearance. If that's so, it is very bad news. Very, very, very bad news."

Sam's eyes got wide. "Are you talking about terrorists or something?"

"I wish," Bella said. "I could handle terrorists with one hand tied behind my back. On a Tuesday. Before breakfast. No, the person I'm worried might be involved is a lot worse than a terrorist." She hesitated, but if she was going to tell him the truth, there was no point in stopping halfway. "She's a Baba Yaga. A witch, like me. Or at least she was."

"You mean there are good witches and bad witches?" Sam asked. "She's the wicked witch and you're the, uh, not-wicked one?"

Bella laughed. "It's not that simple, Sam. Baba Yagas are neither good nor evil. Most of us are a little bit of both, I suppose, just like Humans. Magic has no moral compass; whether it hurts or harms depends upon who wields it and how."

"Are you saying you're not human?" Sam asked. He reached over and put his hand over hers in a gesture that both soothed and moved her. "You seem pretty human to me."

"I was born as Human as you were," she said, turning her palm upward to hold on to his. She couldn't remember the last time she'd done such a thing with a Human. With anyone, really. "But being a Baba Yaga changes you. I'm not that girl anymore. Not really Human, no matter how I appear." She waited for him to pull his hand away, but he didn't.

"What do you mean?"

More secrets revealed. It occurred to Bella that she must trust this man more than she realized. "Baba Yagas drink an elixir called the Water of Life and Death," she explained. "It heightens our innate abilities and lengthens our lives, but being incredibly powerful takes away as much as it adds. In the end, none of us are truly Human, not as you would understand the term. And the longer a Baba drinks the Water, the more powerful and less Human she becomes."

"Is that what happened to the Baba Yaga you think might be causing the fires?" Sam looked understandably dubious.

"Yes and no," Bella said. "Eventually all Baba Yagas have to retire, and Brenna didn't want to. The Water can cause a kind of mental imbalance, if it is used for too long. So the Queen made her retire and cut off her supply of the Water of Life and Death. Brenna didn't take it well." Remembering the cursing and screaming, Bella thought that was probably the understatement of the century. Unfortunately, they'd all thought Brenna would eventually make her peace with it. Apparently, they'd all been wrong.

"The Queen?" Sam said. "The Queen of England is in charge of the Baba Yagas?"

Bella practically spit out her tea. Coughing, she said, "No, Sam, not the Queen of England. The Queen of the Other-world."

"What other world?" he asked, getting up to pour them both some more tea. Bella's hand felt strangely empty, so she put it in her lap.

"Um, you know all those fairy tales you read as a kid?" she said. "Where you could step through a magical doorway and be in another world? The Otherworld is where you would end up if you did that."

"Faerie land?" he said, his face brightening. "It really exists?"

"Not faerie, not exactly," Bella said. "It's complicated. But something like that. Anyway, if Brenna is behind the fires, that's a very bad thing. Without the Water, she isn't as powerful as she was, but she's still capable of causing a great deal of trouble." She shook her head. "Speaking of trouble, what was that unusual issue you had that your friend Tiny thought a witch could help you with?"

Sam rubbed one hand tiredly over his face, wincing visibly when it hit the scarred side. "I'm being haunted," he said. "I think. Or possibly not. I really don't know."

BELLA BLINKED AT Sam. "Well, that's . . . definitive." She looked confused, for which he didn't blame her.

"I'm sorry," he said. "I shouldn't have mentioned it." He noticed she was shivering, so he went over and grabbed the blanket off the bed and draped it over her shoulders. She pulled it around herself, nodding her thanks, and scooted her chair a little closer to his.

"Don't be ridiculous. I'm happy to help if I can. So what makes you think you might be haunted?" Bella asked. "Are you hearing strange noises? Things being moved around?"

Sam shook his head. "Nothing that random," he said. He pointed to the floor about three feet in front of them. "She stands right there and talks to me; I can see her as clearly as I can see you."

Bella sat up straighter. "Do you mind if I ask who *she* is?"

He had to swallow around the lump in his throat before he could answer. "Heather. She is—was—my fiancée. That's who I see."

"Ah," Bella said, her posture softening. "She died in the fire with the other Hotshots, right? The same fire you got burned in?"

"Word gets around, huh?" Sam tried not to sound bitter. "I guess I should have figured that someone would tell you."

"I asked one of the firefighters the other day," Bella confessed. "I wondered what your story was. I'm sorry if I invaded your privacy."

Sam sighed. "It's okay. After all, it was all over the national news when it happened. Half of America knows. I'm well aware that my illusion of privacy up in this tower is just that, an illusion." Like a lot of other illusions, maybe he just wanted to believe it was true.

Bella took one of his hands and held it between both of hers. They were cold, but her gaze was warm enough to make up for it.

"So, she's been haunting you since the fire?" Bella asked. "That was, what, two and a half years ago?"

"Almost three," Sam said. Sometimes it seemed like an eternity ago, sometimes like it just happened yesterday. "But no, I didn't start seeing her until recently."

"Huh, that's odd. Has anything happened that might have triggered the visitations?" Bella asked.

Sam tried not to stare at her, at the red hair and glorious, wild beauty of her. "No," he lied. "Not really. Maybe I'm dreaming it, although it sure doesn't seem like a dream while it's happening."

Bella looked intrigued. "You said she talks to you? What does she say?"

"She tells me to leave," he admitted, shoulders drooping.

"Tells me that I should leave the tower, give up the job. That I shouldn't be here."

Bella raised one eyebrow. "Really? I thought you liked doing this job."

"I do," Sam said. "It's important to me. I don't know why Heather would tell me to quit, but that's what she says, every time. Leave." He wasn't about to mention the ghost's anger over him spending time with Bella. This whole conversation was bad enough already.

"Could she be trying to protect you?" Bella asked. "Because of all the fires this year?"

Sam looked at the worn wooden floorboards. "It's more likely that she's trying to protect everyone else. She says I'm not competent to do the job. That people are going to get hurt because of me."

"That's ridiculous!" Bella said, and steam began to rise gently from the blanket around her shoulders for a minute until she took a couple of deep breaths and calmed down with a visible effort. "You're doing your job just fine, as far as I can tell. You saw Jazz when she was in trouble the other day and called in the cavalry. You've spotted every fire early on."

She shook her head, damp curls flopping. "No, I understand about doubting yourself, really I do. But the ghost, if it is a ghost, is dead wrong about you not being up to the job. Sorry about the pun."

Sam gave a small laugh, inexplicably cheered by her forceful defense of him, even if he didn't think he deserved it. But then reality settled back in again.

"If it is a ghost," he repeated. "That's the problem, isn't it? Because if there isn't a ghost, if it is just my own self-doubt, then I'm seeing things, and that's not good."

Bella gave his hand a squeeze. "PTSD?"

"You know about PTSD?" Sam asked, pulling his hand free and trying not to show how uncomfortable the conversation was making him.

She rolled her eyes. "I spend most of my time in the woods and the deserts, not on the moon. Besides, because of my particular *talents*," she gave the word air quotes, "I end up on the front lines of forest fires fairly often. I just spent three miserable weeks in Montana trying to keep an entire mountain from burning down, some days fighting side by side with firefighters from all over the country. It's an occupational hazard for anyone who lives that kind of life; for someone who has been through what you've been through, it's practically a given."

This information distracted Sam from his own misery for a moment. "Wait—you're a firefighter?"

"Not the way you were, no," Bella said. "I fight fire with magic, the way I put out the fire that had Jazz trapped up in that tree. But sometimes to get at the blaze, I have to blend in with the people who are already there. If necessary, I can act out the role. But believe me, I'm a lot more effective wielding my power than I am an ax."

Sam felt a spark of hope. "Hey, if you can put out fires—"

Bella held up one slim hand. "Some fires," she said. "If I catch them early enough and small enough, like the couple I've put out since I've been here. Once they get to a certain size and magnitude, the best I can do is encourage the wind to die down or the rain to fall, or smother key sections to help out the folks who are fighting it with conventional methods. I'm a Baba Yaga, not a miracle worker."

"Being able to put out a fire with magic seems pretty miraculous to me," he said, but he couldn't help feeling disappointed. For a minute there, it had looked like all their problems were over. The fire problems, anyway. He would still have had to deal with this other one.

"If you know about PTSD, then you know why I'm almost hoping I *am* being haunted," Sam said. "The alternative, that my mind is playing tricks on me, is worse than a ghost."

Bella nodded. "Did they give you anything to take for it?"

Sam glanced at the kitchen drawer and away again. "The doctor prescribed a tranquilizer, but I don't dare take it. Those things can make you drowsy or foggy, and I just can't risk not being alert when I need to be. I'm managing okay without it. At least I thought I was."

"I can make you up something herbal that will help you

relax without making you dopey," she said. "I'm not as good at it as my sister Barbara is, but all Baba Yagas know herbs. And tomorrow, when I'm not so wiped out, I'll be happy to come back and see if I can sense your ghost. Baba Yagas are pretty good at talking to the dead." She tried to cover a yawn, but Sam could see that she was exhausted.

"I'm fine," he said. "Don't worry about me."

"Uh-huh." Bella stood up and put the blanket over the back of her chair. "I'll worry about anyone I feel like. But tonight I'm too tired to do anything useful about it, so I'm just going to head home. We'll deal with your ghost tomorrow."

Sam stood too, looking out the window so he wouldn't focus on how close she was standing to him.

"You should stay," he said, without realizing he was going to.

"What?" Bella looked as startled as he felt.

"You should stay," he repeated. "The worst of the storm may be over, but it is still raining. It's pitch-black out there, and you're already tired and soaked to the bone. Not exactly great conditions for riding a dirt bike. I wouldn't want you to get hurt."

Bella took another small step toward him, tilting her head up so she could look into his eyes.

"And that's the only reason you want me to stay? To keep me safe?"

Sam shook his head. "No. Not the only reason." And he leaned down to kiss her, suddenly realizing he'd been wanting to do it since the day he met her.

NINETEEN

AS SOON AS his lips touched hers, Sam felt passion flare between them like a wildfire that had been smoldering for days and finally been given air and fuel and the space to ignite. All the longing he'd been suppressing flooded to the surface, and judging from the way she kissed him back, he had to think she'd been feeling the same way.

Bella's arms went around him as she went up on her toes, her soft mouth pressed against his, her body stretched against the length of his body. For a moment, the entire world shrank down to the two of them, and then Bella pulled back long enough to murmur something that sounded like, "It took you long enough," before stripping off her damp tee shirt and tossing it onto the floor.

Sam fumbled with the buttons of his own shirt as he gazed hungrily at the vibrant woman standing in front of him. In the end he just yanked it over his head, still half buttoned, and scooped Bella up in his arms. She laughed, burying her head in his chest until they lay together on his bed and took turns removing the remains of each other's clothes.

In the dim light of the fire tower, Sam finally found the freckles he'd been looking for; a few scattered across her shoulder as he nibbled and licked his way down, a couple on the inside of a knee as he kissed his way back up. Then he lost himself in the mysterious new terrain of her luscious curves and soft, sweet valleys until his blood began to burn and all he could feel was her moving beneath him, calling his name as she rose and fell with the rhythm of their dance.

As they climaxed, the full moon broke through the rain clouds briefly, illuminating her face, eyes closed in ecstasy, head thrown back in joyous abandon, and he buried himself deep inside her one more time, feeling the flames of their shared passion burning his soul clean, if only for a moment.

Afterward, they lay curled around each other's damp bodies on the narrow bed, Bella's red curls spilling over his chest, one arm draped across him. Her eyes fluttered with satiated exhaustion, a small smile still playing around the corners of her full lips.

Sam started to move away, and she pulled him closer.

"Where are you going?" she asked.

"Shhh," he said. "I'm just going to grab the blanket and turn out the light. I'll be right back."

Bella chuckled sleepily and waved her right hand. The blanket lifted off the back of the chair where she'd left it and came slowly sailing across the room to drape itself over their entwined bodies. A snap of her fingers and the single lamp in the kitchen went out.

Sam blinked in the sudden darkness. "You're a very handy woman to have around," he said.

"You have no idea," she replied, and proceeded to demonstrate that she wasn't quite as tired as he'd thought.

THE EARLY MORNING sun streaming in the windows woke Sam up at his usual time. For a moment, he thought he'd dreamed the entire thing, but the languid contentment in his body convinced him otherwise. A glance around the tiny space showed that he was alone, and he tried to shrug away the disappointment that briefly lashed sharp claws into his otherwise good mood. It was a night of mutual comfort, nothing more. No point in reading something into it that wasn't there. Couldn't be there.

Then he looked out the window and saw Bella standing on the catwalk, looking out at the mountains, the mug between her hands steaming peacefully into the morning mistiness. She'd clearly made use of his solar shower; she was dressed in yesterday's clothes, but her red hair gleamed like wet rubies in the brightening sun. An echoing brightness seemed to settle into his chest, somewhere around the place where his heart used to reside, before it cracked into shards of broken glass and debris.

Bella turned around when he came outside, shrugging a shirt into place as he walked, and she gave him a smile of such vivid cheerfulness, it put the sun to shame.

"Morning," she said, tilting her head up to receive his kiss. "Sleep well?"

"Like a rock," he said. "A very happy rock." He bent down to sniff at the steam rising off of her cup. "What is that, mint?"

"Um-hmm," she said, eyes twinkling.

"But I don't have any mint tea," Sam said, baffled. "At least, I was pretty sure I didn't."

"No, you didn't," Bella said. "I kind of grabbed it from the caravan. You didn't have any bacon either. Shame on you." She grinned at him, as if daring him to balk at her magical sleight of hand.

Sam just shook his head. "Wait until I tell my grandmother she was right about me meeting a witch. The woman is going to be unbearably smug."

Bella rolled her eyes. "I can't believe that I ended up with the one guy and the one teenager who still believe in witches. What the heck are the odds?"

"Teenager? You mean Jazz?" He clearly needed to make some coffee, because he wasn't tracking well. "Of course she believes you're a witch. She's your niece."

Bella gazed out at the sky, her face studiously blank. "The

view from here is really amazing. I'll bet you never get tired of looking at it."

"She is your niece, right?" Sam refused to get sidetracked by a discussion of the scenery.

"Well, not technically," Bella said, taking a sip of tea. "In fact, not at all. We met for the first time the day she got trapped up in that tree."

"What?" Sam leaned his back against the railing and stared at her. "If she's not your niece, who the hell is she and where is she from?"

"She's Jazz," Bella said, putting her tea mug on the ground by her feet. "And she's from a series of lousy foster homes where she was systematically ignored and abused. She's been living in the forest since spring, apparently. Now she's staying with me for a while."

"Are you serious?" He couldn't believe what he was hearing. "You're harboring a runaway? Do you have any idea what kind of trouble you could get in for that? What kind of trouble she could be running away from? Just because she says she came from a foster home doesn't mean she did. Teenagers run away all the time. She might have parents looking for her. Hell, she might have the police looking for her, for all you know."

It wasn't that he didn't like Jazz—he did, a lot. But that didn't mean Bella could just take her in like a stray dog that showed up on her doorstep.

"How do you know that she doesn't have anything to do with these fires?" he asked, fists clenching at his sides. "Teenagers are often at the root of suspicious fires, you know. For all you know she could be a pyromaniac. It wouldn't be the first time that a fire setter got caught in his or her own fire."

Bella glared at him, crossing her arms over her chest. "Now you're just being ridiculous. Yes, she's a runaway, but she had good reasons. No kid lives in the woods for months if they have something better to go home to. She's not on the run from the law and she's not setting the fires, I promise."

"How can you be sure?" he said, fighting the impulse to step back from the glare of her green eyes. He wished they could turn the clock back to five minutes ago, when everything was so mellow. But he was right about this, and she knew it. "You can't just take her word for it. She could be lying to you."

"She's not," Bella said. "And if you don't believe me, you can ask Koshka. He's as good as a lie detector."

Sam rubbed his face, feeling the stubble scratchy under his palm. "Koshka. You want me to ask the cat if your teenage runaway is telling the truth?"

"I told you, no one can lie to Koshka; it's one of his gifts. And he's not a cat. He's a dragon disguised as a cat. Big, scaly beasts kind of stick out in this day and age, you know."

"Right," Sam said slowly. "Your cat is a dragon."

"What? You can believe in witches and ghosts, but you draw the line at dragons?" Bella scowled at him.

"I draw the line at letting you shelter an underage runaway, no matter how good your intentions are. She's still a child. The system is there for a reason."

Bella gritted her teeth. "In Jazz's case, the system didn't work. It didn't work for me when I was a kid either, which is how I ended up being taken in by the Baba Yaga who trained me. I'm not going to just throw her to the wolves because you think she might be lying. Not when I know she isn't."

Sam drew in a deep breath, feeling it stutter inside his smoke-damaged lungs. "I'm sorry about your past, Bella, but you can't just make up the rules to suit yourself."

She narrowed her eyes at him. "Oh no?" she said in a soft, dangerous voice. "Which part of *powerful witch* did you not understand?" She snapped her fingers, and a flame danced between them, no more than six inches away from his nose.

"Shit!" he said, taking an involuntary step backward, the railing the only thing stopping him from plummeting into the air. "Are you crazy?" He gripped the metal bars behind him with both hands. "You know how the chief said you should leave the area because it wasn't safe? I'm starting to think maybe he was right. Only maybe it isn't safe for the rest of us to have you here."

Bella gazed at him for a minute with suspiciously bright

eyes, then blinked a couple of times rapidly, the fire in her hand winking out of existence. "Maybe he was right," she said in a rough voice. "But I'll leave when I'm damned good and ready to and not before. And if I see one sign of either a cop or a social worker, *someone* is going to get turned into a toad."

Then she turned on her heel and stomped down the stairs to the ground. After a minute, he heard the roar of the dirt bike's engine, racing down the road in the direction of the caravan. Away from him.

Sam sank down onto the hard surface of the catwalk and put his head in his hands. He didn't know why he felt so stunned and bereft. It wasn't as though he thought one night of comfort and passion meant they were starting a relationship. He didn't do relationships anymore; he couldn't bear to lose one more person, and relationships just made you vulnerable.

But he thought they might at least be becoming friends, of a sort, and now it turned out that he didn't know Bella at all. At least not in the ways that counted. And that last thing she did with the flames made him wonder all over again if she could have been involved with the two fires she was found near. He didn't know which he hated more—thinking she might be a fire starter or thinking Jazz might be.

But most of all, he hated the glitter of tears he was sure he'd seen in Bella's eyes right before she left.

BELLA FELT EVERY rock and every bump as the dirt bike bounced too fast down the trail in the direction of home, each shock echoing in her bones and in her heart.

Idiot! She scolded herself as she rounded a curve and almost skidded on the still-wet ground. But she wasn't talking about her driving ability. More like her common sense, or lack of it.

It wasn't as though she didn't know better than to get involved with Humans. Hadn't she learned anything from the past? Not only was Sam frustrating and pigheaded (and just plain *wrong*, dammit, at least when it came to Jazz), but she'd almost lost her temper over it, and that could have been disastrous. The look on his face when she'd created a flame out of thin air right in front of him, that particular mix of fear and horror and disbelief—she'd seen that before. She'd hated it then and she hated it now. And the fact that she'd done it to Sam, knowing what he'd been through . . . It was going to be a long time before she could forgive herself for that.

A lot longer before Sam would forgive her, of that she was sure.

Then there was the little matter of the picture she'd seen on the windowsill when she'd gone to make tea earlier. A large group of firefighters, all in full gear with their helmets tucked under their arms and big grins on their faces as they looked toward the camera. Bella had gotten a jolt when she'd recognized a pre-fire Sam without his scars or the haunted look in his eyes. But that had been nothing compared to the shock of seeing the woman standing next to him, one arm linked through his. The lone female in a sea of men, the woman had a round, cheerful face, a slightly stocky but strong-looking physique . . . and red hair.

For a second, gazing at the picture, Bella had a moment of doubt; was Sam only attracted to her because her hair color reminded him of his lost fiancée? Then she'd told herself she was being ridiculous, and that their intense and inexplicable chemistry was clearly mutual. She'd dismissed the thought as foolish until things had blown up in her face. Now she was back to wondering who he actually saw when he looked at her.

She took one hand off the handlebar and swiped at her eyes, trying to blame the wind and the speed of the bike, but not really believing it. Her chest felt tight and crackly, like the air right before a lightning strike. Maybe she could say her tears were rain, although the sky seen through the tall trees was a determined crystalline blue. The only clouds in sight were the ones that she'd created herself, and she needed to waft them away so she could see where she was going.

In short, she needed to stay away from Sam and get her head

back in the game; focus on finding the Riders and tracking down Brenna, if that's who was behind last night's storm. Sam could take care of himself, and he'd made it brutally, painfully clear that he didn't want her around. Fine. Let the man deal with his tiny owl and his panic attacks and his completely misguided ideas by himself. It was none of her business anymore, and that was the way it should be.

She just hoped that he would keep her secret, and Jazz's.

She wasn't going to miss him at all.

TWENTY

JAZZ WAS SO happy to see Bella return safe and sound, she almost forgot to act cool, and barely stopped her bare feet from rushing down the steps and across the clearing and her arms from forming some kind of crazy hug. Instead, she strolled toward Bella and turned the motion into a victory air punch.

"Excellent job stopping the storm last night," Jazz said. Then took a second look as Bella removed her helmet and swung her leg over the little red dirt bike. For a woman who'd saved the day, she didn't seem very happy. There was a smudge of dirt over one cheekbone and a distinct reddish tinge to her eyes, which were shadowed and tired-looking. Witches didn't *cry*, did they? Maybe using all that magic just wiped her out. That would explain why she'd had to stay at the tower.

Of course, there was another possible explanation, and Jazz was neither too young nor too naïve to figure out what it was. But if Sam and Bella had finally acted on all that simmering attraction that was so obvious to anyone other than the two of them, Jazz had to guess it hadn't gone all that well. *Leave it to grown-ups to mess up something simple.*

"Um, is something wrong?" she asked Bella. Their relationship was still in the shaky and weird stage where neither one of them really knew the boundaries. It wasn't as though they were really aunt and niece, after all. But Jazz kind of felt like that anyway. "I mean, was there a problem with the magic, or, you know, like, Sam, or something?"

Bella shook her head. "The magic went okay. It just took me a few tries to figure out what I was doing wrong. I'll explain it later. I need to get back to the search soon. I'll just make us some breakfast before I go."

Uh-huh. Jazz noticed she didn't answer the Sam part of the question at all. Which sort of was an answer, all by itself, she figured. She hadn't had a lot of experience with boys, what with moving from foster home to foster home and from school to school. But from what she'd observed from the popular girls, if things went well with a guy, you told *everybody* about it. It was only when it wasn't working out the way you wanted that suddenly every other subject on the planet was more interesting, even algebra.

A large gray and brown head appeared in the caravan's doorway. "Nice of you to finally check in," he said in a growly tone. "Some of us worry, you know. Also, didn't we have bacon?"

"You knew perfectly well I was okay," Bella responded, ruffling the fur on his head as she walked by. "And we're going to have to live without bacon today. I sort of misplaced it. Have some cheese instead. You like cheese."

"How do you misplace bacon?" Jazz asked, mostly not caring. She was just glad to eat something other than tuna. She liked it okay, but seriously, not for breakfast. Well, at least not now that she wasn't so hungry all the time.

She followed Bella back into the caravan and slid into a seat at the table. Normally she would have offered to help, but Jazz had a feeling it wasn't a good idea to get in the woman's way right now.

"Never mind," Bella said. "It happens. I'll try and find some time to run into town for supplies today. In the meanwhile, we can all eat what's in the refrigerator already. Just be glad that my fridge doesn't have a mind of its own, like Barbara's does. She once had to eat nothing but cherry pies for days." A few minutes later she slapped a plate of melted cheese and toast down in front of Jazz, who wasn't completely sure it hadn't melted from the heat of Bella's bad mood.

Koshka snagged a piece of cheese almost as big as his paw and made it disappear effortlessly. "Aren't you eating?" he asked Bella pointedly. "All that magical work last night must have used up a lot of energy. You need to eat."

"You're my dragon, not my mother," Bella said. "And I'm not hungry." But Jazz noticed that she made herself some cheese and toast anyway, and sat down at the table opposite Jazz to nibble at it halfheartedly.

After a few moments of charged silence that seemed to send sparks out into the air within the caravan, Jazz and Bella spoke at the same time.

"Is Sam okay?" Jazz asked, as Bella said, "I'm not sure you're safe here anymore. You might want to consider finding someplace else to hide out."

"What?" Jazz lowered her toast slowly back down to her plate as if it had suddenly turned into a poisonous snake. "You want me to leave?"

She could feel the walls closing in around her as history repeated itself. *Of course* Bella didn't want her to stay. No one ever did. Not for long. But Bella had been the one demanding she stick around. It wasn't like Jazz had begged her or anything. Hell, she'd even tried to leave, and Bella said no. So what changed? Was it because Jazz asked about Sam when Bella obviously didn't want to talk about whatever had happened between them?

Bella shook her head, long red curls framing a face that looked more sad than mad. "No, that's not it at all, Jazz. I swear, it isn't that I want you to go. I'm just not feeling good about the situation, that's all. I mean, there's all these fires, and now it turns out there may be a crazy former Baba Yaga lurking somewhere in the forest who might have something to do with them . . ."

Jazz narrowed her eyes. She knew a partial truth when she heard one; she'd told enough of them in her time. "What aren't you telling me?" she demanded. "I'm not a kid. If I've done something wrong, tell me what it was. Maybe I can fix it. Or, like, say I'm sorry, or something."

Bella let out a sigh that sounded like the last balloon at the end of a party giving up the ghost. "You didn't do anything wrong, Jazz. I did. I told Sam the truth, about my magic, and that you aren't my niece, that you're a runaway from the foster care system. He didn't take it well."

"What? Why would you do that?" Jazz could feel unwanted tears welling up in her eyes, and she brushed them away angrily. "I mean, I like Sam, and I guess I trust him, kind of, but he's clearly a do-gooder. You can't tell people like that that someone is breaking the rules; they freak out. Now Sam isn't going to want to hang out with me anymore. What's he going to do?"

"I'm sorry, Jazz," Bella said, looking at the table. "I wasn't thinking. It just kind of came out. I do that, sometimes. Speak without thinking. It's that whole raised in the woods thing." She picked her head up and met Jazz's gaze with obvious reluctance. "He told me I should turn you over to the system, and of course I explained why that was a lousy idea. But I'm not sure he believed me. Hopefully he took me seriously when I told him I'd turn him into a toad if he called the cops on you, but I can't be sure. That's why I wanted to warn you that you might not be safe. I'm sorry. I screwed up."

Jazz blinked. This might well have been the only time in her entire life an adult actually apologized to her for messing up her life. It didn't make things better, exactly, but at least it meant that Bella hadn't changed her mind about liking her. Probably.

"Huh." Jazz played with the tag end of her toast. "Well, I screw up a lot, so I guess I can't hold that against you." She shrugged. "And let's face it, I don't really have any other place to go. Except back into the forest, and you didn't want me to do that."

"I still don't," Bella said. "It's even more dangerous out there than it is here."

"Maybe I'd better just take my chances and stay here with you," Jazz said, trying not to obviously hold her breath. "I mean, if that's still okay."

Bella stared at her for a minute, as if considering factors that Jazz couldn't see. "I've been told I'm not safe to be around," she said finally. "You might want to keep that in mind. I can't promise to keep you safe. Not even from me."

She got up from the table, grabbed her helmet, and stomped out the door, leaving Jazz sitting there with her mouth open and a crumbled mess of cheese and bread on her plate. She pushed it away; she'd lost her appetite anyway.

"Um, was that a yes?" she asked Koshka, only a little plaintively. "I really couldn't tell."

"It was a yes," the giant cat said. He reached out a claw to snag Bella's uneaten breakfast. "Just not a very enthusiastic one. Do me a favor, kid. Don't grow up to be a redhead. Some of them are very moody."

"Did I do something wrong?" Jazz said in a quiet voice. "I've been trying not to be any trouble."

Koshka put his huge paws up on the tabletop and leaned in to lick her face gently. It felt like someone was rubbing sandpaper over her skin, but she liked it anyway.

"You've been just fine," the dragon-cat said. "It's not you. It's her. She's afraid of hurting you."

TWENTY-ONE

"I'VE BEEN AROUND plenty of people who hurt me," Jazz said in a quiet voice. "Most of them tried a lot harder than Bella to pretend they were nice on the surface, when there was a lot of ugly crap lurking underneath. I've gotten pretty good at figuring out who's a threat and who isn't. I know I haven't known you guys for very long, but somehow I don't see Bella as the type. Yeah, she might say something that hurts my feelings, but even that she wouldn't do on purpose."

Koshka nodded. "You are right about that, although it is the 'not on purpose' part she's worried about." He patted the floor next to him. "Come down here and sit next to me. I want to tell you a story, and looking up at you is giving me a crick in my neck."

"I don't think cats get cricks in their necks," Jazz said, but she slid out of her seat and onto the floor anyway. The wood was smooth and cool, and a light breeze crept through the open window over her head, smelling like forest and last night's rain. Some of the tension eased out of her shoulders. "What do you mean you want to tell me a story? We're in the middle of, like, a serious talk."

"It's a serious story," the dragon-cat said. "It's about something that happened to Bella when she wasn't much older than you are now. It isn't really my story to tell, but I think it might help you understand why she is reacting the way she is." He shook himself, so bits of gray and brown fur floated up into the sunbeams, then stretched his long legs out in front of him as he settled into a comfortable position.

"I don't know what happened between Bella and Sam," he started to say.

Jazz stared at her toes. They were pretty dirty. "I have a pretty good idea," she said, and wrinkled her nose.

Koshka smacked her more or less gently with one over-sized paw. "Don't interrupt me, youngling. I'm telling you a story here."

"Sorry, Koshka."

"Hrmph," the dragon-cat said, then waited a minute to make sure she was paying attention.

"As I was saying," he said, giving her a mock glare, "I don't know what happened between Sam and Bella, but whatever it was, it seems to have ripped the scab off a scar that has never really healed."

"On Sam, you mean?" Jazz asked, confused.

"On Bella," Koshka corrected. "It isn't the kind of scar you can see on the surface. Now are you going to let me tell you the story or not?"

Jazz mimed zipping her lips shut and throwing away the key. "As if," the cat muttered. "We should be so lucky.

"Once upon a time, about thirty years ago, there was a Baba Yaga in training named Bella," Koshka said.

"Thirty years ago! But Bella can't be older than her late twenties," Jazz said.

"Most Baba Yagas are older than they look. It has to do with drinking the Water of Life and Death," he said. "Now, about that shutting up?"

Jazz subsided, digesting the fact that Bella was truly magical. It wasn't as though she hadn't known that, but most of the time when Bella wasn't doing some kind of spell, she seemed so normal, Jazz kind of forgot.

"She was still learning under the guidance of her mentor," Koshka went on. "But like most teenagers, she thought she knew more than she did."

Jazz opened her mouth to protest, thought about it, then closed her mouth again. The cat gave a small, satisfied nod.

"Bella's mentor, Berta, had told her many times that it was risky for witches to mix too much with Humans, especially witches who hadn't finished all their training yet. Bella was, in fact, quite advanced in the practice of magic, but she still had problems sometimes controlling her temper. Magic is best practiced with a cool head, or not at all."

Jazz nodded. She'd figured that out already after only a few days.

"Of course, sixteen-year-olds are generally not known for their good sense, or for listening to their elders, and Bella managed to make friends with a Human girl of her own age who lived near where she and Berta had been staying for the bulk of her teen years. Bella and the Human girl spent every spare minute together, although for a Baba Yaga in training, that wasn't much time, and talked about everything."

"They were BFFs," Jazz said, understanding. "It's kind of hard to imagine a young Bella with a BFF."

"A beefy-what?" Koshka twitched his whiskers forward and looked irritated.

"A BFF. Best friends forever."

"Oh. Yes. I suppose they thought they were," Koshka said. "For a time."

"So what happened?" Jazz asked.

"There was a boy," Koshka said.

"Ah. It figures."

"Indeed. Bella and her friend both took a liking to a local boy, who flirted equally with both of them. I suppose you could say he led them on, but they were all young, and I don't suppose he knew any better."

Koshka yawned, showing sharp teeth and clearly expressing his low opinion of Humans in their youth. Jazz supposed that teenage dragons didn't have the same issues. She made a mental note to ask, later. Maybe.

"And then he picked Bella," Jazz said with certainty. After all, she was *Bella*. Even as a teen she must have been seriously freaking cool.

"No," Koshka said. "He picked her friend, Lily. Lily was pretty and blond and cheerful. Bella was, well, Bella. Complicated. And, of course, she lived in the woods and had many secrets, and a mysterious guardian who didn't approve of visitors. Teenage boy visitors especially. But mostly Lily was normal, and of course, Bella wasn't. How could she have been? She was a Baba Yaga in training."

"Oh," Jazz said, disappointed on the younger Bella's behalf. "That must have made her really sad."

Koshka cocked one furry eyebrow. "Sad would have been okay. But Bella came across the boy and her friend kissing one day in a meadow, and she lost her temper. All Baba Yagas have an affinity to a particular element, and Bella's is fire. Then, as now, she occasionally had problems controlling that affinity when she was nervous or upset. And that day, she was very, very upset."

Jazz got a sick feeling in the pit of her stomach, like the time she ate bad clams as a kid. "What did she do?" she whispered, pretty sure she didn't want to know. Koshka's story was clearly a fairy tale, and they rarely ended well for everyone. Not the old traditional ones.

"The boy was mostly just frightened out of his wits," Koshka said. "But Lily was burned very badly. Badly enough to scar her for life, maybe even to have killed her."

"Oh no," Jazz said, tears welling up in her eyes. *Poor Lily. Poor Bella.* "But she didn't mean to harm Lily, did she?"

"No, of course she didn't. Bella was just surprised and hurt and upset, and she lost control for a moment. But a moment was all it took, and the damage was done. Bella was completely distraught at what she'd done, and the boy ran away, maybe to get help, maybe just to get as far away from her as possible, she didn't know.

"So she did the only thing she could do, and went to her mentor for help. Luckily, the meadow where it happened wasn't far from where they lived in their caravan—"

"This caravan?" Jazz gazed around at the small space in wonder.

"Yes, this caravan. It was bigger then." Koshka shrugged, used to enchanted huts that became caravans of whatever size was needed at the time. "Anyway, Berta was able to heal the girl, using her magic and a tiny bit of the Water of Life and Death."

He stared at her intently. "Which she wasn't supposed to do, by the way, and for which she was later punished by the Queen of the Otherworld, so don't expect Bella to use it on you if you do something stupid and break a leg."

Jazz swallowed hard at the thought of the powerful Queen. Bella had told her a few stories about the Otherworld. Now *those* were real fairy tales. "I'll try not to break a leg," she said. "So everything worked out okay. I mean, Lily was healed, and Bella learned her lesson, so it was, like, a happy ending after all."

"Far from happy," Koshka said with a sigh that rattled the windows. "Far, far from it. Lily might have been healed, but she remembered what it felt like to nearly burn to death, and she was completely traumatized. She never spoke to Bella again, wouldn't even see her when she came to try and apologize. Not that it mattered, because once Bella put on such a spectacular display of magic, she and her mentor had to move away."

"Oh."

"As for Bella learning her lesson, well, she learned one, all right, but I'm not sure it was the right one. Berta reminded her—repeatedly and forcefully, since she was still stinging from the Queen's ire—that it wasn't safe for Baba Yagas and Humans to mix. At least, not for any longer than it took to get the job done, if there was one, and never as anything closer than passing acquaintances. And especially not in Bella's case, because she couldn't be trusted not to lose control."

"Oh," Jazz said again, feeling like she should come up with something more profound but failing. She knew all too well what it felt like to be alone, too different to really fit in, or too temporary to make friends. She'd had some, over the years, but sooner or later she'd get shuffled off to some new family and have to leave them behind. "At least she had her mentor. And you."

"She did," Koshka agreed quietly. "And she would tell you she has a very satisfactory life, and indeed she does."

"But now she has Sam," Jazz said. "Isn't that going to get complicated?"

"I suspect it already has," the dragon-cat said. "Plus, of course, there is you."

"Me?" Jazz was confused for a minute, then remembered the reason Koshka had decided to tell her this story in the first place. "You mean, that's what she was talking about when she said it might not be safe to be around her? She thinks she might lose control and set me on fire like she did her friend?" She could hear her voice go up in indignation, but she didn't care. "She would *never* do that to me. I know she wouldn't. I mean, yes, every once in a while she gets kind of twitchy, usually when Sam's around, and maybe lets loose with a couple of sparks or something, but I can't imagine her actually hurting someone on purpose."

"Of course she wouldn't," Koshka said sadly. "But try convincing her of that."

ALEXEI COULD HEAR the witch muttering to herself as she walked in circles around the interior of the cave, occasionally stopping to glare at him or the other Riders, but not actually bothering to interact with them. He should have been relieved by that, but instead, it made him even more worried. Alexei wasn't used to worrying; he was a man of action, and liked to leave the worrying to Gregori, the deep thinker. But this morning, it seemed like there was enough worry to go around.

"Pah," Brenna said as she passed by him on her current circuit. "Interfering brat."

Brat? What brat? Was she talking about him? Alexei had been called a lot of things in his long life, but that was a new one.

Brenna had been out of sorts—even for her—ever since last night. She'd been riding high initially, her skin practically crackling with energy from the magic she'd generated with her torture of the three of them. The storm she'd created had roared and growled like a lion, raging so strong they could feel it even in their cavern underneath the mountain, and a miniature aurora borealis roiled above the cauldron as the spell Brenna cast grew stronger and stronger. Rivulets of water had cascaded down the incline from the cave entrance, adding "wet" to their catalog of misery.

Alexei could hear Mikhail off to his left, still coughing raggedly from the dampness and clutching his side when he thought no one was looking. Alexei himself didn't much care if he was wet or dry; he was like a bear that way, Barbara once said. What he cared about was that at the height of the storm, when Brenna was at her most twisted and triumphant glory, the storm suddenly abated. The winds stopped howling down the small chimneys in the rock, the water had slowed to a trickle, and they no longer heard the crash and rumble of thunder overhead.

Initially, the Riders had all been relieved. Even Mikhail, barely conscious and bleeding pinkly into the puddle he lay sprawled in, managed to muster up a tiny smile. They'd assumed the spell had failed, or that the storm had merely run its course.

Until Brenna let out a shriek louder than any crack of thunder and started hurling things around the cave. She'd kept it up for ages, ranting unintelligibly and cursing in more languages than Alexei had been aware she knew. Her rage had sparked small fires, igniting unlit candles and blowing one lantern right off the wall in a splinter of glass and molten wax and flying shards of copper. Moss shriveled and turned first brown and then gray before crumbling into dust, and the air was filled with dust devils and bits of debris.

The Riders had hunkered down the best they could, with no way to hide or run from the chaos. Alexei had simply put his arms over his head to try and protect it and stayed crouched like that until eventually silence fell like a shroud, broken only by the sound of water dripping and the clank of something falling off the table as it settled back down on all four legs.

When he'd looked back up, Brenna had fallen into an uneasy doze, slumped on the pile of rags she'd piled on a high corner shelf of rock she used as a bed. Even in her sleep she'd muttered and groaned, and now, awake again in the dim light of the dawn, she was doing it still, pacing in circles that she periodically interrupted to pick up something she'd thrown in her fury and place it back where it belonged.

Only the gigantic cauldron still steamed unperturbed on the top of the worktable, the occasional bubble working its way to the surface and letting out a noxious odor as it popped.

"That's it," Brenna suddenly said. "I've had enough of her foolish interference. No one has any respect for their elders anymore." She turned and glared at Alexei, who glared right back.

"Don't look at me, you old hag; you're not my elder. Not by a couple of thousand years. And I wouldn't call this"—Alexei waved his arm around to indicate the dank cave and his captured brothers—"respecting *your* elders."

"I'm not talking about you, you stupid oaf. You're a walking, talking mountain; I don't expect respect from you, or intelligence either, for that matter. I'm talking about *her*. That damned Baba Yaga. She did this. Interfering with my spell. Meddling with things she has no business meddling with. *Thwarting me*." She hissed that last bit through clenched teeth, hair frizzing even worse than usual in the damp air.

Alexei thought she looked every bit the wicked witch who was used to scare small children, even without the iron teeth of the old Russian tales.

As usual, it was Gregori who picked the important element out of Brenna's rambling speech. "There is a Baba Yaga here?"

They exchanged glances, and Alexei could feel his heartbeat echo in his ears. *A Baba Yaga had come. Perhaps they were saved after all.* The relief was almost painful.

"There is," Brenna said, spittle flying from her lips to sizzle in the fire as she spat out the words. "That damned redhead, Bella. I don't know how long she has been here, or what brought her in the first place. Maybe the locals called her in to deal with the fires, idiots that they are."

Alexei's heart sank. Perhaps the Baba Yaga hadn't gotten their note after all. If she came in answer to a summons for help, she could be a few miles away and not even realize they were there. After all, the last time they'd seen Bella, he and Gregori had been racing through Montana on their motorcycles, hell-bent on finding Mikhail. Alexei wasn't even sure Bella had seen them wave as they sped past her, too intent on their mission to stop and chat.

"If Bella is here," Gregori said calmly, with the assurance Alexei lacked, "it is only a matter of time before she finds us and sees what you have done. She will tell the Queen, and this time you will not merely be banished from the Otherworld. You know Her Majesty will have you put to death for this travesty. Best you start running now, before it is too late."

"Pah," Brenna said with a sneer. "Bella may be a Baba Yaga, but I have been one for a lot longer. I have more experience, and even with her pesky interruption, last night's storm did enough damage to the forest to boost my power considerably. I am *this* close to perfecting the spell—there is no way I am letting some snip of a girl stand in my way."

"What are you going to do to stop her?" Alexei asked. "She is a Baba Yaga."

Brenna looked at him as though he were even stupider than she'd thought. "Why, I'm going to kill her of course. The silly thing has left me no choice. If she won't keep her nose out of my business, Bella will have to die."

TWENTY-TWO

BELLA WAS LONG gone, the exhaust from her dirt bike merely a memory on the wind, before Sam finally let go of the railing and stopped gazing at where she had been. He shook himself, as if waking from a dream, and forced his legs to take him inside.

Once there, he stared into the mirror he normally avoided except when he shaved, trying to see the man that Bella had seen the night before. She hadn't cared about his scars, hadn't even seemed to see them. Maybe she was right and what was on the surface didn't matter. But that meant he had to face the truth: that what lay underneath was far uglier.

He couldn't believe how badly he'd behaved. He would have liked to have blamed it on guilt and confusion, but the truth was that once Bella was in his arms, she'd felt so right, he hadn't felt guilty at all. And yes, her conjuring that ball of fire out of nowhere had startled and alarmed him, but he knew in his heart that she wouldn't have hurt him. There was no excuse for what he'd said to her. No excuse at all.

As he made himself a cup of coffee and prepared to go into service, Sam ran their argument over and over in his head. Had he overreacted when she'd admitted that Jazz wasn't her niece? Probably, although he wasn't sure if he was as out of line as Bella had thought.

He remembered vividly the time when he and the other Hotshots had fought a dreadful blaze that consumed over a hundred acres, burning a swath of prairie and over a dozen homes, and killing three people caught in its path. Two of the Hotshots team had been injured that time, one of them trapped under a tree that fell unexpectedly and the other suffering from exhaustion and smoke inhalation. Sam would never forget the look on the face of the teenage boy who finally confessed to starting the fire—no remorse, no apology for those lost or injured, only an almost sexual gratification as he'd talked about watching it all burn.

So Sam thought he might be excused for thinking, just for a moment, that it might be suspicious for a teenager to be wandering around in the forest when there were multiple unexplained fires. Of course, as soon as he'd said it, he realized that he knew Jazz better than that. Hell, he knew Bella better than to doubt her ability to judge someone truly.

The truth was, he'd been taken aback by the fact that she'd lied to him. Or maybe, just let him believe the lies others had passed along to him, which she'd never corrected. Possibly because she was afraid he'd react in exactly the way he had, automatically assuming that if Jazz was a runaway, she should be returned to wherever she came from, regardless of the circumstances.

Even Sam wasn't naïve enough to believe that, although in general he did believe in following the rule of law. At the very least, he figured he should let Jazz tell him her version of the story before jumping to conclusions or taking any action. That was, of course, if Bella would let him anywhere near her not-niece, after the horrible things he'd said.

He picked up the binoculars, already planning his apology speech for when he went out of service (and trying to remember where he'd seen wildflowers growing, in case he needed more than mere words). But the sight of a gray smudge rising toward the sky knocked any other thoughts out of his head.

Thumbing on the two-way radio automatically, Sam continued to scan the area as he said, "Dispatch, this is Sam. I've got a smoke in the northwest quadrant, over by Hansen's Mill. It looks bad. Copy?"

There was a click as the dispatcher picked up. "Copy. How bad is bad, Sam? Do I need to call in folks from outside the county, do you think?"

Sam looked through the glasses again, although the column of smoke was thick enough now that he could see it without them. "Roger that, dispatch. It's about doubled in size since I noticed it a few moments ago, and that's not a good sign."

A few choice curse words traveled through the ether before Willy clicked off his radio. Looking out at the smoke in the distance, Sam added a few of his own. Out of habit, he checked the clearing where the caravan sat, although it wasn't anywhere near the area where the current fire was located. There was no sign of either Bella or Jazz, or, for that matter, her gigantic cat, who Sam was still pretty sure wasn't really a dragon, no matter what she'd said.

He hoped that she'd stay safe, although he was starting to get the feeling that *safe* and *Bella* were two words rarely found in association with each other. Sam wasn't sure if he was more afraid for her or of her, but either way, he owed her an apology, and he planned to give it to her.

As soon as the current fire was out and it was safe for him to leave the tower, however soon that was.

AS BELLA RODE her Enduro through the woods, she passed a few truckloads of firefighters, geared up and obviously heading for a fire. Worried, she glanced over her shoulder toward the caravan, but they were clearly headed in a different direction, and she figured Jazz and Koshka were safe for now. Worse came to worst, the caravan was completely capable of moving itself—and them—out of danger, should it become necessary, although it might be a little hard to explain if anyone saw it happen.

She hesitated, torn between going after the firefighters and helping out there, and following the gut instinct that told her she would find the person setting the fires if she could locate the notch between the two mountains where Sam said the storm last night had originated. In the end, she kept moving down the trail, figuring it was better to stop all the future fires than to assist with just one. Especially since there wasn't much she could do with the woods filled with Humans and their equipment.

But she still felt guilty, heading *away* from a fire instead of toward it, and that emotion gave her a little glimpse into what Sam must feel every time he stayed in the tower instead of going out to fight a fire. Bella's fingers clenched on the handlebars as she flashed back to their fight. She wished she could just check in on him and make sure he was okay; even if he never wanted to see her again, she still couldn't keep herself from thinking about him and worrying about how this latest fire was making him feel.

Focus on the job, Bella, she reminded herself, hearing the voice of her mentor in her head. She steered the bike around a broken branch that was lying over half the narrow roadway and turned off onto a smaller spur—more a path than a road—that seemed to lead in the direction she wanted to go.

Finally, she slowed the bike, stopping it altogether when she felt the first ripples sliding over her skin like cobwebs in a dark basement. Magic. She could smell it in the air, sense it in the tingling at the tips of her fingers and in the small hairs on the back of her neck. She'd been right; someone nearby was using magic.

Of course, it could be some local Wiccan type, sending out an innocuous spell for prosperity or love, but somehow, Bella didn't think so. Whatever she was feeling had too much power behind it for that.

Leaving the Enduro tucked away behind some overgrown berry bushes, Bella crept down the path until the sensation of enchantment on her skin grew even stronger, like tiny waves as they brushed against the shoreline. Peering out from behind a wide and sturdy tree, Bella spotted someone leaving what looked like a crack at the base of the hill. For a moment, she almost didn't believe her eyes, but it was impossible to mistake that frizzy gray hair or the funky long batik skirt, as colorful as always in reds and oranges and yellows, which made it stand out even more in the midst of all the greens and browns of the forest.

It was Brenna. Now Bella just had to figure out what to do with her.

BELLA WISHED THAT Koshka was with her; she'd feel a lot better about bearding the lion in her den with an actual dragon by her side. But of course, one or the other of them had to be at the caravan. It wasn't as though she could leave an inexperienced teenager guarding the Water of Life and Death. So that option was out.

She seriously considered the option of calling in one or both of her Baba Yaga sisters, either of whom would be happy to get their hands on Brenna, especially after what she had tried to do to Beka. But the Queen had made it clear that she expected Bella to handle this situation on her own, and it wasn't a good idea to disappoint the Queen. For a moment, Bella even debated going to the Otherworld to report in to Her Majesty, but in truth, she didn't have anything concrete to report.

Yes, she'd found Brenna in the forest. That was certainly suspicious under the current circumstances. But so far there was no proof that she'd had anything to do with the fires, other than Bella's suspicions, and there had been no sign of the Riders, or anything to implicate her in their disappearance. With Bella's luck, she would drag the former Baba Yaga before the Queen, only to discover that she'd decided to move to the Human lands and take up rug hooking and making moonshine.

No, there was no other choice. Bella was going to have to get a closer look at whatever was in the cave Brenna had just left. Luckily, the older witch had been carrying a basket over one arm, so hopefully she was going out to gather herbs and such and would be gone for some time. All Bella had to do was pop her head inside, see if there was anything that could link Brenna to the fires, and then, once she had evidence to back up her theory, she could call in reinforcements.

Bella crept down the slight incline toward what looked like a shadow, but which she was pretty sure was actually a hole leading into the mountain. She held on to slim saplings as she worked her way toward the entrance, a pungent green odor drifting up from the plants she crushed as she created a new path through the undergrowth. A lone bird let out an alarmed squawk, then winged away as she stopped for a moment at the edge of the woods.

Nothing moved.

There was no sign of Brenna, or anything else larger than the squirrel that stood on its hind legs and gazed at her indignantly before racing up a tree with some treasure held clenched in one bulging cheek.

Goose bumps crept up Bella's arms, but she told herself that she was just being oversensitive. After all, even if Brenna returned before Bella was done checking the place out, a retired Baba Yaga was no match for a young, active one. Not that it didn't make sense to be cautious, with Brenna's history. After all, it didn't take magic to try and kill someone, and she'd already proven she was capable of that. Bella shook the feeling off and bent over to push away a few straggling wild roses that guarded the entrance to the cave, wincing as a thorn caught the back of her hand and lifting the injured flesh up to lick off the tiny beads of blood that welled up in the thorn's wake.

But once she'd inched her way inside, one cautious, sliding step after another, she dropped her hand, the minor wound forgotten in the shock of the scene that greeted her.

The first thing that struck her was the smell. It was beyond rank, some indescribable mixture of raw sewage and the coppery tang of blood and the acrid stink of a chemistry experiment gone wrong, all overlaid with the stench of sweat and desperation. It hit her like a wall, making her stop in her tracks and cover her nose, taking shallow breaths through her mouth instead.

But that was almost worse, since now she could taste it, the fear and the excitement and the magic in the very molecules of the air.

As her eyes adjusted to the dim light inside, what she saw almost made sense of the odor, if only her brain could take it all in. Her mind kept trying to transform what lay before her into something else, something less horrible, less *impossible*.

All three Riders were there, in a cavern whose walls seemed to waver and creep instead of standing still, wreathed in a fog of magic and smoke from a pile of sticks that smoldered under a cast-iron cauldron. Stalactites hung down from the ceiling near the edges of the space like teeth of some great monster, and the damp floor was covered with muddy dust and fluids better not examined more closely.

One part of Bella's attention noticed a worktable bearing the huge cauldron that steamed forebodingly amid a clutter of arcane tools and glass jars filled with oddly colored liquids, but mostly her vision was taken up with the Riders.

Oh, her poor, poor Riders.

She nearly wept to see them, so battered and bruised she barely recognized them, she who had grown up with them since she was a small child. They were encased in cages of some malignant enchantment; that much was clear at first glance. Nothing else could have held them long enough for Brenna—and it must have been Brenna—to have caused the kind of damage that met Bella's eyes.

All three Riders were appallingly gaunt and had obviously been tortured. They were filthy, their clothing reduced to rags, Mikhail Day's usually pristine white leathers a muddy tan, where they still existed at all. The Riders themselves were covered with cuts and bruises in various bilious shades of purple and green and yellow. Alexei's large hands were blistered and red, Gregori had one eye swollen completely shut and numerous open wounds that still oozed blood, and Mikhail . . . Mikhail barely lifted his head to acknowledge her appearance, gazing upon her with an expression of un-mitigated grief and horror and despair.

Tears sprang into Bella's eyes, and one hand went invol-untarily to her heart. "Oh no," she said brokenly. "How could she do this to you? How could anyone do this to someone else?"

She walked quickly to the nearest cage, where Alexei crouched like a captive bear, shoulders hunched and his in-jured hands held uselessly out in front of his body. "Just let me take a look at the magic she is using to hold you here," she said, stomach roiling from the sight of her friends in such distress. "I'll have you out of there in a minute, I swear. Just hold on."

"No, Baba," Alexei rasped, his usually powerful voice reduced to a whisper, as if days of screaming had worn it away. "You must leave. You must leave now. It is a trap."

TWENTY-THREE

"WHAT?" BELLA SAID. She swiveled around, but saw nothing. Maybe Alexei was paranoid and rambling. Who could blame him, after everything he'd been through? "Don't worry, it's going to be okay. I'll get you out of here." She gritted her teeth as she got a closer look at his hands. "The Queen is going to kill her for this."

"Never mind the Queen," Alexei said. "You have to get out of here. Brenna sent out that ripple of magic on purpose, to lure you in. She knows you're in the forest, that you've been stopping her spells from working. She intends to kill you." He gazed at her beseechingly, a single tear dripping into the tangled remains of his braided beard. "Please, leave us, Baba Yaga. Go get help if you can, but you must leave now."

Bella scanned the enchantments laid on the bars of the cage, trying to figure out how to unravel them or tear them down. They were complicated and yet simple at the same time, like a series of ribbons wound in and around one another until you couldn't see beginning or end. Under different circumstances, she would have admired the artistry of the magical work; as it was, she wanted to rip them apart with her bare hands.

"I'm *not* leaving you here like this," she insisted. "I'm not afraid of Brenna. I'd rather not confront her, but if I have to, I will. Don't forget, I'm a Baba Yaga at the height of my powers. She's an old woman who hasn't had any of the Water of Life and Death in a long time. I can take her."

"You don't understand, Bella," Gregori said from his enclosure next to Alexei's. He pointed at the cauldron she'd noticed on her way in. "Brenna has been working on some strange and evil potion, drawing on our pain and immortality, and on the distress she has inflicted on the trees and creatures of the forest with the fires she's been setting."

Bella could feel the muscles in her jaw clench. "So, it really *was* her behind all these fires. I knew I sensed magic on the wind. But I don't understand; what is the potion supposed to do? Why on earth would she go to all this trouble, put you three through all of this unspeakable madness?"

"*Madness* is the right word for it," Gregori said, even his formidable calm seeming to be wearing thin around the edges. "She believes that the potion will give her back her power and her youth, much as the Water of Life and Death does, except this elixir is derived from pain and suffering instead of being created from the Queen's faerie magic."

"That's insane. Nothing can do that." Bella tried spinning tiny tendrils of her own energy into the bindings of the cage in front of her, hoping to find a weak spot.

"I'm not so sure, little one," Alexei said, his tone grim. "The potion isn't finished, thanks to your blessed interference, but I swear, she is stronger than she was. Stronger than you think. You must leave before she returns."

"She can't be that powerful," Bella insisted, still struggling with the magical lock, which seemed to have caught up her strands of energy the way a submerged log can snag a fisherman's hook. The harder she tried to get it loose, the more stuck it became.

"Sometimes it is better to be clever than to be powerful," a triumphant voice said from the bottom of the slope leading into the cave. Brenna stepped forward, teeth bared in a mockery of a smile. "Although I like to think that these days, I am both."

Bella's breath caught in her throat, but before she could move, Brenna pulled a shimmering globe out of the basket she carried over one crooked arm. The orb was filled with a sickly-looking yellowish glow that matched the one Bella could *almost* see hovering around the Riders' cages, if she gazed out of the corners of her eyes.

"You foolish Baba Yagas, always trying to save everyone. So predictable." Brenna tossed the globe into the air once, caught it, and then lobbed it past Bella's head and into the tangled web surrounding Alexei's prison.

The energy spread through the bars and followed the wisps of the magic Bella had sent into the enchantment to try and undo it, flooding her with a jolt of force that overloaded her neurons and short-circuited both her body and her power. Helpless, limbs convulsing, she slid to the dirt floor, and from there, into darkness.

JAZZ PACED BACK and forth in the caravan. When that got too annoying, she went outside and paced out there. None of which made Bella suddenly appear out of the depths of the forest.

She gnawed on an already ragged fingertip, trying to figure out what she was supposed to do. After Bella had taken off on her dirt bike yesterday morning, Jazz had spent the rest of the day alternating between worrying and trying to keep herself busy with cleaning an already clean caravan and practicing the little bits of magic Bella had taught her. Jazz wasn't used to having someone else to worry about, and she wasn't sure she liked it.

When Bella didn't return for dinner, or when darkness fell, Jazz became quite certain: she *hated* having someone to worry about. Koshka tried to reassure her, saying that Bella was a grown woman and could take care of herself. He told her that there was nothing more powerful than a Baba Yaga (except a dragon, of course, and he was the only one of those around). Eventually he convinced her that Bella must have gone to the fire tower to stay with Sam.

"You think they made up?" Jazz asked him. "That would be great."

He'd given one of his openmouthed, fang-filled yawns and shrugged. "Young love. How could they not? Besides, we both know our Bella is irresistible."

Jazz had been so distracted by the fact that he'd said "our" Bella, she'd accepted his explanation and finally gone to bed, expecting Bella to be back in time for breakfast.

But breakfast had come and gone, and they were fast approaching lunchtime. Even Koshka was starting to fret a little, although he tried to hide that fact from Jazz. He'd gone out on a run briefly, saying he needed to stretch his legs, but, she thought, really searching to see if he could find any sign of Bella within the small radius he could cover without getting too far away from the caravan.

When he returned, he shook his head and dropped a pile of dead mice at her feet.

"Why don't you take these to Sam at the fire tower? That owl must be starving by now. When you get there, you can tell Bella it is time to get her ass back here."

Jazz was so worried, she even forgot to get grossed out by the rodents. She found a bag and tossed them inside, picking them up with a piece of cloth she made a mental note to burn later. "Good idea," she said. "It's going to take me a while to get there, without a dirt bike or anything. But maybe I'll luck out and find someone going in that direction who can give me a lift."

To be honest, she didn't care if she had to jog all the way there. She was sure that Bella must be with Sam, in which case Jazz was seriously going to give her crap about making her and Koshka, like, freak out over nothing. All she knew was that Bella was the first person who had treated her like a real human being in years, and there was no way Jazz was going to risk losing that. Or the magic, dammit. Bella had better be at that fire tower.

* * *

ONE GOOD THING *about living for months in the woods*, Jazz thought as she jogged down the main path. *It was better for keeping you in good shape than a gym.* Of course, it helped that Bella's campsite was only three or four miles from the fire tower. Still, she stopped for a moment at the base of the tower to catch her breath before she ran up all those stairs.

Once at the top, she banged on the door with the flat of her palm. "Sam! Sam!"

She could see him put down the binoculars and walk across the room, but waited more or less patiently for him to open the door before she stuck her head in and said, "Where's Bella?"

The fire watcher looked baffled, the eyebrow on the unscarred side shooting up toward his hairline. "Hello to you too, Jazz. Bella's not here. Why did you think she would be?" He waved her the rest of the way into the small space.

"Oh," Jazz said, drooping. "I'm sorry to bother you then. Here, these are for you." She made a face as she handed him the bag of mice. "The owlet is still okay, isn't he?"

"He's fine," Sam said, pointing at the box on the table. "See for yourself."

She went over to check on the little bird, happy to see that he looked to be thriving. "You're taking really good care of him. The mice are from Koshka, by the way."

"Great," Sam said. "Er, tell him I said thank you."

"I will." Jazz patted the owl gently on the head with one finger and then looked back up at Sam. "Are you sure you haven't seen Bella?"

"Not since yesterday morning after the storm," he said. "Why, how long has she been gone?"

"She left the caravan not long after she came back from the shower," Jazz said, trying to keep the concern out of her voice and probably failing. "She was really upset about something and took off to look for her friends some more. And she never came back."

Now Sam looked worried too. And guilty. "I'm afraid she

was upset because we had an argument. I said some pretty lousy things."

Jazz stared at the floor. "You guys fought about me, didn't you? Because she told you I wasn't her niece."

"We disagreed about a few things," Sam said, gazing at her steadily until she raised her head. "But yes, that was one of them."

She met his eyes. "She said you told her she should send me back into the system. You think I might have something to do with these fires, don't you? Just because sometimes kids my age set fires. Well, sometimes people start fires by not putting out their cigarettes carefully enough, and I don't smoke. So I think it's pretty lousy that you just made some kind of assumption because of how old I am."

Sam sighed. "How old you are is why I told Bella you shouldn't be running around the forest by yourself. And yes, I did think, just for a moment, that you could be involved. But I also thought that about Bella, if it makes you feel any better. I'm sorry if I hurt your feelings."

"Pfft," Jazz said. "As long as you're not hitting me with your fists, you can throw all the words at me you want. But you're wrong about me and you're wrong about Bella. She's trying to stop the fires, not start more." The "you idiot" was unsaid, but still echoed loudly between the two of them. Jazz crossed her arms across her chest and glared at him, not impressed when his expression softened.

"Did the people you ran away from hit you, Jazz?" he asked in a soft voice. "Is that why you left?"

"I *left*," she made air quotes around the words, "because the hitting was about to become something much worse. And no thank you very much. I'd rather take my chances with the bears."

Sam winced. "Couldn't you have called your social worker, or told the police? Not all adults are bad, you know."

Jazz rolled her eyes. "Seriously? Have you ever met a so-cial worker? Some of them are nice enough, the ones that haven't been in the system long enough to be, like, totally burned-out. And some of them are total shits who are just picking up a paycheck and don't care at all about the kids. The one I had last was actually one of the good ones. But she was responsible for something like two hundred kids, so I saw her maybe three times a year. She'd come in, check out the house, ask me how things were, with Mr. I'm a Model Citizen standing right by my shoulder, and then go away, grateful that things were working out so well and she wasn't going to have to find another placement for me when she'd completely run out of families to stick me with."

"And the cops?"

"Right," she said. "Like they're going to take the word of some loser who'd been in eight foster homes in ten years over a guy who sold real estate and lived in a house with an actual freaking white picket fence. All he had to do was say he'd taken away my phone and I was acting out to get back at him, and they'd look at me like I was wasting their time." Jazz spoke with the bitterness of experience. She'd tried telling a cop about one of her foster parent's abuse. Once.

"Besides, the kind of crap my latest foster father had in mind, the only way to go to the cops was to let it happen first, and then report it. No way in *hell* was I going to do that."

"I'm sorry, Jazz," Sam said, rubbing one hand over his scars in a gesture she'd seen him make before when he was stressed or upset. She was pretty sure he didn't realize he did it. "No kid should have to go through that."

Huh. "So, you believe me?" Jazz felt her heart lift, just a little. He'd better not be jerking her around.

"I do, actually," he said. "Bella tried to tell me the system failed you, and I was so caught up in my own preconceived notions of the way things should be done, I didn't really listen. I'm sorry."

From what Jazz could tell, he was even sorrier that he and Bella had fought over it, but she wasn't going to rub salt in his wounds by mentioning it.

"Can I ask you something?" he said, looking serious.

"Um, sure, I guess."

"You seem like a really terrific kid," Sam said, stating it

like it was some kind of fact. Jazz tried not to feel all warm and fuzzy, but it was a pretty cool thing to hear someone say. Especially someone she liked and respected as much as Sam.

"Well, duh," she said, as if people said crap like that to her all the time.

He grinned back at her, not buying it. "Yeah, I know. Captain Obvious here. But what I wondered was, if it isn't too personal a question, how is it that you never got adopted? I mean, I think any family would be lucky to have you."

"Damn straight," Jazz muttered. But then she sighed again. "I guess you don't know much about the foster care system, do you?"

Sam shook his head. "Not really, no. Just what I've read in the papers and seen on the news. I know there are a lot of problems."

Jazz just barely kept herself from rolling her eyes again. "There's the understatement of the century," she said instead. "Mostly there are just way too many kids and not enough people who want kids. And the ones they want, well . . . have you ever gone to an animal shelter?"

He blinked at her, clearly not following her train of thought. "Uh, sure. When I was a kid, my parents took me and my sister to go pick out a kitten." For a minute, his eyes looked sad. "Heather, my fiancée, and I were going to get a cat. We just kept putting it off because we were worried about how long we'd be away at a stretch, fighting fires." He looked around the fire tower. "I guess it's a good thing we never got one."

Personally, she thought having a cat would do him a lot of good. Just being around Koshka made her feel better when things weren't going so well. Maybe they'd let him bring one to the tower, if he asked. She shook her head, trying to get her thoughts back on track.

"Okay, so you went to the shelter, and there were probably like a bazillion cats, right?"

"There were a lot, sure. I was only ten, but I remember I wanted to take them all home with us."

"Right," she said. "But you could only take one. So you picked a cute kitten, right?"

He nodded, still not following.

"In any given animal shelter, there are hundreds of cats," Jazz explained. "Lots of them are beautiful, and sweet, and well behaved. Some of them even use the litter box the way they're supposed to, nine out of ten times. But a bunch of them are older, and have a few things wrong with them, and no one wants to take a chance on a cat that might have bad habits, or is, like, an adolescent and maybe a little hyper. So just about everyone takes home a cute kitten instead."

"And you're saying that no matter how terrific you are, you aren't a cute kitten," Sam said.

"And there are a *lot* of cute kittens," Jazz agreed. "I went into the system when I was five, and really, by then I was already too old to have much of a chance of being adopted. People want babies. They don't want kids who are too smart for their own good and have attitude." She grinned at him ruefully. "I have been informed, numerous times, that I have attitude."

Sam gave her the ghost of a smile in return. "Believe it or not, I can see that. But I like your attitude. I'd be more likely to call it spunk."

"Jeez. Spunk? What are you, like, a hundred?" But she smiled to show she was kidding. Then the smile slid off her face as she remembered why she'd come in the first place.

"Listen, this little chat has been grand and all, but if Bella isn't here, I need to keep looking for her." Jazz gazed out the windows at the huge expanse of land surrounding them. "What if she's out there hurt? She could have had an accident on the bike or run into some kind of a wild animal or something."

Sam did that thing with his face that grown-ups do when they're worried but trying to pretend they're not so the kid won't get upset. Jazz resisted the urge to tell him to cut it the hell out. Barely.

"I'm sure she's fine," he said. "She strikes me as a woman who is capable of looking after herself. And speaking of looking, hang on for a minute while I do my rounds. We already have one ongoing fire; I need to make sure there aren't any more."

Jazz rested one hip on the edge of the table so she could talk to the owlet while he went outside with the binoculars. He spent a long time looking off in one direction, his glasses aimed at a dark smudge that Jazz could see with her naked eyes. When he came back in, his face was drawn and pale, but he still made an effort to speak to her kindly.

"Look, why don't you go back to the caravan. She's probably come back by now and is worrying about where you are."

Jazz shook her head. "Koshka would have told her where I went, if she actually came home."

"Uh-huh." It was Sam's turn to roll his eyes. "I believe that Bella's a witch, but really, a talking cat?"

"I thought she told you," Jazz said. "Koshka's not really a cat. He's a dragon disguised as a cat. Of course he can talk." She chose to ignore the fact that she'd been pretty amazed by it when she first found out.

Sam blinked. "She told me. I just thought she was kidding."

"Right. Because people kid about dragon-cats all the time." She tapped one bitten fingernail on the table. "Look, you said there's a fire, right? Do you think Bella could be down there using her magic to fight it or something? That could explain why she didn't come home."

Sam perked up, the sadness vanishing from his face for a moment. "You know, that's probably exactly what she's doing. Let me check in with the county zone warden."

He scooped up what looked kind of like a walkie-talkie and spoke into it. Jazz figured that whatever it was probably worked better in the woods than a cell phone did.

"Hey, Jake, this is Sam in the fire tower. I'm looking for a missing person, and since she has prior firefighting experience, I thought she might have joined in with the volunteers you've got working on this one and just forgot to tell anyone where she was going."

"Got a description, Sam?" asked the voice on the other end of the call.

"You bet," Sam said. "You can't miss her. She's a gorgeous redhead with green eyes. Last seen riding a red Enduro dirt bike."

Jake laughed. "Sounds like she'd have been noticed if she's out here," he said. "I'll check with the team leaders and get back to you, but nobody has mentioned anyone like that to me yet."

"Thanks, I appreciate it. How goes the battle?"

"We've got her about seventy percent contained," Jake said. "If the wind doesn't pick up, we should have her under control by nightfall, thanks to your sharp eyes. I'll keep you posted. Do me a favor, though, and don't spot another one, will ya? We've got guys from three counties here. I'd hate to have to divide our efforts."

"I'll do my best," Sam said. "Stay safe."

"You bet." The radio clicked over into silence.

Jazz looked at Sam. "So no one's seen her."

"No one mentioned it to the zone warden. That doesn't mean she isn't there," Sam said. But the look in his eyes didn't match his reassuring tone.

"Uh-huh." Jazz pushed off from the table. "I guess I'll go back to the caravan. Like you said, maybe she came back while I was gone."

"Let me know if she shows up, if you can," Sam said. "You know, send the cat with a message or something." Just in case, he wrote his cell number on a piece of paper and gave it to her, although the things only worked sporadically in and around the forest.

"Right." Jazz bit her lip. "Sam, did you tell her she wasn't safe to be around?"

Sam grimaced. "Something like that, yeah. She made a ball of fire appear in her hand when we were arguing. It startled me, and I suppose it scared me, flames showing up right in front of me like that. I overreacted."

"Jeez," Jazz said with feeling. "I guess I can see why. But she wouldn't have hurt you. Really."

"I know that. It was just in the moment, well, people say things they don't mean when they're caught off guard." He reached one hand up to pat his face self-consciously. "I think you know why I'm not all that great with fire."

"Yeah. And I'm pretty sure Bella felt rotten about it afterward," Jazz said. "Maybe you guys can make it up to each other when she comes back from wherever she is."

"I felt rotten too," Sam said. "But I don't think Bella is going to forgive me for what I said, and I wouldn't blame her. I'd just like to know she's okay."

Jazz really hoped Bella was. She walked toward the door, then stopped before she walked outside. "Can I ask you something?"

"Sure, anything."

She gnawed on a fingernail for a second, not knowing if she really wanted the answer. "Are you going to call social services on me?" She held her breath.

Sam thought about it for a moment. "I can't say I'm happy about your situation, Jazz, especially if it turns out that Bella is really missing, and you're at that caravan alone." He held up one hand as she started to protest. "I know; you managed on your own in the woods for months just fine. And I respect that, I do. But that doesn't make it right, or a good long-term option."

He rubbed his face, looking tired and worn. "I'll tell you what. Let's see if Bella turns up. If she does, we can all talk about it. If she doesn't, well, we'll have to see. But I promise I won't call anyone without telling you first, and if I do have to call in the authorities, I promise I'll make sure someone listens to you, even if I have to hire you a lawyer and pay for it myself. No matter what, I'm on your side."

Jazz blinked back tears. One adult being nice to her was hard enough to take. Two in one week was enough to break her. If she hadn't been so tough, that is.

"Okay," she said. "I guess that's fair." Not that she wouldn't take off again if she had to, but for now, she needed to stick around at least until she knew Bella wasn't hurt or in trouble or worse.

Because she had a bad feeling it might be all three.

TWENTY-FOUR

JAZZ WAS DRAGGING by the time she got back to the caravan. She wasn't sure which was more exhausting, the long walk, the tough discussion with Sam, or worrying about Bella. Either way, all she wanted was to sit down and not think about anything for a couple of hours. Preferably in front of a video game where things blew up a lot. Ha. Not likely.

Bella's dirt bike wasn't in view when Jazz got back, but it was usually kept tucked away underneath the caravan, so that didn't necessarily mean she hadn't returned. Jazz opened the door and peered around hopefully. "Bella?"

Koshka lifted his head from where he was lying sprawled over most of the bed. "She's still not here. Does this mean she wasn't at the fire tower?"

Jazz sank down onto the bed next to him, disappointment draining what little energy she had left. She'd really been hoping that Bella would miraculously have returned by the time she got back.

"No," she answered the cat. Dragon. Whatever. "She

wasn't there, and Sam hadn't seen her since they had a fight yesterday morning."

"I thought it was something like that," Koshka said in a disgusted tone. "Humans. All those complicated emotions getting in the way of basic instincts. It's just silly."

"You don't think she would have left because she was upset about their argument, do you?" Jazz ran her fingers through Koshka's soft fur, wishing he purred like a regular cat. She could use something soothing about now. "I mean, not forever, but, like, just to go someplace and be by herself for a while?"

Koshka shook his large head, careful not to dislodge her hand. "Not a chance. Baba Yagas don't run away and pout when they're on the job. And she wouldn't have left you. Not for this long. Something's happened. Something bad." He sounded very certain, and it made Jazz's stomach clench.

"What are we going to do now?" she whispered. "Should I go look for her, do you think?"

"Right, and have you disappear too?" The dragon-cat snorted. "Not on my watch." He got up and stretched, then hopped down onto the floor.

"I have a better idea," he said. "I'm going to contact Barbara's and Beka's Chudo-Yudos. It's time to call in reinforcements.

SAM STARED OUT the window at the diminishing column of smoke. It was smaller than the last time he'd looked, but it was still there. Jake had reported the fire at ninety percent contained, but nobody relaxed until that number hit one hundred. Too many things could go wrong.

Jake had also told him that no one had seen anyone answering to Bella's description, although he promised to ask the teams to keep an eye out.

Sam was relieved to know that Bella wasn't out there in the midst of the flames, but he was a lot less happy not knowing where she actually was, or that she was okay. He reminded himself that just because Jazz hadn't contacted him to say Bella had returned, that didn't mean the two of them—and the cat that just might be a dragon—weren't sitting around at the caravan right now having dinner and laughing about how worried everyone had been over nothing. After all, he didn't even know for sure Bella had a cell phone, and even if she did, and could get a signal, that didn't mean she'd actually call him. He wouldn't blame her if she didn't.

He swung the binoculars around from the smoke to the clearing, but didn't see any movement around the caravan. He'd been checking periodically since Jazz left, and did manage to catch a glimpse of her arriving back safely, so that was something, but that was the last he'd seen of her. Even the cat seemed to be staying inside. Of course, a lot of the time he had the glasses trained on some other area, so an entire circus could have come trooping in and out and he might have missed it if he wasn't looking in that direction at the right time.

Still, he didn't feel right about any of it. Not Bella being missing. Not Jazz being on her own. A part of him regretted promising her that he wouldn't call in social services without telling her, but he wasn't going to go back on his word. Besides, after what she'd told him, he wasn't sure that being alone in the woods wasn't a lot safer than whatever she might get sent back to.

He paced back and forth, scanning the horizon as dusk began to settle over the mountains, turning the sky a darker blue that was almost purple. It was killing him to be stuck here, when what he really wanted was to be out searching for Bella. But he couldn't leave his post, not even for that. Not while there was a fire.

He felt like a fool for letting his pride and fear and stubborn insistence that he knew best get in the way of whatever connection he and Bella had begun to have. She was amazing and special and, yes, magical, and he'd pushed her away. And worse yet, he had the awful feeling that if they hadn't had that stupid fight, maybe she'd be home and safe.

If her disappearance was his fault, he didn't know how

he'd live with himself. And if something terrible had happened to her, he didn't know if he could.

BELLA'S BRAIN FELT too large for her skull and throbbed in time with some techno music she couldn't hear. For a minute, she wondered if she'd had too much to drink, like the one time she'd been crazy enough to take Alexei up on his traditional vodka challenge. The way everything was spinning around seemed vaguely reminiscent of that, but surely she wouldn't have been crazy enough to fall for that one twice?

Then her eyes began to focus again, and she could tell she was propped up against a dusty rock wall, bits of which were digging into her ribs, and it all came flooding back. The cave, the Riders, Brenna, and some kind of magical trap that she fell for like a preteen falls for a too-pretty movie idol. Dammit.

Looking down, she saw that her hands were bound with something that looked like greasy black string and felt like iron. She couldn't budge it, and when she tried to pry it off with her teeth, some oily substance embedded in the ties burned her mouth and tasted like old rubber tires dusted with bird shit. Ugh.

Bella gave up on trying to unbind herself for the moment and looked around. Brenna had clearly dragged her into the magical cage where Mikhail Day was already imprisoned, probably because he was in the worst shape and therefore least likely to try and jump her while she hauled Bella in. Mikhail had pulled himself partially upright on the same wall Bella was currently leaning against, although at the moment it looked like it was all he could do to keep from passing out. His face was ashen white, except for a fading purplish bruise around his mouth and a dried trickle of blood under his nose, no longer as straight and perfect as it had been.

The blond man still managed to wink at her when he noticed that she was awake. "You should have run when I told you to," he said hoarsely. "Just like when you were a little kid. You never could do what you were told."

Bella started to shake her head, but stopped when it made her ears ring. Whatever magical whammy Brenna had put on the cages and then set off when Bella was sucked in, it packed a real wallop.

"Sorry," Bella said. "Worst rescue ever."

In the next cage, Alexei gave one of his growling laughs. "Not quite, Baba Yaga. After all, Sun and I came here to rescue Day. That did not go so well either. You may have to get in line for the title."

"And I was going to rescue a damsel in distress," Day added, wheezing a bit. "Since the lady in question turned out to be our not-so-lovely hostess, I think I win the prize for worst rescue."

Bella blinked. "Good grief. We should form a support group."

Brenna shambled over to the edge of the cage and sneered at them all in turn. "Witty banter, how charming. And I certainly hope that there won't be any other ill-advised rescue attempts. I'm running out of room in here." She cackled, sounding uncannily like the wicked witch she was. Bella kind of resented the cliché, but she figured that was the least of her worries.

She took a deep breath, mustering all her focus, and lifted her bound hands in front of her so they were aimed at Brenna. Then she muttered an arcane phrase that should have resulted in a bolt of energy flying across the space between them. Instead, there was a burning sensation, and a few sparks fizzled for a moment at the tips of her fingers before fading into nothingness.

Brenna gave a deep chuckle. "Ha! Nice try, sweetie. Those ribbons aren't just for show, you know. They're binding your magic along with your hands. Can't have you trying anything silly now, can we? You've already been quite enough trouble as it is."

She bent down close enough to the bars that Bella could smell the reek of patchouli oil over the other noxious aromas in the cavern. The woman's many colorful dangling bead necklaces clinked against the bars as she reached one dirty hand through to tug on the ties around Bella's wrists. Apparently satisfied, she straightened back up and gazed around her. "Three Riders and a Baba Yaga. Not so impressive now, are you?"

Bella felt anything but impressive, truth be told. But the Riders were in much worse shape than she was, so it was up to her to get them out of here. If she'd thought the Queen would be irate over her failing to track down the three Riders, that would be nothing compared to how Her Majesty would react if she found out that Bella had found them and then allowed herself to be captured by an aging former Baba Yaga. They'd probably end up playing an epically unfortunate game of "animal, vegetable, mineral." And Bella really, really didn't want to end up as a rock. Not even a pretty, shiny one.

Since there didn't seem to be any way to fight her way out, or magic her way out, maybe she could talk her way out. Somewhere under that demented exterior there had to be some vestige of the woman Brenna had once been. At the very least, Bella had to try and get through to her. If she couldn't convince Brenna that what she was doing was wrong, maybe Bella could at least stall until Koshka came to track her down. Unfortunately, it would probably take a few days before he was sufficiently worried to abandon his job guarding the Water of Life and Death. That was going to take a lot of stalling.

Bella took a deep breath and mustered up what she hoped was a convincingly sympathetic tone. "Look, I know you didn't want to retire, Brenna. And the Queen was just talking the other day about how we needed more Baba Yagas to deal with the increase in natural disasters brought on by Human activities. Why don't you let us go, and I'll see if I can convince Her Majesty to reinstate you. I know all this was just a big mistake."

Brenna laughed bitterly. "The mistake was the Queen's, thinking I would ever be willing to give up the magic and the power of being a Baba Yaga after so many years. Not to mention the youth." She picked up a hank of her frizzy gray hair, and waved it at Bella. "Do you see this? Who would want to look like this, I ask you? It was one thing to don the guise of an old, arthritic woman. It is entirely another to live in it." She spat on the ground in front of the cage.

"We'll explain that to the Queen," Bella said earnestly. "Once we remind her of your long years of service to the crown, I'm sure she'll be happy to give you enough of the Water to at least keep you from aging."

For a moment, she almost thought Brenna was buying it, but then the witch shrugged and twirled her beads around one gnarled finger. "It doesn't matter," Brenna said. "I don't need her or her secret potion anymore. I have a potion of my own."

"The Riders told me you were working on an elixir," Bella said, gritting her teeth so she didn't scream at Brenna for exactly *how* she'd been going about that task. "But they also told me it wasn't working. Let me take you back to the Otherworld. We'll figure something out."

"Ah, but it *is* working," Brenna said, leaning toward the cage. "I've gotten some of my power back already, and soon I'll have the rest, and more. My potion will make the Queen's look like grape Kool-Aid."

"That's not possible," Bella said slowly, as if talking to a not-very-bright child. "There is no way to make such a thing."

"Ah, but there is," Brenna said, pointing one long, bent finger at the large tome sitting on the end of her worktable. "And I found it."

"What, in that dusty old book?"

Brenna cackled. "That's not just some dusty old book, sweetie. That's the lost journal of a man named Pyotr, written long before the Baba Yagas spread out past the boundaries of the lands where they originated."

Bella could feel her heart fall into her boots. "Pyotr? *Mad Pyotr?* But he was insane! What do you think you can learn from the journal of a madman? I thought the Queen destroyed that manuscript long ago." *Hell, they'd all thought that. She couldn't believe it still existed. And that* Brenna *had found it. This was an even worse nightmare than she'd realized.*

"You know how hard our dear Queen finds it to throw away anything of value," Brenna gloated. "I discovered it hidden away in the back of one of the libraries at the palace, while I was wandering around trying to find some way to spend my enforced retirement. It wasn't even locked up, if you can believe it. Just tucked in a silver box on a shelf, along with a number of other oddities. Once I realized the treasure I had, I borrowed it. That's what libraries are for, isn't it?"

"Who was this Mad Pyotr?" Day asked weakly, looking at Bella with a baffled expression. "And why have I never heard of him? I thought I knew everything of importance that happened at the court for the last two thousand years or more."

Bella shook her head. "This was a secret—known only to the Queen and King, and to all the Baba Yagas, who are told the story as a cautionary tale when they finish their training."

"Oh, go ahead and tell them," Brenna said, wandering back to stir whatever toxic brew she had in her cauldron. "They might as well know, since they're going to die because of it."

Bella's heart sank even further, if that was possible. At this rate, it was going to reach China. She wasn't sure what the Queen would say about her sharing the long-held secret with the Riders, but she wasn't going to pass up any opportunity to find out what Brenna was up to. Plus, you know, stalling.

Bella tried to find a more comfortable position against the wall. "Once upon a time, a Baba Yaga found a boy child abandoned in the forest. Or maybe she stole him. Those things happened, back in the long-ago days. Either way, she decided to raise him as a Baba Yaga."

"What?" Alexei's voice was indignant. "But only women can be Baba Yagas."

"Exactly," Bella said, and went on with her story. "She raised the boy in secret, and as he grew, she gave him the Water of Life and Death in the hope of making him magical. It worked, in the beginning, but eventually the Water drove him mad. Or maybe he was mad to begin with and the Water just made it worse. No one really knows.

"It was never intended to be used long-term by a mortal man. Certainly not as often as she gave it to him, or starting so young," she went on. "The Queen, who created the enchanted elixir to begin with, and who is the only one who knows what is in it or by what magical process it is made, designed it specifically for use by the Baba Yagas, all women."

"When you say he went mad," Gregori asked quietly, "what exactly do you mean?"

Bella's stomach flipped over, just thinking about it. The tale was always passed on in full, graphic detail, to ensure that each new Baba Yaga never for one moment would consider making the same mistake. Those details were engraved on her brain like acid, but she thought she could just give the Riders the highlights and that would be good enough.

"Initially, it was fairly benign," she said. "He began to have conversations with imaginary creatures and would stay up late at night tracking the movements of the stars, which he swore contained the code for messages only he could understand. Eventually he moved on to trying to read the future in the entrails of animals, sometimes while they were still alive." She shuddered. As a young woman, this was the part of the story where she'd thrown up. There had been pictures. Magical images projected on a hut wall, but no less vivid for all of that.

"Let me guess," Gregori said dryly. "The Queen finally found out and she was Not Pleased."

"To say the least," Bella agreed. "In fact, I think it would be safe to say she was furious as only the High Queen of the Otherworld can be. She turned the Baba Yaga into a tree, as an example to all. And then hired a local woodsman to chop it into kindling. They say it was a spectacular bonfire."

"What happened to the boy?" Day asked. He was clearly intrigued by the story, and a hint of color had returned to his face.

Bella sighed. "Without any additional Water, his madness seemed to abate, and the Queen considered him to be a harmless victim of the Baba Yaga's poor judgment.

"He was left to wander in the forest, rejected by both Humans for his strange ways and babbling about magic and witches and other things best left alone, and by the Paranormal people (who you will remember had not, as yet, retreated to the Otherworld), for fear of inviting the Queen's wrath."

"In short," Alexei said with a sigh, "they forgot all about him as soon as the Queen was over her fit of pique."

"Probably so," Bella said. "The story says that he spent the rest of his life plotting revenge for the death of the woman he knew as his mother and trying to get his magic back. The book Brenna has was a record of his experiments, as well as a journal that documents the true extent of his madness in his later years.

"From what I was told, Pyotr believed that he could duplicate the beneficial effects of the Water of Life and Death, which were drawn from and acted on the five elements of Earth, Air, Fire, Water, and Spirit, by somehow absorbing the essence of others. But since he did not have the magical ability of the Queen, he thought he could get the same effect by using pain and terror. Not only was this completely wrong, of course, but in his attempts to do so, he left a trail of death and destruction in his wake. The Queen and King finally decided to put a stop to him after his final experiment left an entire small village tortured and dead, from the tiniest baby to the frailest elder. It is said that they had him torn limb from limb between two centaurs."

Bella shuddered and gazed across the room at Brenna. "And after all that, he still failed. He was insane, and what he was attempting to do was simply impossible. All Baba

Yagas know that, and so do you, Brenna. You must give up this madness."

"That's where you're wrong, sweetie," Brenna said cheerfully, waving a wooden spoon that looked like it had been gnawed on by rodents. "You see, I have something that Mad Pyotr didn't have—I have the Riders."

TWENTY-FIVE

BELLA'S HEAD WAS still spinning. Or else she'd completely lost track of the conversation. Of course Brenna was insane. There was always that.

"I don't understand," Bella said, although it took every ounce of self-control to keep her tone even and calm. "What do the Riders have to do with Mad Pyotr's experiments?"

Brenna patted the huge bound manuscript as if it were a beloved pet. "I know you were taught to believe otherwise, dear Bella, but in truth, Pyotr came quite close to solving the riddle of his elixir. I only filled in the missing pieces."

"What missing pieces?" Bella asked, pretty sure she didn't want to know the answer.

Brenna dropped some nasty-looking mushrooms into the cauldron and stirred it three times counterclockwise before she seemed to remember she was in the middle of a conversation.

"Oh, well, poor Pyotr was on the right track, trying to drain the life energy out of the people he killed. He even got it right when he theorized that energy taken at the height of stress and anguish would have more power. But he erred in attempting to take that force from Humans; they simply lacked the vigor the potion required."

"That was a mistake, all right," Alexei muttered.

Brenna tutted, but otherwise ignored him. "After I began reading his journal, I realized that the reason the potion hadn't worked was because Pyotr's main ingredient wasn't strong enough. It needed the life essence of immortals, not Humans. And fortunately, I knew three remarkable specimens." She beamed proudly at the Riders. "How lucky for me."

"Not so lucky for us," Day said, sounding unspeakably tired.

"Ah well." Brenna shrugged. "The whole world is made of winners and losers. Nature is designed that way. The strong survive, and the weak, they feed the strong. Try and think of this as your contribution to the circle of life."

"Your theories are all very well and good, Brenna," Gregori said, "but they haven't worked, have they? Even with all that you have inflicted upon us, at best you have gotten only a temporary boost to your abilities. Perhaps you should consider the Baba Yaga's offer to intercede with the Queen."

Brenna waggled one bony finger in his direction. "Not at all, my dear Red Rider. You see, the timely arrival of the lovely Bella has given me the key I needed to finish my elixir. You might say that she is the final piece of the puzzle."

"What the *hell* are you talking about?" Bella asked, finally losing her already tenuous grip on her temper.

"Now, now," Brenna said. "There's no need for rudeness. I was about to explain, before you interrupted me. It's really quite simple. I was so close already. I was draining the Riders little by little, using their pain and immortality as the basis of the potion. Then I added a second layer, by absorbing the agony of the trees and plants and forest creatures as I burned the forest. That bit was genius, really. Pyotr never thought of doing that."

Bella ground her teeth, but didn't say anything. If she could find out what Brenna had planned, maybe they could come up with some way to stop her.

"You kept getting in the way though," Brenna said crossly. "I used everything I had to create that last big storm, and you snuffed it out before I could get the boost I needed. Very annoying, you and that dratted fire watcher. Well, I'll take care of you now, and deal with him later."

"Leave Sam alone," Bella said through clenched teeth.

"Don't you worry," Brenna said. "You won't be around to watch him suffer. I have bigger plans for you." She gazed at Bella fondly. "I'm going to construct a magical circle, just as I did when I was starting the fires in the forest. But this time I am going to put you and your three Rider friends inside before I ignite the blaze."

"What?" Day said, and Alexei growled. Gregori simply lifted one feathery black eyebrow.

"Oh yes," Brenna said with the satisfied tone of a mathematician who has finally solved a difficult equation. "I'm going to burn you all to death, starting with Bella. The agony of your deaths, plus the anguish you Riders will experience at watching a Baba Yaga die in front of your eyes and not being able to stop it, will create a massive amount of energy that I will channel out of the circle and into my potion. I will have what I want at last, Queen or no Queen."

"She will track you down and punish you, just as she did Pyotr," Bella said, trying to quiet the pounding of her heart. She had no trouble whatsoever believing that Brenna would do just as she'd said she would.

"Ha! That is the sweetest part of this plan," Brenna said. "Everyone who knows the Baba Yagas, including the Queen, will assume that you finally lost control of your fire ability and killed the Riders and yourself accidentally. No one will even be looking for me." She looked positively smug.

"How do you propose to get us all out of the cave and into the forest?" Gregori asked. "Day cannot even walk under his own power, thanks to your attentions. And you can hardly carry us all yourself."

"I won't need to," the old witch said. "Alexei is still strong enough to carry each of you out, one at a time."

"And why would I do that, knowing that you intend to kill us all on the other side?" Alexei asked, crossing his muscular arms in front of his chest.

Brenna smiled a crooked smile. "Because otherwise I will kill Bella right now. Slowly and painfully. At least if you do as I say, you can tell yourself that there is still some chance for escape. Although, of course, there won't be." She laughed, amused at her own whimsy.

Bella thought Brenna was probably right. They would do whatever she asked, in the hope that at some point she would drop her guard and one or the other of them could somehow overpower her and take control of the situation.

"Now hush up and stop bothering me," Brenna said, turning back to her cauldron. "I have lots of preparations to make. After all, I only have one shot at this. You wouldn't want your deaths to be in vain, now, would you?"

Bella would rather not die at all, thank you very much. She just wasn't sure right at this moment how she was going to avoid it.

AFTER A WHILE, Brenna left the cave to prepare what she called the site of her greatest triumph. Day rather doubted the rest of them would view it the same way.

Ignoring the grating of his broken ribs, Mikhail dragged himself across the small, dusty space that separated him from Bella and propped himself up on the wall next to where she sat. He was probably closest to Barbara out of all the Baba Yagas in the United States, but he'd always had a soft spot for Bella, with her fiery hair and cheerful disposition.

"I am so sorry I got you into this," he said to her, leaning his head back against the rocky support behind him.

Bella snorted. "Last time I checked, I got myself into this. Well, with a little help from the Queen. I fail to see how Brenna's madness is your fault."

"Dat's vat ve've been telling him," Alexei said, his thickening accent betraying the depth of his emotions. People looked at the huge man and only saw the size of his body;

after centuries together, Day knew that the enormity of his muscles was only exceeded by that of his heart.

"I'm the one who fell for Brenna's 'damsel in distress' disguise," Day argued, not for the first time. "I saw a pretty woman alone by the side of the road in the middle of nowhere and just had to ride to the rescue on my trusty steed. Er, bike." Sometimes he forgot that his enchanted white horse now bore another outward appearance. It was still a horse to him, even if it looked like a fancy white Yamaha with fringed white leather saddlebags and the world's most gleaming chrome.

Bella reached over and patted his arm gently. "I know we always tease you about your Knight in Shining Armor complex, Mikhail, but truly, that's one of the things I love about you. Gregori and Alexei might not have stopped, but you could never leave a woman in trouble. I think that's a good thing, not a bad one, no matter how it ended up this time."

"Besides," Gregori added ruefully, "you at least have the excuse of being fooled by her disguise. When Alexei and I came looking for you and Brenna appeared, telling us that she'd found you hurt in the woods, we followed her into the trap like lambs to the slaughter."

"Even after she plotted against Beka, it never occurred to us that she might attack a Rider," Alexei said, shoulders slumped. "We were all idiots."

"Maybe so," Gregori said. "But here we all are, and it would seem that time is running out. Perhaps our remaining hours would be better spent coming up with a plan to get ourselves out of this mess, instead of trying to decide which one of us was the greater fool."

"Good idea," said Alexei. "Except everyone knows I am not the brains of this bunch. Maybe one of you has something to suggest?"

The ensuing silence made it clear that no one did.

Finally, Day heard Bella let out a small sigh. "What is it?" he asked. "Aside from the obvious, that is."

"I know it is kind of petty, compared to the rest of our situation, but it really galls me that if Brenna succeeds, not only will she have gained the power she wants, but the Queen and everyone else will think that I am responsible for your deaths. Gah." She hid her face in her bound hands.

"Don't be ridiculous," Alexei said, sputtering. "No one will believe that, no matter what Brenna says."

"Of course they will," Bella said morosely. "Maybe you don't know the story, but enough people do. And once one person in court brings it up, they'll all be talking about it and saying, 'Remember that time when Bella lost control of her power and burned that Human girl nearly to death? And now she's killed herself and the Riders. It's history repeating itself.'"

"You mean that incident when you were a teenager?" Day asked. "That was some kind of an argument over a boy, wasn't it?" The side of his mouth edged up, as he remembered all the young, beautiful women who had fought over him through the years. But Bella's sad expression brought him back to reality. "Sweetheart, you were young and inexperienced. That kind of accident could happen to anyone."

"Well, anyone with the power to set people on fire," Alexei added.

"Not helping, big guy," Day said.

"My mentor Baba didn't think so," Bella said. "She warned me that my lack of control could endanger Humans and advised me to avoid them as much as possible."

"*That's* why you spend most of your time in the mountains and deserts?" Day said, startled. "We always thought you just preferred to be away from civilization, like some of the older, more traditional Baba Yagas."

"I do like the quiet, solitary places," Bella said. "But to be honest, I've always lived in fear of accidentally hurting someone again if I associated with Humans too much."

Gregori gazed at her thoughtfully. "When was the last time your fire ability got out of control when you were angry or upset?" he asked.

She hung her head. "Just recently," she said. "There is a man . . . a Human who watches over the forest during the fire season. We were getting close, I thought. I really liked him."

Pink suffused her cheeks, but Day restrained himself from mentioning it.

"And what happened?" he asked. He'd like to meet the man who could make their Bella blush. Hopefully he'd have the chance.

"We had an argument and I got angry, and flames just appeared in my palm. I know I really scared him; it was terrible."

"What happened next?" Gregori asked.

"Next?" Bella seemed confused by the question, as if she'd already proved her point. "I ran out, ran away. I didn't even stay to see if he was all right or say I was sorry."

"But you didn't actually hurt him?" Alexei said.

"No . . ."

Day reached over and took her hand in his much larger one. "Don't you see? Of course you lost control when you were young. You were still inexperienced and learning how to manage your powers, and besides, you were a teenager. That's what teenagers do. They make mistakes. But you are older now and you have much better control. You would never hurt anyone accidentally."

Bella blinked away tears. "Do you really believe that?"

"Of course I do," he said. "Although I will happily give you permission to hurt Brenna on purpose, should you get the opportunity to do so."

She gave him a crooked grin, but sat up straighter. "I'll keep that in mind."

THE FIRE WAS still hovering around ninety percent contained by late afternoon, but Sam couldn't stand hanging around the fire tower, not knowing if Bella had returned safely or not. He finally gave in and called Tiny, who occasionally subbed for him if he had to run errands or wasn't feeling well, and asked him to come man the tower until he got back.

Tiny, bless him, didn't ask any questions, just put the binoculars and a novel called *The Hum and the Shiver* down on the table, started up the coffeemaker, and told Sam to take as long as he needed. It was just as well, really, since Sam had no idea what he would have told the older man if he'd asked. Somehow, *I'm off to check on a woman I hardly know but can't stop thinking about* didn't seem like the right thing to say, and *Well, you know that witch you people called in? She's gone missing and I think it might be partially my fault* didn't sound any better.

Sam pushed the four-wheeler to its limit and got to the caravan around five. He'd hoped to find Bella, Jazz, and Bella's giant cat sitting outside eating barbeque, but the clearing was silent and still, with only the occasional call of a stellar jay to break the shadowy calm underneath the trees. He felt a shudder run down his back and hoped it was only due to his fear that Bella would answer the door and then slam it in his face. Truthfully, he'd be okay with that as long as he knew she was safe.

But when he knocked, it was Jazz's pale face he saw, under its mop of jagged-cut brown hair. She looked drawn and worried, with circles under her eyes that hadn't been there earlier, so he knew the answer to his question before the words even left his mouth.

"Has she come back?"

Jazz shook her head and opened the door further, silently inviting him in. "No," she said. "No sign of her. I didn't think you could leave the tower while you were on duty. Does this mean the fire is out?"

Sam came in and sat on the couch, his long legs barely fitting in the space in front of it. "No. Almost, but not quite. I was worried about Bella, so I got a friend to cover for me."

"Oh," Jazz said. Then blurted out, "I'm worried too. Really worried. I know she's tough and magic and a Baba Yaga and all, but she wouldn't stay away this long if she had any choice. Something's happened to her; I just know it." She blinked rapidly, fighting back tears. "I know you probably think I'm just being a stupid kid, that she's not really my aunt or any of my business or anything, but she's been so nice to me, and I hate thinking that she's, like, just lying out there hurt or something."

"I don't think you're being stupid, Jazz," Sam said quietly. "I agree; she wouldn't have left her cat, or you, for more than a day. Not willingly. If it helps at all, there have been people moving through the area on their way to and from the fire, and they're all keeping their eyes out for her."

Jazz plopped down on a small green and pink tufted chair, looking incongruous in her worn concert tee and blue jeans on the slightly battered antique. "They haven't seen any sign of her though, have they?" she said, sounding discouraged. Bella's humongous brown and gray cat came over and leaned against her leg, and she reached down one thin hand to pet him. From where Sam sat, it was hard to say who was comforting whom.

"I'm sure she's okay," Sam said. "When we find her, she'll probably laugh at us for being so concerned."

"Yeah, maybe," Jazz said, clearly unconvinced. "But it's a big forest, and I don't even know where to start looking for her. All I know is that she'd been searching for her friends in the east. There's a *lot* of area east of here."

Sam perked up a bit. Finally, something he could do to help. "Actually, I think I can narrow it down quite a bit from that," he said. "When she came to the fire tower the other night during the storm, she wanted to know exactly where it started. I was able to point her toward a notch between two hills to the east where I saw the first clouds and lightning strikes begin. Maybe that's where she went."

But then his excitement drained away in the face of the realistic limitations they were facing. "Of course, I don't know how much ground we can cover with just me, a teenage runaway, and an oversized cat. We're going to have to try and get some other folks to help search, but right now most of the local volunteers are fighting the fire. It's going to take some time to find people who are available to search for a missing person, especially since we don't have any evidence that she's really missing, other than our gut feelings."

"Not to worry; I've called in reinforcements," said a gravelly bass voice. "And who are you calling oversized? I'll have you know, I'm a perfectly normal size for a dragon disguised as a cat. You should see Barbara's Chudo-Yudo. He's masquerading as a gigantic white pit bull, and I swear, I've met trucks that are smaller."

Sam could feel his jaw drop open, but it took him a moment to gather himself together enough to shut it. He blinked at Jazz. "Did that cat just talk, or am I losing my mind?"

Koshka laughed, a bizarre sound coming from something with whiskers and ear tufts. "So you believe in witches but not in talking cats? You have a very limited worldview, Human. You might want to work on that."

Jazz just shrugged. "I know, it's a little weird, but you get used to it."

Somehow Sam couldn't imagine getting used to any of it, but before he had a chance to say so, there was a thumping noise from the back of the caravan and a cupboard swung open to reveal what looked like a swirling void filled with fireflies. A scent like a summer breeze and lavender and something sweet like honey or mead filled the space, and then two women walked out of nowhere, bent over slightly to fit through the confines of the cupboard door.

Once inside, they straightened up and faced toward Sam and the others; two stunningly beautiful women, both wearing swords and determined expressions, but otherwise completely unalike. The one on the left was tall and imposing, with a cloud of black hair, head-to-toe black leather, and a scowl that didn't bode well for anyone who got in her way. The one on the right was a tanned, willowy blonde in a patchwork skirt and tank top, whose smile for Sam and Jazz didn't distract his attention from the fact that in addition to her silver sword she seemed to be carrying at least three knives, one of which she tucked into her long braid as soon as she determined that neither of them was an immediate threat.

"Hello, Koshka," the brunette said. "Chudo-Yudo sends his regards. Want to introduce us to your friends and tell us what the hell is going on?"

"Baba Yaga," the cat said, making a kind of bow in her direction. "This is the girl Jazz, whom Bella has taken under her protection. Jazz, these are two of Bella's sister Baba Yagas. Barbara is the dark, crabby one, and the pretty, yellow-haired one is Beka, who is in charge of the western third of the country."

"Nice," Barbara muttered. "Dark, crabby one indeed." But she did make an attempt at a smile. "And who is your other friend, pray tell?"

Sam stood up. "My name is Sam Corbett. I work in the fire tower near here."

Koshka head-butted him in the back of his knee, almost knocking him over. Sam was pretty sure it was an affectionate gesture, but it was hard to tell for sure.

"Sam is a Human Bella has become involved with," the cat said bluntly. "They're in love, and he knows who and what she is, so you can speak freely in front of him. She has been training the girl, so the same applies to her."

"Wait, what?" Sam said, taken aback. "Bella and I aren't in love. We hardly know each other."

Barbara, the darker one, let out a tiny chuckle. "In my experience, that doesn't seem to make much of a difference." Beka nodded, eyes twinkling, as if they were sharing some joke he didn't know the punch line to.

Koshka sighed, and Sam could swear that he saw a trickle of smoke eddy out of the cat's nostrils. "Fine," the cat said. "Have it your way. So you don't think of her all the time, even when you're trying not to? Couldn't describe in minute detail not just how she looks but how she smells, what shade of green her eyes are at twilight, how you feel when she smiles at you?"

Sam swallowed hard. He'd been in love once before; he knew all the symptoms. He'd just been so sure it would never happen to him again, certainly not now and not with a woman like Bella.

"Of course I like Bella," he said hoarsely. "She's wonderful, but that doesn't mean—"

The woman named Barbara gazed at him with amber eyes

that seemed to see into his soul. "Never mind all that romantic nonsense. Would you tear the forest apart with your bare hands to find her?"

Silently, Sam nodded, swallowing hard.

"Good enough for me," Barbara said. "Let's go get our girl."

"But, wait," Sam said, not quite believing he was arguing with a cat. And two witches who had somehow walked out of a cupboard.

"*What?*" Koshka said in the tone of someone who is rapidly running out of patience.

"You said we were in love. But surely Bella isn't in love with me." *How could she be?*

The dragon-cat snorted. "She may not know it yet, but she is. Now, can we go find her so she can tell you so herself?"

TWENTY-SIX

AFTER A BRIEF discussion, it was decided that Sam would lead Barbara and Beka to the part of the forest where he thought Bella might have gone. That settled, he was left with one pouting teen and what he was pretty sure was a pouting cat, although it was hard to tell underneath all the fur.

"I should go too," Koshka said with a growl. "But I can't leave the Water of Life and Death unguarded. I am not happy about this."

Barbara's dark brows drew together, and she exchanged an indecipherable look with Beka; some kind of Baba Yaga shorthand, Sam concluded, although he had no idea what it meant.

"Maybe you should come along and bring the Water with you," Barbara suggested. "I have a gut feeling we just might need it."

Koshka groomed his whiskers with one immense paw. "Is that so? Well, I'm all for anything that allows me to join the search. But you're going to have to carry the flask. Bella tried to make me wear a harness once. It did not go well."

Sam could well imagine. "I'll carry it if you want," he said.

The women traded another one of those looks, and Beka shook her head. "That's okay," she said. "I'll just throw it in my bag." She indicated the patchwork purse she'd been wearing that matched her skirt and looked capacious enough to hold half the contents of the caravan if she deemed it necessary.

"Uh-huh. Don't trust the human with your magical drink," Sam said, not at all offended. "I get it."

"It's our responsibility," Barbara explained. "It would be like a cop letting someone else carry his service revolver around. Just not a good idea." She spoke like someone who had once argued with a cop about that very thing, and Sam remembered that Bella had mentioned that one of her Baba Yaga sisters was married to one.

"What about me?" Jazz asked plaintively. "I want to go look for Bella too."

Now it was Sam's turn to communicate silently with the others, and he was glad to see that they all agreed, although he knew that Jazz wouldn't be so pleased.

"You should stay here," he said. "Just in case Bella does come back, so she'll know we're all out searching for her."

Not surprisingly, Jazz rolled her eyes. "You could leave a note," she suggested a tad acerbically. "You know, something that says: *Worried about you, gone searching in the east. Come find us if you get back.*" She tapped her bitten fingers on the arms of the chair.

Beka smiled at her. "Sam's right, Jazz. Not only is it important to have someone manning the home base, just in case, but we have no idea what we could be walking into out there. Anything strong enough to prevent Bella from returning could turn out to be very dangerous indeed, and she would never forgive us if we let anything happen to you. She has grown very fond of you, you know."

Sam thought he'd never seen anyone look so stunned in his life.

"She mentioned me to you? Bella did?" Jazz said, eyes wide.

"Of course she did," Beka said, and Barbara nodded in agreement.

"Oh. That's . . . Oh."

"So you'll stay here?" Sam asked. "Please? Just in case she comes in hurt and needs help?"

Jazz sighed heavily. "Okay. But you'd better find her and bring her back."

"Count on it," Barbara said, a touch grimly, and Sam suddenly felt sorry for anyone who stood in her way.

ONCE OUTSIDE, THEY ran into an unanticipated problem. Koshka summed it up, gazing at the three Humans and himself and then sniffing Sam's four-wheeler pointedly.

"There is no way we are all going to fit on that thing," he said. "Besides, it will be easier for me to follow Bella's trail from the ground. How do you suggest we handle this?"

Sam was at a loss. Bella had taken her dirt bike when she'd left, so there were no other vehicles. Barbara just shrugged.

"You can lead us on the machine," she said. "Beka and I can keep up as long as you don't go too fast. We're both in good shape, and Baba Yagas have greater endurance than your average Human. When we get closer, we'll leave the four-wheeler and you can join us on foot."

"It's miles," he said.

Beka grinned at him, looking way too perky to be anyone's idea of a wicked witch. "I surf for hours almost every day. I'm a lot stronger than I look. And Barbara, well, she's exactly as strong as she looks. Don't worry about us; we'll be fine."

"But what about Koshka?" Sam asked. "Won't his paws get sore?"

The cat gave a good imitation of one of Jazz's eye rolls. "Dragon, dude. I could run all day and all night and into next week if I wanted to. And then make toast."

Sam figured there was no point in standing around and arguing. Especially with a cat. Dragon. Whatever. They took off down the road with him on the four-wheeler in the lead, the two women jogging behind him (Beka with her skirts hiked up and tucked into her belt), and Koshka running alongside them.

Five or six miles later, they came to a halt when they reached a place where the four-wheeler couldn't go any farther. Barbara and Beka looked like they'd been out for a leisurely stroll; Sam was impressed despite himself. And if anything, it made him feel a little better about Bella—obviously Baba Yagas were made of pretty tough stuff.

Beka peered dubiously into the overgrown trail Koshka had his broad nose pointed toward. Briars and ferns competed with less picturesque weeds to make a narrow aisle that was more greenery than path. "Are you sure she went this way? I mean, yes, it's aiming in the direction of the notch Sam told us about, but wouldn't she have taken a better route?"

"That's actually about as direct as you can get from here," Sam explained. "The road through the national forest doesn't go in that direction. In fact, there isn't really *anything* along that route, as far as I know. No houses, no hunting cabins, nothing."

Barbara and Beka exchanged glances. "Sounds ideal if you're a deranged former Baba Yaga looking to hide out," Barbara said.

"Besides, Bella left me signs," Koshka said, as if that should have been obvious to everyone else. When they all gazed around without seeing whatever he was referring to, he snorted and waved one large paw toward the base of a nearby tree. "She left them at my eye level, not yours."

Sam still couldn't see anything, but apparently the two women could, because they nodded happily and started plowing through the underbrush that grew up into what was probably some kind of animal trail. Sam abandoned the four-wheeler and followed along, but his scarred lungs soon began to protest at the speed they set, even when the path grew clearer. He could feel his lungs laboring, and hear the ragged rasp of his breath as he fell farther and farther behind the others. Sweat dripped off his forehead and into his eyes, stinging almost as badly as the briar thorns did.

Finally, he came around a corner to find Barbara and Beka waiting. Beka's pretty face was creased with concern; Barbara just looked annoyed.

"We have to move faster than this," she said, arms crossed. "I have a bad feeling we're running out of time. Can't you pick up the pace a little?"

Sam struggled to catch his breath, hands propped on his knees as he gasped for air. "Sorry," he said. "You go on. I'll catch up when I can."

Koshka appeared out of the shadows, startling him, although apparently the Baba Yagas were used to it, since they didn't even twitch. "His lungs are damaged from the same fire that gave him those scars," he explained to Barbara. "I'm amazed he made it this far." The cat sounded more admiring than critical.

"Oh," Barbara said. "Well that won't do, will it?" She held out one hand to Beka without taking her attention off Sam, and the blonde dug into her bag until she found a silver flask embossed with a large, ornate letter *B*.

"Here," Barbara said, giving him the flask with only a momentary flash of hesitation. "It's an emergency. The Queen will just have to understand."

Sam straightened up, still wheezing. He stared at the container but didn't reach for it. "Is that the Water of Life and Death you've all been talking about? Bella told me it was only for Baba Yagas. Is it safe?"

"Safe for you to drink or for me to give to you without permission?" Barbara muttered.

Beka grimaced in sympathy, but said to Sam, "I promise, it is safe. In small amounts, anyway. I gave some to Marcus, my husband, when he was badly injured in a fight. And he married me anyway." She grinned at him. "Just be careful to only swallow a mouthful. It's potent stuff."

"Do you want to find Bella or not?" Barbara demanded.

He definitely did. If that meant drinking some magical potion, well, he'd take his chances.

He tried to take a deep breath, but ended up with a coughing spasm instead, one that seemed to go on and on, ripping and tearing at his lungs until Barbara finally thrust the flask into his hands and helped him to hold it to his lips.

Liquid sunshine ran down his throat, burning and soothing at the same time. His mouth was filled with an explosion of flavors he didn't even have a name for; sweet as honey, dark as chocolate, potent enough to make his head spin. Underneath the swirling, heady lusciousness of it, he caught a hint of something bitter and musty—death in the midst of life, just as its name suggested.

For a moment, Sam was so overwhelmed by the taste and aroma and sensation of the Water, he almost forgot to breathe. But when he finally remembered to, he was shocked to discover that he could take a full breath for the first time since that fateful day. In fact, he couldn't remember the last time he'd felt so full of vitality and energy, as if his entire body was functioning at its full capacity.

Barbara gave him a look that seemed to indicate she knew exactly what effect the Water of Life and Death had had on him, but then replaced it with her usual scowl and said, "Do you think maybe we could get back to looking for my lost sister now?" Sam was beginning to suspect that at least half of her attitude was a deliberate put-on. Of course, that still left the other half, so he just nodded and started to run.

THE END OF the trail spilled them out at the base of a large hill covered with straggly bushes and spindly trees. As soon as they'd taken a few steps into the open, Koshka let out a strange low, deep noise, part hiss and part growl. Something about the sound made the hair stand up on the back of Sam's neck, and he suddenly believed that the dragon story might just be true. A family of flickers flying overhead quickly changed direction, obviously deciding they had someplace else to be. Sam didn't blame them.

"Koshka?" Beka said. "What is it?" A large knife had somehow appeared in her left hand, and her right hovered over her sword.

"I smell magic," the dragon-cat said. "Nasty, unpleasant magic." He swung his massive head around, sniffing the air. "Stay here. I'll be right back."

It was a mark of how agitated he sounded that even Barbara did as he said. The three of them hung back in the trees while they waited for the cat to return. Sam tried to reconcile the normality of the deep green forest surrounding him with the fact that he was standing in it with two witches out of Russian fairy tales, waiting for an enchanted dragon disguised as a cat to come back and tell him if they'd found a third witch. In the end, he just gave up.

Koshka reappeared a few minutes later, looking disgusted as only a cat can. He sat down in front of the others, rubbing one paw over his dark pink nose. "Pah," he said. "You should be grateful you stayed here. It's disgusting down there."

"Yes, but did you find Bella?" Barbara demanded.

The dragon-cat shook his head. "No, but I found where she was until recently. There is a cave down below; its entrance is almost completely hidden by an old rockfall, but once you know it's there, it isn't hard to spot. I checked it out, and it is empty now, but it reeks of magic—magic and blood and pain. Bella's dirt bike is there, and her scent is still fresh, so she can't have been gone long. I can smell the Riders too, and it looks like there were some kind of cages and a setup for doing magical work. The place stinks of Brenna. God, I hate the smell of patchouli." He rubbed his nose again, sneezing.

Barbara's face was set and grim. "Cages?"

Koshka nodded. "And blood. Whatever Brenna has been doing in there, it hasn't been very nice."

The thought of Bella being held captive by a crazy, powerful witch and tortured, or worse, made Sam's heart race. She had to be alive—he still had things to say to her. And if this Brenna had harmed her . . . well, he had a sudden urge to be not very nice too.

"Can you track where they went?" he asked Koshka. "And does anyone have an extra knife they can lend me?"

TWENTY-SEVEN

KOSHKA LED THEM to the mouth of the cave. From there, they didn't need his ability to trace a scent; Sam and the others could see the scuff marks where more than one person had walked through the dirt and leaves, and they simply followed the disturbed ground as rapidly and quietly as they could.

But nothing could have prepared them for what they saw when the trail ended.

Barbara held out one arm to keep them all from stepping out of the shelter of the trees and revealing themselves. At the edge of the tree line there was a clearing, much like the one where the caravan still sat, except that the foliage had left a larger space, with more open sky overhead.

The clearing itself was lovely, filled with wildflowers and touched by the golden rays of the early evening sun. But within it was a sight so appalling, Sam thought his heart would stop from the sheer horror of it. A perfectly round circle of flames roared like a beast in the center of the clearing, reaching red and orange fingers toward the sky. He could barely see through the smoke and the five-foot flames to where Bella and three men stood, one man leaning heavily on the other two, all of them clearly trapped inside.

"Oh my God," he whispered. Barbara's iron grip on his arm was all that stopped him from running into the fire to try and pull Bella out.

"Wait," she said, barely loud enough for him to hear over the pounding of his heart. "We've got to be smart about this. Look."

She pointed off to one side, where an old woman with wild, frizzy gray hair, wearing a long batik skirt and tunic and a tangled mess of dangling beaded necklaces, watched from outside the circle. The woman was about a third of the way across the space, too far for them to hear her, but Sam could see her lips moving as she held up an empty glass container, aiming its mouth toward the strengthening flames. For now, the fire seemed to be staying put in its circle around those trapped inside, but it was obvious that eventually it would slip its bounds and move inward to consume the four within.

"Is she *singing*?" Sam asked incredulously.

Beka pressed her lips together until they turned white, and she shook her head. "Chanting. She's doing magic. It looks like she is trying to pull the energy from the fire into that bottle she's holding, but it isn't something I ever saw her do when I was growing up, so I have no idea what the hell she's up to."

"Other than burning Bella and the Riders to death," Barbara added grimly.

"Wait," Sam said. "You knew her when you were growing up?"

If anything, Beka's face grew even paler. "She was my mentor," the blonde said quietly. "She found me as a child and raised me, training me to be a Baba Yaga."

"Until she tried to kill you not too long ago," Barbara said in a dry tone. "Now, can we focus on the situation, please?" She tapped one booted foot on the ground as she thought out loud.

"Beka and I can put out the fire if we work together, but

as soon as we try to do so, Brenna will sense the magic, and she could probably collapse the flames in on Bella and the Riders before we can get the fire completely out." She and Beka looked at each other helplessly.

Koshka cleared his throat, sounding like rocks grinding together. "I have an idea," he said. "But in order for it to work, I'm going to need Sam to do something really hard."

"I don't have any special powers," Sam said. "I can't do magic. So I don't see what I can possibly do. But I'll leap through those flames if that's what it takes to help Bella." Hell, doing nothing was killing him anyway. There was no way he was going to stand here and watch her—and her friends—burn to death. He'd already lost too much to fire.

"What I have in mind is going to be even tougher than that," Koshka said. "And probably more dangerous."

Barbara raised one elegant ebony eyebrow, and the dragon-cat went on.

"I need you to distract Brenna. And there's a pretty good chance that doing it will get you killed."

Sam swallowed hard and then looked across the clearing to where Bella's red hair could barely be seen behind the growing wall of smoke.

"I don't care," he said. "As long as it gives the rest of you a chance to rescue Bella. Just tell me what you want me to do."

TWENTY-EIGHT

SAM WAITED UNTIL the count of fifty, giving Beka and Barbara time to get into their positions at opposite sides of the clearing, staying back in the trees outside of Brenna's view. Koshka disappeared, leaving Sam alone to brace himself for confronting the scariest woman he'd ever seen. It didn't really matter; for Bella, he would have taken on a horde of angry Mongols.

Finally, he walked into the grassy meadow, stopping six feet away as Koshka had insisted. Up close, she didn't look all that scary. Just some old hippie in a ragged funky skirt, standing around chanting to herself. Until she turned and locked her gaze on his and he could see the raging madness staring back at him. A bead of sweat trickled down his neck, and he suddenly felt every beat of his heart thumping in his chest.

"Hello, dear," Brenna said, smiling crookedly at him. "Aren't you supposed to be stuck up in your tower, watching the world burn down around you while you do nothing?"

Well, she obviously knew who he was. That was kind of a surprise. The viciousness of her comment was an eerie contrast to her pleasant expression, but he didn't let it rattle him. If that was what she wanted, she'd have to do better than to echo his own constant thoughts back at him.

"I've come for Bella," he said. "And her friends. Let them go." He held out the gleaming silver knife Barbara had pulled out of her boot earlier and handed to him, although he had no illusion that it would be any real threat to this honest-to-badness wicked witch.

Brenna looked at the knife and at him and let out a peal of laughter. "What are you planning to do with that? Put a marshmallow on the end and roast it? You've already lost, Sam. In a few moments I will finish the spell and your girl-friend will be burnt to a cinder." She made a tutting noise and shook her head. "That does seem to happen to the women who hang around with you, doesn't it?"

Her form began to shimmer and shift, as if it were enveloped in a glittering cloud. Sam rubbed his eyes with the hand not holding the knife, and when he blinked them clear, Brenna was gone.

In her place stood the familiar form of his lost love, Heather, clad in her fire gear, looking just like she did in the picture he had in the tower of them with all the other Hotshots, taken right before the beginning of that last season. Her helmet was tucked under one arm, but she held the other one out to him beseechingly, and said in Brenna's voice, "Go home, Sam. Go home. There is nothing you can do here."

What the hell? Sam took an involuntary step backward and then stopped as comprehension hit him like a freight train.

"You. It was you all along." His fingers clenched around the hilt of the knife. "It was never Heather haunting me. It was you, trying to drive me away from the fire tower. Lady, that's *low*."

Heather's figure shimmered again, replaced by Brenna's scowling visage. "You should have listened to her instead of trying to be a hero. Now you'll get to depart this life with the rest of them." She shook her head. "Don't you know that knights in shining armor died out with the dragons?"

Sam heard a strange sound from the forest behind them, something between a cough and a roar, and a huge gout of flame came out of the trees and hit Brenna full force. Before Sam could blink, all that malice and menace had been reduced to a pile of ashes. A tiny trickle of smoke floated up from the place where she'd been standing.

A gleaming brown and green dragon the size of a van slithered out of the woods and said, "Not all dragons, you bitch. And *nobody* hurts my Baba Yaga."

As Sam stood frozen to the spot with his mouth open, Koshka shimmered, much as Brenna had, and returned to his guise as a harmless, if overly large, Norwegian Forest cat. The cat sat down and casually began to lick one paw, as if it hadn't just been a mythical creature who'd turned their powerful enemy into a charcoal briquette.

"Nicely done," the dragon-cat said to Sam. "You kept her attention long enough for me to get into position and change forms. And you're not even dead. Way to go."

Sam snapped back to life and turned around to see Barbara and Beka walking toward the fire, arms raised high and fingers crooked, as if beckoning to the sky. In response, a cloud mass overhead turned from white to gray to black as he watched, and rain poured down to put out the fire. As soon as the flames were gone, the deluge stopped as suddenly as it had begun.

Without any conscious intention on his part, Sam's feet moved in Bella's direction, and in a moment he was clutching a soaking wet redhead to his chest, hugging her as she squeezed him back, laughing and crying and kissing all at the same time.

"Aw, get a room," the dragon-cat said, picking its paws up as it walked into the circle and shaking the water off with irritated little flicks.

But he came over and joined them, leaning against Bella's legs so hard he almost knocked them both over.

"Count on it," Bella whispered in Sam's ear. "Count on it."

* * *

BELLA RELUCTANTLY LET go of Sam and looked up at him in amazement.

"What?" he asked.

She just shook her head. They'd deal with it later. "I'm awfully glad to see you. Surprised, but glad. I wasn't sure I'd get the chance."

"You should have known I would come for you," he said.

"I wasn't sure anyone really knew I was missing," she said ruefully. "I had visions of you all sitting around thinking, 'Gee, she's taking a long time in the forest,' but not worrying about me because I'm a Baba Yaga." She coughed a little, her lungs still adjusting to blissfully smokeless air.

"Are you kidding?" Koshka said from his place at her feet. "I thought he and Jazz were going to try and search the woods tree by tree." He preened. "Luckily, they had me."

Bella bent down to kiss him on top of his furry head, ignoring the hacking up a hair ball noises he made when she did it. Then she went to go give Barbara and Beka each a quick but heartfelt hug before getting on her knees to check on the Riders where they were sitting on the slightly charred grass in the middle of the circle, or in Day's case, lying down.

The other two Baba Yagas joined her, looking grim.

"What the hell did that witch do to you?" Barbara said with a grimace. "Nothing personal, but you guys look like crap on a stick."

"A very big stick though," Alexei said, wiping his sooty face with an equally grimy hand and simply smearing the blackness around. "At least in my case." He coughed loudly, the sound getting progressively rougher.

"You'd better take a look at Mikhail. Brenna captured him first and he really got the brunt of it," Gregori said. Despite being as covered with dirt and bruises as the others, he still managed to look as though he was about to sit down to drink a cup of tea before starting his afternoon meditation. It was only when Bella saw the haunted look in his eyes that she could tell that he wasn't as unshaken as he might try to appear.

The Rider wasn't kidding, Bella thought, as she moved over to sit next to Day. There wasn't a part of him visible that hadn't been beaten or burned or otherwise abused. She was pretty sure he had at least a few broken bones, and she didn't like the way he held his ribs when he coughed. Always fair skinned to go with his blond hair, the White Rider was so ashen now he was living up to his name.

"Hey, old friend," she said. "It is good to see you again. But you've looked better. You'd better heal up fast so you can go back to impressing the ladies."

Mikhail grimaced. "No more ladies for me, Baba Yaga. I'm going to take up skydiving instead. I think it's safer." He coughed again, and Bella saw a bright bead of red appear at the corner of his mouth.

Trying not to sound alarmed, she turned to the other two Babas and said, "I don't suppose either of you happened to bring any of the Water of Life and Death with you, did you?"

Beka pulled Bella's own silver flask out of her bag with a flourish. "Ta-da! Koshka insisted on coming with us, and we couldn't just leave it behind. Besides, Barbara had a feeling we'd need it, and Barbara's feelings are never wrong."

"Well, hardly ever," Barbara said, winking at Bella. Bella was pretty sure that the other woman was referring to how long it took her to realize she was in love with Liam, the Human she ended up marrying.

Bella took the flask and held it up to Mikhail's mouth, and he took a long swallow. A little color crept back into his face, and some of the more obvious wounds on the surface began to mend before their eyes, but he still lay there, clearly in pain. Bella bit her lip and gazed up at Barbara in question.

The cloud-haired Baba Yaga knelt down beside Bella and put her hand on his chest, feeling the same irregular and stuttering heartbeat Bella had sensed. The three Baba Yagas exchanged wordless glances, then Barbara, the oldest, held out her hand for the flask.

"The hell with the rules," she said. "And the hell with

any possible long-term consequences. They're the Riders. They've served the Baba Yagas and the Queen for thousands of years. Whatever it takes." Bella and Beka nodded in agreement.

Barbara lifted Day's head and put the flask back to his lips. Gregori pursed his own lips in a silent whistle when he saw how much of the Water of Life and Death she was giving him.

"Is that going to cure him or kill him?" he asked, sounding more curious than critical.

"You're about to find out," Barbara said in an acerbic tone. "Since you're up next."

Each of the Riders got a huge dose of the Water, although none as large as Mikhail had gotten. Barbara put the container up to her ear and shook it, obviously trying to estimate how much was left inside. Then she handed it back to Bella, who was still trying to stop coughing.

"There's only a drop or two left in there," Barbara said. "And it sounds like you need it. Go on, then."

Bella obediently upended the flask, feeling the Water of Life and Death hit her system like an infusion of atomic energy that smelled like flowers. Sighing, she staggered to her feet, with the help of a hand from Sam.

"Thanks," she said, including everyone in that. "You have no idea how good it is to see you all." Then she glanced around. "Hey, what happened to Brenna?"

"Don't worry about her," Barbara said with a straight face. "She's toast." Then she and Beka cracked up, a rare sight for the usually stern Barbara, and even Koshka let out a dragonish snort.

"What?" Bella asked. "What did I miss?" She'd been so busy worrying about the Riders (and being happy to see Sam), she hadn't even thought to ask how they'd defeated Brenna. Stuck in the circle behind a wall of flames, she hadn't been able to see whatever happened. She just assumed her sister Babas had dealt with Brenna somehow.

"You should probably come and see," Beka said. Koshka led the way, his tail held proudly high.

It wasn't until Bella was gazing down at the pile of ashes that she figured it out. "Koshka!" she said. "You didn't!"

The dragon-cat scratched one ear with a hind foot. "Yes, I did. She asked for it."

Bella bit her lip, torn between laughter and trepidation. "I'm pretty sure the Queen wanted her alive so she could, you know, kill Brenna herself."

"In that case," Koshka said smugly, "I've saved her a lot of trouble."

"I hope the Queen thinks so," Barbara muttered. She patted her pockets fruitlessly.

"What are you looking for?" Beka asked. "Gum? A camera so we can take a selfie with our former nemesis as a warning to all those who would seek to take us on?"

Barbara made a completely nonmagical sign with one finger. "No, you twit. I'm looking for something to put *that* in, so we can take it to the Queen as proof."

Sam pulled a slightly crumpled bandana out of his jeans. "Will this do?"

"It's not very dignified," Beka said, sounding uncertain. She rooted around in her large bag but clearly didn't find a better alternative.

"*Dignified* and *Brenna* don't belong in the same sentence," Alexei said, and spat on the ground. "It is better than she deserves."

Bella couldn't really disagree. She knelt down and used a flat rock to shovel as much of the ashes as she could onto the disconcertingly cheerful red and white cloth, and then the motley gang of three Baba Yagas, three Riders, a former firefighter, and one very smug dragon-cat set off for the caravan. It was going to be a long walk, but at least they didn't have to spend it looking over their shoulders.

BY THE TIME they got back to the caravan, night had fallen in earnest. An owl swung past silently as they entered the clearing, winging its way back out into the woods they'd just walked through. A sliver of moon rose over the trees, and stars twinkled gaily. Bella wondered if the world had gotten more beautiful or if she was just grateful to be alive and have the Riders back.

A teen-shaped torpedo barreled out of the door as the group approached, whooping and grinning from ear to ear as she gave Bella a huge hug.

"You're okay! You're okay!" she said, before stepping back and trying to pretend she hadn't gotten carried away. Bella wasn't sure which one of them was more embarrassed, but if anything, that just made her treasure the gesture more. Jazz went on to hug Sam too, and kiss Koshka soundly on the top of his head.

"You found her! You brought her back!" she said to Sam. "I knew you would." She stared at his face, but didn't say anything.

"Hey, it was mostly me, you know," Koshka said. "Although Sam helped. A little."

"We helped too," Barbara said. "But you don't have to hug us." Bella choked back a laugh. Barbara was definitely not a public display of affection kind of woman.

"I'm glad to see you too, kid," Bella said, putting one arm around Jazz. "As you can tell, we found the Riders. Also, Brenna is dead, so we don't have to worry about her anymore."

Jazz started humming something under her breath that sounded distinctly like "Ding-Dong! The Witch Is Dead" until Bella gave her a dirty look. She indicated each of the Riders in turn.

"Jazz, this is Mikhail Day, Gregori Sun, and Alexei Knight. Boys, this is my pseudo-niece, Jazz. She's been staying with me for a few days," Bella said.

"Day, Sun, and Knight?" Jazz said, cocking her head to one side quizzically. "Really?"

"It is a fairy-tale thing," Alexei explained. "Very long story."

"No doubt," the teen said. "Maybe you can tell it to me over dinner? I made sandwiches, just in case."

"I like her," Alexei said approvingly. "She made sandwiches."

"Tuna?" Koshka asked.

"I hate to break up the party," Barbara said, "but under the circumstances, I think we should probably report to the Queen right away. If not sooner. She isn't going to be happy if some tree sprite flits through to the Otherworld and tells her what happened before we can."

Bella swallowed hard. "Good point. You boys can eat your sandwiches on the way while we travel."

Day looked down at the stained and torn remains of his formerly pristine white leathers with dismay. "I can't go in front of Their Royal Highnesses looking like this. It's disgraceful."

"I suspect that just this once, she will forgive us," Gregori said. "And it is not as though we have any other clothing to change into. Eventually we will have to find where Brenna hid our motorcycles, but for now, I believe Barbara is correct. It is time to go tell our tale to the Queen."

"I hope she is in the mood for a horror story," Alexei said glumly.

"At least the story had a happy ending," Jazz said, trying to cheer him up.

"It isn't over yet," Bella said. "And whenever you're dealing with the Queen of the Otherworld, happy endings are definitely *not* guaranteed."

TWENTY-NINE

JAZZ WATCHED IN amazement as the three Riders devoured the platter of sandwiches she'd made; she wasn't even sure they stopped to chew. Of course, they all looked like they hadn't eaten much lately. She'd seen that same gaunt and weary look on the faces of some of the street kids she'd hung with on her travels out to Wyoming, although none of them had been as bruised and battered as these guys. Even the giant one with the cool braided beard seemed beaten down and tired almost beyond bearing. She hoped this Queen person didn't give them a hard time.

Jazz had the feeling none of them could take much more.

Despite what she'd said about them eating on the way, Bella made more sandwiches and got a bottle of vodka out of the freezer, which seemed to cheer the Riders up immensely. Except maybe the one Bella called Day, who pretended to be cheerful but couldn't hide the sadness in his eyes.

While they ate, the Riders cleaned up the best they could, each of the Baba Yagas helping with soap and water and, occasionally, a hint of magic to at least cover up the worst of the damage to their clothes. Jazz thought they all still looked pretty pathetic, but she wasn't going to be the one to say so.

"Will you be gone long?" she asked Bella, trying not to sound whiny. It had been a long time since she'd had someone to care about, and after spending all those endless hours worrying about Bella, she wasn't looking forward to them being separated again. Not that she was kidding herself into thinking they were going to stay together forever or anything, but she'd been hoping for a day or two before they went their own ways. To be honest, it was kind of freaking her out, seeing Bella getting ready to head out the door again. Even if the door was a magical cupboard that somehow led to an enchanted kingdom.

"It's hard to say," Bella said, looking almost as strained as she felt. "Time can move a little strangely on the other side. We could be back in five minutes, or it might not be until tomorrow morning." She sighed and turned to Sam. "I don't suppose you'll still be here when we get back?"

"I really should get back to relieve Tiny and check on the owlet," he said, reaching his hand out as if to take hers and then pulling it back again. "But I'll hang around for a little while, just in case you do get back right away."

"I think I'll stay and keep him company," Koshka said, not meeting Bella's eyes. "I realize there's no Water of Life and Death to guard at the moment, but I'd feel better watching over the caravan, just in case."

"Ha," Bella said. "You just don't want to face the Queen and explain how you crispy-critter-ed Brenna." She and the dragon-cat stared at each other for a minute, and then she shrugged. "Fine, stay here. You save my life; you get a pass."

"I guess I don't get to go meet the Queen and see the Otherworld," Jazz said, only a little bitterly. "Since I didn't, like, get to go on the big rescue mission or anything."

Bella gazed at Jazz thoughtfully. "Actually," she said, "I think you should come along."

"*Really?*" Jazz said, jumping up and down.

"Really?" Barbara and Beka said in unison.

"Huh," Koshka said. "Interesting."

Bella shrugged. "Yes, really." She leaned over and kissed Sam on the cheek, blushing a little as she did it.

"I'll talk to you soon," she said. "Assuming that the Queen doesn't turn us all into a bowl of fruit."

SAM WATCHED THE cupboard door close behind the crowd of people who had just trooped through it like a clown car in reverse. He still found all this magical stuff pretty amazing. It was like waking up one morning to find yourself living in the midst of a fairy tale. Although the Baba Yagas (with the notable exception of the horrible Brenna) were nothing like any witches in the tales he'd read as a child. For one thing, they were a heck of a lot hotter.

Especially one of them.

"Well, I'm glad that's over," Koshka said. "Hopefully now things will get back to normal. Dragons don't enjoy drama, believe it or not. We're mostly fans of napping and eating."

"I don't much enjoy drama myself," Sam agreed. "I hope the Queen isn't too hard on Bella for coming back without Brenna."

Koshka narrowed his cat eyes as he looked up at Sam. "You really *do* like Bella, don't you? I approve." His tone made it clear that if he didn't approve, they would be having an entirely different discussion.

Sam could feel his hands clench and made a conscious effort to relax them. "I do," he said slowly. "More than I would have thought possible. But I can't see a woman as beautiful as Bella wanting a scarred ex-firefighter. She could do a lot better."

"Pfft," Koshka said. "I didn't see anyone like that in the woods just now. I saw a man who stood next to a raging fire and faced down a dangerous witch. Seemed pretty damned brave to me. You didn't even scream when you saw a dragon coming toward you. Much." He gave a snicker.

Sam was fairly sure he hadn't screamed . . . although he might have taken one giant step backward. Koshka in dragon form was *impressive*.

"As for the scars, maybe you should go look in the mirror."

Huh? Sam went into the tiny bathroom and peered into the mirror there. He put one hand up to touch the left side of his face as his reflection stared back at him with wide eyes and a stunned expression.

It was impossible, but his scars were faded; still visible, but much less obvious than they had been. They no longer stood out in ridges that yelled for attention, having become instead simply a flaw that people might notice without the horror they used to elicit. It must have been part of the healing powers of the Water of Life and Death that Barbara gave him to fix his lungs so they could move faster. He'd been so focused on everything that occurred afterward, he hadn't even realized that the Water had not only healed his lungs; it had healed the scars on his face as well.

He wandered back out into the main area of the caravan, head spinning. "Man, that's going to be hard to explain," he muttered.

"She didn't care anyway," Koshka said. "The poor girl was so distracted by her attraction for you, she barely managed to accomplish the tasks she'd been sent here to do, finding the Riders and stopping the fires." He gazed meaningfully up at Sam. "Most of the fires were being caused by Brenna all along, you know. Your season should be a lot quieter from now on."

A sudden realization hit Sam like a semi. "So Bella's accomplished both of her tasks. I'm glad, of course, on both counts, but does that mean you'll be moving on now?"

Koshka shrugged, like a mountain of fur during a seismic shift. "That's what Baba Yagas do," he said simply.

Sam paced around for a minute, fighting a rising tide of feelings he didn't know how to deal with. Finally, he said, a tad abruptly, "I've got to go take care of my own job. I'll radio Tiny when I get close to the tower and tell him he can leave. That way he won't see my face. Tell Bella when she gets back that I'm glad it all worked out okay."

Then he walked—almost ran—to the door of the caravan and bolted for his four-wheeler. Suddenly the fire tower seemed like the only safe place in a world where the rules weren't what they'd been a week before and the future held the certainty of a whole different kind of torment.

KOSHKA WATCHED THE door vibrating with the force of its closing and blinked a couple of times. "Was it something I said?"

Humans. He'd never understand them.

He turned his large head to look around the empty room and said plaintively, "HEY, isn't anyone going to feed the cat?" When there was no answer, he marched up to the kitchen area, jumped onto the counter with a thud that rocked the entire caravan, and opened the cupboard with one paw.

Knocking a can of tuna onto the floor, he then pounced on it and ripped the top off with a delicately extended claw.

Some days it felt like he had to do *everything* himself.

BELLA FELT LIKE she was at the head of a very odd parade: three kick-ass Baba Yagas, one of them slightly singed around the edges; three Riders, more than a little rough around the edges and the middle and the sides; and one crop-haired, teenage Human whose expression kept morphing from amazed to intimidated and back again. The only thing they lacked was a Pied Piper playing a flute.

As always, the Otherworld was a glorious riot of colors, sounds, and smells. Their current path led them past a field of chatty blue carnations five feet high, all babbling at once about whatever local gossip amuses flowers. Rainbow-hued butterflies swooped and played in the air above, so involved in their game of tag (the one that was "it" turned to a solid color for the duration of its turn, apparently) that they never even noticed the unusual band walking underneath them.

The spicy odor of the carnations vied with the lemon-scented stream that flowed next to the path, its lavender-tinted waters filled with orange and green fish. A water sprite waved to them as Bella and the others went by.

As they approached their destination, Jazz shifted so she was closer to Bella and said in a not-very-quiet whisper, "That's a castle!"

Bella grinned at her affectionately. "Where else would you expect the King and Queen to live? A teepee?"

"Yes, but it's huge. And so . . ."

"Fairy-tale-like?" Bella sympathized with Jazz's reaction. On some level, you never got used to the grandeur of the royal palace, no matter how many times you saw it.

"Wait until you meet Their Highnesses," Beka said. "Brace yourself for shock and awe, Otherworld-style."

"Mostly just brace yourself," Barbara said. "And pray the Queen is in a good mood."

As they crossed the immense velvet green lawns in front of the castle, Barbara stopped a bearded gnome in bright red shorts and an embroidered yellow linen shirt and asked him where the royal couple could be found.

He doffed his pointy red hat, trying not to stare at the Riders, and suggested that they look on the polo fields. "I believe there is a match on at the moment," he said. "Baba Yagas, sirs, miss." He bowed and scuttled off in the direction of a group of courtiers playing croquet not too far away.

Beka sighed. "Well, there goes keeping a low profile. Everyone in court will know we're here within ten minutes."

"You think it will take that long?" Alexei said. "I would bet on five, if I was a betting man."

Barbara snorted. "Which you are."

"They play *polo* here?" Jazz asked, focusing on the part that impressed her.

"Sure," Bella said. "Only the players are elves and they ride on unicorns."

"Wow," Jazz said. "It kinda sucks that I don't have anyone to brag to about this stuff."

"You can brag to us," Mikhail said kindly.

She rolled her eyes. "You guys are, like, the weirdest peer group ever."

Nobody argued with her.

AT THE POLO fields, it didn't take long for them to be noticed. The spectators at the edge of the crowd pointed and whispered among themselves, and the news spread through the hundred or so people there like a wave, so that by the time they arrived in front of the royal dais, all attention was on their party. Behind them, Bella could see courtiers converging from the direction of the castle as well. Out on the field, play was suspended as those taking part gradually realized they'd lost their audience.

They approached the King and Queen and bowed low, Jazz only a beat behind the rest.

"Your Majesties," Bella said. "We are sorry to interrupt your afternoon's entertainment, but you instructed me to bring the Riders to you, and so I have."

"OMG," Jazz said. "The Queen is *gorgeous*." She hovered behind Bella, clearly feeling less than her usual brash, confident self in the face of such glory and pageantry. Her eyes were so big, she reminded Bella of Sam's little owlet.

The Queen, whose hearing was abnormally good, allowed a tiny smile to flit over her perfect lips at the compliment, but her expression grew grim as she took in the battered and emaciated appearance of the Riders.

"What is the meaning of this, Baba Yaga?" she said in a shocked voice. "Who has done this to My Riders?" She reached out one slender hand for that of her consort, shaken in a way that Bella had never seen before.

Bella bowed again and took a deep breath. Her Baba sisters came to stand on either side for moral support, although since she had been the one given the task, it was up to her to report.

"I apologize in advance for the use of a forbidden name," Bella said, feeling her stomach knot up in anticipation of the Queen's ire. "But it was Brenna, Your Majesties. Brenna was responsible for first kidnapping and then torturing Mikhail Day, Alexei Knight, and Gregori Sun. And when I tracked her to her lair, she then attacked and imprisoned me as well. If it weren't for Barbara and Beka, and the aid of a brave Human, the Riders and I would all be dead now."

There were gasps from all around them, but the Queen simply pressed her lips together and looked furious.

"And why in the two worlds would Brenna do such a thing?" the King asked, thunderclouds forming on his forehead. Literally.

"Yes, Baba Yaga, what could she or anyone else have to gain from such despicable behavior?" the Queen asked. "Are you quite certain it was her?"

Bella gritted her teeth. "Quite certain, Your Majesties. When someone hits you with a magical trap then tries to burn you to death, there is no mistaking her. As for the why, apparently Brenna found the lost journal of Mad Pyotr and was attempting to 'improve' on his potion to extend life and increase power. She believed that she could achieve this by draining the Riders' power and immortality, along with channeling torment from the natural world through fire."

"*Mad Pyotr's journal?*" A vein throbbed on the Queen's alabaster brow. "Where on earth did she get that book?"

Bella clasped her hands in front of her, knuckles turning white. "Er, she told me she found it in your library, Your Majesty."

A small shrubbery nearby burst into flames, and one of the three moons overhead suddenly canted slightly to the left. The wiser of the bystanders all took a step backward.

But the Queen simply took a deep breath and shook her head. "Unfortunate," she said. Then she focused her razor attention on Bella again. "And where is Brenna now?" she asked in a voice that didn't bode well for the woman in question.

Bella and Barbara exchanged glances, then Barbara stepped forward and held out the bandana full of ashes. She untied the ends so that the King and Queen could view the contents.

"And what, precisely, is *that*?" the Queen asked, wrinkling her regal nose.

Bella grimaced. "I'm afraid that is all that remains of Brenna, Your Majesty. My Chudo-Yudo took the attack on me rather personally."

There was a moment of silence as everyone present held their breath.

Then the King gave a loud laugh and said ruefully, "So would I if anyone dared to attack My beloved."

He patted the Queen's hand, and she smiled at him fondly before saying, "Ah well, I suppose it could not be helped."

She made a gesture, and the ashes rose up out of their ignominious wrappings and swirled around like a miniature glittering tornado. When the air cleared, there was a silver statue of Brenna in the process of melting, metal flames captured in the act of immolating her.

"Let this be a reminder," the Queen said in a soft but still menacing voice, "of what happens to those who would threaten Our Baba Yagas."

THIRTY

THE QUEEN BECKONED to the Riders to approach her, and Bella and her sisters stepped back, grateful to have the Queen's steely glance aimed at someone else for a bit.

The King and Queen exchanged looks filled with concern, and the Queen actually rose from her throne-like, bejeweled seat to give each Rider a kiss on the cheek. Alexei practically turned pink with pleasure at this unusual display of affection from the normally chilly and distant royal.

"We have been most concerned for your welfare," the Queen said. "And We can see that Our apprehension was not without reason." She put one slender hand on each Rider's chest in turn, and if anything, her expression grew even more distressed.

"We are grateful to the Baba Yagas for rescuing you and bringing you safely home to Us, but sadly, We must tell you that while they were in time to save your lives, their efforts came too late to save your immortality." She shook her head with regret. "We are sorry to say that you are now as mortal as any Human, and there is nothing We can do to change that."

A few of the more sympathetic courtiers burst into tears

at this pronouncement, but the Riders themselves barely reacted.

"I wish we could say we were surprised by this news, Your Majesty," Gregori said. "But we had already come to such a conclusion ourselves. We only needed your ability to sense magical essence to confirm it." The three Riders bowed again, Mikhail taking a little longer to straighten back up than the others. Bella could tell that he was still feeling guilty, but she didn't have any idea what to do about it.

Barbara took one step forward. "Your Majesty," she said, and then hesitated before going on. "Does this mean that they aren't the Riders anymore?"

Bella's heart squeezed, and it was all she could do not to start crying too.

"I am afraid that is true," the Queen said, going back to sit next to her consort, who placed his hand gently over hers. "It is hard for Us to imagine a world without the Riders, but the Baba Yagas will just have to manage on their own from now on."

"But what about Mikhail, Alexei, and Gregori?" Beka asked. The youngest and most softhearted of the three Babas, she had tears openly streaming down her cheeks and did nothing to try and conceal them. "What will happen to them now?"

The Queen straightened up, her diamond-tipped crown sparkling in the artificial sunlight. "They will stay in Our lands, here in the Otherworld, of course, for as long as they like. They will be tended to and cared for as they recover from their ordeal, as the beloved friends to Our kingdom that they are. They have served long and well and deserve a rest. Their every whim shall be indulged, and they shall lack for nothing as long as they are Our guests."

The Riders exchanged glances among themselves, obviously in agreement about something as yet unsaid, and Gregori stepped forward to bow deeply to the Queen and King.

"Your Majesties are most gracious, as always, and we will happily and gratefully accept your generous invitation to stay here while we recover. It has indeed been a long and difficult time, and we are all tired and in need of healing."

The Queen bent her head gracefully.

"But," he went on, "we belong in the Human world, having spent most of our long lives there. And none of us would be comfortable sitting around and doing nothing; it is simply not in our nature. So when we are well again, we will return to the world and see who and what we are now."

The Queen's countenance showed her dismay, and even the King, normally the more accommodating of the two, looked tempted to put his royal foot down.

"But how will you cope?" he asked, almost plaintively. "You have been the Riders for thousands of years. Everything will be different now."

"Not everything, Sire," Gregori said, sounding as calm as if his entire existence hadn't been turned on its head. "I will still have my wisdom, Alexei his strength, and Mikhail will still be absurdly charming. I assure you, we will learn to cope with our new limitations." He gave them all a small smile. "Perhaps it will be a new adventure. Such things are good for the soul."

The King turned to his consort. "My treasure? What think you of this plan?"

The Queen tapped a lacy fan against her chin, then swirled it outward in one graceful movement. "We are disappointed, of course," she said. "But it is their choice. They will always be welcome here, should they change their minds. No matter what, We wish them well." She shrugged. "After all, they have always been more than Human; perhaps they have gifts as yet untapped, even though they will no longer be immortal."

"Your Majesty," Barbara said. "I have a confession to make. And a question."

One white eyebrow lifted. "Indeed, Baba Yaga? And what would that be?"

Barbara held out Bella's now-empty silver flask. "When we rescued the Riders, their injuries were most grave. The initial dose of the Water of Life and Death we gave them was insufficient to heal them, so on my authority, we gave them a much larger quantity than would normally be used. And a small amount was given to a Human, the one who helped us to find and rescue the Riders from Brenna."

"Under the circumstances," the Queen said, "that seems quite reasonable. We would have done the same. No apologies are necessary."

Bella bit her lip. She was pretty sure Barbara hadn't been asking for forgiveness.

Barbara clearly considered saying something along those lines and thankfully thought the better of it. "Ah yes, Your Majesty. Thank you. But actually, I was concerned for the Riders." She paused, obviously not knowing what to call them now, since that name was no longer theirs, and then forged on. "No one I know of has ever been given that large a measure of the Water of Life and Death. Will there be any side effects from their ingesting so much of such a powerful potion? They won't go mad like Pyotr, will they?"

"Only time will tell," the Queen said. "Even We do not know the answer to that question. Although I can say that since the Riders were never merely mortal to begin with, it is unlikely that madness will be an issue. What else might come of this, no one can know."

Then, as was her habit, she dismissed what she could not control and returned her focus to what she could.

"Baba Yaga," she said to Barbara. "You and Beka will go with all haste to fetch the journal of Mad Pyotr and all of Brenna's magical supplies, including any of this potion she so misguidedly created. You will bring them back to Us, immediately if not sooner, so that We may see this book destroyed once and for all." The "as it should have been in the first place" went unspoken, but the palace librarian turned very pale.

"Yes, Your Majesty," Barbara said, looking relieved not to be scolded (or worse), and she and Beka gave the Riders big hugs, bowed once more to the King and Queen, and hurried off. As they were leaving, Beka made the universal sign of a telephone with her pinkie and thumb and mouthed *Call me* at Bella before following in Barbara's wake.

The now-former Riders were ushered away by the Queen's healers, and finally only Bella and Jazz were left standing in front of the royal couple, Jazz still hovering uncertainly behind Bella as if trying to see everything while remaining more or less invisible.

The Queen sighed heavily. "We congratulate you on fulfilling the task We assigned you, Baba Yaga, although one might wish that the end results had been less heartrending. Still, at least the Riders were rescued and Brenna thwarted at last."

Everyone stared at the new statue, and one unfortunate lady-in-waiting made the mistake of tittering loudly.

There was a puff of multicolored smoke.

"Darling, was that really necessary?" the King asked, gazing at the small, bewildered-looking lizard nestled amid a pile of pale pink silk, most of its crimson and orange body curled up in a high-heeled shoe.

"I expect it will wear off in a day or two," the Queen said to him. "And you know how I hate being interrupted when I am speaking."

She turned back to Bella and pointed her fan at Jazz, who suppressed a squeak. "Baba Yaga, were you going to introduce this interesting creature to Us, or were We supposed to guess her purpose here?" Thankfully, she sounded more amused than put out.

"I was just awaiting the proper moment, Your Majesties, since there were other more urgent matters to be dealt with first."

The Queen nodded. "Quite right. But since those matters have been dealt with . . ."

Here went nothing. Bella tugged Jazz out to stand by her side. "Your Royal Highnesses, this is Jazz. She is a Human girl who I found living by her wits in the forest and took in for a time during the recent unpleasantness. She is clever and independent and quite talented. I took it upon myself to test her on some basic magic skills, and she is surprisingly good. I am convinced she has the potential to become a Baba Yaga in her own right."

Jazz looked stunned at this introduction, but the Queen and King seemed intrigued, as Bella had hoped they would be.

"We have been saying that the Baba Yagas are spread too thin these days, have We not?" the Queen said to her consort. "What with the thoughtless tendency Humans have of upsetting the balance of nature. What think you?"

The King stroked his pointed black beard thoughtfully. "She is quite old to be starting training, Baba Yaga," he said to Bella. "It is usual to start with a much younger child."

"Yes, Your Highness," Bella said. "But I believe Jazz will learn fast and do well. And one advantage of starting with someone older is that, in theory, she could be ready to go out on her own much sooner." She put one reassuring hand on Jazz's shoulder, feeling the girl shaking. She smiled at the King. "At least she is an orphan, so that much is traditional."

The Queen turned her piercing glance toward Jazz and gazed at her searchingly. Apparently she found whatever she was looking for, because she said, "Very well, child. Show Us an example of what you can do."

"No pressure," Jazz muttered under her breath. But Bella could feel her gather her focus as she was taught, and slowly a tiny illusion formed in the air, a miniature version of Koshka standing on his hind legs demanding food. Although small, it was a perfect replica, right down to the attitude.

The Queen's mouth edged up ever so slightly, and she brought her hands together in brief applause. "Nicely done," she said. "Although I would not do that one in front of the dragon, if I were you." She bent down toward the girl, beckoning her closer.

"Is this what you truly want?" she asked Jazz. "It is not an easy life, to be a Baba Yaga, although it can be a long and rewarding one."

Jazz lifted her chin. "More than anything, Your Majesty. Especially if it means I get to stay with Bella and Koshka. They're the best people I ever met."

Bella felt a flush of warmth, even though she knew that in Jazz's life, that bar was set pretty low.

"I like her," the King said decisively. And that was that.

The Queen made most of the important decisions in the kingdom, but on the rare occasions her consort voiced an opinion, she always listened.

"Very well," the Queen said, clearly ready to get back to watching her polo match now that the difficult issues had been dealt with. "You are officially Our newest Baba Yaga in training, under the reliable care of Bella. We shall expect regular reports on your progress."

As Jazz returned to Bella's side, her face lit up like it was Christmas morning, her birthday, and an unexpected snow day, all at once. The Queen added, "She will need a new name, of course."

Jazz rolled her eyes and said under her breath, "I don't think so. There are too many people around here whose names start with *B* already."

THIRTY-ONE

WHEN BELLA AND JAZZ ducked through the cupboard door that led back into the caravan, Jazz was struck by an unaccustomed feeling: she was home. Truly, honestly, home at last. She knew it would take a while before she stopped waking up each morning expecting disaster and rejection, but she was also convinced that no matter what happened, Bella would never toss her away or give up on her.

This realization was enough to stop her dead in the middle of the room, where she stood for a moment quietly hyperventilating until she could get a grip. The caravan was quiet; there was no sign of Sam, and Koshka was curled up on the bed, snoring quietly.

As Bella plopped down on the couch, the dragon-cat opened one eye and said, "Oh good. You're not a bowl of fruit."

"Not this week," she agreed. "Also, the Queen agreed to let Jazz train to be a Baba Yaga."

He opened the other eye. "The kid stays?"

"The kid stays."

"Booyah," he said. "Alexei owes me twenty bucks." He

stretched leisurely and oozed off the bed in typical cat fashion, then walked over to lean heavily against Jazz's legs. "Welcome to the family, kid. You're going to do just fine."

She patted him on the head, trying not to act like some kind of snively wimp. "Yeah, it will be cool," she said. "Probably."

The dragon-cat snorted, clearly not fooled for a minute.

"Speaking of cool," Bella said casually, "will you two be cool if I go find Sam? I should probably let him know how things turned out."

"Uh-huh," Koshka said. "You know it's the middle of the night, right?"

Bella looked out the window where, in fact, it was completely dark except for a small glimmer from the lantern by the door. "Oh," she said.

Jazz reached over to check her phone, which was sitting on the counter, and rolled her eyes. "Since when is nine o'clock the middle of the night?" she asked the cat. "I'll bet Sam is still up."

"I hate to run out on you when I just got back," Bella said, her forehead creasing.

"Are you kidding?" Jazz said. "I get to live with a witch and a dragon and learn how to be a Baba Yaga. I'm great. Go do what you gotta do." Then a thought hit her and she said, "Um, Bella? I'll still get to stay with you if you and Sam get together, right?"

Bella got up from the couch and gave Jazz a big hug. "I don't know if there is any possibility of that happening—Sam and I have some pretty big issues to overcome, and I don't even know if he *wants* to get together. But rest assured, there is no way I am letting you go.

"Besides," she added, "if I did, you'd probably turn into a juvenile delinquent. I'd hate to have that on my conscience."

"That would really suck," Jazz agreed. "For you, I mean. I think I would kind of enjoy being a juvenile delinquent. I'd get to hang out on street corners, spray graffiti on random buildings, and wear a leather jacket."

"I'll tell you what, Jazz," Bella said. "How about you skip the first two and I promise to buy you a leather jacket."

"And my own dirt bike?"

Bella grinned. "I guess you'll need one to keep up with me. Deal."

"Cool," Jazz said. "Now stop stalling and go talk to Sam."

"We're going to have to have a discussion about which one of us is the parent figure here," Bella muttered. But she disappeared out the door anyway.

Jazz and Koshka stared at each other.

"What do you think the odds are that things will work out between them?" Jazz asked.

Koshka shrugged. "I only bet on sure things. Human emotions are way too uncertain."

He gave a big, sharp-toothed yawn and walked over to the kitchen area. "By the way, the first duty of a Baba Yaga is to make sure that her Chudo-Yudo gets fed. We should probably start working on that part of your training right away."

ALL THE WAY to the tower, Bella tried to figure out what on earth she was going to say to Sam. *I really, really like you* sounded completely lame, and honestly, not strong enough to encompass the way she couldn't stop thinking of him, even in the midst of disaster, and woke up every morning from dreams in which he was heavily featured (and usually barely dressed).

I know that things between us are weird and I'm barely Human, but how do you feel about dating? didn't come across any better, and she completely dismissed *I think you're the most gorgeous, kindest, sexiest, most wonderful man I've ever met* out of hand.

By the time she parked the Enduro at the base of the tower, she was down to *I'm so sorry I almost set you on fire, but hey, I'm a passionate woman and that can be a good thing* or *Screw it, I think I love you*. She almost turned around and went home.

But before she could chicken out, the door to the tower opened and Sam stepped outside, bending down to peer at the ground below him.

"Is that you, Bella?"

She opened her mouth to greet him but was rendered speechless by the sight of his perfect body clad only in a pair of denim cutoff shorts that showed off his muscular biceps, taut abs, and strong legs. So instead, she just ran up the many stairs as fast as she could, driven by the need to have her arms around him as soon as almost-Humanly possible.

Apparently he felt the same way, because as soon as she reached the platform at the top of the stairs, Sam grabbed her and hugged her so tight she felt her ribs creak. Then his lips were on hers and they were kissing as if only the contact of their mouths would keep the earth spinning on its axis.

The only problem was, after a few minutes of deep, soulful kissing, she was no longer sure it really was. Certainly her world seemed to have tilted sideways, and gravity had changed so that all her mass was drawn into Sam's orbit.

"Hey," she said breathlessly when they finally came up for air.

"Hey yourself," he said, gazing down into her eyes as if she was the center of his world too. It was a heady feeling and one she'd never had before.

"I just thought I should come by and tell you that everything went okay with the Queen," she said.

"I'm glad you did," Sam said, feathering a series of butterfly kisses down the side of her neck. He drew in a deep breath. "I wasn't sure if you would come by before you left, and I have a lot to say to you."

Bella smiled up at him tenderly. "I have a lot to say to you too. Would you rather talk before or after?"

Confusion made his brow wrinkle. "Before or after what?"

"This," she said, and pulled off her tee shirt to toss it across the railing. Then she dragged him inside the tower—not that it took much dragging. The rest of their clothes hit the floor soon after, and then they were in his bed, kissing and touching and caressing each other as if each of them had been starving and suddenly presented with a feast.

And what a feast he was, she thought, all that smooth skin over firm muscle, from his wide shoulders to his broad chest with its sprinkling of hair so crisp under her fingers. Then her explorations led to his flat stomach and muscular thighs, and from there to her favorite part, rigid and upright, feeling so thick and right in her hand.

She loved the sounds he made deep in his throat as she stroked his silken length lightly, then straddled him and guided it between her legs. She'd meant to draw the moment out, but neither of them could wait, and so she tilted her hips down as he shoved up, and then they were together, as the universe intended, moving in unison with eagerness and softness, loud moans and low laughter, biting and nibbling and stroking everywhere until they exploded at the same time in a rush of passion and joy.

As the moon rose, they lay together in a haze of satisfaction, still touching with idle pleasure, delighting in being in each other's arms.

Bella sighed, running her hand over the now-less-obviously scarred side of his face. His healing was a kind of miracle, she thought. But then, everything about him was a miracle to her.

"I can't believe my scars are so much better," Sam said, echoing her thought.

She raised herself up on one elbow to kiss the place where they had been. "I never cared about them, you know," she said in a low voice. "I always thought you were the most handsome man I'd ever met. Everything you are shines through your eyes, scars or no scars."

"You say the most amazing things," he said. "And what's more, I even believe you when you say them."

"So you should," Bella said with a laugh. "Baba Yagas don't lie. Well, hardly ever, anyway, and definitely not about something like that."

Sam was silent for a moment, running one hand up and down her hip as she snuggled up facing him. "The difference in those scars is going to be hard to explain," he said finally. "Not that I'm sorry to be rid of the worst of it. Of course the scars inside are going to take longer to heal, but somehow now I can actually believe that someday they will."

"What are you going to do?" Bella asked. It hadn't even occurred to her that being miraculously healed was going to make things awkward for him, but of course it would.

She could feel his shrug more than see it in the semidarkness.

"I'm going to claim a family emergency came up," he said, his tone fraught with an emotion she couldn't quite identify. "I'll request a sub for the rest of the season. There's always someone on the waiting list; in fact, I'm pretty sure Tiny said he had a cousin who'd applied for the job around the same time I did. If he's still available, Tiny will show him the ropes."

"I'm sorry," she said softly. "I didn't mean to screw up your life. I know how much you value this job."

He shrugged, which brought a few body parts even closer in interesting ways. That distracted them for a minute, until he added, "It's okay. When I come back next year—if I come back next year—I'll just tell everyone I had reconstructive surgery. People have been suggesting plastic surgery since I got these scars, so I suspect they won't find it hard to believe, although in reality, there is no way that doctors could have achieved this result."

"Oh," Bella said. "That's a clever solution." She kissed him again, her lips smiling against his. "It's nice to know you're not just another pretty face."

He leaned down and blew a raspberry against her belly in response, then put his arms back around her. "What about you? What's going to happen with Jazz?"

Bella grinned, happier about this than anything else that had happened. Well, almost anything. She was pretty stoked about Brenna ending up as a pile of smoking ashes. And, of course, there was Sam. At least for this golden moment out of time.

"The Queen gave me permission to train her as a new Baba

Yaga," she said, glee humming in her voice. "I'll have to come up with a way to explain her, and fake paperwork, of course, but if I can't do that, I'm not worthy of the title *witch*."

"You definitely bewitched me," Sam said, although he sounded a little sad. "I think it is great that Jazz will have a home and someone to take care of her."

"But?" Bella said, hearing the word he'd left unsaid. She hoped he wasn't going to ruin this lovely afterglow with some sort of lecture on legalities and proper procedure.

He sighed and kissed her bare shoulder. "But, to be honest, I'd been thinking that maybe you would be willing to let me travel with you for a while. Or maybe, you know, forever."

His words seemed to hang in the air like smoke from an unseen blaze.

"Forever seems about right," Bella whispered past the lump in her throat. Joy bubbled up like champagne through her veins. "As long as you don't mind risking being set on fire when you make me mad."

Sam's smile lit up the night. "I'll just have to do my best not to make you mad," he said. "But if I do, I'll distract you one way or another until you get over it."

And then he proceeded to demonstrate something very distracting indeed.

IN THE MORNING, Sam called the FMO, the fire management officer who was his immediate boss, and explained about his "family emergency." He didn't have any problem sounding emotional, although of course the reasons weren't exactly the ones he used in his explanation.

When he was done with that conversation, he called Tiny, only partially sidetracked by the glorious sight of Bella sitting cross-legged on his bed in last night's clothes, combing her long, curly hair and looking fulfilled and smug.

"Morning, Sam," Tiny said in greeting. "Not another fire, I hope?"

"No," Sam said. "No fire. In fact, I have it on good authority that the rest of the season should be much quieter."

There was silence on the other end of the phone. "She did it, then. The Baba Yaga. She found out who or what was causing the fires and put a stop to it?"

"She did." Sam grinned at *his* Baba Yaga across the room. "Very permanently, I'm happy to say. You shouldn't have nearly as much trouble from now on."

"Well, that's grand news," Tiny said. Then he paused again. "What do you mean *I* shouldn't have as much trouble? Don't you mean *we*?"

This was the part Sam hadn't been looking forward to. He was going to miss the fire tower and the job, but mostly he was going to regret not spending time with this remarkable man who had accepted him with an open heart when he'd had so little to give in return.

"I'm leaving for a while," Sam said. "The rest of the season, anyway. I'm hoping I can figure out a way to come back for next season, but I'm not sure. I've already let Bob at the Forest Service know, and he's sending a replacement in a couple of days. I was hoping you could fill in until the new guy gets here. I'm sorry about the short notice. It's kind of . . . complicated."

"Huh," Tiny said. Then he chuckled, which was the last reaction Sam was expecting.

"This wouldn't have anything to do with a certain red-haired witch, would it?" Tiny asked, laughter in his voice.

Sam should have realized he couldn't fool his friend. And that he shouldn't have worried about letting Tiny see his new and improved face, since the older man knew all about the magic. "It does," he admitted. "For one thing, in the midst of some pretty crazy stuff that came down in the last few days, my scars were partially healed. Which is going to be pretty tough to explain to anyone other than you."

"Seriously?" Tiny said. "That's fabulous! Wait until I tell Lisa. She's going to be so happy for you." Sam could hear a muttered conversation in the background, as Tiny apparently couldn't wait to share the news with his wife.

"Lisa's ecstatic," Tiny reported. "But I get how it could be tricky to hang around after something like that. What are you going to do?"

"Well, that's the other thing," Sam said, still finding his amazing good fortune hard to believe. "Bella and I, that is, we're going to be traveling together. I mean, I'm going to be traveling with her and her um, niece. That is—"

Tiny let out a huge guffaw that echoed down the phone lines. Either that or Sam could hear it from Tiny's cabin near the base of the fire tower. That seemed distinctly possible.

"I get it, Sam," Tiny said. "You're a lucky man." He paused. "And she's a lucky woman to get you too. I hope the two of you are very happy together."

Sam gazed across the room at his magical miracle of a woman. "I'm pretty sure it's that kind of fairy tale," he said. "We may not live happily ever after, but we're definitely going to give it our best shot."

SAM PACKED UP all his things while they were waiting for Tiny to get there. It didn't take long—it was a small space and Sam had packed light anyway, not really caring what he had besides clothes to wear and basics like soap and toothpaste. Bella helped him, putting his books into one box and his few decorative items into another.

She stopped suddenly, standing still with a framed picture in one hand. Sam, looking up to see what she was doing, realized what she was holding and walked over to put his arms around her from behind, so he was looking at the picture over her shoulder.

"That's my old Hotshots crew," he said. "We took that picture at the start of the last season we had together."

"I thought so," Bella said quietly. He couldn't tell what she was thinking. "So I assume that's Heather." It was a statement, not a question. After all, there was only one woman in the photo.

"Yup," Sam said. "I guess Brenna must have come up here sometime when I was out, either running or visiting you, and saw this. Or maybe she saw it on the Internet. This photo was everywhere, after the fire. Somehow she found out what my story was and used this picture to make herself look like Heather. I guess she figured she could get me to leave the fire tower if she 'haunted' me long enough."

"She didn't know you very well then, did she?" Bella said tartly. "Bitch. I'm glad it didn't work, but it was still a low blow."

Sam shrugged. "Compared to what she did to the Riders, it was pretty mild, but she did make me question my sanity there for a while. My guilt over losing Heather and the others was so strong, it gave her an easy card to play."

"And now?" Bella asked.

Sam gently turned her around so she was facing him. "Are you asking if I'm still feeling guilty, or if I still have feelings for Heather?"

Bella hid her face in his shirt for a moment, then picked up her head and looked him in the eyes. He felt like he could fall into the green depths of hers and never come up for air.

"Both, I guess?"

He searched inside, trying to find the most honest answer to give her. She deserved that, and more.

"I think that part of me will always feel guilty for surviving when none of my friends did," he said in a quiet voice. "I don't know why I was saved, what I could possibly have done to deserve life when everyone else died. But I do know that I intend to make the most of the gift I have been given. The last few weeks have taught me that."

He put his hands on her shoulders. "And yes, a part of me will probably always love Heather. She was a wonderful woman. But she is my past and you are my future. If I am very fortunate, I will get to spend many years proving to you just how much you mean to me, not as some kind of replacement, but as you, the cheerful, fiery, magical Bella, who I love very, very much."

Tears glistened in Bella's eyes, and she whispered, "I'll take that," before turning away to place the picture reverently on top of the other items in the box.

* * *

BELLA AND SAM walked into the caravan, each of them carrying an armload of Sam's possessions. Sam had the owlet in its box balanced carefully on top of his load.

"Sam!" Jazz shouted, running over to give him an awkward hug, bags, owlet, and all. "Does this mean you and Bella made up? Did she tell you I'm staying with her and training to be a Baba Yaga? I'm magic! Are you coming with us?"

"Take a breath, youngling," Koshka said, giving her a gentle swat on the behind with one giant paw. "Maybe you want to let them put down their burdens before bombarding them with questions and inappropriate public displays of affection?"

Bella tutted at him. "First of all, we're not in public, and second of all, there is nothing inappropriate about Jazz being excited to see Sam. Since we're all going to be traveling together, I think it is just as well that she is in favor of the idea."

"Yay! You *are* coming with us! That's the best news ever." Jazz danced around the living area, and Bella couldn't help but think what a far cry she was from the prickly, defensive teen she'd been when they first met. Of course, they'd all changed, Bella maybe most of all.

Well, all of them except Koshka. Dragons didn't change much, other than to assume their disguises and take them off.

Bella knelt down in front of the dragon-cat who had been her constant companion since she was a child. "Is this okay with you, old friend?"

Koshka blinked his round green eyes, gazing first at Jazz and then at Sam. A pink tongue darted out to lick the tip of Bella's nose affectionately.

"Of course it is," he said. "I would have been quite peeved if you had come back without him." He scratched behind one tufted ear pensively. "There is just one thing though."

"What's that?" Bella asked, slightly apprehensive. After all, he was her Chudo-Yudo and a powerful mythical creature; he could ask for just about anything.

The dragon-cat gave her a serious look, then yawned, showing a sizable array of very sharp teeth.

"We're going to have to get a bigger caravan," he said. "Because there is no way I am sharing a bed with the two of you."

Bella and Sam couldn't have agreed more.

EPILOGUE

Dear Bella,

I was so very happy to hear about your new-made family. I liked your firefighter very much; he was courageous and loyal, and clearly loves you deeply. You deserve that, and more. And I think young Jazz will make a remarkable Baba Yaga. Someday she may even surprise the Queen.

I appreciate the invitation to your wedding next year. To be honest, I do not know where I will be by then or what I will be doing, but I will make every effort to attend. You are very precious to me and always will be, even though I am no longer a Rider.

Thank you for your concern, but I am doing as well as can be expected. Physically, I am quite recovered, so I have left the Otherworld and returned to this one, where no one knows who I am and I can be spared the pitying looks. For now, I am content to be in a place where I can be alone and think and perhaps figure out who I am as plain old Mikhail Day. Alexei and Gregori are on their own journeys as well, but hopefully we will all meet up at your wedding.

By the way, it may be that Barbara was correct. I have been showing signs of an intriguing new ability that the Queen thinks might be the result of the unusually large dose of the Water of Life and Death we all got. I am not without some trepidation about this development, but at least it will give me something to focus my attentions on.

There is only one thing I can say about my future with any certainty, and that is that I will absolutely, positively, and without exception be staying away from damsels in distress.

Affectionately yours,
Mikhail

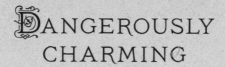

MIKHAIL DAY WAS rather enjoying the sound of the rain on the metal roof as he read by the warmth of the crackling red and orange fire. Rain was one of the things he liked about this side of the doorway; it never rained in the Otherworld, although there was always plenty of moisture to balance the heat of eternal sunless summers.

He'd always taken pleasure in the time he spent in the Otherworld, that enchanted land where the Paranormal folks had gone to live permanently after retreating from the encroachment of Humans. But after six months spent there healing from the horrific wounds he and his fellow Riders had suffered at the hands of the deranged former Baba Yaga Brenna, he'd grown tired of the perfect weather and the pitying looks and had retreated to the anonymity and imperfection of the mundane world.

The Queen's generous parting gift of a sack full of gold coins (almost certainly not the kind that disappeared the day after you used them) had purchased him a year's rent in this rustic cabin deep in the woods of the Adirondack Mountains. Built to provide an austere but comfortable writing space for an author who then discovered he couldn't create amid that much quiet, the cabin was miles from the nearest road and as private as Day could wish. The coins had bought him plenty of supplies, but most of all, they'd gotten him what he truly wanted: nobody else around.

Much had changed in his life in the last year. Brenna had stolen more than his immortality with her torture; she'd stolen his abiding self-confidence, and his identity as a Rider. He couldn't bear to be around his brothers, his fellow Riders, who had lost all that and more because of his error in judgment. Mikhail had no idea what he was going to do with the rest of his now-limited life, with the exception of one vow: he was *never, ever* going to help a damsel in distress again. The last time had cost him too much.

A piece of wood snapped and sparked in the fireplace just as thunder crashed overhead. May in the Adirondacks could be chilly and volatile, but it was still better than being out in the world. Mikhail gave a small sigh of satisfaction as he turned the page of his book, an amusing mystery he'd picked up in his travels that took place in the imaginary town of Caerphilly, Virginia, a setting as far removed from witches and faeries and magical mayhem as was Humanly possible, and where all the murders happened to people he didn't care about.

Let the rain fall and the wind blow, he thought, taking a sip from a glass of deep red merlot. He might not know what he was going to do with the rest of his life, but for now, doing nothing was just fine with him.

JENNA QUINLAN STARED down at the inert mass that a few minutes before had been her beloved if ancient Dodge Colt, and said a rude word. Then she said a couple more, just in case the gods hadn't heard her the first time.

Not that they seemed to have been listening lately. It hadn't been a good few weeks.

First there had been the shocking, impossible news from

her doctor. Then the fight with her now-ex-boyfriend, followed rapidly by being fired by her now-ex-boss.

She'd gone into work a couple of days after her talk with Stu to find her belongings in a box on the top of her desk and Mitchell standing next to it with his arms crossed and a miserable expression on his face.

"Sorry, Jenna," was all he'd said. "Stu and me, we go way back. And his father's company sends us a lot of business." He'd handed her a pathetic severance check and the box with her Hello Kitty coffee mug perched on top, and that had been that. It wasn't as though she loved the job; being a personal assistant wasn't as glamorous as it sounded. But after the first two blows, the third one practically knocked her off her feet.

She'd spent days calling around town looking for work, only to find that Stu's influence had preceded her there in every instance. Then she started feeling as though she was being watched.

It was subtle at first. A glimpse of the same unfamiliar face on the bus, an anonymous figure lurking in the shadows across the street from her apartment. One day she came home to find scratches around the edges of her locks and signs that someone had been inside, riffling through her belongings. She had no idea what on earth anyone thought they were going to find, but she suspected Stu's less-than-delicate hand there too.

Jenna hoped it was Stu. The alternative was a lot more frightening.

In the middle of the night, she'd woken up with the memory of her grandmother's voice ringing in her ears. "When it happens," the older woman had said, holding on to Jenna's hand with surprising strength for someone with one foot in the grave, "and it will—don't stay in the cities. *She* can find you in the city. Too many eyes and whispering tongues that no one can see. Run to the woods, far away from everything and everyone you ever knew. Run, girl, run as far and as fast as you can."

The next morning, Jenna had taken what little money she had in savings, grabbed the go bag she always kept on hand more from paranoia than any true belief that she'd ever need to use it, and taken off toward upstate New York. There was a cabin deep in the woods there that had once belonged to a distant cousin. Jenna's grandmother had inherited it long ago and passed it on to Jenna when she died. She'd never even been to the place. But under the current circumstances, that was a good thing, since no one would think to look for her there . . . assuming she could actually find it. In theory, all Jenna had to do was follow the handwritten map the cousin had given her grandmother, hike in with her bag of supplies, and hole up until she could figure out the answers she needed.

Her world might have been rocked on its axis, but Jenna Quinlan wasn't just going to curl up in a corner and give in to fate. She was going to run and hide, yes, but only so she could fight another day.

OF COURSE, THAT plan would have worked better if her transmission hadn't seized on this back road in the middle of nowhere. One minute she'd been driving along, watching the rampant green underbrush for errant deer and other un-expected hazards, and the next, her poor car had given one last agonized *thunk grind whine* and then slid gently into a gully on the side of the road, its steering completely frozen and the engine as dead as the life she'd left behind.

Jenna banged her head gently against the steering wheel a few times, but not surprisingly, that neither fixed the car nor improved her general attitude. Wind whispered in through the open driver's-side window, bringing with it the luxuriant scents of late spring in the mountains, barely touched by the intrusive burnt-rubber aroma of technology self-destructing. Birds flew by singing their coquettish flirtations in alternating keys. Jenna had never felt so alone in her life.

And yet she wasn't truly alone, was she? Not anymore. And that fact meant she didn't have the luxury of sitting in her car and crying, as much as she might feel like it. Doing nothing was no longer an option.

"THERE'S NO MISTAKE, Ms. Quinlan. You're eight weeks pregnant. These things happen," the doctor had said, not unsympathetically. She supposed he'd used those words with other bewildered and slightly indignant twenty-nine-year-old women, all of whom said much the same things as she had.

"But I am so careful," Jenna had protested anyway, knowing there was no point but needing to say it out loud. "I'm on the pill, and I use condoms, *and* I watch the calendar. Plus my current boyfriend has a vasectomy, for God's sake! It's not possible."

The doctor leaned back on his stool, his golf tan dark against the pristine white of his coat. Brown hair starting to go gray at the sideburns added to the professional air he projected. Jenna had never seen him before she'd gone into the clinic that day, so she had no idea if he was as competent as he seemed. It didn't matter, since the test results couldn't be argued away.

"No form of birth control is one hundred percent effective," he said, looking at the clock on the wall and not at her. "Vasectomies do fail, although not often. Yes, the odds were against it, but as I said, these things do happen." He finally met her eyes and gave her a tentative smile. "I understand that you hadn't intended to get pregnant, but at your age, you might want to consider that it will only become more difficult to do so later on, should you decide you want to have children. Perhaps you could look at this as a miracle, rather than a disaster?"

Jenna had swallowed down bitter irony and just shaken her head instead. The doctor could utter any platitudes he liked, but she knew what really lay at the heart of this so-called miracle: curses simply couldn't be thwarted.

And as curses went, this one was a doozy.

She sat in the car for a moment or two more, remembering that day when everything changed. Then she squared her shoulders, grabbed her duffel bag out of the trunk, slung her purse across her chest, and set off. According to the map, she couldn't be more than ten or twelve miles away from the cabin. A manageable hike in decent weather.

When the rain started falling an hour later, she almost laughed.

AT FIRST, DAY mistook the pounding on the door for a part of the storm. After all, there was no reason for him to expect visitors, not out here in the middle of nowhere. But when he finally got up to answer the persistent knocks, he got the sinking feeling that the storm had come to him.

A bedraggled woman stood on his doorstep in the pouring rain, and his first impulse was to slam the door in her face.

But she had clearly come as far as she could; her pale face was twisted in pain and she shivered convulsively beneath a denim jacket that was as soaking wet as the rest of her. Long black strands of hair hung down in twisted ribbons like seaweed in the vanishing daylight, reminding him of an ocean creature he'd once dated briefly in his more adventurous youth.

Mostly, though, it was her eyes that captured and held him; they were a strange shade of icy blue, large and wide and luminous with trepidation, surrounded by long dark lashes decorated by tiny droplets of rain. A duffel bag dragged in the mud behind her and an incongruously cheerful Hello Kitty purse was slung over one drooping shoulder.

He couldn't send her back out into the storm. But that didn't mean he had to be nice about it; Mikhail Day the charming Rider was dead and gone. He is someone completely different now, and happy to be so.

"Lost?" he asked briskly, his own voice sounding strange in his ears after months of silence.

The woman blinked water out of her eyes. "Not at all," she said. "This is the Holiday Inn, right?"

"Very funny." Mikhail reluctantly held the door open a little wider. "No holidays here. No inn, either. But I suppose you can come in until the storm passes."

The woman looked justifiably unimpressed by his less than gracious welcome, but she walked through the door anyway, parking her duffel bag on the mat next to it along with her soggy sneakers, and gazing around with a mixture of caution and curiosity.

Day knew what she saw: a simple one-room cabin built with clean lines and simple elegance, but no frills. The large double-sided fireplace heated the kitchen space on one side and the bigger living area on the other, its warmth barely reaching to the neatly made double bed in the loft space overhead. Almost everything was crafted out of wood: the floors and ceiling, walls and cabinets. The only color came from the royal blue comforter on the bed and the subtler blues and greens of the couch and recliner. All of it had come with the cabin when he rented it; only a few treasured keepsakes belonged to him, arrayed atop the fireplace mantle or tucked away out of sight in a small ebony chest.

"Um, are you here by yourself?" the woman asked. One hand hovered over a pocket of her purse and he wondered idly if she had some kind of weapon in there. Not that he cared.

Day sighed. "Not anymore. Look, you're perfectly safe here, if that's what you're worried about. Why don't you take off your jacket and hang it over the kitchen chair nearest the fire so it can dry. I'll go fetch you a towel." He looked at her again. "Or two."

She did as he suggested, limping noticeably as she crossed the floor to reach the other section of the room. After she placed her jacket on the chair, she turned to stand in front of the fire, holding her hands out gratefully to the warmth.

"Did you hurt yourself?" Day asked, not bothering to try and sound like he cared.

The woman nodded, spattering rainwater over the polished wood floor. "I was doing okay, but then a couple of miles back I slipped on some wet leaves and twisted my ankle. It's swelling up pretty nicely, or I would have kept going. I'm sorry to bother you. I'll wrap it in something and warm up a little, and then I'll be on my way again."

Right. Day might not be charming anymore, but even he wasn't going to send a woman out into the pouring rain as night fell. For one thing, he rather liked the bears that lived in the neighborhood, and he'd prefer to not give them a temptation they might regret later.

"We'll see," was all he said, tossing her the towels and letting her use them to dry her long hair and the worst of the wetness on her clothes. Finally he relented and fetched a pair of loose linen pants with a drawstring waist and a long-sleeved cotton shirt—both of them a dark green, not white. Never white. Not anymore.

"You're dripping all over my floors," he said briskly. "Put these on and we'll dry yours by the fire. It won't take long."

She hesitated for a minute, then took the clothing, waiting for him to turn his back before dropping what she was wearing to the ground with a sodden *plop.*

Day's mouth quirked up when he turned around again. She was slim and tall for a Human woman, probably five nine or so. But he was six three, with broad shoulders and long arms; his clothing made her look like an adorable, slightly damp child.

No, not adorable. Just silly. At least that's what he told himself. Either way, it was hard not to laugh. Fortunately, his unwelcome guest clearly had a good sense of humor, and grinned back at him as if she could tell how ridiculous she looked.

"I have clothes in my bag," she said. "Unfortunately, I'm pretty sure they're almost as wet as the ones I was wearing. So thanks for lending me these."

"Better that than to have you ruin my floors," he said. "Do you want to tell me what you're doing up here in the middle of the woods?" He gazed at her milky white skin, dark hair, and wide eyes. "If you're looking for the seven dwarves, they live in the next forest over."

"Thanks, but I prefer my men on the tall side." She looked up at him, as if reconsidering her words. "And, you know, friendly."

"That doesn't answer my question."

"I know," she said brightly. "Got any tea?"

Day rolled his eyes but put the kettle on top of the stove anyway. "How about a name?"

"Sure," the woman said. "Steve."

Day glared at her, his blond brows drawn together. "Very funny," he said. "I meant, what is your name? Or should I just call you Snow White?"

The woman's teeth chattered together and she moved closer to the fire. "I'll tell you what: If you give me that cup of tea, you can call me anything you want."

Day poured the hot water into a pot filled with tea leaves and let them steep for a few minutes before letting the dark aromatic liquid slide into a mug. Then he held it up in the air, just a tantalizing couple of inches out of reach.

"Jenna," she said. "Jenna Quinlan. And you?"

He handed her the mug, smirking a little. "Mikhail Day. Nice to meet you, Jenna Quinlan."

"Uh-huh," she said, not believing it. "Did you say Michael?"

"Sure," Mikhail said. New life, new name. Why not? "Michael Day. You can call me Mick."

As Jenna sat drinking her tea, her chair pulled as close to the fire as she could get without actually being inside it, Mikhail rooted around in one of the kitchen cabinets to find his first aid kit. What with one thing and another, he and the other Riders tended to get a bit banged up as they traveled around assisting the Baba Yagas. Banged up, blown up, and occasionally stabbed just a little. Especially huge Alexei, who liked fighting and drinking almost as much as Mikhail liked women (and fighting) and Gregori liked philosophy (and fighting).

He suppressed a sigh as he pulled out the supplies he'd need to wrap Jenna's ankle. Even with their supernaturally fast healing, they'd often had to resort to the bandages and salves that Barbara, the herbalist among the Baba Yagas, had supplied them with. Now that he wasn't immortal, Day had no idea if his powers of rapid healing remained or not. But it probably didn't matter, since the Riders were Riders no more and the Baba Yagas would have to manage without them from now on.

Jenna's eyes widened at his muttered cursing. "Is it that bad?" she asked.

Mikhail shook his head. "Sorry, no, I was thinking of something else." He turned his attention to the slim ankle and shapely foot he held in his hands. Other than the obvious swelling and redness, there didn't seem to be anything wrong with her ankle. Or the rest of her, not that he was looking.

"It doesn't seem to be broken," he said. "Just a bad sprain. I'll wrap it for you; that ought to help. But you're not going to be able to put much weight on it for the next couple of days."

Her porcelain complexion turned even paler at his pronouncement. But she sat up straight in the wooden chair, her chin raised defiantly. "I'll be fine," she said. "I'm tougher than I look."

That might be, Mikhail thought as he glanced from her duffel bag to her mud-caked sneakers to her lightweight jacket, all dripping wetly onto his floors. *But you're sure not equipped for a long hike through the woods. Who or what are you running away from?*

Then he reminded himself sharply that such things weren't his business anymore. Hopefully she was as tough as she said, since she was going to get no help from him beyond a bandage and a place to warm up for a night. He was out of the rescuing business for good. Truth was, the way things ended up when he tried to help, she'd probably be better off with the bears.

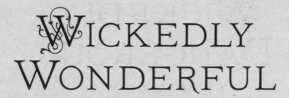

WICKEDLY WONDERFUL

A BABA YAGA NOVEL

Known as the wicked witch of Russian fairy tales, Baba Yaga is not one woman, but rather a title carried by a chosen few. They keep the balance of nature and guard the borders of our world, but don't make the mistake of crossing one of them…

Though she looks like a typical California surfer girl, Beka Yancy is in fact a powerful yet inexperienced witch who's struggling with her duties as a Baba Yaga.

A mysterious toxin is driving the Selkie and Mer from their homes deep in the trenches of Monterey Bay. To investigate, Beka buys her way onto the boat of Marcus Dermott, a battle-scarred former U.S. Marine, and his ailing fisherman father. Only by trusting her powers can Beka save the underwater races, pick the right man, and choose the path she'll follow for the rest of her life…

deborahblakeauthor.com
penguin.com

M1736T1015

M883G1011